I0760965

# EXTINCTION

*One man's journey to hell and back to save the earth from extinction*

S O Lessey

ISBN 978-1-954345-33-1 (paperback)
ISBN 978-1-954345-34-8 (hardcover)
ISBN 978-1-954345-36-2 (digital)



Rushmore Press LLC
1 800 460 9188
www.rushmorepress.com

Printed in the United States of America

# CONTENTS

## Part IV

*Quarantine*



## Part V

*Asylum*

## Part VI
*Death*



## Part VII
*Extinction*

# PROLOGUE

March 2020—the peak of the coronavirus spread panic around the world. The world's powers have failed to contain the virus, and death tolls are steadily climbing to frightening heights in this twenty-first century. The worldwide panic had become so ingrained in everyone's psyche that the superpowers have now started to play blame games with each other in a foolish attempt to claim the top-dog position while the populace continues to suffer from the biological and economic fallout.

I myself have been subject to rigorous quarantine procedures and seen the dark side of virus control systems from the inside out and the conditions under which normal citizens will be subjected in order to allay the fears of politicians. With the progress of the virus, its greatest friend remains complacency from the populations around the world, of which a lot still exists.

This story examines a hybrid version to the COVID-19 virus, COVID-20, and what could have happened in an unmitigated and unchecked COVID universe. This scenario will lead the protagonist, William Huxley, through the darkest parts of his very own being, confronting the demons plaguing the earth, along with his own, while searching for his missing sister, Elizabeth. Join Bill on his journey toward freedom from a pervasive pandemic that brings the world to its knees in a fight against extinction and the survival of the entire human race.

# Part I

# OUTBREAK

*November 1, 2019*
*0 Deaths*
*0 Cases*

# 1

# THE NOVEL CORONAVIRUS

The break of November's workweek started with a lazy Monday morning on the third, with my body aching from limb to limb after an intense ride around East Manhattan Sunday evening. Rolling out of bed at eight thirty was a bit of a task, with a serious case of the Monday blues ravaging every joint and muscle in my body.

I stumbled out of bed and into the kitchen, dragging a bowl from the cupboards while sitting near the island, eyes still partially closed.

"Wake up, sleepyhead," spoke a gentle voice from the balcony. "I already made you breakfast, it's there on the dinner table. Now come on, you have to reach to class soon."

My eyes opened wide now at Liz's voice, my older sister of thirty-three, commanding me to surmount the challenges of genetics. I wandered over to the couch with a fresh set of neatly cut fruit and cereal, finished with a cup of soymilk and chia seeds poured into the bowl. I turned on the news to catch a glimpse of the morning show before heading out into the rat race while nibbling on a tangy piece of orange. My nose wrinkled at the taste while Liz came over to sit with me while she had her morning coffee.

A natural brunette and a tall five feet eleven, Liz was of slim built and liked to keep in shape, as was our common upbringing. I was a little over six feet and would like to think was also that fit, but the truth was always a little less flattering. Her eyes were bright and smile warm, with a chiseled nose bridge and strong jawline. She was always the leader of our pack and ferociously pursued her academic research, a path that I tried to follow but was always lagging behind.

The news was filled with the upcoming democratic nominations and debates, with politicians duking it out on the same side like mortal enemies and Trump usually having a laugh on the other end, licking his chops at their growing confusion and disorganization.

"They're gonna get eaten alive if they're not more careful," Liz remarked as she took another sip of her piping-hot coffee and intently focusing on the drought of female candidates, which she openly hoped for Kamala Harris to dominate, which just didn't materialize.

"It's all a gimmick. you know, a larger engine that has already determined the outcome," I said. "At this stage, it's all about TV ratings like a South American telenovela."

I laughed, but Liz didn't fully appreciate the comical side of it. She took America's democratic process very seriously, an active supporter of the "Vote or Die" marketing ploy in the previous couple general elections.

She got up as I was finishing breakfast and walked out on our fifteenth-floor apartment balcony in East Harlem on 106th Street looking out at the East River, looking unusually clean, sparkling under the early morning sunshine.

"Don't let the sunshine fool you," she said as she huddled up in a jacket before heading out.

The wind was strong as a harsh winter threatened the end of the decade, creeping up on us New Yorkers, waiting to catch an unsuspecting traveler who forgot to double up on his layers before walking out into the street.

"So what's up with you today? Any mutant virus plague lying around in the lab you looking to release?" I chuckled at her.

Her wry smile in response indicated that that was not the first time she had to respond to such an accusation.

"No, but I am supposed to get some new imported cultures from China today," she replied. "I'm hoping to see if my research could branch out a little. I'm a little tired of analyzing those viruses, postrelease, just to craft a vaccine after the fact. I want to understand more about the virus itself—its history, culture, moods, and evolutions so I could probably get some new juice for my book."

Liz was an eternal optimist, one who couldn't stay in one space for long without conquering the field, then moving on to something else that sparked her interest. She had graduated from Toulouse University in France with her PhD in microbiology and infectious diseases, particularly in the area of the spread of zoonotic viruses in Eastern countries of Taiwan, Hong Kong, and Bangladesh. She was the smartest person I knew, and her focus over the past few years were on resistance genes in humans and how they played a role in limiting the effect of viruses such as swine flu (H1N1) and bird flu (H7N9), the latter being a deadly version of the original bird flu strain with a 36 percent mortality rate. She had come back to the States in 2018, hoping to branch off more into microbial and enzymatic engineering, focusing on the manipulation of viruses and their respective strains.

I, on the other hand, was the dunce of the family, compared to our oldest cousin, Zack, who was running a surgical clinic in Iowa and making upward of half a million a year. I started to get ready to head out to school, the New York University Global School of Public Health, trying to complete graduate work as a research assistant and hopefully get a grant to continue research in a PhD field similar to sis.

I took a short shower, flying out of the bathroom shivering as the hot water was at a minimum, with the winds of winter swooping in mercilessly. I strapped on my T-shirt and fixed my hair, taking a shave and nicking my neck because I was rushing to head out. Liz had a late meeting at eleven, but my classes started at nine; and it was already seven thirty, so I threw some hair gel into my six-inch curls so my intentional look of a Latvian brunette man-child with a potbelly and curly afro was now complete.

I said goodbye to Liz and swung my tote bag over my shoulders while heading out for the bus stop on 106th to move on down to upper SoHo where the school was. I stopped off at Washington Square, admiring the droves of people skating, walking hand in hand, and enjoying the simple park that gave a home and meeting place to so many. Walking down Washington Place Street, I could feel the clean air gradually dissipate into a ruckus of swearing and jackhammering that sung a sweet chorus to me, saying, "Welcome to New York."

The road safety barricades forced me to skip around several trips and safety hazards as pebbles flew onto the wall and made a dent into the tile finish a few inches in front my face. I nimbly walked on smoke and escaped from the sewers giving a contrasting sharp smell to the somewhat fresh air elsewhere. This scent ushered me inside the Global Health Campus on 726 Broadway to the screen at the university entrance indicating the room while classes were scheduled. It was already 9:05 a.m. when I reached in because of the wonderful traffic on a Monday morning in Manhattan.

I opened the clean timber entrance doors with the stainless steel handles of room 503 on the third floor and made my usual loud entrance and hustled to the back of the class when everyone gave me their death stare for interrupting the guest speaker we had on today—Englebert Noistruyen, a Swedish researcher and expert in the field of the history of deadly viruses throughout the world.

"Latvia," he began as I settled down, "was one of the worst hit areas in the mid-1300s by the bubonic plague. Rats—rats, everyone—rats were everywhere, the vermin running through the streets like people in the running of the bulls in Pamplona, Spain. *Yersinia pestis*, this being the bacteria that caused the plague in humans, coming from the fleas of the infected rats. The first few cases originated in Kyrgyzstan and spread the world over, causing 200 million deaths. Bodily fluids of the dead oozed on to the streets of Italy and Paris alike, accelerating the spread of the virus, decimating European populations by one-third, a zoonotic virus as well coming from these mammals and small rodents."

I listened intently to the lecture as he went on to describe the Plague of Justinian, the third plague, and smallpox killing 56 million people in the fifteenth century.

"The twentieth century, however, was one that had most scientists and virologists excited in the latter half of the century following the Great Influenza, or Spanish flu, which took out 50 million people in 1919, but served to shape most medical response mechanisms since then," the speaker continued. "Clothing, vaccines, quarantine approaches—they were all based on the Spanish flu and even new research on responses to what are called coronaviruses, a relatively new type of family of viruses that attack the respiratory system of humans, is based on that one pandemic.

"Middle Eastern respiratory syndrome, MERS, and severe acute respiratory syndrome, SARS, are all coronaviruses which are zoonotic in nature, coming from camels and bats respectively. So the question is, even though these diseases have, for the large part, been contained and managed by world health agencies and their various combat mechanisms—in the grand scheme of virus history—is there more to come? What are the major threats on the horizons of modern medicine?"

I raised my hand to ask a question but was quickly overshadowed by Jenny, the class know-it-all who was right up under the lecturer and obviously seeking his favor.

"Professor," she shouted in her high-pitched suck-up voice, "if the driving force behind these zoonotic viruses are small mammals who carry the disease, then isn't it reasonable to assume that as our immune systems adapt and improve based on our living environments and lifestyles, wouldn't their systems do the same? Or even the relative nature of their hardiness or remoteness and our weakness from our respective lifestyles remain at odds and thus give birth to these viruses?"

"You are precisely correct, child," shouted the professor.

Jenny smiled wide for the class to revel in her brilliance, and the professor went on to explain her epiphany.

"As humans move to more and more remote areas of civilization—a phenomena which planners call *urban sprawl*—will eventually force interactions between man and animal where they normally would never exist," the professor expounded. "The result of that is not only an external interaction but also a biological one where you have the human on one side, evolving only due to more buildings and concrete, whereas this animal's immune system and evolved viruses have grown to deadly proportions in the most remote and harsh conditions from the corners of our earth. This, by far, is the seed of the greatest threat to global public health on this earth—a coronavirus that doesn't spread indirectly to the lungs like the bubonic plague and others did. No, this attacks the lungs directly and spreads like the winter winds in New York, the novel coronavirus, and we, as a civilization, are not ready."

# 2

# PATIENT ZERO

The entire class sat slack-jawed as the professor spoke to a crescendo as if concluding an upcoming blockbuster that would rock the world theatres and libraries. I must admit, though, I too was intrigued at the prospect of something beyond MERS and SARS and how public health organizations would cope with an outbreak of something like that.

His lecture went on for a few more hours, until lunchtime came and a ping sounded on my phone from Petra, my partner, inviting me to lunch and disrupting the entire classroom in the process.

"Well, by the watch of Mr. Huxley, I believe that takes us to lunch," the professor said. "So let us proceed with caution to these public spaces, as from this morning's lecture, you can see the consequences of complacency. Good day to you, and don't forget your papers are due online this Friday."

Everyone hustled out of the lecture hall as if a plague had just gotten released, and I headed out to get my bike and ride down to Lafayette Grand Café, down on Great Jones Street. I rode to a series of honking horns and more swearing that came across muffled as the wind speed picked up momentum and a few snowflakes kissed my nose and cheek.

After clipping my bike to the bike rack outside the café, I found Petra, also a microbiologist who worked out of a private lab I met at a conference in Las Vegas in 2017. A peck on the cheek then led us inside under the warm lights as she ordered goat cheese ravioli, bacon, and eggs, while I took my usual fries and macaroons to support my already larger-than-usual breakfast.

"So what is up with you today other than first snow?" she smiled with a small blush and formed dimples while explaining a routine day at the lab just examining samples and forming papers for the next conference—this one due to be in Geneva, Switzerland.

I was so envious of her work as it took her all over the world while I was stuck in Manhattan.

"Hey, things could be worse, you could have still been stuck in Florida with your dad reviewing his memoirs." I nodded in acceptance that such a projected plight would have been worse.

We talked for hours on end about seemingly nothing as we could hear the wind attacking the glass mullions and, I know, my bike.

"Poor Betsy," I exclaimed, giving remorse to my trusted steed that had been shepherding me around New York for almost five years now.

"I'm a little jealous, actually," she said.

I looked at her, surprised.

"Who, of Betsy? C'mon, you can't seriously think you could compete with Betsy—her perfect form, easy wheels, and baby blue fixings," I laughed. "You wouldn't stand a chance!"

She turned her face and let out a "hmph" as I fed her the last of my fries before we dusted our hands and said our goodbyes before riding back to campus.

My expectancy was raised after the morning lecture for something equally intriguing in the afternoon, but alas, it was not to be. So I snoozed my way to the 4:00 p.m. mark before heading out to Central Park for a nice ride in the evening, finally ending with me sitting on the edge of the lake north of Bethesda Terrace, just taking it all in. I spread out a towel on the lawn just looking out at the crimson sky and its reflection on the lake. I took out my phone to take a few shots to add to my Instagram stories and TikTok in order to appear to still seem relevant to the youth of today.

I nodded off for a tiny nap, taking me to a chilly twilight that woke me suddenly with a slight panic. I looked about and put on my thin framed glasses to see where I was. It was still the park; but there was a strange, eerie feel that descended upon the scene—a strange fog, a shadowy man in the distance with a black cloak, and people lurking everywhere. Bothered by the environment, I took the bike straight to the apartment and rushed inside before the night could move on any further.

Nausea and vomiting then set in when I reached home, accompanied with a blinding ocular migraine that put me out of commission in my bed until late that night.

* * * * *

In the wee hours of the morning, I garnered enough energy to come out to the living room to see Liz on the balcony. I went outside to meet her.

"Hey."

"Hey, fighter, how've you been?" she said with a slight chuckle."

"Lousy," I responded, holding on to the balcony railing for support.

"You'll be fine, don't worry."

"So how was work today?"

"Well, yesterday . . ." She paused a little before answering. "Very interesting, actually. For a change, I got a few samples coming to me yesterday, new samples from China that speak of something uncharted."

"Was it a novel coronavirus?" I laughed while she watched me with surprise.

"How did you know that?" she said, her tone serious all of a sudden.

I paused and realized she wasn't joking, so I told her about the lecture this morning and that my knowing was purely coincidental.

"The truth is, I've had it for a while, just didn't pay it any mind until I saw an e-mail sent from the Wuhan Institute of Virology flagging those samples as potential pathogens and offering to pay a handsome amount for the analysis of the strains and projections of a possible outbreak."

"Well, you know once you're talking virus modeling, I'm your guy," I said.

Stemming from my strong background in math, I always helped her with the virus modeling to predict the spread of viruses based on georeferenced microbiological GIS data and hospital records. I also could use the money to help with student loans and this year's tuition fees, so the project piqued my interest even more.

We spoke briefly on it again for the night and not much after that. Liz was steeped in work, not leaving the apartment for days at a time, walking around with journal papers and a furrowed brow for most of the day. I didn't get involved until perhaps the latter part of November where I started to work my magic and after structuring the Fourier-based models, hardwired it into codes before having a Russian online team generate the models for me before sending them back. It took them a few days to run the models; no computing power we had here could even come close to their systems. Then they sent the results.

No sooner had the results come in than I got an email from Liz speaking about a news article in Wuhan from the *South China Morning Post* titled "Case Number 1 of COVID-19, November 17, 2019." It was about a fifty-five-year-old woman from the Hubei Province in China contracting the disease that local doctors said could only be described as a new strain of the SARS virus. It seemed to originate near the wet markets of China where all sorts of animals were killed, skinned, and sold raw for the millions of patrons passing through on a weekly basis. Although the virus was in its early stages, it already showed aggressive symptoms of affecting the woman's respiratory system, with no treatment seeming to help.

The panic I had felt earlier in the month seemed to return, with my model projections not helping the situation. But as a scientist, I was obligated to share it with Liz, and so I did, hitting the Reply button on her mail to me.

I lay back on the sofa, eating a grilled cheese sandwich, staring out the window into the nothingness of space, thinking about the potential of this case. But I held personal reservations that this virus was so far away, like the bird flu, that we have no reason to be concerned.

*If nothing else, it's a great research opportunity to get some good papers in the market and build some of my credibility*, I said to myself.

* * * * *

I headed out the next day, still not seeing Liz but having a renewed vigor to pursue the professors to work with me to publish my work on the modeling of the potential virus. Of course, no one wanted to sponsor the paper as it was too early in the game and the paper would only serve to spread panic. My field, unfortunately, was the unpopular form of science that clashed with other field like public relations and often ended up the loser in that battle.

A few days later, our dean announced research opportunities coming up in China for the Infectious Disease Department, partnering with the Wuhan Institute of Virology and exploring the hinterlands of the Hubei Province to conduct said research. I was very excited when I heard about this and couldn't miss the opportunity. I sent in my application early, hoping to get word as soon as possible.

By December 1, I got positive news of the opportunity and was told to pack my things and get ready for an all-expense-paid trip to the eastern megacities of China. I was overwhelmed with excitement and couldn't wait to tell Petra who was less than excited for me, knowing that I probably will be gone until January, missing our second Christmas season together because of work. I promised to make it up to her, but for the sake of my career and science, I explained I couldn't pass up the opportunity.

She of course didn't understand and went into a flying rage about me constantly choosing work over her and not being considerate of her feelings. She was right, of course, but she knew what she was getting into when she first met me.

*I have never changed my modus operandi before, and I'm not about to start now*, I told myself despairingly.

I e-mailed Liz as well to tell her the news, but she was already off to Amsterdam to a conference of her own. From there she would then head to Taiwan before returning in February.

* * * * *

A few other infections then trickled in early December, my focus now glued to the Chinese market and how they reported and coped with the virus that didn't seem to be going away. The International Committee of Taxonomy of Viruses (ICTV) then gave this virus the name of COVID-19—that is, the novel coronavirus of 2019 and SARS-CoV-2, the disease that causes the virus or the second coming of the SARS Coronavirus. Quite a mouthful for newscasters to say but just the right amount of words for us scientists.

*The year 2020 is going to be epic*, I thought. *I can't wait.*

# 3

# TO SAVE A SOUL

"Be prepared for cave diving" were the words of Lance Ingibjörg, the team lead researcher for the expedition to China.

Lance was at least six feet four of almost pure muscle, coming from a triathlete background and somehow ending up in infectious disease research. He sported blond hair and a receding hairline with a stone jaw you could break a brick on. His Icelandic heritage did help put me at ease, considering our mission was to dive in a cave full of infected bats, hoping to find the most infected one and capture it.

Our first meeting was carded for December 5, a Friday evening after classes, as the bulk of the campus would be empty. We were heading out there with five researchers and a guide from the local Hubei Province. It was the Thursday before that, and for some reason, I still felt a little queasy from the month before, never really shaking the stomach bug. I tried laying off the milk and minimizing the sugar intake I would normally have, but nothing had a reasonable impact. I decided then and there that my answer could be in eating more natural food, so I opted to head to the market for some fruits and see what a stronger supply of natural vitamins could do for my stomach.

I took my bike and rode down to corner Broadway and Seventeenth Street to find some tents up in the Union Market, a rootsy farmers' market full of unexpected and fresh produce and meats, just what I was looking for to soothe my stomach. It was every color and hue under the sun there—tomatoes the size of my fist, onions, oranges, carrots, red carrots, purple carrots, radishes, leafy greens, and every cut of meat you could want. I took out one of those reusable bags and went to work, getting everything I needed: bananas, apples, oranges, grapes, turnips, radishes, squash, lemons, ginger, sweet potato, fresh bread, fresh fish, bell peppers, etc.

When I was done, I had every color in the bag and had to get another bag to carry it all. The hard veggies went in one bag so I could slide it into my tote, and the other bag I placed in a sling over the bike handle. I felt as if I overdid it a little, but hey, what's life without living? I was very happy with my haul, so I asked Petra to meet me at my apartment so I could cook something for us to eat.

I found myself coasting down Fifteenth Street, feeling the proverbial wind in my hair and all of a sudden, I found myself in an alley and had to make a sharp turn, nearly riding over something on the ground. I put my foot on the ground to balance and went back noticing the thing I nearly rode over—it was alive. I looked carefully at the creature and realized it was a bat, but it was no ordinary bat; it was a flying fox, one of the largest bats in the world! My heart started to race a little, but I did know that the back alley of the market was known to trade in exotic wildlife, if you caught it at the right time.

I waited a little to see if someone would come out and claim it, but my heart was too soft. I couldn't leave it there, so I held it by its feet and put it in a cotton towel I had and gently lifted it up, looking to carry it home with me. The poor thing didn't even fight; it probably barely had any energy left in its muscles.

"Don't worry, kiddo, we're almost home," I said. "You'll get a nice place to rest once we reach, almost there."

It took me fifteen more minutes of faster than normal biking to reach the apartment in East Harlem. Night had just started to fall, and I opened the door, closing it behind me, and didn't even notice Petra in a bath towel waiting on the sofa to welcome me. She was pissed at first I didn't take any interest, but as soon as I turned over the cloth, there it was—the flying fox. The beast was huge.

Petra let out a gasp and scream when she saw it and immediately went in to change before calling her friend who was a vet.

I snatched the phone out of her hand, yelling, "No, we can't call the vet, they would take him! We could see about it, no worries."

She was shocked to see the passion with which I furiously went cleaning its wound on the giant, meter-wide wings. It honestly looked like a wiener dog with wings and fox-like ears. It sported a pointed snout and a nose just like a small dog. I went in to my room and got out some antibiotics and Ivermectin, a serum to reduce inflammation and help the healing process.

*These foxes are fruit bats, so thank goodness I have a lot of fruits*, I thought as I took out several fruits to feed it, but it wouldn't budge.

Then I peeled a banana and brought it to its nose. It was like magic; its head started bobbing up and down, until its jaws clamped on to the tip of the banana, breaking off a piece and chewing sideways like a camel pup. It looked so cute doing it that Petra and I smiled, watching it eat like if it were our own child.

"So what's the plan?" Petra asked sharply.

"Umm, I dunno yet, nurse it back to health?" I said. "See what I could do just to keep it here for now—at least until it's back to full health."

She nodded in acceptance, and I could see she hoped for a speedy recovery, only because she didn't want to be stuck in the apartment with it alone.

It was a little scary but also very adorable in its own way. We took turns napping outside with the bat, listening for any whimpers to go out and give it attention or medicine. I fell asleep on the final shift on the couch, groggily jumping out of sleep when the sun started to enter the room and the bat actually left the table and jumped onto the sofa, trying to squeeze between myself and the sofa to get away from the sun and snooze on its own. I smiled when I saw it. Settling in, I dozed off, getting a chance to recover from the night of mayhem.

* * * * *

Evening soon came, and I had to rush out to campus to the first meeting of the expedition, so I asked Petra to look after the bat until I got back, promising pizza once I returned, to which she agreed. I reached the campus hall tired and met the other team members, Yue

Hi, from the University of Beijing, Natalie Dassen, Rick Ortega, and Lance. Lance got the meeting off the ground, explaining the details and background of the bats we were about to study and saying they are predominantly horseshoe bats—a tiny bat of a few inches with an upturned snout and large ears, which truly looked like an alien creature when I studied its form.

The intent of the study was to capture a few bats, take blood samples, and test these samples for the presence of the COVID-19 or SARS virus. It seemed pretty straightforward, so we got our schedules and list of support material we would have to purchase in order to read up and be ready for the exercise, giving context to the physical activity. Honestly, all that was on my mind was our own bat and how he was doing in the apartment.

So as soon as Lance dismissed the team, I darted out of there, taking up some pizza by the corner spot, and sped up Broadway to reach home. I arrived at 6:00 p.m. and checked my messages to see if I got anything from Liz, but nothing yet. The weekend was wide open, and I wanted to make good use of it nursing the bat back to health.

"So we got our schedules today," I said to Petra nervously, a sign she picked up on and folded her hands immediately.

"And?"

"Well, we'll be leaving on the twentieth of this month, full-on cave diving and stuff."

She scoffed at the premise before she realized what I was really asking.

"No no no, I am not taking care of that thing for you!" Petra screamed. "Look at it!"

"Who, Jimmy? Naw he won't be any trouble at all, look at him," I countered as the flying fox sat quietly next to me, nibbling on a banana while watching up at us intently and chewing away like nobody's business, looking like the cutest thing in the world.

"Jimmy!" she shouted back. "Ugh."

"What, you don't like it? I had a pet when I was younger called Jimmy, well actually, his name was King—but hey, Jimmy works."

She watched me with a scorn of derision.

"It would—if you were keeping it as a pet!"

She caught me red-handed; I did want to keep Jimmy as a pet. But nature willing, of course, I will nurse him back to health and let him fly. I wouldn't want him to become an invasive species in the region, so I would have to keep him until he was fully healed and I could release him in Australia or something near his kind.

I looked in Jimmy's eyes.

"What are you doing all the way out here?" I asked him, lifting him up like a baby to give him a burp.

* * * * *

A day passed routinely, and Jimmy was getting really strong. He crawled everywhere in the apartment and then started hopping from place to place. What a sight it was to witness this thing's giant wingspan fully extended. In the day, he hung upside down on the chandelier, looking like a massive cocoon ornament in an eclectic form of interior design. I got him a large owl cage so I could take him around for walks and stuff, give him a bit of fresh air rather than being cooped up inside all the time.

He was a grey-headed flying fox with a golden mane of the mature male of its species. I would often scratch his mane, and like a dog, his eyes would narrow and give off the most alluring of squeaks as if pleading for me to continue. It was 8:00 p.m., and I brought out the cage, placing a banana at the bottom of it for him to eat. He immediately swooped down from the chandelier and picked up the banana, eating it in the cage. I had a black cover for him to make him feel calm as we walked through New York.

I walked out to the East River, and the pale moonlight was relaxing so I took off the cover for him to get some air. It wasn't the cleanest, but still it would help. Jimmy immediately came up to the edge of the cage, sniffing and grabbing on to the bars, squeezing it with his little wing spurs. My stomach then started to act up again, so I had to head back, skipping a little to speed up the return, heading to the toilet as soon I entered the space. I threw up but felt a little jaded.

"Are you okay, dear?" Petra asked, seeing me looking a little pale.

"Yeah, yeah," I replied. "Just a little tired, that's all."

I reached out to open the cage to let Jimmy out, and I noticed he was very on edge, fidgeting about in the cage. And as I reached in to release him, he darted out, flying on my arm and biting me in the process, drawing blood on his fangs.

I screamed out in pain, and Petra came over, aghast, immediately turning her rage toward Jimmy while I calmed her down. Jimmy, who was crawling about the ceiling, started to calm down—so much so he started to hang from the chandelier again going to rest. It was barely ten at night.

I got out some antiseptic solution and a cotton swab to clean out the scratches and placed a bandage on it.

"You look like a tiger scratched you," Petra said.

"All the better," I smiled. "It'll toughen me up when the real deal comes in Wuhan."

# 4

# BAT HUNTING

I woke up the next day filled with angst over the trip and other reports of new cases of patients exhibiting pneumonia-like symptoms in Wuhan, right on the eve of our trip. I tried my best not to pass on that anxiety to Jimmy, so I opted to carry him to classes, as it was a pet-friendly campus. Petra grew in her frustrations as I got closer to the bat, but there was a mystery and allure about the creature that drew me to it.

We were to have our second team meeting about the trip as the departure date was only a few days away. Lance started the meeting with strong optimism as usual while I snuck a peak to make sure Jimmy was doing okay under the cover I had over the cage.

"Hey, Harry Potter, why don't you leave Hedwig alone for a bit so we could focus on more pressing matters at hand?" boomed Lance, prompting a giggle from the other team members.

I guess it was true, a nerdy guy walking around with an owl cage looking for Hogwarts Express in New York is an alluring concept, I thought quietly.

"We'll be heading deep into the Shuangfenshang National Forest Reserve in upper Hubei. An ancient temple there, Luojia Ancestral Temple houses a group of monks who would help us in the trek. There is some difficult terrain, so best be on your peak physical condition to keep up.

"Carabineers, coats, nets, headlamps, cots, blankets, basic toiletries, and a cellphone camera should be sufficient. I'll send out a full list later tonight, so make sure you head out and get your supplies here and we'll do a spot check before departing JFK Airport in a few days. Our flight leaves in the early morning, eight hours to London, and we cross to the other section of Heathrow by skytrain before connecting to a United flight into Wuhan. That flight is about twelve hours."

Everyone scratched their heads upon hearing the long flight times. I thought I would probably walk with my books to stay active on the flights. I wondered what we would find there as it seemed like a pretty exciting space to explore from the images Lance showed us—beautiful, even. But it didn't take away from the fact that those spaces were ridiculously remote, and being the city boy that I was, I had to expect physical pain and suffering.

*Oh well, can't be much worse than what I'm facing in grad school,* I joked to myself, sneaking another peek at Jimmy.

Lance continued with his safety briefing and guidance on basic knots and specific guidance on shoes and clothes to get and where we could go to find them. I didn't have much time left, so I went out shopping around the city, carrying the cage wherever I went. I was always on the move, borrowing books from the library to get familiar with the flora and fauna, checking updates on ResearchGate and Elsevier in order to stay apace with any more coronavirus stuff in China.

After getting all the stuff I needed, I reached home and spent most of my time talking with Petra and enjoying her company for the last few days before I left. I fed Jimmy before heading back to my books and took him out to let him spread his wings a little in the apartment. His bruised wing was healing nicely I thought, so it was easy for me to focus on my work, even when he crawled up on the sofa for attention. I fell asleep on the couch and woke up much later in the night, so I figured it best to head to the bedroom after putting Jimmy in his cage with some food.

I looked at the chandelier, the couch, walls, kitchen, cupboards—nothing.

I checked the bedrooms, bathrooms, cabinets—nothing.

I started freaking out.

Then I rechecked the bathroom and saw the small window left ajar. I screamed to the top of my voice.

Petra came out of the bedroom, startled.

"Hey, what's wrong? Why are you losing it?" she said.

"You left the window open!" I freaked. "Now Jimmy is gone, gone, and never gonna come back! Oh my god why would you do that?"

Petra immediately went into defense mode, accusing me of ignoring her and spending all my time with Jimmy.

"It felt like a competition with that thing, that beast!" she shouted back at me.

I was hurt, so before I did something I would regret, I stormed out the apartment to look for Jimmy, up and down the East side. I walked, calling him out with whatever strength I had left. I felt dizzy, harrowed from the whole experience. Within the hour, I returned to the apartment, flustered and confused, my brain fogging up from the ordeal and pain from losing my friend.

I dropped onto the sofa and tried sleeping, but Jimmy was still on my mind. I tried thinking of places to look for him, the bat now becoming an obsession. I only knew him for a short time, but we formed a very simple and natural bond between man and beast that I truly appreciated, filling a gap in my spirit I didn't know was there.

My breathing became labored, and tremors afflicted my palms as I dripped sweat. Hate filled my heart when I thought of Petra.

*How could she do that to me?* I said inwardly, convinced that it was a sign of things to come. *A control freak obsessed with dominating my attention and time.*

Finally, by early morning, my breathing settled and the sweating eased up. Dawn broke the horizon, letting light right into the living room. And then I could hear it—squeaks coming from the couch.

I looked to my left and could see him. It was Jimmy—he came back and was snuggling next to me to catch a break from the bright sun. A warm smile dawned upon my face, and I came to a realization that I couldn't leave him with Petra. I would have to take him to China.

"So it's settled, buddy, we're going to China!" I said.

I was so happy to see him, I didn't even realize that Petra left a note for me on the kitchen counter.

I opened the folded piece of paper and it read,

> Bill,
>
> Our time together was a great one, filled with more ups than downs. But I fear that something has taken over you over the past few months that is making you very different to the man I once knew. You have become obsessive, impulsive, and insatiable when it comes to your work, to the point where I don't even know if you are aware of my existence anymore. I need some time to think and be by myself. I have never reached this far with someone else, and I too fear that my dependence on you has damaged me in more ways than I would have hoped. I wish only the best for you, but I also feel I need to take stock when the relationship is posing a danger to my own mental health as well. You need to focus on yourself and take care of yourself. This road you are heading on is a dangerous one that doesn't have an end. Please reconsider your trip to China, for our sake.
>
> Love,
> Petra

The letter dug a deep wound in my heart, a wound that I feared would not heal anytime soon. But the work meant too much for me, I couldn't give it up on the guise of an empathetic cause.

*She will be here when I return. We will reconnect then*, I convinced myself. *The little break will do us fine for now.*

I folded the paper and placed it in my wallet, promising to return to it sometime in the near future.

I looked over to the sofa and could see Jimmy watching me with his beady eyes, interested in the tumultuous energy in the apartment that morning. I also noticed that my sickness seemed to have gone away again.

*Oh well, must be a good omen for the trip then*, I told myself. *It's probably best to focus on that and power through to the end.*

I smiled and started roughhousing with Jimmy again. He liked nothing better while giving him a banana for breakfast as he squealed with delight. My flight was in less that twelve hours, but I had to visit a vet friend of mine to give Jimmy all the shots and papers he needed and the licenses that I needed in order to have him come along on the trip.

I probably spent over five thousand dollars before everything was sorted, so packing took some time and I had to pay extra for the overweight portion of the luggage. He spent most his time on my shoulder, crawling about from side to side like a capuchin monkey, tugging on my sleeve when he was ready for a treat. Everyone loved Jimmy too—well, everyone but Petra. They would give him head scratches, which he would quickly let out a cute squeal to prompt them to play with him more.

I borrowed a book about the history and culture of the horseshoe bats and the caves they occupied in the hinterlands of China. I read specifically about the many scientific stories about the populations and how they migrated about the continent in search for food and good weather, but there was also the lore. The lore was quite interesting as well. The story of the Chinese *yaoguai*, or supernatural demons, spoke of a creature that lurked in the caves called a *yangshing*, or vampire, that lived in the caves and fed off the yang, or energy of humans and animals.

Other articles speculate that what locals saw was really the horseshoe bat, but given its strange features, they gave it supernatural powers, as most cultures would. The illustrations showed a tall and slender creature using the winds of the clouds to carry it over villages and clans, with an army of bats accompanying them on their hunts. I noticed the bats were fairly compact and aligned pretty accurately in scale to the horseshoe bat's size, but whether it is anatomically correct is another story.

I opted to pursue this story no further, returning to the safe haven of scientific papers and virus modeling to pass the rest of the time. And just like that, it was time to check in and meet the others at the departure lounge in JFK Airport. It was time for the hunt to begin.

# 5

# THE WUHAN INSTITUTE OF VIROLOGY

The trip to Heathrow on the eighteenth took about eight hours, give or take. I took the time to catch up on the reading about the area and a little more about their culture. The area apparently was very rural, with little connection to the outside world beyond earthen tracks that farmers would use to bring their produce and meats to the regional market in Wuhan.

There were several stories centered around the *yaoguai* and the original concepts surrounding the afterlife emerging from old Chinese folklore and religion. The *Diyu*, or the Chinese version of hell, was an elaborate take on Dante's *Divine Comedy*, the concept of a multileveled sort of purgatory designed to torture souls. In this case, this place is one to help souls shed their past burdens in preparation for reincarnation.

The early writings were found in the *Jade Record*, or *Yuli*, which is a series of artistic impressions of the judges of each of these spaces called the ten Yama kings in the early age of the Song dynasty in 960–1279. I looked at the paintings, and they were truly a graphic masterpiece, reinvigorating my interest in graphic novels when I turned twenty but somewhat fell away as the matters of the world crept in. As my mind drifted off to think about how these concepts intertwined with world history and our own expedition, the plane swiftly hit the tarmac, and I woke up to squeaks from Jimmy out of the bouncing of the giant aircraft.

Lance remained very businesslike, while Natalie and Yue gossiped in their matching pink suits and jeans that made their figures as enticing as possible, especially Natalie who had the form to fill out her clothes nicely. Rick came from behind and bumped me on the shoulder, letting me know that he knew I was ogling in the plane aisle and that I should keep it moving. We had a lengthy layover and dragged ourselves to terminal 4 of Heathrow via a skytrain before boarding a United flight, not looking forward to another long pull in the air. For this twelve-hour stint, I spent most of my time worrying about Liz and where in the world she could be.

It was over a month since I had last heard from her, and I wondered if everything was okay. Several unanswered e-mails didn't help the situation, so I thought to send something to her colleague of whom she spoke often, Peter Ogsden, a virologist from the Sweden Virology Center. I met him once.

Peter was a handsome, tall Swedish man over six feet with blonde hair and a goatee to match. His area of specialty was designing virus serums which could then be converted to antidotes and vaccines in mass production. With him being a brilliant mathematician, I often admired his level of mastery over epidemic modeling and projections; and I thought it may be useful to have him take a look at my current projections of the COVID virus.

*No harm in making it more accurate, I guess*, I wondered.

The time passed quickly, and we soon arrived in China on Saturday morning. The time zone difference shot us forward in time pretty quickly, which meant Christmas was only a few days away now. We got off the plane a little disoriented but found customs and immigration were surprisingly easy on us. We filtered out into the lobby and saw a well-dressed Chinese man holding up a sign with Lance's name on it. He took us to our hotel, the Yinhai Mountain Villa, which was just a block away from the Wuhan Institute of Virology.

We arrived at the villa a little after 10:00 a.m., Saturday morning, and I felt as if I hadn't slept for days—Jimmy too. We got our keys and went straight to our rooms, dropping on the bed like a sack of potatoes. I opened Jimmy's cage, and he too dragged himself to come right under me, knocking out to a point of solid unconsciousness.

Sometime later, I awoke and felt the urge to do more research. I took out my laptop and continued researching the Chinese horseshoe bat.

The horseshoe bat is tiny, with barely a three-inch wingspan, but it has monster fangs and a face only a mother could love. The most peculiar feature is its nose, a smashed-in facial feature that had a ring in the shape of a horseshoe, making it look constantly disgusted with whatever it was looking at. It is a tiny menace, but one we would conquer.

As I was looking at the creature on the screen, I swore I noticed a twitch. I squinted and peered closer, and its lips were pursed. And then it bore its fangs and flew straight at my face. I flew back shouting, and then realized I was only dreaming.

I looked around the room in darkness, watching Jimmy fast asleep, beads of sweat gathering on my forehead. I went to the bathroom and washed my face not knowing what time of the year it was, watching myself in the mirror to ensure I wasn't losing my head before going back to bed.

* * * * *

The rest of the night was less than restful, so I woke when a stream of sunlight entered the room with a less than hospitable glare, Jimmy just as annoyed as I was.

"C'mon, boy, time to get at 'em," I said to my furry friend.

I went in and took a shower after rubbing down Jimmy with a wet sponge, feeling ready for the day. As I headed into the medicine cabinet for toothpaste and started brushing my teeth, I noticed something. It was a scar, a tiny scar on my forehead, on the right side. I passed my hands on it to make sure it was real, and sure enough, it was real. The ridge covered about two inches of my forehead, with a slight scab forming over it. My mind immediately went to the bat, but I thought that was impossible. I put it off as some accident in the darkness of the room that I probably didn't feel.

After shaving, I headed downstairs with Jimmy, ready to get breakfast. We met the crew downstairs, and they welcomed us like long-lost relatives.

"Hey, looky here, it's Hedwig and his pet," Lance joked. "Funny of you guys to finally rise from the dead."

Everyone laughed comically as I fed Jimmy a banana from the buffet. He scarfed it down with gusto, and I just had some eggs and Szechuan noodles with corn ears while everyone babbled around us.

"The professor is waiting for us, so we'll go meet him at ten," Lance instructed us.

Everyone nodded, but I found this strange.

"So the professor works on a Sunday too?" I said. "Man, the Chinese really do work all the time."

This remark was met with silence.

"Umm, Bill, it's not Sunday, it's Monday morning," Lance responded.

A jittery laugh broke out, but they noticed my genuine concern with a furrowed brow.

"Two days?" I gasped. "We slept for two days? I didn't even feel it. Maybe the jet lag hit me a lot harder than I thought. Oh well, best just to make the best of the situation."

The crew laughed at me some more, so I headed back to the room quickly to get dressed with my usual track pants and T-shirt for our meeting, brushing off the odd circumstances.

Professor Li-Sang Lee, a distinguished emeritus professor of the Microbiology Department was a leader on the continent for his research into *Citrobacter* and its resistance and communicability in humans and animals alike. We met him in his massive office. He was a short but intentional individual, barely five feet tall, with glasses hanging on the edge of his nose bridge and a strong handshake that pushed even Lance back a few inches. He seemed to be in his sixties and spoke extensively of his research in Wuhan and the eastern China megacities of Shenzhen, Beijing, Shanghai, and a couple inner cities like Chengdu and Chongqing.

"This virus is novel, as the taxonomy denotes, a truly exciting time for science but a tremendously dark one for humanity," the professor began.

I was surprised at his sullen tone, given only a few cases were discovered. But perhaps there was something that he knew that no one else understood.

"The basic *Citrobacter* is not a common feature, its proteins and organisms have unique shapes and properties which make it remarkable but also very virulent and deadly. The few cases we have seen so far have proven to be difficult to treat but even more difficult to contain," the professor continued. "In the realm of normal medicine, this is a problem, and from my simple level of medical expertise, I could see the difficulty it would pose if it were to spread. But we are scientists—we look at it for what it is in relation to new knowledge gracing this planet. And make no mistake, it is new, and yet, it is as old as Chinese mythologies itself. We are simply now discovering it, a phenomena that no doubt emerges from the growing interaction with remote areas of wildlife and humans whose state of existence is becoming less and less primitive and more technologically advanced.

"This is where you all come in. This disparity that exists between the remote animal world and modern man is a fact. You cannot change this fact, but we can learn more about it. This is the thought of Mao Zedong that facts and truth are two separate realities. Our job is to put in the work to bring the facts together and formulate a truth that is not only absolute but relevant."

He was inspiring, a true beacon of science and its mission to help humanity survive, grow, and prosper. I was pumped up to help, glad now that I stuck to my guns to come along on the trip. Petra—at least, for now,—is a distant memory to my current reality.

"And that, what do you have there, young man?" Professor Lee pointed to Jimmy.

"Oh, this? This is my pet flying fox. His name is Jimmy," I said.

I took off the cloth a little, and the professor looked in. Jimmy was hanging upside down, taking a nap. But something was different. As he came close, Jimmy's wings started to tremble, to vibrate; he didn't wake, but he was giving off a warning signal of sorts.

I closed the cage and apologized.

"He probably is just tired, a long flight, you know."

The professor nodded but also sported a wry grin, almost a condescending grin for my attachment. But I chose not to dwell on it and so let it be.

"Since the first case, there have been ten more," the professor said. "The virus's capacity to spread is, well, catastrophic. It warrants a level 4 biohazard controlled lab and suits in order to contain the spread of a fully matured infection."

I was shocked to hear this, making me take our mission a little more seriously.

"Your work will go a long way in helping us find the origins of the virus in those bats and hopefully be able to get their DNA and begin the process of mapping the genome of a vaccine. The area you are targeting is as rural as rural China comes. The rice farmers of the Shuangfenshang Nature Reserve plant beautiful rice terraces that adorn a thick forested area. The upper reach of this area is where you will find the Yaojing Cave, just past the Ancestral Buddhist Temple. It is indeed a very picturesque view, and the experience I am sure will be, at the very least . . . memorable."

I didn't like the professor's pause on the word *memorable*, but I guess it was too late to be chicken now. I had to man up and put my curls in a tight man bun and get ready for the hike of my life.

Lance thanked the professor for his kind words and announced that we would leave at dawn the next day after our evening meeting to review the technicalities and check each other's gear.

* * * * *

Lunch was mostly quiet with rice and more noodles. Jimmy was getting a nice array of cucumbers and melons of all colors—yellow, green, red, and even an orange one. He was pleased because they were different levels of sweet and seedless as he hated watermelon seeds. His chewing was humorous, and it picked up the mood of the entire team.

Yue went on giving us stories of her early years with the professor and doing her first set of microbiology grad studies with him. Her praises knew no end and neither did her learning. I felt at ease with her words, so I opted not to be so harsh on him mentally, even though

Jimmy didn't seem to like him. The camaraderie grew as Rick caught me a couple other times still ogling Natalie. Even Jimmy looked at me with a judgmental sigh. We met that evening to go over the final set of details, our gear, guide and supplies that we would have to carry mostly on our backs in the final stretch.

"So how do we actually catch the bats? Is it like hand fishing or noodling cuz that is some terrifying stuff to go through if you've never done it before," I recounted some early days with Liz when we spent some time in Texas with a couple of her colleagues and a noodling adventure I could never get out of my head.

"It is fairly simple," replied Lance affirmatively. "This net I have—this will be key in placing it over the mouth of the cave. We then gently approach and remove the bats caught in it and take the measurements we need."

"So why is the net so thin?" Natalie asked. "Wouldn't it break?"

"No, it is intended to be as fine as possible to the point where it's almost invisible so the bats' sonar won't pick it up. They get caught in it, but it is gentle on their skin so it doesn't cut them."

I understood, and then I took out a carabineer and asked him how far the cars would be carrying us, hoping for an answer of 'all the way.' But Lance loved a challenge, so he would never go in a place that would be that accessible, and I suppose the more remote, the better for the research too.

"Duanjiawan, the upper reaches of the Median Reservoir past the Luojia Temple and the Shenghua Fishing Village. Beyond there, the terrain is foot access only. As I said before, one of the monks will accompany us as we look for a spot to camp out and conduct the research."

Everyone accepted the specifics and collected our protective gear that resembled full-on biohazard suits but lighter.

"Are you gonna bring Jimmy with you up there?" Lance asked, confused.

When I responded positively, he advised against it as the trek would be much more difficult holding a cage in my hand.

I thanked everyone for their company and retired for the night, hoping for a good night's sleep in order to make Lance's 5:30 a.m.

wake-up call. I didn't sleep a wink all night, probably still concerned not to miss another entire day of time and risk being left behind.

* * * * *

*Right on time*, I thought.

A commanding knock came at the door, which startled Jimmy who woke up and headed into his cage, anticipating the adventure ahead and keen not to miss a second of it.

I packed my giant camping bag and hung the cage on its side while Jimmy crawled on my shoulder to enjoy the run in the free wind of the country. Flying foxes weren't native to Wuhan, so he was like a kid on an expedition to Disneyland the entire way there.

We assembled and piled into the four-wheeler that Lance rented, a suitable vehicle for the monster of a man. We stocked up on some dried foods, and for me, I sneaked in some sweets and frozen fruit snacks for Jimmy that I know he would appreciate. And then we were off.

It took about a half a day to get to the nature reserve, and we passed on very impressive infrastructure similar to a highway in the States, which made our run much easier. Wuhan's city center consisted about 8.9 million people, so everywhere we went was flooded with foot traffic. The larger metropolitan area, I understood, was around 19 million—staggering population numbers, the likes of which we were not accustomed to in the United States.

We passed a few nature reserves well along the way, a river near Mulan Tianchi, right next to a massive solar farm the size of four football fields. Thousands of people lined up for entrance into the reserve as if it were the Rio Carnival. Within a few hours, we passed through several of their suburban towns, Huanghuilong, Sifanchong and Langjiachong before entering Lujiawan. The roads gradually became smaller and bumpier as we progressed farther inland, reaching more rural areas resembling something from a Discovery Channel documentary. The green was so lush and the air so fresh. I guess whatever I was breathing before couldn't actually be considered air, which was a stark contrast to the urban areas in the city center.

We pulled up to Luojia Ancestral Temple around lunchtime—or, at least, I assumed it was—and when we got out the van, it was truly a sight to see: a tall Chinese pagoda temple with red-brick roofs and green trims that curve off the edge and shoot straight up to the heavens at least eighty feet. The stairs to the temple were mossy and steep, at least fifty steps before you even reached the ground floor.

Lance asked us to come along, so I left all my stuff in the car before taking on the ascent. By step number 25, I was about to puke. I rushed out at the beginning, which I realized was a bad idea. Jimmy realized I was struggling, so he flew to the roof of the temple to await my arrival.

Ten minutes later, I finally surmounted the final step, my jersey drenched; and Lance was at the top already, barely breaking a sweat. The girls were already at the top but was also out of breath. Rick was breathing heavily but not tired. I adjusted my glasses and wiped it as we took in the evergreen forest surrounding it; birds chirping and butterflies were everywhere in the garden. I marveled at the number of people that were there; they were in the inner court of the temple saying prayers and placing incense on a mantel specifically designed for just that.

After some time, a bald, elderly monk emerged from the back of the temple and bowed to us all; and we returned the favor. Lance introduced him as the abbot of the monastery, and he seemed happy to see visitors come to their end of the world to experience its many wonders. He motioned for us to come to the backyard and sit among the garden—a beautiful garden filled with flowers, butterflies, and birds that chirped all morning to welcome the midday sun.

He shared some noodle soup with us brought by one of the other monks, a much younger fellow probably in his thirties and full of vigor. Apparently, he was our guide. He had very little or no teeth. Brownish-black plaque that had a deep red hue ate away at his entire row of teeth, leaving a hobo-like smile on his face. I was told this was the infamous betel nut chewing habit that many countries in the Pacific had, a nut that grew from palm trees that people chewed incessantly with some lime and a palm leaf. The extracted juices give the body a natural high that stays with them throughout the day.

The abbot went on to give a discourse of the history of the valley and the stories of the five sacred mountains of China and the pillars that hold up the heavens from the earth. He also went into some detail about where we were about to go, a place called Huangxiang Shan, or "Mountain of Illusions."

"The caves are a very complex network of subchambers," the abbot began in broken English. "My only advice is to stay on the left as the right goes too far inside with a mazelike feature that may be difficult to navigate and even return alive."

Although the abbot spoke broken English, what I gathered from his stories was that no one usually traveled that far inland. It was not that it was forbidden; rather, there are some peculiar and almost sinister stories of disappearances and witchcraft located in those inner reaches. He then picked up on the tension growing in the group, so he opted to change the topic on more about the other side of Chinese mythology and the divine beasts of the cosmos.

"The vermillion bird, she rules over the south," the abbot began. "The azure dragon, the east; the white tiger, the west; and the black turtle, the north. These four beings hold the balance of the world on their shoulders—in particular, the turtle who actually carries it on his back, aided by several elephant apprentices."

We chuckled at the rich tale and told him a little of what we are going to investigate. He nodded and advised to be careful of the tiny bats as they can be nuisances and were known to carry a series of sicknesses. We accepted his blessing, and he sent us on our way with Fu, the younger monk, who would accompany us for the rest of the journey.

Each of us left with sandalwood incense, which the abbot specifically chose out for us. I felt really honored, and I bowed last to him before taking leave of the temple.

"And don't forget your friend." He smiled to me as he pointed to Jimmy, chuckling at the connection between us.

Heading down the steps were far easier than the other way around, and we settled into the truck as Fu guided our way. The remaining distance was a little over an hour, moving into the Shenghua Fishing Village and getting an additional treat of roasted tilapia fish before proceeding on. Duanjiawan was right after along the country road 13, and we broke off the beaten path to park near a friend of Fu's house, making brief introductions and getting ready to hike the rest of the way.

"Right behind the pools is where the caves are. There are about four of them, so we will head to the highest one," Lance explained.

I looked over my shoulder, and Jimmy was right with me, ready to make the trek. Once we strapped up all our gear, we hit the trail.

The path was just a few meters wide, too narrow for any vehicle, and carved out by a watercourse, making a narrow trench in the center of the hard, light brown rock. I felt good heading up the first thirty minutes, sipping water along the way and giving Jimmy a sip from time to time. But after that, the trail went to less than a foot wide with tall grasses lining the sides, not all of them friendly. Some of them were as sharp as a razor, hooking on to my clothes and ripping alongside until it caught my skin, drawing blood for the first time on the trip. I shuddered under the afternoon winter sun. Even though covered to some extent, we still had a sharp trek that took some climbing skills to master the rise. After the first hour, we finally arrived at the first pool.

It was on a platform on the top of that portion of the hill, and you could oversee the entire region as the cold, strong forest winds rushed through to meet me. I could see the rice terraces alongside us, with gorgeous shades of green, checkered with brown straw hats from the farmers knee deep into the ice-cold mud fields checking their crop under the winter winds. The pool hadn't completely iced over yet, but a small wash of my hands felt it nearing that point quickly.

Lance shouted for us to continue the trek in an attempt to make good time of the sunlight, and so we did. A couple more hours, and we were all completely out of it, making our last steps that our body temperature and strength could allow. Lance reveled in the snow, and Fu continued to lead the pack until he stopped suddenly, putting up his hand. There, in the gorge on the left, the massive final fourth pool and an even larger mysterious cave sitting right behind it.

# 6

# THE MERMAID'S APPETITE

We all hustled to the front of the cave that had an outcrop on its right that could protect us from the icy, strong winter winds. It was around 6:00 p.m., but the sun apparently set late here as in London, so we had a little more time to make camp.

I dropped on the floor like a dead man, the only thing getting me moving again was the ice-cold winds jolting me to action. Lance was the obvious first to assemble his tent, getting a fire going, before helping the rest of us get our tents set up and things unpacked. That was going to be our home until the New Year, so it was best to get comfortable.

I unpacked all my stuff in the tent as we each took some basic foodstuff to roast on the open fire. We had to plow through some mud to get to this point. The lake was completely iced over—thin ice, though, not the kind you could stand on. It made a perfect platform to reflect oncoming cold gusts into the cave that was set right behind us, making haunting whistling sounds as it moved in and out of the cave, like a rock monster breathing.

Lance continued checking our nets and medical gear to make sure we were ready. The first attempt to catch a bat was due at midnight. I looked around for some water source but couldn't find any, frozen underground I guessed. Everyone continued with light chatter over the open flame while my eyes drifted over to the mouth of the cave. My breathing got a little labored, and my eyes almost felt hypnotically entranced while disappearing into the depths of the cave. It felt like something was luring me to come inside, until Jimmy squeaked, waking me up from my daydream. I looked around and felt a little lost.

*Get it together, man*, I told myself, feeling some strange forces coming into play up on the mountain.

We were advised not to sleep too deeply before wake-up call at eleven, so I retired to my tent to try and catch a few hours' sleep before action began again.

Time moved quickly, and I was the first to emerge. I waited around the dead campfire until the others woke up. Lance was second, then Rick, and then the girls.

We started crocheting the ends of the net to make sure there were loops we could affix to the ends of the cave. Lance retrieved a rope ladder that Fu nailed on one side of the entrance to the cave, scampering up the other side as well, taking a gentle stroll as if the rock were horizontal. We took out our notebooks to carefully record the number, names, and the data from the little bats. The sun had just gone down a few minutes before, and the chatter from within the cave got louder, so we waited until the net caught something. We also put on our lighter biohazard suits to prevent any skin breach from an infected bat.

Soon there were hundreds then thousands of bats flying out from deep within the cave, but none caught on the net. This frustrated the entire team, but we could wait another day to try to catch samples. Lance pulled out some extra netting and tried lacing it on top of the other one, navigating his way through the stream of bats coming out the cave's mouth. It looked like a giant blowing black smoke out into the sky, a scary concept if ever I saw one.

Within the next hour, we could see the lower edge of the net shake violently.

"We caught one," Lance announced, first to carefully pull the bat from the net, holding it under a blanket so it wouldn't bite or stress any more than it had to.

We took hair, skin, blood, and muscle tissue samples, placing the items in separate petri dishes and recording the unique identification of the sample before tagging the creature. It was so small, but it scared me after what I saw in my room back in the hotel. It wriggled incessantly like a flying chinchilla with huge ears and a smashed-in nose. We let it go before hearing a couple more caught in the trap. Rinse and repeat until we had about ten samples for the night. Traffic was slowing up around 1:00 a.m., but most of them probably were feeding on the outside now.

We went on securing all the data, everyone taking a different sample and then writing down the data others would have taken like a form of quality control. We finished around three in the morning, so we all had some hot cocoa before heading in for the night.

I lay on my back, hearing the whirring of the wind outside and placing my hands under my butt to try and garner some warmth. Jimmy was lying next to my shoulder, seemingly okay with the temperature within the tent. I could hear snoring from my side, not sure which one of the crew had a sinus problem, sounding like a freight train, making it difficult for me to fall asleep. I looked up at the tent apex, and my mind drifted off on the bats and the cave.

My eyes started to get heavy, dropping on my face every second like a lead weight was tied to them. I then heard some footsteps coming from outside. The wind seemed distorted, owing to someone blocking its natural flow. I rolled my head sluggishly to the flap, wondering what it could be.

It opened, I looked hard, but didn't see anything. And then I felt a warm waft of air come from the left side. It was soothing, like a hot spring or bowl of soup that attracted my attention. I turned over, and there sat Natalie, resting on one hand, leaning over toward me. I stammered a little, and her left index finger reached out and sat on my lips, abruptly bringing me to silence.

Her hips were curved into the form of the rest of her body under a purple tank top and pajama shorts, her Polish background screaming out in the soft white skin she now rubbed along my leg. She started crawling to my face, her eyes piercing, staring into my soul, while her rosy, voluptuous, pink lips pursed ever so slightly up into the air as it drifted toward mine. Her breasts hung over my chest, with her now on all fours hovering over me. It was enchanting.

I felt absolute surrender in my spirit, a slice of heaven descended to meet me that night. I arched my shoulders slightly to meet her lips with mine. Her nipples brushed against my chest, dragging across left and right, making them hard, a slight squeak emerging from her mouth, followed by a tongue.

The squeak continued, until it turned into a shrill of intense decibels, and she started retreating. I winced and turned my head, covering my ears in pain, closing my eyes until I opened them bright.

I shot up from my sleep, but no one was there. It was just Jimmy, flared up and wings extended, coming over to me as if he chased something out, something that was far from human. I couldn't head outside until my morning wood would give me a little break. I lay back down to ponder the reach of whatever was starting to haunt me.

I took up my phone and checked my images to review my research. Unwilling to head back to sleep, I searched "The Painted Skin," the Chinese version of a siren that haunted men in their sleep, coming to them from their subconsciousness, drawing them out in their sleep until they brought them to their deaths, and draining their life energy and leaving them in a coma. I took out a mirror and looked at myself. A dark spot was left on my neck, looking like a hickey but something that went deeper. I rubbed my face, trying to keep myself awake until I could fight it no more, drifting off before the dawn.

* * * * *

I didn't hear or feel anything until I heard shouts coming from outside. I bundled out of bed, feeling like vines held down my arms and legs, a sinking feeling at the pit of my stomach telling me not to move. I rolled out of the tent, which started to feel like a bad idea when the winds picked me up. I had to beat a hasty retreat until I suited up properly. I headed out to a new fire and wondered where everyone was.

"Why is it still dark out here? Did I barely get any sleep?" I asked.

"No, asshole, you slept all the way through. It's almost one o'clock in the morning," Natalie barked. "We all had to cover your shift, but now the wind took our net into the cave, so Fu and Lance went in after it."

I looked her up and down, feeling uncomfortable but slightly aroused, her look of disgust refocusing me.

The cave was open, and a part of the net beat in the breeze as some bats still were coming out. I opted to head in after the guys to try and help. It was the least I could do, given I slept through an entire shift.

I turned on the headlamp on the suit and headed in. My first step caused me to fall almost five feet in, which was a massive drop to toss any sense of ego from spelunkers. I got up, dusting myself off, and looked around. A wave of bats came at me and was still coming as if they were angry about something. Their shrill cries penetrated the suit controls. Jimmy was still on me, but he clung on to my back, watching out for me from behind.

There was bat mess everywhere. A burnt igneous rock rose from the floor in the form of sharp stalagmites to which I held on to move around. The cavern was large and deep. There was nothing you wanted to do more than shout for the other guys, but of course this would draw unwanted attention to yourself. I had to clamber up a few steps before hitting what I considered solid ground, a polished limestone finish adorning the bottom of the cave posing a particular challenge to stay upright.

I tried walking carefully inward, but it was no use; the cave sloped beyond a forty-degree decline. Eventually, I just lost my footing, falling flat on my face and sliding inward until I came to a stop a few minutes later. I groaned as I fought the slippery nature of the now wet rock and black puddles I was standing in to get a good view of the place.

Looking around, I could see that the rock patterns were fairly uniform but now much deeper into the cave, trickles of bat colonies were still coming out from inside. I continued walking in. The dripping of condensed ice winds and the careful steps of my clumsy boots were the only sounds echoing far into the recesses of the cave chambers. I found myself walking for a few minutes well until I eventually came upon a fairly solid path that took me on a gentle incline. I followed it inside, but the space to walk was getting narrow and short, to the point where I had to crouch to keep moving forward.

The path then suddenly turned to mud, like arable soil mud. And just like that, a series of cuplike lilies started to shoot up. I recognized them as mermaid wineglasses, a rare type of underwater lily that grew on some unique ecosystems across the world. I carefully waded through them; and as I touched one, it shriveled up and looked like it died, turning brown and limp. I touched another and then another, and the same thing happened. It was as if this forest lilies just parted for me as I approached. Jimmy now squeaked continuously, sensing the same strange things I was seeing.

I started walking faster until I stepped on something stiff. I shone the light below and saw the lilies covering something. I moved them away with my hand; and then it was there—a human face, lying face up, pale and drowned to death. I looked closer, and it was Rick!

My heart skipped a beat, and I turned around and saw the entire path that I had made started growing back ferociously, to the point where it looked like a wave was coming to swallow me whole. Jimmy let out a scream, piercing the walls of the caves, and I could hear rustling from a distance. I ran toward the depths of the cave until I could feel I was getting to higher ground. But a wave of bats was also incoming from the other side.

I huddled down on all fours until thousands of bats passed by. I could feel them scratching my back as they flew from seemingly all directions, but I couldn't do anything. Lance and the others had to be in the cave, so I pressed on, eventually moving upward in steps until I reached a dead end. I looked up at the ceiling and could see a strange sign written in Chinese:

盖亚将生活

I didn't know what it meant, but I took a picture of it and paused, thinking where next to go. And then I heard crumbling rocks, coming from before. I ran back to the pool and saw the lilies still rushing toward me, making a strange tingling sound like tiny bells that sent chills up my spine. There was a chamber to my right, so I darted in that direction, looking for any clues as to where the others may be.

I came to a grotto, and there they were, Lance and Fu, lying on the floor, a stench of methane escaping from the chamber, bubbling up through a pool in the center also filled with the wineglasses, their leaves crawling out to consume the guys. I ran to them and beat off the plants, and as I looked up, I could see a shimmer of false movement—someone or something was up there. I didn't wait to see what it was.

I slapped Lance awake and threw some water on him, and he came to pretty quickly and was able to help me with Fu who had no helmet on. Lance's gear was also ripped up pretty bad, but he had enough strength to help me pull up Fu and head back up. We darted through the lilies quickly near Rick's corpse and struggled over the first limestone slide, groaning and yelling with every pull we had to make, the methane leaving us disoriented. I felt like I had no strength left in me, and as we headed over the apex, we could see the rope ladder the girls dropped. A deep sigh came from us as we hauled Fu up the ladder, struggling to pull ourselves out of the cave before spreading out in front the fire as we all coughed uncontrollably for a while, while the girls started patching us up.

The cuts and bruises were small, but for some reason, it felt as if we had gone through a war. I screamed like a little girl when Natalie put some alcohol swabs on my bruises. Lance tried to keep a tough face while Fu placed on his.

"Wait, where's Rick?" Yue asked in a panic.

I watched Lance's face, and he returned the gaze, both of us responding with dejected silence as the fire continued to crackle viciously under the winter gales.

# Part II

# EPIDEMIC

*February 9, 2020*
*813 Deaths*
*37,552 Cases*

# 7

# PANDORA'S BOX

It was Christmas Day, but it was one we would all like to forget as Lance organized a small memorial for Rick, putting the expedition on hold for the rest of the night. The girls wept as Fu gradually regained consciousness under a tank of oxygen. There was a sullen mood where the windswept snow quickly smothered any candles we had out on Rick's pictures below. Even Jimmy sensed the mood and stayed in his cage in the tent all day, brooding the loss. Part of the net was still up, and from time to time it still caught a couple bats. I pursued with the research methodology, determined for Rick's death not to be in vain.

We struggled to stay focused for the next week, frightened of what was to come, tempted to go in and get Rick's remains as his dead face loomed over our spirits. I had to keep an eye on Lance as he was most likely the one to do something as silly as that. He blamed himself for Rick's demise as he took the time to try and confide in me what we witnessed in the cave. I remained just an earnest listener and no more.

Our last day on this cursed hill arrived, and no one needed to know anything that might upset them more than the trip already had. The final day came and went with little action; everyone was just happy to leave the place with enough data to make the resulting paper a credible one. We began our trek downhill under strong winter storm conditions. My eyes could barely stay open as we made our way past the first bend. I looked back up the hill to the crest near the lake, and I saw a shadow overlooking us. As I squinted to get a better look, it was gone.

I sped down the descent slightly, trying to escape the paranormal grasp of the cave. Soon enough, we came to the van. I nearly shed a tear when I saw it. The girls broke down completely, crying uncontrollably, hurrying to get into the van to curl up under its warmth.

Lance walked into the driver's seat and drove off in silence, dropping off Fu and thanking him for all his help before reaching in to the Wuhan Institute to meet the professor. Our beards were full, and hair was strewn all over our faces. The girls had an unusually disheveled appearance to their normally put-together ensemble.

We related our tale to him, he offered his condolences while he took the raw data from us, and offered it to his assistant to send off to their lab for analysis. He advised that we get some sleep as our flight was later that night. We headed over to the cafeteria to get some lunch and a stash of fruits for Jimmy before heading to our rooms to pack.

I couldn't sleep; it was all too much on my conscience to bear. I just sat on the bed, thinking about the event, and took out a separate journal and started taking notes and sketches. I was a scientist, and the only thing I could use to combat these strange occurrences was what I knew best—science.

We packed our stuff and headed out to the airport to check in. I looked over and saw a newsstand and took out a paper. There was an article about the virus and how it was sweeping through Wuhan. We were so preoccupied with our research that we forgot the dire circumstances that were projected. Five dead and eighty confirmed cases were the statistics on January 3, 2020. And while the source was from Chinese national newspapers, where censorship and government control was a possibility, I went to my model to see what the numbers projected. It was correct to within 10 percent. That scared me a little, owing to the projections that the model had to come.

My thoughts were interrupted by the call to board on the PA system, so I took Jimmy through customs and was relieved to be heading back to comfort in New York. I couldn't take a minute more of that experience. It left me jaded and exhausted, but in Lance's case, he left with a heavy burden on his shoulders. He left final instructions with everyone to submit their individual trip reports to him within five days, and he asked us to remain scientific in our observations—no doubt trying to manage potential hysteria and credibility matters.

* * * * *

The flight took us a couple days in the air. But we returned within a day, thanks to shifts over varied time zones. I eventually returned to the apartment and immediately hit the bed before letting out Jimmy and leaving some fruits out for him to eat. I slept for eighteen hours before waking up feeling like I've been hit by a truck.

I made some savory continental breakfast that hit the spot after so much noodles and soups I had to endure. I took a shower that felt like something I haven't had since I left, concluding that my skin and body just got accustomed to New York water and developed a liking to it. I started work immediately on the trip report and handed it in the same day, being careful to omit any paranormal inklings I might have wanted to include, even though that version would have been more accurate. I peeked into Liz 's room and saw it was very messy, so I assumed she was back and probably out to work.

* * * * *

I got ready and headed into school the next day to meet with everyone to discuss the next steps of the study. When we met, everyone was in better spirits as the girls took turns petting Jimmy—something he looked forward to every time coming to class.

Lance took a deep breath to announce that the department had launched an official investigation into Rick's death and that the police was involved, partnering with the Wuhan Institute and authorities. None of us were particularly surprised, but it still was a criminal investigation that we never had experienced before. Lance announced that we got the results of our research, so he gave each of us copies in USBs to review the paper and send our comments over to him to finalize the paper for publication. We all thanked Lance for the opportunity and the support and urged him not to blame himself for anything; there was nothing more we could do. He nodded and thanked us for our commitment before sending us on our way.

I rushed home to read the preliminary draft, curious about the results of the data we collected. I speed-read the paper about twenty times before settling down to properly go through the product, understanding and internalizing the results.

It said that almost 80 percent of the bat samples we collected had traces of some virus; the genome of which was classified as a coronavirus but a special one. I looked at the samples' microscopic analyses, and it was a virus like I had never seen before: virions were everywhere, and the proteins and membranes were thick and oversized, looking like a mutated version of what I saw before. This bothered me, and upon reading the analyzed data, it aligned perfectly with what the professor was alluding to—a respiratory zoonotic virus that attacks the lungs directly with an aggressive contagious property that allowed it to spread airborne. It was frightening that it originated from those horseshoe bats, but that would at least confirm that we could use those bats to try and find one that survived and develop a vaccine from that bat's antibodies.

I sent my comments to Lance, which were minor in nature, waiting for Liz to come home and give her the update. She never showed, though, which worried me a little. I went online and saw that she never responded to any of my e-mails. I saw her friend Peter respond to say that he hadn't heard from her for a while, so I naturally kept the pursuit up and let him know once I heard anything.

* * * * *

A week had passed, and on January 10, we had a hearing with the dean to confirm the contents of our trip reports and why we knew Rick was dead. I said what I could, and because I actually saw his dead body, they grilled me the most. After a harrowing two hours, the team met after and Lance brought us a copy of the published paper in *The Journal of Infectious Diseases*. It was satisfying to read through it, and the dedication went to Rick posthumously, which heartened the team to a smile.

I headed home with the paper, still perturbed after the entire committee hearing, but I read the paper some more, looking particularly at the virus components and structure. I went to my e-mail to check on something, opening some old e-mails from Liz that she would have sent. This paper basically dubbed the virus the "novel coronavirus (COVID-19)," as the first case was in 2019. I opened up Liz's paper and noticed it was almost identical to this one, except the virus structure was different.

The proteins weren't that thick, the envelope and the genome all looked simpler, yet the symptoms and mode of transmission described in the paper was the same, except for airborne transmission. Then I realized something. The virus wasn't the same; it was evolving—and at an alarming rate, at that.

I wasn't sure how to proceed, but I knew for sure the virus that was published with us was not COVID-19. If I had a choice, I would call it COVID-20; and if the authors of the paper used Liz's words in the new paper, that means there was a possible cover-up and the symptoms may in fact be a lot worse than they are making it out to be.

* * * * *

A few days passed, and I was in and out of school, doing what I could to try and find Liz. I saw the team from time to time; but they looked exhausted, constantly sweating, and Yue even coughed a couple times.

Was it too crazy to think it had reached the United States? Was it virulent enough to cross those seas? And with air transport being as common as it is, for the mutant virus that exists, that would surely not be a problem.

January 25, 2020—the first newspapers on the stands read my worst fear come true: "Coronavirus Now Worldwide, the First US Case."

# 8

# RAGNAROKKR

Things were now very serious. Even if the wider public hadn't realized it yet, the fact that a thirty-five-year-old man who just returned from Wuhan visiting family had it—there was no limit to where the virus could reach. The man was admitted to a hospital in Washington and was treated for his symptoms.

I wasn't sure what to do; but as the virus started to spread West, the emphasis on virology and microbiology and their ability to churn out relevant research toward a vaccine would dominate the landscape. I returned to what felt comfortable, which was running my models, and started adjusting mathematical algorithms to cater to the true structure of the virus and its abilities. And the results were frightening to say the least.

I tried to find as much information as I could online about the virus and potential projections that experts would have done, but there was nothing.

*That's strange*, I thought, after using all the major search engines and realizing that everyone simply reported on data to date and no one was willing to share any projections—it was almost as if the information was being controlled. *They must be trying to minimize panic and widespread chaos.*

And I understood this, but sometimes, I think it's also necessary to have faith in humanity and sharing the information would at least make it known how serious the problem is and for people to start adjusting their lives.

Later that day, I got a call from the office and a series of e-mails from the dean implementing a work-from-home policy, limiting working in the office to essential services only. I was shocked to see this and wondered if they were the only one rolling out this strategy.

I stayed close to the news and noted that most politicians simply made the ideas of the virus a political football, with the upcoming US general election the major thing on their minds. With newscasts now becoming an unreliable source of current data without sensationalism, I had to keep my eyes glued on the academic community and the information they produced.

"God is an American," said one man interviewed in Iowa on an MSNBC morning news, an approach that categorized the early global response to the virus that seemingly took things very casual, the state of the economy being more important than protecting the people. Most people continued partying and was concerned about spring break and showing off their beach bods among thousands of other spring breakers. After what I saw in Wuhan, it was impossible to take the virus lightly.

I set up a conference call with our team and noticed all of them were also in their houses working from home. They were all sweating profusely and showing slight symptoms of hypoxia. This concerned me, so I kept the discussion light, realizing that I was the only one of our group to not get any serious illnesses or show any symptoms.

*C'mon, Liz, where are you?* I wondered. *I need you here now.*

Jimmy was happy to be flying around in the apartment once again, but he too knew there was something wrong. My propensity to have everything delivered and disinfected before letting it into the apartment space was seen as strange.

I spoke to Petra on the phone, but she was pretty distant since my return, only wanting to spend a bare minimum amount of time talking and always rushing toward something else that seemed to be more important to her. I went into Liz's room and started going through her stuff to find some clues as to where she could be. I found an iPad just sitting on the dresser, so I took it out and tried cracking the password. It took me an hour to crack the password using some online routing software and proxy servers, but I got in.

Searching through the tablet was like going through Liz's mind; it was a network of papers and mind maps that chronicled her research goals for the next two years. The host resistance gene structure and parts were a key of her research, breaking down the level of virulence of a particular virus to the level of acceptance of hosts and focusing her research there. The host resistance she was writing was composed of three parts: the specific cellular receptor that controls viral entry, host cell structure and resistance, and, finally, the strength of the host's immune system. Her most recent paper seemed to focus the most on the first part and doing some gene splicing work to improve the resistance of that specific cellular receptor, blocking the virus from entering the body from the onset. It was an interesting read, but what I really needed were her e-mails to track her down.

I tried as much as I could but couldn't hack the mail server to access the messages. I sat frustrated in the room but wasn't sure what my next move could be. Thinking aloud, I started searching for her papers online about what I just read on the tablet—nothing. All the dark corners of the internet didn't have even a scent of what she was working on. It's as if no one was interested in it or even pursuing it.

I tried calling around different airlines but found nothing of worth, so I picked up a face mask from the set we got in Wuhan and opted to take a walk to Central Park with Jimmy. Reaching into my tote bag for a cigarette, I found my journal, so I started writing down the information I knew so far and the players involved—the Wuhan Institute, Liz's company, Peter, her friend from Texas, and me, which were all I had. I layered all that I knew onto her research and the fact that I couldn't find the information anywhere, so I placed a big question mark; a riddle I would have to solve along the way.

*I should test the market,* I thought.

And so I spent most of the night and day working on a paper of my own, one that chronicles most of our activities in Wuhan and relating it to the modeling I was doing. My paper would show the virus crossing the 100,000 threshold of confirmed cases by early March, reaching 1.7 million deaths by June, and the rest I just put speculative data until I could have more in my series to validate and verify the model for greater accuracy.

After finalizing the information, I sent it to our faculty head and asked him to sponsor the article, seeking peer reviews and critiques from some major players in the field. He wrote back with long queries of the data and sources with specific concerns over the interpolations and validations of the model. I tried to answer most of his questions, but it became an effort in frustration as he basically was telling me in a nice way to tank the research and he won't sponsor the article.

*Is it a global commitment by the leaders of the field to contain those projections?* I mused. *I understand trying to control public perception, but if the virus is coming regardless, then shouldn't the different countries go into shock earlier rather than later? Doesn't the population have a right to know?*

I thought they did, so I started my own blog, setting up a WordPress website on some cloud-based hosts out of Russia and published my stuff there.

Within a couple days, my site was taken down for "sedition and anticybercrime concerns." I was in shock but not surprised. There definitely was something funny going on, and I had to get to the bottom of it.

I went over to Lance's apartment to talk to him about Liz and to find out if he has any leads he could send me on. He stayed in an apartment on West Twenty-Fourth Street, part of a complex of high-rises next to the picturesque highline, the elevated repurposed train line for pedestrians. I buzzed in and went to see him, smiling as I entered.

I couldn't believe what I saw. He was barely a shadow of the Icelandic giant who would brave waters thick and thin for his fellow man. Now, he was gaunt, sweating bullets, and had a red complexion that made me very concerned for his health. He almost looked like he didn't have much time left.

"Lance, h-h-hey, buddy, how you keeping?" I said.

He responded with some vicious coughing, jumping up to a seated position as he did.

"Bill, good to see you," Lance said. "As you can see, I'm not doing so well. I'm not sure how much time I have left, as the doctors have never seen anything like this, COVID-19 being the closest fit. But I gather they are still not sure."

I stayed quiet to his concerns so as to minimize his worry.

"I dunno, Bill, but something makes me feel like those bats we saw weren't carrying an ordinary virus—*ordinary* by our standards, of course. And I think that Prof Lee knows about it."

He coughed uncontrollably for a few minutes before settling back down to talk.

"I believe with strong fervor that something is amiss and that we were actually at ground zero in Wuhan," Lance continued. "Those bats—they remain the key to the entire puzzle, Bill, and the world, well, the world doesn't have as much time as they think. Here in the States, we seem to be taking it very lightly, not that anywhere has really given the virus the attention it deserves. It all seems to be a coherent massive lie, a fabrication designed to level the playing field in a continental power struggle that you or I know very little of."

I nodded in agreement before giving my opinions of what had happened, using Liz as an example of something fishy going on and that she may know where next to go in order to manage what is to come.

He agreed and coughed as he did, pulling out a business card for a friend of his in Greenleaf Canyon in Topanga, Los Angeles, who owned a private airplane school.

"This is my buddy Travis, just tell him I sent you," Lance instructed. "He recently made some odd trips to the Pacific and China that has his mind going a little crazy too. I think it would be worth your while."

I thanked him and updated him on the experience with my paper, and he said he wasn't surprised, advising that everyone was very risk averse now for the virus information to reach public and that governments are shutting down potential sources of leaks.

He smiled at this conflict, looking at me with piercing eyes. "You know, my *amma* always told me stories from Nordic lore, stories to try and guide our world today. I never believed in any of them. They always seemed to be for another time—another world, almost—when it was a norm for Vikings to go from land to land, conquering and pillaging for the sake of growing their empire. A long and unending winter. This was the main sign for the trigger of *Ragnarokkr.* She called it *Fimbulwinter*, or a winter with no end.

"Tell me, Bill, when was the last time you saw a winter this long and cruel in New York? I haven't, and maybe this is just the ramblings of a dying man, but I know that a darkness is sweeping over the earth, one that no man knows how to stop or even slow down. Tell me, Bill, why do you have such firm resolve against the coming plague?"

I had never heard Lance this pessimistic; it was scary to see. I had never thought of the virus as a coming plague, but I suppose it was an apt assessment, given what we knew to be true and what we have experienced firsthand. But why indeed was I so embroiled with this fight for survival? After a few seconds of pondering his question, only one thing came to mind.

"Liz, Liz is the reason I keep fighting," I told him. "She has been with me through thick and thin since my father left us when we were children and mother died. I had no one else, but she stayed with me. She believed in me, as I now believe in her. I will not rest until I find her. If her discovery yields something of greater importance to the world, then so be it. But the affairs of men is one mangled in a complex web of desires and unholy intentions. I would rather stay out of that as I have no desire for power or glory."

He stopped and looked at me.

"Yes, yes, Bill, find your sister, this is the only way," Lance encouraged me. "The world has no more room for martyrs, and it is easy for someone in your position to fall prey to its allure. Turn on the plight of the world for now, find Elizabeth, and get her to safety. Should this coming plague be divinely ordained, then you ought not to stand in its way. It is not worth the pain that it would cause your heart—a burden that you may not be able to carry."

His tone dropped, and his mind drifted to something afar, perhaps Rick's plight, which is yet to leave his spirit.

"It haunts me, Bill," Lance got back to me, a gentle tear rolling down his cheek. "I still see his body dropping behind me below the floor of lilies, a gentle tingle of bells to signal the mermaids have caught their prey. I wish I could help, but there was nothing, nothing more I could do."

"I know, Lance, we all knew the risks of that trip," I reassured him. "No one blames you for anything, you acted professionally and in accordance with the principles of the history of daring scientists to come before you. And as a result, we have made a contribution to the world understanding of the virus and its origins. We could ask for no more."

Lance exhaled loudly, still bothered by the entire scene and how it all played out.

"The truth is, I haven't been able to sleep properly since I returned. This virus that we have contracted seems to be well beyond what everyone else has gotten."

He held up his palms to show purple fingers with sweaty reddened bulbous ends, a sign of strong hypoxia. This prompted another string of coughs that made him wince at the pain on his chest.

I patted him on the shoulder and bid him farewell, hoping he would make a recovery before I returned.

* * * * *

Greenleaf Canyon was a quiet town in an otherwise very busy city center on the West Coast. I didn't know what it would hold, but at this stage, I thought anything would be better than just sitting down waiting for things to get worse. I bought my tickets and packed my stuff, ready for another leg of the journey toward finding Liz.

# 9

# GHOST TOWN

It took a while to get my affairs in order, arranging for payment of my rent and utilities before I would return to New York. I was able to connect with Lance's friend Travis, and he welcomed the visit out at Green Canyon in LA, and he even offered to have me stay at his house for the time being there. I thanked him for his kindness and made my last set of preparations before heading out.

My flight left New York, heading to LA, on January 31, 2020. It was a short flight, comparatively speaking, and I had no issues with Jimmy and moving him around domestically. As I landed, I picked up an *LA Times* newspaper from the newsstand and noticed that the situation has changed overnight. The WHO had declared a global health emergency for the coronavirus. At this stage, 213 deaths were recorded, and 9,826 cases were confirmed.

I had to take a seat at the news.

*The virus is spreading like wildfire*, I thought. *We had just returned from Wuhan where the virus had now started to take hold of the city, but there wasn't any widespread panic anywhere. This is crazy!*

I wasn't sure what to think other than it was more urgent than ever that I find Liz and make sure she was okay.

I pulled out my laptop to check my mathematical models, and again, my projections were within 10 percent of the actual results. I calibrated my models again with the new data, hoping my data would drop. It didn't.

I folded in the papers, got some coffee and fruits for Jimmy, and took a cab to take me out to Greenleaf Canyon.

* * * * *

We departed LAX in the morning and arrived at the canyon within a couple hours, turning into Greenleaf Canyon Road and moving onto the Gold Stone Road amid the thickets reaching the homestead where Travis and his son lived. He came out and greeted us with open arms with his seven-year-old boy, the spitting image of his daddy.

Travis looked to be in his early forties with long blond hair and blue eyes to match, with a built similar to Lance, as if they originated from the same Viking clan in Iceland. We had a good laugh about the trip and spoke about the unusually hot sun that started roasting the landscape over the past few days coming out of an unusually cold winter season by LA's standards. He carried us to our bungalow, which was on an adjacent lot near the main house where we put our things and unpacked a little before returning to the main house to chat with him on the porch.

"I hear Lance isn't doing so good" he started in a grim tone, in stark contrast to his upbeat welcome. "He called me a while back, told me to expect you, and he had a lot of end-of-the-world talk spewing out from his chew hole. I tell you, as I told him, no disease is gonna take out no Viking, he's been through much worse. He's gotta be able to pull through this one, he just gotta."

I could hear the crackle in his throat. Lance clearly meant a lot to Travis, perhaps high school buddies or maybe they grew up together. Either way, I didn't want to feed the fire too much by talking about Lance out of context.

I gave him a short update and the positives of the visit, pointing out that I was looking forward to heading back to New York soon to update him on the trip.

"Oh, you're a good one, son," Travis told me. "Now I see why Lance likes you. Well, hey, let's go get some grub, you guys must be famished."

His chirpy redneck tone resonated with my spirit, keeping it up and moving forward.

We started chatting about the coronavirus, and I told him about our research trip, leaving out the sad details so he would understand why we were there. He was very attentive and thoughtful, appreciating the salient details of the story and thus making an impression of what was to come. He did mention that there was some stirring going on in LA, but it only started a little over a week, with certain businesses becoming more restrictive in who they see such as private dentists and doctors, asking the nature of the case, and whether it was emergency in nature.

"Well, I had a few fillings I wanted to get sorted, but I was shit out of luck, so I just took care of it the old-fashioned way—tying a string to the tooth and slamming the door," Travis said, laughing out loud at his story and proudly showing off the two missing incisors from the top row, laughing even harder when he saw myself and Jimmy wince a little at the sight.

"And what about this little fella? Where did you get this beaut?" he remarked, playing with Jimmy's mane, which the flying fox loved all too well.

I related the story, and he was fascinated by it all, telling me that he too was a collector of wild birds and fish and asked if I would like to see the collection. I responded in the affirmative, taking a casual walk out back into the forested areas until I could hear loud chirping and squawking from within the trees.

"You see, I believe in keeping birds and having them as wild as possible so their populations can flourish."

He showed me the massive trees to the back that had bird nets draped over the canopies where several of the trees grew, but it allowed a massive enclosed area for his large exotic bird collection. There was a rainbow belt of birds in flight as he came close and threw birdseed into the air for the masses of parakeets and yellow crowned parrots to join. We continued walking along the paths; and I could see macaws of every color—scarlet, hyacinth, yellow, green—and toucans with their multicolored plumage caressing the outer greens of the large oak trees.

I looked closely and even picked up some tree boas, bright green and blue, slithering over the extended bare branches situated coolly under the shade of the canopies. I marveled at the sight, and my hand drifted through the chain-link fence to touch one of them. But they were too far, projecting their hypnotic allure from their poise and majesty.

As we walked further into the estate, I could feel the environment temperature drop as we approached what Travis called his "land of mermaids." I didn't think it was the best choice of words, based on recent experience, but I suppose he knew where he garnered the inspiration from. A stream started flowing alongside us on the path, and there were little splashes from the aerated water when it crashed onto rocks, spilling on to the pathway, making it slippery on some areas. I could now hear the rush of the stream as it passed under the path via a bridge, emptying into a large pool at the base the size of a football field.

"Gentlemen, this is the land of mermaid," Travis said.

My eyes opened wide, trying to take it all in at once. Water hyacinth covered most of the water entry, and the rest were lotus lilies. Every color of lotus possible graced the pond—pink, purple, white, and even a soft yellow—covering different areas of the natural pond, with the water gently snaking through each and every one of them. There was an area near the edge of the pond that was open, and I jumped when Travis suddenly threw a handful of what looked like fish food and some green bushes.

A cascade of reds and yellows bubbled from under the lotus into the open water, thrashing on the surface, making a big scene, fighting for a morsel of food. They were rare Japanese koi fish, Travis explained, the rarest of the rare, bred from a few parent fish from the legendary Dainichi clan from Japan. He sported the most legendary fish that drifted through the lake like they owned the space. At least 1.5m in length and the girth to support it, a sea of Showa, Sanke, and butterfly koi moved through the pond seamlessly, giving a show fit for royalty—a true spectacle to behold. Jimmy peered carefully over my shoulder, his beady eyes glued to the event.

From the far end of the pool, I could see the lotus then raise ever so slightly above the water level and then start moving. Something was under it; something was coming. I thought it was an alligator as it was definitely something big. The lotus then peeled off the back of the creature, and as it did, it came to the surface and revealed itself—a school of West Indian manatees. I smiled when I saw them, the fabled mermaids of the seas that often gave pirates nightmares when they saw them moving in the distance; their graceful, fluid movement had its own temptation under the surface.

The gentle creatures carefully skimmed the surface for the pieces of greens and chewed them down using their massive jowls. Each creature was over four meters and weighed close to 450 kilograms. They were the true giants of the pond but moved about, carefree, which brought a smile to my face, a satisfaction that had Travis break out in laughter.

"Well, ya know, Bill, I try my best, and it brings me joy to come in and interact with these animal spirits," Travis said. "I feel at rest, you know, even amidst a world terror. But tell me, how can I really help? What do you need?"

I told him about my predicament and how Liz upped and left and that I couldn't find her. I told him that it's also quite possible that she simply moved through private planes to wherever she was headed as she was very comfortable with those.

"Why would you say she's comfortable, why not just use a main airline?"

"She has a pilot's license for that size of plane, and she prefers flying those planes than sitting in a passenger seat," I told Travis. "She flew a lot when we were younger, and I suppose if she is in fact on the run, she would be trying to keep a low profile. That type of plane seems to be the best way to do that."

Travis nodded. "Well, before you came, I did search my database with all my businesses, but I didn't see that Huxley name come up over anything, so she definitely didn't pass through my empire."

He saw my face drop when I heard that.

"But fear not, we small airplane operators are a tight group of people, so I'll make some calls and see what turns up, okay?" Travis assured.

"I would really appreciate that, Travis. I need to find her. I wouldn't be able to forgive myself if anything were to happen to her."

"And nothing will. We'll find her before you know it. Now come on, let's go check out my begonia collection."

I happily concurred before retiring to the main house for a late dinner. At the end, he gave me a card for a colleague of his called Truman Pakrit, an Indian-born American citizen living in a coastal town in California called Secuit Canyon on the outskirts of Western Malibu.

"He runs a private airplane show too," Travis added. "He would know if you sister has passed through."

I nodded in gratitude for his help before heading to bed in our cottage, pondering the possibilities where Elizabeth could have run off too.

* * * * *

Bright and early we graced the roads of LA to try and beat the heavy traffic, heading out west to the Malibu shoreline. It took us about a couple hours to reach out there and another half hour past West Malibu before reaching the Secuit Canyon. It was more barren than Greenleaf, but you had a beautiful view of the coast here.

The address Travis gave me came up to a rundown hangar with no plane in it. We honked the horn a few times before a pudgy short, brown man with a sharp nose and warm brown eyes emerged, speaking in what I would consider a perfect American accent. He had a stern smile and brought us inside his office, a twenty-foot container fit out with lights and AC parked right next to the old hangar.

"I've been expecting you both," Mr. Pakrit said of Jimmy and me. "Travis told me everything, so let me start by saying I'm sorry what happened to your sister, but have you considered going to the police?"

I stammered and told him I would prefer not to as I felt that I would have a better chance of locating her.

Mr. Pakrit shrugged his shoulders and brought up some records on his computer showing that Liz Huxley did not use his services.

"However" he started, "there was one lady that I think may fit the description of the person you are talking about. Do you have a picture?"

I took out one from my wallet to give him.

"Yep, that's her," he smiled, reaching into his files and taking out the documentation for a Joan Winslet, an alias Liz seemed to have entered the premises with. "She paid me quite handsomely too, much more than the usual rate to take the plane to god knows where. She said she would send me the location where she landed when she got there. I haven't heard from her in a few days."

"Is that common?" I asked, confused.

He replied no, but it was some good business that he couldn't refuse.

I nodded, and then I saw something in her file.

"Hey, what's that?"

He looked at the file and noticed a business card in it.

"Hmm, first time I noticed that," Pakrit said.

I took it out and read, "Secuit Divers' Lodge—for all your diving needs."

"Hmm, a diver eh? Well, that place actually isn't that far from here, about a few miles driving west, you can't miss it," Pakrit instructed. "It's on the coastal side of the highway."

I smiled and thanked him for his time before heading back into my rental Dodge Raptor and speeding off into the western wilds to find this dive shop.

* * * * *

"Liz and I dove a lot," I explained to the front desk clerk, Lilly. "I just wanted to know where she went and whether we could head out there today."

She watched me with great skepticism, so I took out my ID and picture of Liz without divulging the fact that she was using an alias. Lilly begrudgingly helped me out, showing me the dive records and even gave me Liz's dive log. That was exactly what I was looking for. The log showed her exact location, dive depth, and what she went out looking for. But I think I know.

We always went wreck diving when we were younger. Once life and adulting caught up with us, we had to leave it behind; but we explored some of the most sought-after dives the world over. I'm sure that whatever clues she left behind for me to find her, it would be at that dive site, so I met up with the resort's dive master and asked him for some assistance to head out to the dive location.

He willingly said yes but asked me to pay a little more as no dives were scheduled for that day. I understood and paid it anyway, eager to see what the depths of the pacific had in store for me. He gathered the gear and stocked up the car before heading out to the beach to meet with a local fisherman to load the boat we would use.

The dive master, Fred, was very fit and seemed to be in his early fifties with a tan and face that made him seem Hawaiian. I didn't know for sure, but he also offered to accompany me on the dive after inquiring to what level I was certified to dive. After placing the oxygen tanks and other equipment into the boat, we were on our way.

"Hey, you know, you didn't tell me where we're headed," I told Fred.

"Just off Catalina Island, a wreck there—that is where your friend went," Fred responded. "She dove by herself and spent a little over an hour at that depth, probably a little under sixty feet. This area is known to have sharks and poisonous lionfish, so make sure you head down with a speargun—you may need it."

He saw the nervous look creep over my eyes, but there was no time for that now.

I suited up as best as I could and jumped into the boat.

*Let's see what surprise you left for me, Liz,* I told myself. *Let's get this show on the road.*

# 10

## CATALINA ISLAND

Catalina Island was one famous for tourists and locals alike and known as a playboy's paradise. Named after St. Catherine by the Spanish conquistador Sebastian Viscaino in the early 1500s, the Native Americans who lived in Catalina Island before were quickly ushered off the island that they called Pimu before the island was established as a place for the rich and famous to enjoy. We, of course, had other plans for the space as the boat ripped through the turquoise waves heading off the island into deeper waters near one of its popular wrecks.

The Grumman G-21 Goose flying boat was a popular seaplane that was downed with four occupants. All survived the crash, but the submerged plane became a popular dive site that everyone wanted to go and see. Both Liz and myself went to see it in the early 2000s and always loved heading there and taking pictures in front the propellers.

The sea spray was glorious under the morning sun, wetting my face and body to keep it cool under the strong rays. Jimmy was loving the new experience as well. As we approached the dive site, Fred cut the engine and had our boat drift to the general area before starting to suit up. I kindly asked him to sit that one out as I was pretty familiar with the space and needed someone to watch Jimmy for me while I was down there. He advised caution and reminded me of the different safety measures to employ once down there. The dive was over two hundred feet deep, so it wasn't that simple.

I suited up and took up a dive canister of enriched air while connecting the regulator to the O-ring and strapping up my buoyancy control device (BCD). I looked over the boat edge and noticed some movement at the bottom. It looked unusual, knowing how graceful fish moved underwater. Still, I didn't fight it. So after testing my equipment, I put on my masks, goggles, and fins before heading down below with the speargun. I gave Fred an okay sign and patted Jimmy on the head, leaving him in the cage so he wouldn't follow me down.

I rolled into the water, making a tremendous splash upon entry, as the underwater world opened up for me once again. It had been close to five years since I last dove; so I took it slow, equalizing early and as often as possible, as I went down to deeper quarters. The first sixty wasn't bad, even though my jawline was feeling the squeeze on the mask. A few exhales through my nose quickly sorted that out.

I felt the temperature getting colder as I descended, as the surface got farther and farther away. There weren't much currents, and the visibility was a little over twenty feet, which was pretty good at that time of day. I used the compass to head toward the wreck, passing straight into a kelp forest as Liz and I did so in the past. The kelp looked like long, green tentacles streaming up from a bottomless ocean, waving in the current like ghosts. I navigated past the forest and swore I saw something move again in between the kelp, like a sharp dart to stay out of my sight.

Several schools of fish swam alongside me, keeping me company as I headed down. The freedom of the ocean set my mind at ease. However, few could prepare for a descent beyond the 80-foot mark as you just stare into sharp nothingness, a horizonless pull of no visual guides forward or backward as you begin propelling forward with nothing but your headlight, compass, and faith to guide the way. Beyond the 150-foot mark, I passed a sea of plankton, which made the rest of the journey darker, like night underwater. I had to turn up the light to make sure I could see a few more feet in front of me. It was nerve-racking, moving forward slowly and not knowing.

*This is the root of all fear,* I thought, trying to keep my mind busy.

Then out of a cloud of dust, a reef shark's nose emerged, drifting across my path like a water snake, blind to my existence, just going about its business. My stomach dropped a few feet, but I spread my legs to pause my forward motion and just let the currents pull me forward. I exhaled hard and closed my eyes before continuing on, beating my feet a little slower to allow my surroundings to soak in a little more before transitioning to another depth. I checked my SPG gauge and saw that I still had a little over 2,500 psi in the tank. That was still good, but a lot of air was lost because of the shark.

I continued drifting downward until I finally reached the bottom at a little over two hundred feet. The pressure was so strong, I had to ascend a little to equalize as my ears started to feel as if it were going to blow. My mask started to fog up as well, so I had to look up and clear the mask of water. And as I looked down, it finally came into sight—the propeller from the Grumman Goose, sitting at the bottom, growing algae for a school of parrotfish to nibble away at.

I drifted forward to the wreck and gently swam around it, a breath of nostalgia coming over me as I looked at the pink algae–covered propeller. It was still beautiful, after all these years. I had to take some time just to sit on the bottom on sand, pondering life without Liz and wondering when everything got so hectic that I couldn't do any of this stuff anymore.

I took a deep breath and noticed that my tank was already down to 1,800 psi, which was strange since I didn't come very far. I lay on my back, staring up at the blackness of the plankton layer and noticed bubbles coming out from under me.

It must be a leak in my regulator, I surmised. I have to search the wreck fast.

I checked the tail and wings carefully, overturning as much steel as I could without stirring up too much sediment and making the water too murky to see anything. Eventually, I came to the propeller covered in purple hydrocoral. I remembered that this was where Liz and myself took our picture. I stood where I did then, and there it was, something was tied to the grill of the plane behind the propeller.

I reached into the grill, but I couldn't grasp it; the object was far within the bow turret so I had to stretch. I felt a shimmy behind me and jumped. Upon turning around, I could see a dust of sand in the air; something was there. I could see something moving, so I started squinting my eyes as my heart beat faster. And then suddenly, a shark appeared! But it was an angel shark.

I breathed a sigh of relief, exhaling heavily, as the beautiful creature was just curious, moving about me as if to say hello. I pushed my way in and finally got it. It was a flash drive stuck in a watertight bag with a symbol on the bag, "L." I got it. I was so happy, I forgot to check my air.

I clipped on the bag to my suit and gradually started heading back to the surface, looking back at the wreck, feeling a deep longing for times gone by. As I gently followed the currents on the route back, the light started to return slightly before reaching to the kelp forest. I was still at a little over 180 feet deep, and while navigating the forest I felt a sudden, strong downward pull. I gasped as something dragged me down, but it was hidden between the kelp.

I started to panic as I descended rapidly and my ears started to hurt, my jaw feeling like it could fall off. I looked below me and saw a hand—a hand holding my fin and dragging me below. I breathed so fast, I couldn't think straight. I got pulled into a coral valley, and as I hit bottom, I could see the creature. I shone the light in its face, and it screamed underwater. It was a weird phenomenon to witness, like a person struggling to breathe but still able to get out a low-pitched roar against the underwater pressure.

It exposed its gaunt, horrid face staring right back at me. I was horrified. The creature had the same purple fingers Lance had, but its hands were at a much deeper phase of decomposition. Its face was drawn and teeth mangled. It didn't have gills, but it also didn't seem to breathe. It had a dark complexion to its jagged, rough skin as if it didn't even belong in the ocean. It was feral, wild, and wasn't thinking; all it did was drag me farther down until I caught on a piece of dead coral.

I could feel my secondary regulator hose catch on it, and the creature kept yanking me forward until the hose snapped. The hose went into free flow, air escaping to the surface unhindered.

*My air!* I thought.

I couldn't panic; I had to stay focused. I turned against the current to face the creature and drew for the speargun then fired a shot right at its head. To my horror, I missed. I had to fight to reach behind me to reload, my breathing starting to feel labored. I loaded the gun again and got off another shot—this time, impaling the creature's skull. It went stiff, drifting with the currents and twitching under its reflexes like a zombie while a strange, oily mucus-filled fluid oozed out its head.

I started gasping as I turned around, heading up to the surface. My ears felt like it was bleeding, yet still my ascent couldn't be too sharp as my body wouldn't be able to take the depressurization. I looked over to the kelp forest, and there were more of the creatures. From afar, they looked like undead mermaids but with humanlike feet. They quickly went to the area I struggled with the first creature, and it was a feeding frenzy—they ate their dead comrade whole. All that was left was a mass of silt kicked into the water, making visibility difficult.

I wasn't sure what my next move was. I was out of projectiles, and I had to pause for a few seconds to allow my ears to adjust. Then I noticed they saw me and started coming in my direction. I continued swimming up, barely seeing the surface, and I knew I hardly had any air. I let go of my signal and blew my horn for the boat, hoping Fred was close by.

Within the last few feet, I looked down; and nothing was there, they couldn't come to the surface. I breathed a sigh of relief and drifted the rest of the way, manually inflating my BCD on the surface so I could float. I felt myself blacking out, but I could see something in the distance coming to get me. I made it—just barely.

* * * * *

The soft, firm words of a female woke me up on a hospital bed in Malibu Urgent Care Hospital. I looked around and saw Travis there, pumping his fist in victory when he saw me awaken. All I could hear was an intense ringing in my right side that wouldn't stop.

In the next few hours, the doctors debriefed me of my condition. I had blown my right eardrum and had high levels of nitrogen bubbles in my bloodstream, not to mention I lost a lot of blood.

"How?" I asked the doctor.

He showed me a large gash on my foot, right next to my calf. Travis kept my spirits high, bringing some fruit and muffins for me to eat, and he also brought Jimmy, whom I was very happy to see. I hugged Jimmy continuously as he squeaked uncontrollably, everyone joyful in the moment. After the euphoria died down, I saw Fred and asked him about my wetsuit and whether he saw a bag attached to it. He nodded, and Travis brought over my iPad with the flash drive for me, knowing I would want to immediately view it.

The drive had two files on it, a PDF file and a picture. I opened the picture and saw it was one for a Dr. Francis Drake, an associate professor at Cornell Medical University in New York. The PDF was labeled "2," so I opened it. Travis and Fred watched it with me. It was a paper that followed on the last one she sent, continuing on her story of controlling the coronavirus through strengthening specific cellular receptors, but this paper had a little more detail, written like a journal entry:

> I write to you today on the heels of what I consider to be a global conspiracy. By now, I am certain the virus has spread, and nations would be reeling from the economic implications of the same. China would be the first to feel the hit, leaving Russia, Great Britain, and America to fill the void of top economic power easily. But this is just the beginning.
>
> As the virus spread, world powers will struggle for economic dominance as the rules of the games will start to change. Owing to human nature, many will remain complacent, and even more will die as the virus makes its way through all 7.74 billion of the world's population. There is something larger and more sinister at stake than anyone could scarcely comprehend. We must remain vigilant.
>
> I have begun work on developing a mechanism through genetic splicing to boost the strength of the virus-resistant genes in humans, in particular, our specific cellular receptor, which is challenging but not impossible to do. Many now want my life, as they are

> now aware that I will no longer be their instrument of death to millions in a fight for economic supremacy. In this time of desperation, a chosen few will have to take up the heavy mantle of survival and do all that it takes to save the human race from extinction.
>
> As many would realize by now, the virus is a living entity, a part of something distant that is whole and is evolving with every passing day, becoming more virulent and deadly as time goes on. Our saving grace, however, will have to be our tenacity and faith, we must be unwavering. A large wave is about to hit the free world, and we must be ready to act.

I paused to ponder the severity of the concept Liz was referring to—extinction. And even though all things are possible, I didn't consider the stakes that high. But if she says it is that large an issue, I have to treat it that way.

I looked over at Travis, and he nodded, as if to say he understood where I would go next. He offered to make the arrangements for me to return to New York within a couple weeks. But until then, I had to rest and recover from my wounds so I would be fully ready for the next leg.

# 11

# THE HAMMER HAS LANDED

I was greeted to coronavirus news every morning on every news channel on American television. It was getting tiresome, given they were saying the same set of facts over and over again. I got very restless waiting to recover, until after a week, I discharged myself from the hospital as I couldn't sit idly by anymore. I soon after boarded the plane and wished Travis all the best, promising to return shortly to carry our conversation on the virus further.

On the plane, I pondered the concept of genetic splicing to improve a host's resistance to a virus. It was a brilliant concept, but that was Liz for you—an out-of-the-box thinker who believed so strongly in herself there was no problem in the world she didn't think she could solve. It was, however, a blessing and a curse in that, to this day, I can never say I know for a fact that she was involved with anyone. She was married to her work, and she made no apologies for this; but still, I always thought the human in her must crave for support and human intimacy at some point in time. The closest person to that concept had to be Peter, but then, even he didn't have a clue of where she was. She kept him in the dark, but I got a sense he was in love with her, whether that was reciprocated is another matter.

*There was no worse fate,* I told myself, *to give someone your heart and soul and have them not mirror your sentiments.*

But she was never a person to have regrets; she was confident in who she was and the path she chose in life—all else was secondary.

I didn't have such strong resolve, but I also couldn't help but admire from afar. This came off as a double-edged sword as—even though I admired her—she cared greatly for me and thought highly of me. Many times I didn't think I deserved it, but here we were, completing the ouroboros cycle all over again. The pressure was on now for me to live up to her expectation, and I didn't plan to disappoint.

I touched down at JFK on February 9, 2020, It was early morning, and as I got a taco from a concession stand, I could see the morning news—this time, the story was different. Apparently, the WHO declared the virus an epidemic. At 813 deaths and 37,522 confirmed cases, the virus has now crossed another threshold, with no end of the spread in site.

All the expert analysts spoke of flattening the curve and working collectively as a society to bring harsher controls to curb the spread of the disease, but what I saw of that disease was that their efforts would be an exercise in futility. I didn't want to waste any more time on the news, even though I was a little jarred to see how fast it had reached epidemic status. I sighed heavily before catching a cab to head back to the apartment, taking a quick shower before hitting the beaten path again—this time, to meet a friend and update him on my progress.

I buzzed in at Lance's apartment building on West Twenty-Fourth Street to see how he was doing. The room was unlocked, so I turned the knob. Upon entry, I could see a few building staff cleaning up the place. I greeted them, but they were scared of Jimmy, a fear I've never seen before so I didn't press. I told them I was there to see Lance, and they looked at each other, perplexed. I tilted my head like a confused dog before asking them to explain, and then, I had to take a seat. Lance had died. I didn't know what to think—that giant of an athlete, in peak physical condition, was taken out by this virus.

I was in shock, and then worry overcame me. I immediately called around to reach the other members of the research team, Natalie and Yue, but they too had passed on. I was struck with grief, my face wrinkled with agony and flush with pain. I sobbed uncontrollably. The severity of the virus had finally hit home. The deadliness of the virus was merciless, leaving no room for recovery. I had to steady myself.

I washed off my face and looked around the bathroom, seeking some sort of reprieve from my current condition, some sign that I was just a bad dream. It wasn't. I had now grown out a beard, looking even more like I was a hobo from East New York. I wiped my face clean before leaving the apartment, continuing on the mission—a mission that seemed to be growing in importance by the minute.

Within an hour, I arrived at the Cornell School of Medicine on corner East Seventieth and York on a busy but still very cold Sunday morning. I walked into the tall, cream multistory building sporting a dull facade with individual air-condition units littered about the building walls. Inside the building, I requested an audience with Dr. Francis Clarke. The secretary guided me inside the elevator, noticeably disturbed by Jimmy's presence and my disheveled demeanor. I went up to floor 6 before emerging onto the foyer and being asked to sit in the waiting room.

I waited, and I waited. In typical university professor style, I waited a little over an hour before he agreed to meet with me. He was the first today that wasn't bothered by Jimmy, but he wasn't amused either. Very cold and business like, I introduced myself as Liz's younger brother and that I was trying to track her down. He mentioned he hadn't seen her for the year so far but that she ran as a teaching assistant for him and had a small office at the end of the floor. He feigned ignorance over any emotional plea I would make about her whereabouts and just kept pointing me to her office.

I went into the office and cracked the wooden door, making a tremendous noise, so much so I had to give a loud apology as the space was as quiet as a library. She had a small desk, and the room seemed to be in shambles, as if someone went through her things and went through it in a rush. I too started searching, and Jimmy helped where he could by sniffing around. I found nothing of note and sat on her chair, taking a long breath, trying to catch myself in the musty-aired office with an old carpet that probably produced pathogens worse than the coronavirus.

I looked around again and noticed she had a few pictures on her desk—three in total—all recent, except one. It was one of our trips that we would have taken over a decade ago, our trip to Zenobia in Cyprus. Another dive site had to be there, but a very unique and dangerous one at that. I remember cutting myself on the wreck, and the cut had gotten infected. I was rotten company for her on her only vacation for that year. That had to be my next target. I had to go quickly.

A splitting migraine then came over me as I went back down the corridor to thank Dr. Clarke, but he didn't allow me to revisit. I left the building, taking a taxi to head back home, the blinding light from the ocular migraine obscuring my view. I reached home, drained of all energy; so as I entered, all I looked for was the AC remote and a blanket. Then I realized I didn't use my key to enter.

I got up quickly and headed to my bedroom to see it completely ransacked. Liz's bedroom was in the same condition.

*I must've left it open and someone came in and thrashed the place,* I concluded. *But then why were all my valuables left untouched?*

I locked the door behind me and let out Jimmy for a little exercise. There was still a bright light coming from the veranda so I got up to close the drapes. I noticed graffiti painted on the glass. It was a face—my face with a knife through it, bleeding out on the ground.

My heart started to pound faster. I closed the drapes and locked the door to the balcony. The chase was just about to begin.

# Part III

# PANDEMIC

*March 11, 2020*
*4,023 Deaths*
*118,610 Cases*

# 12

# A PARANORMAL MURDER

*What do I do now?* I thought. *Someone definitely wants Liz's research, and they're clearly quite powerful, which is why they were able to track me down and leave me a message.*

I slept most of the day but awoke, barely able to get any real sleep. I stumbled out of the sofa and headed into the room to straighten out my things. Moving into a public space wasn't an option, so I took Liz's picture from the desk and packed all my essentials in a suitcase before calling a cab to head out.

The cabbie was a Syrian man. He started shouting at me in his language, angrily forcing me to try and find another cab. I consoled Jimmy, as he wasn't accustomed to that much negative energy. He was usually the star of the show, but now, people didn't see anything but the difference in species. Others just saw him as the virus incarnate, a demonic spawn of Satan that was the root cause of all bad things that were happening to them.

Pondering the predicament I was now in, I figured it best to carry him around in the cage under the cover. At least he wouldn't be visible and could probably catch up on some sleep too. I had it much harder this time around, trying to get all his papers and mine in order for the trip. But eventually, I was able to secure it and headed into another cab—this one, more tolerant of my situation but still eking out a few extra dollars, a premium for his inconvenience, as he put it.

We passed through an unusual route, moving along the west side of Manhattan. Everything looked so hectic, more so than usual. People with masks on their faces were now more common than ever. I remembered when passengers in transit to Beijing were always wearing masks; we called them the "Far East ninjas," which, in hindsight, might have been a little racist. But now we were all forced to be the same ninjas. I could see the Statue of Liberty poised out in Liberty Bay, reflecting now what liberty meant to me. It was odd how one of our greatest impositions on freedom will be done on ourselves—an internal, domestic threat that was eating us alive from the inside.

All talk of terrorism and weapons of mass destruction were now over; it was now about the readiness of our public health institutions to deal with a calamity well beyond the scale of 9/11 and far deadlier.

*How did we get here?* I mused, scratching my head at the concept. *A mutating airborne viral disease that attacks complacency and domestication. Maybe if I were more outdoorsy, fitter, better eater, healthier in general, I would have a stronger immune system, and yet that wasn't my greatest threat to life. Someone has a target on my back because there's a chance that I could stop the problem. No more Greta Thunberg, the Swedish champion of the earth, a hero in my eyes and worthy of all the titles she received and maybe even more.*

The tables now have completely turned as the global discussion now centered on survival of the fittest. I laughed maniacally as I thought of the prospect in disbelief, the cabbie Asif looking back at me in the rearview mirror, perhaps wondering if he needed to take me to a mental asylum and whether he was in danger or not.

I placed my left hand over my eyes and breathed heavily, overwhelmed with the enormity of the situation.

*What am I doing?* I asked myself. *Why am I positioning myself in this situation? Where are you, Liz? Why did you leave me? I need you, I'm scared.*

I broke down, sobbing in the cab, but quickly realized now was not the time. I was smack-dab in the middle of the cover-up, and I had to respond. I had to rise to the challenge.

We pulled up in front of JFK Airport. I looked at the entrance and witnessed the bustle of passengers moving in and out like ants, a submissive wave of energy that moves apace but with no real purpose for the most part. I stood at the center of it, everyone moving around me like I didn't exist. All the white noise drowned out my thoughts; the wrinkles in my skin started contorting as tears started to form.

*No, I have to be better than this, I have to press on*, I convinced myself. *This nonexistence—this anonymity—this is my only weapon.*

Being an unknown was my whole life, and now, it was my only advantage—blending in. I wasn't like Liz, but that's okay. It had to be. It was the only thing I knew how to be.

*I have to make this work*, I thought.

I scratched my head and walked into the terminal building. It was time to move on. I hooded up and headed to my gate with speed, trying to stay in public places. I paused for a moment, realizing that it was different running from something a little bizarre, not knowing what I was running from. I sat patiently at my gate and waited for the Virgin Atlantic plane to pull up before boarding for Heathrow.

* * * * *

The ride was pretty smooth, and I felt a sense of relief reaching English soil. At least I felt it was a little farther from what I would consider the scene of the crime. I stayed in the airport hotel to freshen up before embarking on the connecting flight, sleeping like a log in my room. Breakfast was also restful, and I opted to put on American news channel and backtracked the DVR to see what the morning news was in the US that morning.

He was killed—Dr. Clarke was murdered in his office.

I let out a loud gasp, starting to sweat on to the white hotel robe that I put on before going into the shower. I entered it, my mind racing with thousands of thoughts all at once. I tripped over the shower curtain, tearing it off its hinges and stumbling into the shower, but the steam and flow of the water were not able to cool my hot head this time.

I started blowing out against the water, forcing droplets against the wall. I blew harder and harder and harder until I could feel a full-blown panic attack set in. The room started spinning, I looked up at the ceiling to try and restore my vision, but it wasn't coming back. I covered my eyes, hoping for things to settle, but they weren't. I crawled out the bath to try to find my antipsychotic pills, but in my state, I couldn't find them, I fell flat on the floor, passing out under the pressure.

* * * * *

A call to my room woke me up from the troubled slumber.

*Must be my wake-up call,* I thought, my head still jumbled.

I answered with a trembling voice, and they asked if I was okay. I responded affirmatively. I took my meds to settle my head, a couple Xanax pills to mitigate the anxiety. Jimmy looked worried, so I smiled I played with him a little, trying to laugh off whatever residual tensions the meds may have left. I got on another pair of jeans and hoodie before heading back to Heathrow and boarding the flight to Cyprus.

* * * * *

It was shorter than expected, just over six hours; and I got time to think, recognizing that I had to stay ahead of my pursuers. There was no way they could think I would be heading to Cyprus, so I kept faith in that until I was proven wrong.

I and Jimmy landed in Lanarca Airport on February 28 in the morning, with time barely moving at all. The airport had the modern finish of Heathrow, but the land had the feel of something much older. I only had my tote bag and a carry-on, so I walked around Lanarca to just free my mind a little. Cyprus was simple. I could see a picturesque mosque in the distance overlooking the lake, so I decided I would start there.

The mosque was named after Hala Sultan Tekke (or Mosque Umm Haram), the wife of Ubada bin al-Samit, a well-known companion of the prophet Muhammed. The mosque was beautiful, a credit to the Sufis of Cyprus. It was adorned with all ancient architecture and arches overlooking a lush garden and pagodas perched on the edge of the salt lake.

I stumbled upon a ceremony being performed at the back of the mosque—a dhikr, or devotional Sufi whirling, as my friend Abed always used to remind me. He too was a devout Sufi and always educated me on the practice of the whirling dervishes, most prominent in Turkey but also seen in Egypt. The white cloth and dress danced with the host as they moved about in a form of active meditation. Similar to the revolving solar system, the Sufi whirl was done either singly or in a group while chanting devotional prayers.

I leaned on the pillar and watched the practice in amazement, a much-needed distraction to my newfound reality, reminding me of simpler days with Abed. A reed flute and kettle drum were all that we needed to set the mood to the soothing poems of Rumi. The spirit of the practice calmed my soul. I listened a little more, sitting on the edge of the steps, to take in what might be my last remnant of rest for a long while. I also spied my hotel beyond the lake near the beach. I bowed to the group; though they couldn't see me or whether it was culturally appropriate, I did it still in thanks for the ambience of peace they provided.

The hot afternoon sun caught me in midstride as I walked north toward the beach, just east of the lake. I stopped in front to look out at the surf, with the groynes perfectly poised among the sand to scatter the view of the cool blue ocean cascading on the shores filled with people, cheerful and full of life. It brought me a smile.

I went into the Flamingo Hotel and checked in before heading to the third floor, and the view there was simply mesmerizing. They left me a tray of fresh fruit, bright pink dragon fruit, red rambutans, and large pineapples, which left a heavenly scent in the loft that nearly made my fears and anxieties go away. All I could hear was the sound of the waves and children playing in the light surf.

*This couldn't be so bad*, I thought, and then my mind drifted to the doctor, and it couldn't leave the thought.

I pulled up my laptop to search what had happened to him, but the police simply classed it as a robbery went wrong, concluding with a stab wound to the neck. They had some pictures, so I looked at them closely.

*I'm no expert, but they sure don't look like stab wounds*, I inspected. *They look more like bite marks.*

I noticed them because of how clean the puncture wounds were and how his clothes were ripped apart when there was barely any blood left. Something looking like teeth marks also encircled the neck wounds. His hands showed the same hypoxia from which Lance suffered—purple on the edge and bright red palms.

*These aren't ordinary killings*, I concluded. *But I supposed these aren't ordinary killers.*

# 13

## A HAUNTED WRECK

The murder scene haunted my thoughts that night. Despite the cooling sounds of the waves crashing on the shore, I knew no rest. I couldn't shake the fact that the wounds were the shape of the tongue of the beast I fought off on Catalina Island. Like a flexible dagger with a diamond cross section and sharp ridges, it could easily stab an enemy, sending the body into pulmonary shock, leaving little or no trace of blood behind. I felt my neck to ensure all the muscles and bones were still there before closing the laptop to ponder my strategy for the near future.

Windows and doors were closed, so I let out Jimmy and started a healthy conversation as if I were talking to a grown man. I spoke aloud as Jimmy was poised on the coffee table devouring the rambutans with gusto but still keeping his head up to listen, lest I be offended.

"So what now, friend, where do we go from here?" I started. "I have enough savings in my account to carry me for a little over a year, although I don't think work will be on much people's minds soon enough if the virus keeps spreading. From my memory, there were five places that Liz and I went on dive vacations—Catalina Island, here in Zenobia, Cyprus, Maui, Bali, and a remote space in the Pacific on a little island she called Chuuk. It was originally called Truk, but for some reason or another, the name was changed to Chuuk by modern nautical experts, each area boasting of their own lore and allure.

"I never actually dove with her there, but she spoke of its beauty a lot. Knowing Liz to be the organized person that she is, those spots will have flash drives in locations where we took our trip photo together—a place only the two of us will know about. Each should piece together a puzzle that should, in the end, give me the genetic splicing information needed to be able to find a stop to the virus before all is lost."

I looked up at Jimmy.

"Sounds pretty simple, right?" I told my friend, as if he understood what I said. "But why am I so anxious? Oh yes, there is that matter of the undead mermaids and the murderers who are hot on my trail to end my life before anything could come of it. And I do agree that all this is very heroic and worthy of a Sherlock Holmes spinoff, but I can't help but think about myself in the whole thing and my desire to find Elizabeth.

"Everything else in my mind is secondary, the unfortunate reality, however, is that even if I were to pursue Elizabeth, would my trajectory be so much different to what I am doing now? It is highly likely that the two paths will coincide, and knowing Liz as I do, she would have ensured it to be thus."

My hands were trembling with fear and excitement so much that sleep eluded me that night as well. I was barely able to contain my drive to move at first dawn to the local dive resort up the street. Even with this renewed fervor, I still couldn't get past 4:00 a.m. without gently drifting off to sleep and letting my body have its way—if even for a short time.

* * * * *

The sky broke the horizon the next morning in an orchestral spout of pinks and oranges that heralded the coming of the golden orb. I woke groggily and stumbled my way into the bathroom, brushing my teeth and showering as my manner of method would demand. Jimmy went to sleep, carefully hanging from the ceiling fan and gently swaying to the force of the air-conditioning's stream of airflow within the loft's confines. I gave him a little tap on his wings to wake him up so I could give him a sponge bath to which he promptly scuttled into his cage and huddled behind the blinds to return to sleep. I didn't bother fighting him so I took up a couple apples and grapes and headed outside, walking north toward Zenobia Blue Oceania Dive Resort.

On walking there, I noticed that very few people were out yet, except one man in his fifties, with a Greek scruff and white apron, sautéing a series of vegetables in a skillet on an open fire.

*Ahh street food, I love street food*, I said to myself.

And it looked really good, so I asked for that in the best possible sign language I could muster, to which he responded "Souvlaki" in a booming, godlike voice. I nodded in acceptance, taking in the fresh sea salt in the air that was constantly draining my sinuses as an early morning cleanse.

The dish was flat bread cut open at the sides to form a pouch like a tortilla but soft and supple. It was stuffed with freshly sautéed garlic, cucumbers, and onions and tomatoes, atop rolled fish or some other form of meat. He drizzled olive oil over it and a pinch of salt and oregano with a generous squeeze of lime to top it off and some wedges with a Coke. It was smoking hot and still searing within the bread, so I had to keep moving it from palm to palm while taking bites heading over to my table.

After setting Jimmy's cage down on the side, I dressed my dish with generous amounts of the local harissa sauce, which had me blowing, to give my palate a chance to breathe under the overflow of flavor and rich tastes that really hit the spot for me. I barely swallowed before chasing with the Coke, which gave a perfect balance of modern diet and traditional cuisine that went straight to my brain, forcing me to take a deep breath, tasting the sweet aroma that was Cypriot life. Some of the pepper came off my top lip and burned incessantly, so I had to quickly find a standpipe to throw water over it as it started to swell under the fire of the hot pepper. I didn't mind the pain as I returned to my seat slightly disoriented, looking over at my watch to see the time.

I could see the clock turn to 8:00 a.m., and then my vision became blurred. I zoned in to the watch face and saw the seconds hand slow to a crawl before speeding up rapidly. I closed my eyes to collect myself, nervously returning my gaze to the watch face that shockingly said 9:00 a.m. now.

I looked around me to see if anything else strange was happening but noticed nothing in the immediate vicinity.

*What is happening?* I thought, holding my head as it throbbed slightly.

I had to stay on the move, so I got up and, against better judgment, started moving along the coast toward the dive shop.

I met the dive master, Andreas, at the resort, just as they were opening up. He could speak English well, so it wasn't difficult to communicate. After telling him that I needed to visit the MS *Zenobia*, the wreck of a 172-meter-long Swedish carrier that sunk off the coast of Lanarca on its maiden voyage, he promptly had me finish some paperwork before loading the boat on the harbor to head out. Before long, we were off, the sea spray just as cool and crisp as I remember it, a generous headwind taking back my short curls that tickled slightly as I rocked backward.

Within forty minutes, we were within the dive site, hovering over the target, which was a little under 150 feet below. He went ahead and cut off the engines before prepping the dive gear. I told him I would go down myself, but since this dive was advanced, he insisted he would rather accompany me to ensure my safety. I didn't fight his protest so as not to raise suspicion, but I was concerned for his safety. Jimmy was still fast asleep, so I left him on the boat with the driver, assuming he wouldn't be too much trouble.

Andreas gave me the okay sign, signaling his readiness to submerge. I put in my mouthpiece and went on below—this time, checking to make sure I didn't have any leaks while descending into the bright blue depths. Thankfully, this time, there was no kelp as it would have been a psychological difficulty for me to surmount.

Andreas led the way to the wreck, and we reached the portside of the wreck pretty quickly. We encountered no issues so far, just a friendly loggerhead turtle that came to say hello as he gracefully glided past us. I took the opportunity to swim ahead as I knew exactly where I needed to go, deep within the bowels of the *Zenobia*. A few lionfish swam past with the blue glow of the surface reaching the surface of the wreck easily. I gently moved forward into the wreck, careful not to disturb the old piece of machinery.

I looked out at the control panel, which was still in pretty good shape, considering that it has been sunk since the early 1980s. Some areas of the control room were covered in coral polyp, and I had to resist the temptation to just walk on the deck and keep my buoyancy just right to stay afloat and weightless so as to minimize any incidents. I pried open the door to the first lorry deck. It was dark, as the light was not able to penetrate that far, so I had to put on my headlamp and watch my step. I held the speargun upright and motioned for Andreas to do the same.

Even as our bubbles caused a little stir in the rusted deck and as we passed through the tall containers, I could see some cargo was bound for Africa, Syria, and other Middle Eastern empires. The sunken cargo was a great loss indeed, but I was not here for the treasure that some may think they hold. I was here for a different kind of treasure on the bottom deck.

I pressed on, using the containers to pull myself forward, until we came upon an opening to slip further below. I could see such a hole approaching, and then I could hear an ominous, rusted creak coming from below. I looked down for bubbles but saw none. We clenched our butt cheeks tightly as we headed to even darker territories. I looked back, and I could see something on Andreas's face. It was fear. He knew something—something he didn't mention before as he motioned for me to end the dive. I shook my head in disagreement but signaled him he could leave if he so desired.

We proceeded deeper still, and I could hear another creak. As I passed by one of the containers along the middle of the ship, the creak got louder, until suddenly it turned into a loud crash on my left. As I turned left, it was too late. A beast that seemed reptilian with the jaws of a saltwater crocodile and fangs of a vampire bat dove out at me, reaching forth to claim me as its own. I could feel a heavy thud hit my side, pushing me forward, it was Andreas. He too was able to escape the crushing pressure of the beast's jaw, but there was no time to lose. My curiosity got the better of me and I shined the light on the creature before darting off.

It was decayed—a decayed crocodilian beast with two froglike legs and vampiric teeth with small, red eyes. It thrashed its way wildly, propelling itself forward. We swam at full stretch, spotting the next hole and quickly went down under to the next lorry deck. There was no time for caution, so we swam until we could break some distance between us and the creature.

Andreas found the final hole, and as he was about to dive there, we saw over fifty other creatures on the other side of the hole. They looked like the undead mermaids I saw off Catalina Island, except much less graceful. Like mutated trolls, they stood motionless until they saw us. They sprung to life, their low groan turning to a loud hiss, as their red eyes started popping open. We dove under just in time to evade their rush, the crocodilian and the mermaids fighting it out above deck.

I swam viciously to the port edge of the lowest lorry deck and found exactly what I sought—a music box with "Elizabeth" marked in encrusted diamonds on the top. I grabbed the box and used my momentum to break open a small hole in the hull, taking some scrapes to the skin and letting off a little blood. I looked back and saw Andreas follow, and he was bleeding heavily. I did not notice that the croc took off Andreas's right foot, and he was bleeding out.

I grabbed the top of his dive tank and pulled him along, asking him to kick as we rose to the surface. They couldn't reach far because of the light, and then I could feel a strong jerk backward—they had Andreas. They were eating him from the feet up, about ten of the creatures in total. The light caused their skin to form sores, and pus burst out under the water, causing them to be prey to their cannibalistic kin themselves.

Andreas, in one last fight for freedom, blew his water horn. The noise shattered the silence of the ocean, and I looked at him—in shock, twitching uncontrollably, his lower torso devoured fully. I had to leave him be. I shot the speargun to the largest of the beasts to buy me some time before swimming away.

Then, with horror, I now saw the boat diver, freediving and passing me, trying to save Andreas. He had keen ears but was unaware of the dangers that lay below. I swam past him, as I know he couldn't have known the vicious reality of the deep. They devoured him within seconds. I shed a tear in my mask for them before reaching the surface and clambered on to the boat deck.

I dropped to the floor, throwing off my mask and fins and releasing a blood-curdling cry to the heavens, clutching the music box close to my heart, the price and burden too much to bear.

# 14

## A ZENOBIAN PROPHECY

I could feel the sun bearing down on my chalk-white skin, tearing at the flesh like a raven picking the eyeball from a carcass. I was filled with emotion; I wasn't sure how to describe it best. Rage, or anger, or despair—I felt lost, and my body felt it more than I did.

I threw up in several convulsions on the deck. Jimmy was hysterical in the cage, so I let him out, and he immediately came to my shoulder, licking my face as if to console me. I peered over the edge, and a trail of blood pooled at the surface and streamed up from a point below where I could see dark masses of muscle and those twitching red pupils looking up but can't approach. I stared back at them with hate, and Jimmy also looked over the edge, hissing at them as well, which surprised me that he had some idea what I was looking at. And then I realized I still had the music box.

In all the frenzy, I had forgotten the music box, but it was time to get out of these haunted waters. I had to leave quickly before people started searching for them, and they will probably connect me to their death so I had no time to waste. I drove the boat back to the harbor, less shocked than the first time. But I still felt shaken every time I saw the creatures and their daggerlike tongues waving at me, dancing in their mouths like snakes, waiting for their next target to add to their piles.

I staggered off the boat, and another boat driver gestured to the boat and the equipment as if to say that I can't leave the ship just drifting and I had to tie it off to the mooring and take off the dive gear. I ignored his pleas and went straight to the hotel, feeling like a walking ghost myself. I went into the shower and bathed for nearly an hour, trying to wash off the horror of what I had just witnessed, but to no avail.

I screamed incessantly in the bath before rushing out to take more Xanax and antipsychotic drugs to calm down my body. The music box was just staring at me from the ground, so I took it and wound it up before opening it. It played a song that Liz loved playing for me on the piano, Minuet in G minor BWV from Christian Petzold, a classical tune that she said was an apt spirit of our childhood—"an emergence of struggle," she would dub the piece.

There on the lid was taped another flash drive in a waterproof baggie. I smiled at her ingenuity and the lengths to which she went to keep the papers secret. Written on the bag with a marker, her note said,

See Father Leo.

—L

I plugged in the flash drive and saved it on my system. It had a picture of a priest with Liz, the name of the file saying "Leo" and a PDF named "3." I opened the PDF and saw that it was in fact the third paper of her series. This one named "An Investigation into the Genetic Properties of the Specific Cellular Receptor of Humans and Its Ability to Resist Infectious Diseases." This paper dove deeply into the properties of the specific cellular receptor and how it usually goes about its job on a day-to-day basis fighting off common colds and infections, stopping viruses from even entering the host's body.

She spoke at length of her frustration at the lack of versatility of the property of humans and how even new strains of old viruses could get past the receptor. She referenced her final set of tests of white mice where she deliberately tried to change the structure of the receptor through genetic splicing, ending mainly in failure, except for one.

"Test subject D-0X1 demonstrated the ability to repel the virus by preventing receptor binding and endocytosis," I read from her paper. "Instead, the virus acted as if repelled by the plasma membrane. Here lies potential for more."

She went on to talk of the possibility to begin trials on coronavirus cases and whether genetic splicing of the receptor could be altered enough to have this same effect on the virus, even in a mutated state. I breathed out heavily as I read the paper, its assertions groundbreaking at the least and life changing at best. It was nearly three in the afternoon, and I know people would start to get suspicious. I booked my flight for Hawaii next, heading to Houston from Heathrow. But first, I had to find this Leo gentleman.

I packed my stuff and paid the front desk, asking them for directions to the nearest church. It led me to a basilica, about thirty minutes from the hotel, called the Church of Saint Lazarus. I walked slowly out of the cab, asking for him to wait for me while I seek out the father. The sun started to set behind the cross of the ragstone church, its spires in the same unassuming rock finish as the walls. We grew up attending catholic churches, I and Liz; but I always marveled at the architecture and attention to detail of older churches, especially Eastern Orthodox Churches. The windows were adorned with stonework moldings and iron gates giving off a slight prison feel to the space, which wasn't too reassuring.

I cracked open the door and witnessed a total transformation on the inside, as beautiful golden wall paintings decorated the hallway walls, with ceilings over twenty feet high. This truly was a sight to behold—the old Coptic church withstood the test of time and retained its archaic beauty and charm, with stone arches opening up to the main chamber and wooden stacidia flanking both sides of the main walkway. The dome at the center provided a grand backdrop to a golden Horus that hung with grandeur over the church as if blessing the congregation from above. Hand-painted artwork of holy angels took over the main templon, anchored by a golden cross at the top and fit among golden frames and columns that draw your eyes to their majesty.

I was lost into one of the paintings when a voice came from behind me.

"Lazarus," the voice began, "he was dubbed a saint, and after much political turmoil, the people won a great battle to keep his remains here."

I turned around and saw an elderly gentleman, very soft-spoken and slim, amble out from one of the side doors. He was wearing a simple cream garb that dragged on the floor; his bald head shone under the refracted sunlight from the setting sun. I felt at ease around him, but I feel I still showed my nervous disposition.

He motioned to me to come to the back of the church with him to have tea.

"Green tea okay for you?" he asked politely.

I nodded, carrying Jimmy with me, which piqued his interest.

"What do you have there?" he asked me again.

When I gave him a peek inside, he chuckled and remarked about how cute Jimmy was and then told a story of a bird he had in his forties that was the best companion he ever had. We laughed a little, and with few words, we both knew who each other were. As his tea cup rested on the table, his face got more serious as greater business was at hand.

"Strange things, strange things walk the earth, Mr. Huxley," he began. "Dark things that were here before but have only now resurfaced on the earth to try to claim it as their own. Your Elizabeth, she cares deeply for you and also places you in high regard. But you will need this belief, as your journey is about to become a harrowing walk through the proverbial 'valley of the shadow of death.' You must fear no evil, my child, anchor your belief in the goodness and life of humanity. In there, you will find solace."

"So when did you see Liz, was it recent?" I asked in reply.

"Oh yes, a little over a few weeks ago, but she didn't say where she was going," the priest said. "A mysterious girl—your sister. She said that you will come shortly thereafter and that mysterious things are about to start happening here in Cyprus before spreading across the world."

"Father, was anyone else with her? Did she leave anything of worth, any more messages?"

He shook his head. "She said she would be gone for some time and that you should not worry, that she can take care of herself.

She also mentioned that your path will be littered with danger and horrors beyond your usual contemplation and that you must be prepared for the worst."

He then remembered something else.

"Oh, she also mentioned that a 'Fimbulwinter' soon approaches and with that will come your greatest fears, but she also said that you must persevere, like the patron saint of this church."

I watched him, skewing my gaze. "Did she really say that?"

"Well, she might as well have." He took another sip of his tea as he broke into another smirk. "Come, let me show you something."

He carried me far to the back of the church in an attached building behind his chambers. The old rusted door creaked open as it was pulled in a surprisingly rough manner by the father. I could see a stone coffin, adorned with artwork and a painting on the lid of the coffin of a man covered in a shawl with crosses. An aura hovered about his head.

"This—this is the famed tomb of Lazarus, boy," the father began, "the tomb where he was finally laid to rest after he had risen from the dead, his final resting place. You see, life and death, Mr. Huxley, are claimed as not being real, they are not tangible in this world, for reality is something spawned of truth, and truth is unchanging in the dimensions of space and time.

"Reality is beyond these two, it lies beyond these concepts and humans. Well, we are very powerful beings who can find the truth. We can rise above life and death if we so choose. You are destined for a great battle, and it will test you well beyond your limits. Promise me, boy, promise me you will stay in pursuit of the truth, in pursuit of reality, only in this space can St. Lazarus guide your wavering hand."

He reached out to me and took my right hand in his left while reciting a prayer in Greek, his right hand now rising to the ceiling as if to receive some heavenly blessing. The silence that followed was shattered by the pop of a horn, and I jumped at its sound.

Before leaving, I hugged the father and thanked him for his kind words, looking once more at the tomb and space, a haunting but holy presence imprinted on my mind's eye for life. I stepped out the building and entered the cab to an irate driver. After apologizing to him for taking so long, he sped off to the airport as if in a hurry to collect other passengers.

I left the cab and gave him a tip that forced him to shout angrily at me in a foreign language I didn't have time to try and decipher, so instead, I still waved at him calmly and headed out. Jimmy and I went through the lines with no issues, and I waited at my gate for the boarding call, pondering the horror of the undersea creatures and the growing complexity of the web Liz had left behind. My nerves felt frayed, and the stubble on my face itched viciously under the irritability of allergies and the two dead men.

After boarding, I was tired but dared not sleep, so I stayed up, trying to piece together a mind map, stringing Liz's thoughts on a single page. I could see where she was headed, but the biggest challenge lay within the gene-splicing phase of the experiment and the method and constituent enzymes used to give an upgrade to that specific cellular receptor. I spent the rest of the time tinkering with my model, trying different factors and properties of the virus to improve its accuracy so as to take my mind off the current reality.

The plane soon arrived in the UK, and we deplaned at Heathrow with few incidents before connecting to Houston en route finally to Maui. I passed through the food court in Houston IAF and got a few tortillas and fruit, feeding them to Jimmy along the way, noticing security guards eyeing me suspiciously. I thought nothing of it at the time and kept walking until I reached a diner nearby the artificial tree sculpture that made Jimmy want to get out the cage and play. I gave him his banana, which he ate voraciously, a nearby couple turning up their noses at me in the process.

Out of the reflection in my glasses, I could see a few officers congregating at the end of the hallway, motioning to come closer to me. I got up and started walking, then speed-walking before skipping between the lines of hundreds walking in the opposite direction. I had to lose them. I darted into the washroom and noticed I was alone, so it was easy to take out a couple of backpack straps I affixed to Jimmy's cage and had him come under my hood. He poked his head out like a kangaroo joey under my hoodie. I peeked out the door and saw a group of three guards walking against the crowd moving farther into the terminal. Jimmy's ears flitted as they passed by, and their hands had signs of the hypoxia, their fingers turning blue black on the end and swelling slightly. Their jawlines were hardened, forming as if made of stone, with the flesh peeling off and hanging as if partially shred.

I quickly zipped out and joined the throngs of passengers moving in the opposite direction, drafting the crowd and almost getting picked up in the momentum like in a mosh pit. I reached the terminal building safely and sat at gate 16, on edge, looking over my shoulder for the ghouls' return. A sigh of relief fell over me once we boarded, the plane announcing its plans for takeoff and beginning its approach onto the tarmac before speeding up and taking flight.

*I need to be smarter*, I admonished myself. *I have to find some way not only to outsmart these beasts but also to confront them in some way. They clearly don't like light, so that might be my biggest asset.*

I started researching the backstory of the *Carthaginian II*, an old whaling vessel wreck off Lahaina in Maui, Hawaii. Humpback whales were a common attraction in the coastal town, and at this time of the year, I'm sure I would find some active pods in the region.

*It has been so long since I interacted with the gentle giants*, I thought, longing to hear their bellows again, to listen to their serene cries as they dwarf all other forms of life in the ocean.

This trip had the promise of danger and death written all over it, but I would not have another die for me in my own pursuit

"This time, I get it done right," I whispered into the nothingness.

# 15

# PANDEMONIUM

Kahalui Airport was in sight, a simple but elegant set of structures set out amid the red rock of Maui adjacent to the gentle surf of Kanaha Beach. We arrived in the early afternoon under blazing Pacific heat that forced me to start sweating as I disembarked from the flight. Airport security was fairly gentle, and moving through from one phase to another seemed reasonable. Most of the airport spaces were open air, so we depended on the flow of air from the outside for cooling, which was not much in comparison to coming from the cold of UK and New York.

I stopped by the canteen to get some Burger King and another California franchise while sitting at the open-air seating and watching each passenger pass by, eyeing them for any strange movement. I had truly become a paranoid person, suspicious of everyone and everything. I took off my glasses, rubbing them firmly as they burned as I did, the stress of the situation starting to show with my now full beard.

I could now see a few passengers moving with face masks and little hand sanitizers, the scourge of the virus reaching even this tropical paradise. My hands trembled as I replaced the glasses before taking a deep breath and taxi drivers started hassling me for a ride. I looked at them but felt like I was looking through them. I took out Jimmy, and they immediately retreated.

We opted to walk along the circular to Kanaha Beach just to gather my thoughts. The walk took a little over half an hour, but I didn't mind as the walking did me well after the long flights, and I noticed a carpet of flowers taking up the edge of the road right onto the sand of the beach. I left my shoes on the side of the road and headed to the beach. Jimmy dove off my shoulder and into the bushes of the morning glory runners. Everywhere you looked, the purple flowers cascaded down the beach and adorned the sand with a thick green backdrop and sweet flower that Jimmy quite enjoyed.

The neck pillow from the flight was still around my neck, and I lay on it immediately where I stood under the shade of a few coconut trees while looking out at the waves. The ebb and flow of the water was therapeutic; the surf rolling onto the soles of my feet and returning to its mother teased my senses as a few cars drove past on the elevated roadway.

*How could my reality be so different to what is before me now? How could this paradise be in jeopardy? What did it possibly do to bring this on itself?* I thought.

I could then see a few tourists on the higher part of the beach. A few of them started coughing incessantly, and I felt uncomfortable staying there. As the sun started to set, I walked along the boulevard. Bougainvillea of all colors draped the streets in their pinks and oranges. I managed to hitch a ride eventually to carry me to the other side of the island near Lahaina.

As we drove, the driver was very pleasant and cheerful, just as I would expect in a tropical paradise such as Hawaii.

*A little pricey*, I thought as he explained his fee.

But there was no point negotiating at this stage.

I lay my head back as he inquired about Jimmy, what breed he was, and how old he was. And after Jimmy got his sought-after pat on the head, we were off. We drove slowly along Main Street as the driver started pointing out different sights to us.

I feigned interest so as not to offend him, but as we started to approach the end, a strange man appeared by the traffic lights. My eyes gravitated to him. He was short, Eastern European, dressed in all black, and blue fingers and slightly swollen palms. It was the man I saw in Central Park a few months back.

Dread steamed off his black shades and broad-brimmed hat. He was a man with loose skin with little to no muscle definition. Jimmy started going ballistic in the car, hissing and scraping the window to get at the man. I quickly pulled him off the window so as not to have to pay the driver any damages, but there was that strange man, still ambling through the streets and using his black umbrella as a cane. He hobbled over to the other side as we waited by the red light.

As the lights turned green, I looked back at the man, but still he continued walking past the lamppost. And then he stopped, as if someone called his name. His head rotated sharply, but the rest of his body remained perfectly still. I could see the edge of his eyes under the shades; his irises were blood red, and he saw me.

We continued down the highway, and my mind started concocting all sorts of strange theories about the odd gentleman. His presence felt different from the others; he felt conscious—self-aware, almost. I started inquiring about the coronavirus and whether there were any cases in Maui yet, but the driver shrugged his shoulders nonchalantly. His happy-go-lucky attitude seemed to flow over in responsiveness to pending crises too. He did mention that a lot more people than usual were wearing masks, but he didn't think there was a need for it, and I didn't press the matter further.

I started drifting off as I leaned on the door on the left side of the vehicle when I heard a tremendous crash. The driver was able to steady to vehicle, and I looked out the window to see the silhouette of two guys driving a large pickup truck trying to ram us from the side. The car we were in was a small taxi, but the driver held his own. He didn't ask any questions, only to match the challenge of the pickup with an advance of his own, clipping the vehicle, forcing the van to lose control, and sending it off the edge of the highway into a ditch over eight meters deep. The truck flipped over and smashed whatever life was in the van.

The driver pumped the brakes and introduced himself as David, apologizing for what he called "asshole kids" who found themselves on a holiday and wanted to act as if in the movies. But he did express a need to flee the scene, so he turned the car around and headed to the north of the island instead of the south where we were originally heading.

"You could stay with me in Kahakuloa," David advised. "My wife and I have a spare room for you and Jimmy, it's the least I could do."

I took up David on his kind offer. Little did he know that the trouble would soon follow him home, so I knew I couldn't stay long without endangering him and his family.

As we turned and headed in the opposite direction, the accident fading from sight, I noticed two figures emerge onto the highway. The men from the vehicle survived, and I was sure they would be hungry for more.

* * * * *

Kahakuloa was a little over an hour away in a rural coastal area on the north coast of Maui. It was a quaint town with churches and bakeries scattered about, serving the small village and townsfolk who passed through from time to time. David showed me to his farm, which was on a beautiful spread on the heights of the area climbing the ridges of Pu'u Kukui, the tallest peak on the island. He introduced me to his wife, Jenny, a sweet middle-aged Hawaiian dressed in a beautiful floral dress and wore a smile that lit up the room. She welcomed me to their home and showed me to the guest room at the back, right next to the chicken coop and a couple Australian shepherd dogs, Stan and Jeff.

I set my stuff down and came back out with Jimmy to David calling the dogs to help him with the herding of the cattle and sheep that were out at pasture grazing under a massive Banyan tree. Those trees are common in Hawaii, but this one was huge. The aerial roots climbed out of the ground for life, and the roots descending from the branches directly to the ground looked like the tree had long, flowing hair. I walked up to it and passed my hand on it; Jimmy was attracted to it too, quickly ascending its trunk into the foliage and hanging from one of the gnarled thick, old branches that reached out like an old sorcerer.

As night approached, the wind from the cool night ushered in and blew against the aerial roots and vines, causing an eerie whistle to emanate from the tree.

"That big guy I call Granpa, the oldest tree on the island," David recalled the tree's story. "It has been in my family for centuries, some people even say that ghosts live in the trunk of the tree."

We laughed heartily, but Jimmy quickly scurried over to my shoulder, both of us quite wary now of the reach of the tree and its vibe. Jenny made us loco moco, a traditional dish of rice covered in beef burger smothered in thick gravy and runny yolk with local herbs and black peppers. I didn't realize how hungry I was until I started biting into the rich dish, savoring every last morsel left on my plate. Jimmy was just satisfied with his fresh-cut melons and bright yellow pineapples.

It was great having a home-cooked meal again as we went outside on the porch to relax a bit after such a wonderful dinner, sitting in those old-timey rocking chairs that always felt like they were about to break down on you. Jimmy quickly headed out to the open air to spread his wings, and David came out to have a gentle evening chat.

We spoke for a little over an hour about the space and life on Maui, the lifestyle and culture, and how that would be likely to change with the virus. He was still reluctant to talk about the virus, his position being that talking about it would speak it into existence, so I didn't push the concept any further than it needed. The air was quiet, with only the sound of one of the dog's tails hitting the wall of the single-story barn, as we spoke outside, overlooking the bay. Very soon, the silence was broken by a haunting whistle that echoed over the ocean, a sad tune that sounded like a depressed animal whining before bellowing into a low groan.

Visibility went to a bare minimum, and eventually, the bay disappeared completely. A strange mist took over the coast and started approaching the farm, gradually rising over the ridge and into the barn and pasture. I asked David if that was normal, and he said it was a little thicker than usual but told me not to worry as it was already nearing eight and he was ready to retire before hitting the road again early in the morning.

I thanked him for his hospitality again and opted to stay outside until Jimmy returned, and then I could hear screeches off in the distance. I took up a shovel and ran to where the sounds were coming from, ending up right next to the massive Banyan tree. I looked up and could barely see the canopy of the tree, its vines moving as if possessed by a spirit. Jimmy scurried over to me and clambered on my shoulder, hissing at the tree as if it were alive.

"Hey, take it easy little guy," I said, patting him on the head to calm down, but he wouldn't let me.

I glanced back over to the tree and saw some movement near the roots.

"Hey! Hey, who goes there?" I shouted. "Come out from there, hey!"

My shouts fell on deaf ears, and then I could feel something rest on my shoulders and fingers. I looked over on the other shoulder and saw Jimmy was gone. The mist flowed like water around me, waist high and cloudlike, as if I was atop a mountain peak. I swung around and saw no one, and the mist quickly formed into a tornado, kicking up to my head.

My heart was racing, and I reared the shovel in an attempt to go into the mist. I couldn't use my eyes, but I had to feel the pulse of the earth, so I closed them. And then I felt a gust of wind from the right, and I struck it, connecting with a large object. The mist reeled and retreated slightly, as if alive to the touch. I could see the feet of something inhuman. Its toes were sharp and decayed, its skin was torn off the top, and the same phlegm-like fluid oozed over its bruises.

I went closer to it, but then the eyes—the red pupils, that is—lit up.

The creature got up and started advancing to me, I clenched my jaw and readied the shovel for another blow until I could hear screams coming from behind this creature. It was another one, running toward me, with Jimmy on his back biting its shoulder.

The creature howled in pain until it fell onto the floor in agony, eventually becoming stiff. Jimmy bared his fangs and now faced the larger creature, its neck half torn off the joints from my first blow. Jimmy wasted no time and went straight for the chest, biting into the muscle tissue, prompting another scream from the beast. The mist parted and retreated as if it too felt the pain of the bite.

I came down on the larger creature with another blow on the back of its neck, and it fell on the ground, screaming in pain, as if burning alive on an open flame. Jimmy retreated, satisfied with his defense of me, and clambered on my shoulder again.

The creatures' bodies started to disintegrate before my very eyes; and as one turned over, its red eyes leaped forward, causing the sclera to bulge until it exploded—before he too melted into the grass, leaving a sticky black mass behind. The mist then gradually retreated to the ocean, and the tree settled to a calm.

In the distance, on the road below, I could see the outline of a person, and then, he—or *it*—was gone.

# 16

## THE CARTHAGINIAN II

I felt a chill run down my spine. The series of peculiar events following my arrival in Maui left me out of breath and with some remnants of my childhood arrhythmia. Jimmy squeaked victoriously as he came up to me for a pat on the head, which I was happy to provide. But still, I was in shock on how he was able to topple those large foes.

"I think I underestimated you, boss, never again, partner in crime for life," I told the flying fox.

He liked the prospect of being made partner and spread his wings to make himself big under the moonlight that now showed off a clear bay and quiet ocean—no sign of any mist left over.

We ambled over to side room where we were to sleep next to the barn and heard the door fling open. It was David, sounding hysterical and rushing over to make sure I was okay.

"I heard some noises, is everything okay?" he asked me.

I nodded in the affirmative but also didn't want to worry him unnecessarily, so I left out the main ordeal when explaining it was just the tree up to its usual tricks in the wind. He breathed a sigh of relief and patted me on the shoulder, with Jenny peering out from behind the door, more scared of the night than anything else. I assured her there was no reason to be alarmed, but she was still very nervous about the entire ruckus in the still of the night.

Upon heading into the side room, I cracked open the door, and a foul smell rushed out through the room. I had to cover my nose just stay standing. After leaving the door open for a bit, the air lightened a little and wasn't too bad, so I took a shower and put on pajamas, hitting the bed like a sack of large Idaho potatoes, hoping to drift off to sleep. I couldn't. I got up and turned on the light, and Jimmy was up too and wide-eyed, ready for another bout with the ghouls and the Granpa tree. For the first time, I now noticed a back door located right next to the cabinet.

The whistling of the wind continued, its strength picking up as the night went on. The door was stuck, so I got a crowbar that was lying around and pried it open, the hinges breaking off in the process. I froze stiff, hoping not to attract any more attention than I already had. I walked down into a dark and dingy basement that seemed to end up right below the barn. There was no light switch, so I took out my diver's headlamp and looked about, and the place wreaked of animal feces.

I looked up and saw the floorboards of the barn with spaces in between the different pens allowing all sorts of refuge to escape beneath. I could see some of the excrement leaking off the boards in a small bulge of wet film before releasing on the floor below, but oddly enough, that wasn't the smell I was looking for. After walking around a bit, I noticed there were several wine barrels randomly scattered around the room, at least twenty of them. I looked at one and bent over to take a smell and immediately got knocked back by the strength of the pungent odor.

The crowbar had its work cut out for it as I used it as a lever to pry off the lid that was nailed shut. I covered my mouth and nose this time, hoping to prevent the smell from taking me out. I noticed that the barrels were filled to the brim with brine.

*Brine doesn't smell like that though*, I wondered, sticking the crowbar in and stirring the contents like a bowl of soup, only to see several decapitated human heads float to the surface.

I threw up on the side, hustling to return the cover on the barrel.

*How did David not react more violently to the accident on the highway? That seems strange*, I thought back. *And he's also quite keen on having us stay here. Is he human?*

My thoughts were cut short as I could hear footsteps approaching. I ran off to the corner and stood with the crowbar in my hand, clenching it tight enough to bend the solid iron bar. It was David.

He cautiously walked down into the basement with a shotgun in his hand, squinting as he did, looking for any signs of movement like a panther hunting in the night. I tried to stay still, and then I noticed a rat scuttle across on the other end of the room. David let out a loud shot that startled the animals above, causing a loud ruckus in the barn. The rat lay dead on the ground; his shot was surprisingly accurate as he ventured deeper and deeper into the basement.

He noticed the barrel lid was slightly propped open, using his gun to lift it off. He didn't even flinch at the smell. It was now or never.

I ran over to him as fast I could and strafed right to evade his first shot. He was on to me and got off a shot, hitting me right in the left thigh. But I was on him. The adrenaline flowing through my glands was too strong for me to feel any pain, and with a loud scream, I bludgeoned him with the crowbar, sending him hurtling to the floor. I took his shotgun and motioned for Jimmy to leave.

I packed our things and ran outside, taking his car keys that was left on the mantel and leaving that cursed hill.

"You think I killed him, boy?"

Jimmy looked up at me with his beady eyes, lost to my question.

I wondered if David was a ghoul as well.

*He must have known the creatures that came for us and was waiting to kill us and share our bodies with them and keep the heads*, I deduced. *Ugh, what could he possibly do with the heads?*

"This place is psycho," I told Jimmy. "C'mon, let's just drive back to Lahaina like we originally planned and dive to the shipwreck and get out of here."

I found myself increasingly on edge as the pressure to stay out of the ghouls' hands rose with every passing encounter.

Within half an hour, we got out of the arterial connector road and came back onto the Kahekili Highway that circled the island. It was a relief to hit the highway; not a car was seen on the smooth road that had a crisp, almost silent sound to the ocean along with it—no waves, no currents, just placid under the clear night sky. I took out a banana to give Jimmy, thanking him for his help, and kept driving the winding road, fighting to stay awake.

We reached the northern apex of the mainland a little after midnight, the winds whipping up with surprising coldness biting my skin. My breathing was rapid, and as I moved farther north, my exhaling started to produce a cloud of smoke. This shocked me, and I nearly lost control of the vehicle when I saw it. I was accustomed to producing these vapors at the death of winter in New York but definitely not in Hawaii in early March. This was ridiculous.

As the road continued, I noticed a man sitting on the cliff's edge, on the northern peak, just off the highway, on a trail that moved off into the ocean cliff on the seaside.

*Could it be the same strange man dressed in black from earlier?* I thought as I sped off the main road and drove up to him, Jimmy scaling my shirt to his usual spot in anticipation for some further confrontation.

I looked out, and as I got closer, I could only see his back. He was only wearing shorts in this cold weather, holding a bamboo rod and line pitched over the edge. The man seemed to be in his late seventies, bald and a local from the area. I immediately relaxed, only to be brought to a fright again as a loud, explosive rush of water erupted behind me. We jumped out of our skin and turned around to see that we were standing next to a blowhole—the Nakalele Blowhole, to be precise, as written on the signage near it. There was also a short lighthouse right next to us for oncoming vessels.

All of a sudden, I felt very naked and exposed; the old man then started to chuckle at my trepidation. Again, he seemed to be in his seventies; some advanced wrinkles and a potbelly anchored him pretty firmly to his spot. He coughed vigorously first before addressing us directly.

"Welcome, strangers, welcome to Whale Point," he began. "It's my personal hotspot for midnight fishing and taking my mind off the strange happenings here in Maui of late, and judging by your current state of fright, you have had some encounters with the daemons as well?"

"The what? What did you call them?" I inquired sharply.

He smiled and motioned for me to take a seat next to him, and so I did while he put his palm on the sandy floor and clicking for Jimmy to join us, which the flying fox was more than happy to oblige. The old man gave him a fig, and Jimmy chewed with a face of glee, looking like a camel chewing sideways to savor the flavor even more, bringing out more laughter from the old man.

"My name is Kaiko," the old man said. "I am a nomad in these parts, I live where I please on this island of my birth, I fish to survive and know where and when to get the best catches. There is something about you, stranger, an intensity of purpose throbs through your veins. Tell me, what is your story?"

So I gave him the full rundown, leaving little out, as it seemed like he could handle the full story before returning to my original questions about the daemons.

"The daemons," he went on, "are the product of an unholy alliance in the early years of our interstellar cluster. After the three gifts of the Cosmic Dreamer was brought forth, they, in turn, gave birth to the deorums, daemons, and titans to rule over the twenty-seven-planet solar system. It was all part of the original one dream. But then came the greed and thirst of the daemons that fought for the astral realms. This sparked the greatest war the universe had ever seen.

"Many died—most of which were the titans—before the deorums, in the end triumphed, banishing the daemons to the hellish realms at the bottom of the cluster. One such titan, Gaia, is seen as the protector of the earth, so her followers worship her and hope and pray for the day when she would return to this planet to save it."

"Save it from what?" I asked, and he looked at me quizzically.

"From us, my child. The daemons are a secret society that has been living on this earth from since the first Indo-Aryans existed north of Egypt over five thousand years ago. They operated from the shadows, releasing plagues on the population to level our occupation of the world when they think we have gone too far and dominated a planet they believe belongs to them as the descendants of Gaia."

"What do you mean by 'gone too far'?"

"Our population, my son," he clarified. "I am not sure if you are aware, but at certain times in history, cities have become too powerful for their own good, their capital cities becoming godlike symbols, imbuing their leaders with power that make them want to claim the entire globe. That is when the followers of Gaia intervene. The Antonine Plague, Justinian Plague, bubonic plague, smallpox, Spanish flu—they all came as eradication tools that threatened the most vulnerable in the society, establishing a cull that reduced our population to points where the daemons were satisfied.

"Our population in the 1800s started at 1.2 billion, in the 1990s moved to 6.2 billion, and now approaches 7.8 billion. With no sign of stopping, humans have truly claimed this planet for themselves and have refused to let any other inhabitants share in its spoils. The daemons look down on this, so they have let loose another plague onto the world."

"Well, I mean we can't fully say that a plague is loose on the world—an epidemic, maybe. But definitely not a plague," I said.

"Oh, these are not my words, son, they are from your governments," Kaiko said grimly. "They have finally declared a pandemic the world over, for two days now, with 120,000 cases and over 4,000 deaths. But trust me when I say this is just the beginning."

I leaned back on my hands and exhaled loudly, a large plume of frosted air drifting into the sky. The old man smiled when he saw my distress.

"Take it easy, son, worrying won't get your task done any faster," he consoled. "It's best take it in stride and move forward with a light heart. That's what I do. It works fine for me."

He shrugged his shoulders gently before groaning as he rose to his five-foot-tall frame.

"Hey, um, where are you heading?" I asked.

"To my boat. I'm docked right at the bottom of the cliff here," Kaiko chuckled. "Nothing much seems to be biting. I should probably head down and sail to the other side."

"Hey, wait, are you heading near Lahaina? We wanted to dive there, there's something of my sister I need to find, but the roads don't seem to be too safe anymore."

He pursed his lips and licked his finger, lifted it to test the wind.

"Sure, what's life without some thrills? I'll take ya, don't mind the company myself."

Jimmy squeaked in appreciation as I went to the car to grab my stuff. I clambered down the cliff behind the old man, nearly toppling over the edge a few times well. The tide was low, so we had to wade into the shallow waters onto his boat, a boat that wasn't too shabby itself. Kaiko was the captain of an old forty-foot tugboat; moss covered the hull, but she looked seaworthy and clearly had its share of life stories. I looked around to see where his crew was but found no one, just a young mute boy he called Cliff, who was always eager to help at a moment's notice.

Cliff drew up the anchor, and Kaiko started the boat's engines. The old tugboat ran surprisingly quiet, barely disturbing the drone of the early-morning stillness and lapping of the waves in the now-frigid temperatures.

We sailed around the northwestern point of Lipoa, heading toward Lahaina Beach. Within a couple hours, we started to approach where I remembered the *Carthaginian II* ship to be. Kaiko himself had some idea, so he killed the engines as a small speck of light started to break on the horizon. The silence of the night on the ocean was deafening, even Kaiko spoke in whispers as he handed me a mask and flippers on to which I added my headlamp.

I waited to get my diving gear and noticed both Cliff and Kaiko were just leaning on the hull, waiting for me to dive in.

Jimmy was as puzzled as I was until I had to ask, "Um, do you guys have tanks?"

"Oh shucks, where are my manners? Here you go," Kaiko chuckled, handing me a small tank, or what we call a SCORKL.

I watched up at the sky for strength, just realizing that in Kaiko's era of freediving, scuba tanks and modern diving suits almost never existed, so they developed an extreme amount of lung capacity, allowing them to do fishing and oyster harvesting in fairly deep waters. He also gave me a harpoon, winking at me in the process, as if I was now fully protected.

My heart sank a little, but I couldn't lose focus. At that moment, we were probably just above the *Carthaginian II*, and I had to get going. I dove down under, heading into the blackness of the water, visibility limited to just a few feet ahead. I kept the harpoon at the ready for any more of those creatures and placed the light on very bright as the dive shouldn't be more than a hundred feet deep. I descended easily to the lower depths of the harbor, noticing the massive structure as it started to come within my visible range.

It was definitely the massive whaling ship that I remember, over a 100 feet in length, with a 22-foot beam and weighing over 130 tons. The main masts were broken, but the nettings and bowsprit were still intact, giving the fearsome image of a harbinger of death for whales everywhere. I headed over to the poop deck, and I remember making fun of Liz calling it that, only to realize later she wasn't joking. Several lionfish and frogfish were everywhere as light started to break into the waters, giving an eerie sheen to the fluid currents.

I could see the bag and flash drive nailed to the deck, so I carefully pulled it out and stuck it in my wetsuit to try to keep it dry. I could feel some shaking behind me, so I spun around and saw dust kick up on the lower deck. I readied the harpoon in case, but then I saw a small white tip reef shark emerge, simply startled by my presence. I shuddered a bit as the water felt as cold as I've ever felt it, so it was time to get out while I still had some air left in the SCORKL.

As I rose to a little over sixty feet, I could feel my ascent slow a little. I tried my best to adjust to the different pressures along the depth column, but suddenly, I heard a series of clicks. I jolted forward and turned around to shine my light and saw a pod of humpback whales! It was a spectacular sight to behold. There were at least five of them, ranging from close to seven meters for the babies to closer to twenty meters for the three adults. They started whistling to me, as if to say hi as they gently swam by. I couldn't help but break into a smile, trying to join them in their run.

The ease and the rhythm to which they moved was hypnotic, and I swam alongside them, ultimately grateful to have a chance to see them up close. And after a few minutes, I could see the pod just break into higher gear, speeding up, making it hard to keep up with them. I decided to let up and take the cue to start heading up until another one started swimming by me. I was ecstatic.

I continued swimming by it, side by side, until it was right next to me. This one was barely inches away from my body. I was so happy, I did a clockwise rotation in the water like a drill, hoping maybe the whale would do the same. I smiled; I felt like time slowed to a nanosecond; and I watched this whale carefully, the pod now far out of reach from me.

*Wait, why is the pod gone?* I asked myself. *Whales don't move separately, where did this one come from?*

No sooner had I thought that, my spinning ended up on the whale's eyelid, and it opened its eye, a little larger than an orange. And as it opened, crusts of its skin peeled off, decayed and dead—its iris blood red!

I jumped back ferociously, scared to death of the massive creature. It turned with venom toward me, and I swam as hard as my body allowed. Most of my hearing in my right ear was gone, but I had no choice; I had to rise quickly. And as I rose to the final few feet to the surface, I could see the whale's massive jaws rip open, drawing me back into its throat, sucking me in.

I breached the surface, but so did it; and as gravity had its way with me above, water pushing me back to the surface, the whale erupted into the air. I felt myself get sucked down into its gullet, stifled within its body. It swallowed me whole, I wanted to panic, but I couldn't give up, not now.

*This corpse bride will not have me today*, I told myself as I kept the SCORKL on my mouth so I could still manage a few breaths as I forced my way down its throat under its peristalsis action.

She took me for her own prey, trying to force me into the stomach where the dangerous acids were. I felt my body rotating under the pressure of the bride's throat muscles. I still had the harpoon so I turned it on its edge to have the spur stick outward. Once I made one more rotation, I could feel the piece of steel grip. The whale convulsed slightly, and I could feel my body move upward a little. I pushed and pushed until I breached the throat.

A rush of water started to filter in as the whale seemed to have opened its mouth again. It hit me hard, but I hung on for dear life as the harpoon stayed affixed to the bottom of the creature's throat. And with the force of the water, I tore along its stomach until it split right open.

I was hurled out the beast's body, drifting into open water, the SCORKL breaking free. I only had a little energy left in me, barely fighting to survive. I looked down and saw a shadowy figure beneath watching, its red eyes piercing the dark waters, glaring at my survival and will to live with disdain. I then felt a pull on my neck as the corpse bride drifted along the ocean current, half burst open and disintegrating away—all twenty-five meters of it.

I blacked out, with no more air in me. I started taking in water, choking on it—an unstoppable rush through my body, threatening to explode my life from inside out. A blazing-hot sun scorched the back of my eyelids, forcing them open and wreaking havoc on my skin. A squint is all I could muster in my dazed state, noticing Jimmy sleeping right next to me, cuddled on what I could only think to be the captain Kaiko's poop deck.

As I rose to my feet, I could feel every last bone in my body crackle, hesitant to produce motion beyond the state of death I thought had befallen me. I sat up and looked around—everywhere was just ocean, not a sign of landmass, just Cliff scrubbing the deck as his usual task and the captain on the edge of the ship smoking a pipe while leaning over the railing. My clothes were in tatters, and the bag was gone.

I limped over to the captain, my energy nearly drained, inquiring about the status of the pack. He returned a warm smile and a few kind words.

"Well, Mr. Huxley, welcome back to the land of the living," Captain Kaiko said. "We all thought we lost you to that horrid beast. Thankfully you have the fighting spirit of a Bengal tiger."

"So it was you that saved me then," I said. "I-I don't know what to say, I am eternally in your debt, Captain, but I'm afraid that if we don't have the bag, then all that would have been for naught. I need Liz's bag or . . . or else . . ."

The captain barked off a few laughs before taking out the bag, handing it over. I rushed to give him a hug, and he reminded that even if the bag were gone, my life was more than naught and that I must never forget that.

He called to Cliff to bring some fruit and fried fish from the kitchen, a meal I took down with the voracity of a pack of hungry wolves. Jimmy was still sleeping, so I made a tiny tent for him where he lay and allowed him the pleasure of some more hours' sleep.

"It seems to be a little after midday, Captain, but I know not where we could possibly be," I said, worried. "Are we still in the Pacific? Are we just floating at the mercy of the currents of the wide ocean? Have we anything to fear?"

Captain nodded in dismay at how easily I could get riled up.

"Worry not, son, you are correct to say midday, but I fear you refer to a day ago. It is now a Friday, March 13—Black Friday—and we are currently floating northwest of the Hawaiian Islands, somewhere in the north Pacific Ocean. We're safe out here for now—that is, until you give us a heading to continue. I figure you may be running out of friends right around this here time, so I guess I have a couple more months I don't mind sticking around for, just a few more stories to add to my collection."

I bowed to the captain in reverence, thanking him for all that he was doing for me. Had it not been for him, I would probably have died in Lahaina.

My clothes stank of dead fish guts and puke, producing a pungent odor that may be detected on land from here, so I retired shortly to a chamber below and took a sponge bath, throwing out the clothes I had on. The smell still lingered, but at least it was good enough for me to lie on the bed without blocking my nose to stop smelling myself. My back stung like a thousand jellyfishes were left to rest on my bed, the sunburn from the midday sun causing all sorts of skin layers to burn clean off, leaving almost pure muscle and pain centers that worked all too well.

Limiting movement was my only resort to try and minimize the pain, and I did so while taking out my laptop to watch the fifth paper in Liz's series. And so it was—a file labeled 5. I saw another picture of a Dr. Fujiakawa of Udayana University in Bali, the last trip on my list to complete the five, so that was the second to last piece of the puzzle.

Liz wrote about the process of gene splicing adopted, the isolation of the RNA—a compound similar to DNA but single stranded as opposed to double, with slightly different constituent compounds. Liz wrote about more experiments with mice where she was able to successfully and repetitively isolate the RNA and work toward splicing it. Liz detailed the synthetic development of a set of five specific small nuclear ribonucleoproteins, or snRNPS, to attach themselves onto the intron of the premature RNA (the pre-mRNA), bonding with it and falling away, forming a new spliced RNA—the mature RNA, or mRNA. Unfortunately, she was only met with frustrations with these experiments. The snRNPS just refused to either form as a cluster capable of forming a bond with the intron or the RNA just rejected the compound altogether.

The experiments lasted months on end, and she described several times about the dejection she felt about the consistent failings of their trials while the novel coronavirus continued evolving and growing at its projected rate, infecting millions at this time. Her numbers were staggering to hear, knowing that—notwithstanding the current pandemic status of the disease—the confirmed cases only lay at 120,000. This implied that there may be much more to come.

Liz ended her paper in a sad note, explaining that she just doesn't know what her next step could possibly be—if she should abandon the concept of gene splicing to upgrade the spectral control receptor completely and try a different strategy or not. I felt heartbroken for her, knowing that giving up wasn't in her nature; I knew she would continue fighting to find some success, so I too had to keep moving forward.

Emerging from the cabin with a sense of purpose, I gave Captain Kaiko the heading. He was all too happy to set sail for the South Asian island located deep in the Java Sea. We agreed that it would be best to stay far from human contact for a while as our bodies all had healing to do from the last set of encounters with the daemons.

We set sail firstly for the Philippine Sea, trying to reach the Java Sea by avoiding the main landmasses completely. Within a week, we were able to pass through the strait between Taiwan and Manila, the Babuyan Islands being our guide to fair weather. The sea waves showed mercy on us through something Kaiko called the "charm of the water goddess," a handcrafted necklace of rare shells and oysters he kept on his person at all times. Passing closer to land as we entered the South China Sea, we could spot thousands of vessels lining up at the major ports, fighting to enter against what could only be considered stricter entry controls due to the virus.

A floating mountain range of masts high in the air littered the ports, seamen shouting and screaming at the top of their lungs, while hundreds of watermen ferried passengers and small cargo neatly in between the larger ships. Scurvy, smallpox, dysentery, and fever swept through those sailors like a plague itself, wiping out thousands each year.

"This one," Kaiko remarked, "will only be a little while."

Thankfully, he knew these waters so well, he could find a private, remote port or two along the way to restock supplies, ale, and diesel for the boat, allowing us to return to sea as quick as possible. Kaiko was happiest when he had ale on the boat, a temporary but certain means to pass the time that felt endless on our voyage. Things, however, changed once we reached the middle of the South China Sea—the weather, it was like it was enraged.

The stormy seas and windswept waves knew no calm to satiate their fury. Our little boat was tossed about like a ragdoll under the stresses of the mighty ocean, a strong mist accompanying the storms so visibility was down to almost zero. I tried my best to help the captain and Cliff, but to little avail. The elements were far too overpowering, so it was up to Kaiko to shepherd us through the angry channel and take us to safety. I lost count how many times I threw up on the deck, but still, I wrapped myself in woolen clothing to try and keep warm in the harsh conditions.

We stayed for days in soaking-wet clothing, the virus seeming inconsequential at the time as our body fought our internal as well as our external demons. The salted meat from the pantry started going old and was now covered in tufts of mold and tasted like rotting carcasses. The water did not do much to ease the burden on our stomachs. We all had to resort to drinking the ale as it was at least drinkable under the conditions, leaving us drunk for most of the day and arguing or fighting for our lives by night. We all looked like marooned sailors now with crisp, burnt red skin and fully grown, matted beards, scaring off all unsullied townsfolk who dared try and have decent conversation with us when we stopped at port.

Another week passed, and it was only the captain and myself on deck. Cliff caught a nasty strain of scurvy that had him bedridden for an entire day, now leaving his duties for me to fulfill. For the first time in the South China Sea, I could now see a clear sky. We cheered for the moment with whatever energy left in us. I lost close to 50 pounds in the journey so far, and I couldn't have weighed more than 150 pounds. My body became weak from the limited nourishment and the harrowing conditions we were forced to endure.

# 17

# LAST BOAT OUT OF BALI

By night, I lay flat out on the deck, staring up at the sky, as the boat rocked fairly vigorously from side to side. Compared to what we faced before, it felt like my mother rocking me to sleep. One constellation after another showed itself in the sky, Orion being the brightest of the lot. And then I could hear some whispers from afar. I quickly sat up and looked around, searching where the voice may have come. A haunting tune of a witch danced among the waves, lapping onto the tugboat's keel, a harpy song being played intermittently to add to its intoxication.

*Oh what I would do to find the embrace of a woman now*, I thought, far from any human contact.

It had been close to six months since I felt the embrace of a real woman, but it was almost as the sea knew this and called to me still.

"Hello, Hello, I am hear, come for me!" I shouted to the open ocean, a strong mist now coming in from where I called, quickly racing over the ocean surface and slowing down as it reached the ship hull.

It took its time consuming the ship, crawling up its sides with a sensual allure, and spilling over onto the deck like a glass of fine port overflowing in its own bounty. I had little to no energy to resist, so I simply savored the opportunity to hold this woman, to hear her sing into my ear. And soon enough, she came, dressed in a translucent silk gown, walking toward me with the grace of a Spanish dancer but with the skin of a celestial maiden born and raised in the Pacific—an exotic masterpiece that truly could not be for the eyes of men but for some divine being, rewarding me for my perseverance. I unfortunately did not have enough blood in my brain left to comprehend and answer. This was an experience for which I simply had to feel and be present.

Her skin was perfectly tanned and smoother than a freshly picked rose petal; her hair long enough to cascade onto her waist as water fell continuously along her slender, curvaceous figure. Her outstretched arms reached for me, holding me in a soft embrace. Her lips, full of juice and succulent moisture, met my dry, brazen, charred skin and fed it to the point where it gasped for air in satisfaction. Her breasts touched my chest and made it difficult to fully embrace her figure. My arms just weren't long enough as she giggled in my failed attempts.

*A jade empress—my jade empress—has come to save me from my ordeal to give me a taste of life so I may remember what I still fight for,* I told my hypnotized self.

She used her left leg and wrapped it around my lower back, grinding on my right thigh, while her other leg stayed hyperextended backward. My brain could not think, my heart could not beat, and, for some reason, my lungs could not breathe.

I gasped for air, reaching out for some sort of support to breathe but found nothing; the deck was totally covered in mist. I could not breathe, not even a little, and I started choking, I grabbed my neck to release the grasp of whatever was holding me captive, and then I looked again at my jade empress. I looked into her eyes for the first time and witnessed the horrid blood iris staring back at me. With this, the illusion started to fade, the sky gradually disappeared, and all that was above me was water—layers and layers of water, as I kept submerging under the boat.

An anchor fell right at my side, so I grabbed it, the force of the pulley yanking me from the beasts below that had to loosen their grips as I took to the boat once more, gasping for air as I rose above the surface, coughing incessantly as I was tossed on to the deck. I threw up stale saltwater with a myriad of junk and sand from the bottom of the seafloor that found its way into my body.

Kaiko gave me a good, hard slap on the back, forcing me to upend the rest of the junk from the pit of my stomach, as I lay there, learning my lesson of the temptation of the sea.

Kaiko showed me the charm once more, saying, "The goddess is not always benevolent, her other side—the temptress—often emerges from the depths of the ocean to satisfy her carnal sins. Woe, woe be onto the weary patriarch who thinks himself infallible."

The winds still swept cold, but I had no energy to get up. I lay there until morning, reflecting on the temptation that was, the sweetness of the experience that reached into my very soul, poisoning its desire for more.

* * * * *

"We're almost there!" shouted the captain as he announced we had finally reached the Java Sea on the king tide, the currents of the oceans blowing in our favor, taking us in the direction we needed to go.

This was the final week, and well beyond all logic, the little ship and its elderly captain safely shepherded us to the bay of Sungai Telaga Waja, an inlet on the east coast of Bali, south of the Beji Harum Temple. The mud flats were well submerged under the king tide, allowing us enough draught on the ship's hull to make all the way to the temple and comfortably dock on the moorings.

My knees shook violently as I stood on the wooden pier, and then I ran to the temple and dove on the land, laughing maniacally, scarcely believing that we had made it safely. Ripe mangoes were in abundance around the temple gardens, hanging off the trees in plenty, in a wide array of bright hues. Eventually, I noticed a monk emerge from the temple, holding a set of traditional prayer beads in his hands.

He sat with us and spoke gently, bringing some water to our aid, as I drank it greedily, with Jimmy living in the tree, eating his fill after the long ordeal. The palms of my hands were hard as chalk, my spirit felt chafed with the harshness of the sea, and even the old man looked pretty battered, notwithstanding the fact that he held the ship in one piece when all else seemed lost. The monk started reciting some Buddhist prayers for us before inviting us in, to have a bath and shave before returning for an evening dinner.

As we approached the main temple, I noticed statues perched on the roof of the main building—twin dragons racing toward a rising golden sun, almost holding it afloat.

The monk noticed my interest in the symbol and proceeded to explain, "The twin dragons represent the universal forces of life and death, fighting for the golden sun of immortality, the inescapable reality."

I spun around and looked at him. "Reality, you say?"

He nodded and smiled, as did I.

* * * * *

We slept for a couple hours but woke up for evening prayers with other monks and evening dinner with the group. The space was alight with candles and incense that filled the air with a hazy spirit of enlightenment—a feeling that permeated through the very being of the temple, the golden statues, and intricate adornments on the railings and the bodhisattvas. The food served was group style in the still of the night, thick mangrove trees, and the tides pushing and pulling the sand beneath us and surrounded us. Our meal was in the form of thalis, only once before had I had it in Indian restaurants in New York, a dish of pita bread surrounded by smaller bowls of stews, peas, chutneys, and rice that you can spin around and enjoy the flavors as they mix together on the palate. I ate with the care and dexterity of a sloth as my stomach didn't fully recover from the trip and to prevent throwing up any more than I had to.

The head monk joined us for dinner, his peaceful presence emanating throughout the temple. His equanimity was soothing, but I refused to get sucked into a false sense of security as I cautiously watched the roots of the mangrove trees around, lest the daemons would leap out and attack everyone, taking us out one by one. I realized how paranoid my mind must sound, but those two weeks on the seas could do that to you. My mental energy was drained. Words weren't necessary that night; I simply ate in silence. Kaiko and Cliff did the same, as Cliff was finally able to get to his feet after his long bout with scurvy.

After dinner, I went out to the water's edge and looked out at the water and mangrove trees, the sky forming a sharp backdrop to the scene. The stars started to come alight in the night sky, one at a time, with clouds streaming in to overtake them when they can. A chilly wind whipped over the lagoon and into the temple, but there was an eerie feel to the breeze.

"You know, the stars are here as a gift to the sons of humanity," the monk said to me as he came up to me. "Many take it for granted, but those out of the city, we can still see them and appreciate their nature, as it is similar to ours."

"And what nature is that?" I asked, looking at him.

"Stardust, a complex structure of hydrogen and carbon that forms the birth of life itself—stardust."

I smiled in return but noticed the tension in the monk's face before asking what was wrong.

"The darkness you face—it threatens even the stars," the monk added. "Their life sustains us here on earth, even if many do not know it. There is a deep reality to the fact that we feel at ease to get lost in its beauty in the night sky. Fight on, my son, the world needs you to stay fighting for the living. Have faith you will do well."

I said no more for the night, just to internalize the master's vision, the simple yet profound nature of the message. Within a few hours, I returned to my chambers to get some more sleep, the scars of the ocean journey etched all over my body. A horde of sandflies pervaded the air near the lagoon, ravishing the newly peeled flesh on my legs.

My dreams were lucid that night, but upon awakening, I couldn't remember a thing. I only saw several scratches made by my left hand's bloodied fingernails on the wall. The pain burned.

* * * * *

We had to keep moving, so we woke and had breakfast before heading out on a scooter along what seemed to be busy roads as early as 8:00 a.m. I lost track of time and wasn't even sure what day it was;

all I knew was that I had to meet this professor at the university that day to get more insight on Liz's research and to keep unlocking the puzzle.

We thanked the monk for his kindness and headed out on a scooter, Jimmy taking a front seat to the action on my helmet, enjoying the nice sun out even though the wind was still quite nippy. We drove along several coastal roads before crossing the causeway onto Pulau Serangan, the mainland highway. Within a couple hours, we made it to the university on the PB Sudirman Road, pulling up through the trademark rock-hewn flames on the entry gateway to the university.

I went into the university hospital, asking for a Dr. Fujiakawa, a Japanese geneticist of whom Liz often spoke in her distant e-mails to me from the Pacific. He was an expert in gene splicing and provided groundbreaking work on snRNPs, allowing most of the scientific community to perform genetic splicing in half the time it would usually take them. Just as with Dr. Clarke, I had a long wait in the hospital to see Dr. Fujiakawa, a wait that made me nervous as Kaiko waited outside with Jimmy and Cliff while I suffered through the endless persons streaming into the emergency room and inpatient theatres, coughing and wheezing incessantly to get help.

I was called in to his office, and he was not at all what I expected. A half-African half-Japanese individual in his late fifties shook my hand with a decisive firmness and grace that must have taken him decades to develop. I immediately felt comfortable in his presence and asked him how they were coping with the virus.

This was followed with a long sigh before he related his unending stories about the overwhelmed nature of the health sector and the long hours hospital staff had to work just to cope with the extra traffic and the stress with the increased risk for no extra pay. I empathized with him being on the front line and all before segueing into my query of Elizabeth and how much of the papers he knew about. Surprisingly, he knew quite a lot and pointed out that he supported her greatly in her research, prodding her along where most professionals in the field already turned their backs on her.

He thought her approach to use gene splicing to improve a human's genetic resistance to the virus was a novel concept and had a good shot at working. He told me her only problem obviously was finding the right snRNPs to bond with the introns, a task that even he couldn't surmount. We spoke for a little over an hour when I realized that he had no more information than I had, so before leaving, I inquired if he knew where Liz was; and after he responded in the negative, I asked if she had an office here, and he gladly showed me the way. I was happy to hear this and waited for his assistant to let me into Liz's office at the end of the corridor.

Upon entering, I saw a similar scene to the one in New York, only this one had different pictures on it and a letter with no address asking it to be opened at the "Gateway to the Heavens." I thought the comment was strange until I remembered she mentioned once that she loved a temple in Bali beyond all other sites she ever visited around the world, a place called *Pura Lehur Lempuyang*, as written on the letter. It was the tallest temple in Bali, sitting on 1,700 steps and 1,200 meters above sea level.

*It has to be the last site*, I concluded.

I took what pictures I could and set out to the good doctor's office to warn him of any strange visitors, citing the incident with Dr. Clarke and wishing for him to remain safe. He thanked me for my kind words and genuinely wished me best of luck in pursuit to find Liz. With that, I headed back outside to rejoin Kaiko and the others before heading out from the busy streets of Bali to the forested eastern edge of the country where the temple stood towering over its surrounding greenery.

We stopped briefly at a gas station to fill up on our diesel supplies as we loaded it in the tray. We took the coastal road route and rode for miles on end while making frequent stops along the way, brushing off thousands of sandflies we encountered, which were really starting to become a nuisance. We passed several other Hindu and Buddhist temples along the way. The Balinese landscape truly reflected a space of fluid spirituality that gave a deepened but esoteric experience that was truly unique and haunting at the same time. The locals dabbled in superstition, just as much as they did spirituality, giving ethereal explanations for every occurrence that could possibly happen to tourists in the area.

The ride continued for a few more hours along the Ida Bagus Mantra coastal road before swinging inland and experiencing a sharp increase in the ruggedness of the terrain and steepness of the climb. Rice terraces also littered the Balinese hillsides, with hundreds of farmers wearing straw hats toiling under the cold winds that approached an icy tinge as we got closer to the temple. We broke east again and headed up the mountain, keeping the scooters in first gear as they strained to go up the dirt roads of Pura Lempuyang Luhur in the village of Apang, aptly named, so I knew we were on the right track.

The wind was strong on the temple grounds in these hills of Bisbis, my nose starting to turn blue as the winds quickly changed directions with strong gusts. Jimmy huddled under my hoodie for some protection in this cold afternoon haze that now enveloped the space. Visibility was brought down to a little over twenty feet as we began our climb up the 1,700 steps into the temple that sat on the top of the mountain.

My legs burned as I tried climbing up the stone steps covered in moss, made even more slippery with the frigid temperatures. I looked up to the top and noticed a strange piercing structure shooting through the haze, peeking over the clouded condensate that has taken over the space. We were close so I had to press on. Within an hour, we barely reached the top, and I dropped to my knees in exhaustion, the dramatic weight loss from the sea voyage taking its toll.

I struggled to fill my lungs at this height, the air being very thin, forcing me to take shorter and more rapid breaths. I took out a banana from my knapsack, sharing it with Jimmy to keep up our strength. Kaiko too seemed tired, but he pushed through, getting off the ground and swishing away the cloud of vapor that had gathered around him.

"Well, at least we don't have any more sandflies," I pointed out to lighten the mood, mustering only a thumbs-up from the crew who were anxious to get the mission over.

I looked over the other side of the grounds and noticed another mountain it overlooked—Mt. Agung. I stumbled over to the eastern end of the temple. And then suddenly, the haze started to clear to reveal the eastern gate of the temple, the mystical "Gates of Heaven."

The winds were still icy, but even if through squinting, the sight was a marvel in its own right, a set of split gates that rose over forty feet high, adorned with rock flames resembling a tuning fork for a giant. It shot up from the temple base and announced its presence over the eastern lands. I noticed that Jimmy remained relatively calm while we were up here, so the daemons must have had trouble ascending to this place for whatever reason.

The majesty of the architecture of the split gates almost forced you to stand between them, and I took a deep breath in and closed my eyes, absorbing the energy that the mount possessed. And then I heard water. I looked at Jimmy, and his ears twitched a little too, looking to his right. I had to walk through the gates and saw a sharp drop-off behind and a sheer drop-off coming right after. There was a strange excavation at the top of the mountain that formed a sort of small cave where the ice formed, melting and falling below where a bush of bamboo grew strong and tall.

I took out the letter from Liz and proceeded to read it, standing behind one of the split gate columns to try and get some shelter.

William,

It is with great love that I write my final letter to you before I move on to fulfill my final destiny. Unfortunately, this is my end of the road and where yours now begins. As you would have seen, my research has hit a roadblock, and you still remain the key to the entire puzzle. By now, you would have met Dr. Fujiakawa, my learned mentor and, unfortunately, the only true friend that I have left in the scientific community. Keep his friendship close, as the time will soon come where you will need it.

I have no doubt that you would have had encounters with the final evolution of the virus, the daemon creatures that feed off the life of humans and move with the mist. They are a formidable and dangerous enemy and will stop at nothing until the virus has spread to every corner of the world and infected every living being so they may control humanity and feed their titan savior, Gaia.

I have faith in your spirit, William. You are strong, and I need you to be even stronger—the world needs this now. I know you would have followed my guidance and found the Gates of Heaven atop the highest mountain in Bali. There, for some reason, the daemons cannot reach you. I believe it has something to do with the water. They also cannot stand being burned and impaled through the eyebrows—at least, that is what I have seen so far.

Save the water for your greatest challenge, William. For everything else, use your cunning and wit to survive against their kind, but they are soon to move into high gear, and we all do not have much time yet. Come to me at these coordinates—5.304, 162.904—at a place called Point Vauvillier. Here lies an uncharted island in the Pacific where I will be heading off to next. I believe it to be the daemons' breeding nest and my last chance to find what I need to secure the snRNPs I need.

I long to see your chubby face again, brother, to feel safe in its simplicity. But I fear this challenge, for the first time, may be too much for me to bear, but I go still, as I cannot sit idly by and see humanity suffer when I know there is something I can do, even if they too don't understand the mission.

So for now, this is farewell, little brother. I wish you all the mercies in your travels. Please be careful and remember always to fight on.

Love,
L

Tears welled up in my eyes and blew with the wind as I tried to gather myself. Kaiko listened carefully to the entire story before patting me on the back and grabbing my shoulders as I sobbed and fell to my knees.

"Come, William, we must remain strong," the old captain said. "We have to keep pushing forward. It is what your sister would want."

I heard his words, but my emotions left my vision in a blur. He realized I needed some time to myself, so he took it upon himself to continue on, carefully walking over to the bamboo grove that sat in a puddle of crystal-clear water.

"Hey, be careful!" I shouted to him as he precariously went over to the bamboo, hanging on to the sturdy stalks until he reached the pool at their base.

He carefully took out his knife and cut an inch-wide piece of bamboo and hollowed it out before scooping out some water and saying his own silent prayer before returning. After returning, he took out another piece of bamboo and whittled it down to a makeshift endcap, corking the water inside the bamboo vial that we sought to guard with our lives.

"I know that island, William, it is not as far from Hawaii, but it is just north of San Cristobal of the Solomon Islands and off the Bismarck Sea. We could make it there within a week, once we get the supplies we need."

I wiped my nose, which felt so cold now and I wasn't even sure I still had a nose. I looked at Kaiko and smiled.

"Then come, let us not waste any more time," I told him. "We have our heading, we have our instructions. It is time to stop running. It is time to take the fight to them. Let us get what we need and move with haste. Our destiny waits for us on that island. Let us not disappoint those who wait for us."

Kaiko nodded as we bowed to Ishwar, the god to whom the temple was dedicated, and we carefully descended with renewed purpose and grit flowing through our veins.

After several stops along the way, we had the supplies we needed; and upon returning to the Beji Tirtha Harum Temple by sundown, Kaiko immediately begun work on repairing the ship to make it stronger to take the open ocean currents once again. Work on the ship was difficult as the tide was in and the currents were strong under the high winter winds. The head monk of the monastery didn't say much that night beyond giving us our supper. I could see his concern over the winter-like weather that was soon upon us.

After a few hours of work, approaching midnight, the mist and sandflies were almost unbearable. Something was amiss, and I didn't waste time loading up the ship. A haunting, low drone then sounded over the mist, the same one we heard in Maui before the daemons appeared.

"We gotta go, Kaiko."

I ushered him on as I boarded the ship. He hustled as best he could, the mangrove trees starting to rustle unnaturally in the wind. In a single fell swoop, Cliff drew up the anchor, and the ship was off, ready to head back to the open ocean to face the enemy head-on, on our terms.

# Part IV

# QUARANTINE

*April 30, 2020*
*163,000 Deaths*
*4,156,689 Cases*

# 18

## AN UNCHARTED ISLAND

Back on the deep seas wasn't as bad as I thought it would have been. Heading out on the currents gave a sense of open freedom that left the confinement of the marshes behind. We passed the corner of Pineda Island called the Devil's Tear before breaking into open ocean and landless horizons.

Kaiko possessed nearly flawless navigation skills and really put that to use steering us through the Banda Sea south of Indonesia and the narrow straits of the Ceram and Halmahera Seas before returning us to the south Pacific Ocean. It was a feat on its own as we reached the open frontier, Kaiko taking in some celebratory shots of ale to toast to the moment. I joined in but remained focused on the matters at hand—the chance to finally meet Liz again.

Oh what a yearning for her I felt, the safety of like minds meeting again on a planet that was out to end our lives because we refused to be beaten by the pandemic. The captain and I both shared a few cigarettes as Jimmy climbed the shrouds on the ship to keep his muscles active on the weeklong voyage.

The mission was filled with verve and flair in the first couple days, but by the third day on the ocean, that quickly wore off, leaving me tired and haggard again. I scraped off the wooden cabin walls with my bloodied fingernails, and we grew matted beards soaked in ale and puke. Under my eyes stayed permanently swollen as my face lost more muscle mass, the sea aging us at least twenty years over the period of the journey—at least three days passing under heavy winter conditions and stormy seas without a speck of land in the distance to give us any semblance of hope.

The crew started to fracture as we were all complaining to each other about each other. One time, a fight broke out between Cliff and myself over how long we had been at sea, leaving me with a bloody nose and Cliff with a cracked rib. I started to seriously question the captain's navigation skills until finally I confronted him about it.

"When will we reach? How do I even know we are not lost at sea turning in circles?" I complained.

Kaiko took particular offence to this, shouting at me to take back my words. And when I refused, we got into a scuffle of our own, rolling around on the deck, until Cliff doused us under a bucket of stale fish guts, which got us to stop, forcing us to get cleaned up before continuing our argument.

Upon our return to deck, we noticed the argument wasn't as important as we made it out to be. And then, Kaiko's voice bellowed over the winter winds like the voice of God, "Land ho!" We all cheered with glee, and Jimmy bounced up and down on the deck as we danced our way well into the night.

I looked closely. The island in Point Vauvillier mentioned by Liz was tiny, but something definitely was strange about it. The currents started to take us to the landmass, and immediately Kaiko knew something was wrong. A strange mist enveloped the island, and a sharp rock range was scattered about the shores of the reef that encircled the island.

Kaiko had to be sharp, flexing his skills as the helmsman. He needed us to distribute the weight on the boat on each side, depending where he needed the boat to go. The seas were stormy and waves torrential as a storm came in over the island. We dodged one, two, three sections of the reef and was coming upon a fourth one—there was no escape.

We hit the reef with a tremendous thud, throwing us forward, leaving us strewn across the deck. We recovered quickly and continued the thrust forward, but the reef had ripped in to our hull on the starboard side. We were taking in water. With half a mile to go, we had to make haste.

Kaiko spotted a remote beach near a grove of mango trees he would try to beach us on. The lower deck was now covered, and we couldn't bail the water fast enough, so we just had to brace for impact. Fifteen-foot waves brought up our rear and lifted us over the sea level, dropping us like a sack of potatoes, smashing the ship into little pieces.

I grabbed onto Jimmy, and we all dove into the waters, each of us wearing our life jackets just in time. We swam the rest of the way, settling into a sheltered mangrove that gave some protection under the strong winter winds.

"Everyone okay?" Kaiko asked as we came ashore, standing in knee-high water among the rhizome roots of the mangrove trees, crickets chirping in the background under a moonless winter night.

Everyone nodded before pushing through the slush and mud of the mangroves before reaching dry land, dropping onto the bush-covered dirt road, throwing up what remaining saltwater was left in our bodies. I spotted a large tree across the road, so we sought shelter from the storm under there—at least to survive the night. Our clothes were soaking wet, and we were all in danger of catching serious hypothermia, so we all tried to stay close and conserve our body heat.

The night wore on, and I started trembling under the stresses. I only remembered eventually waking up slightly when some light entered as a group of elderly villagers came to our aid as they were out to do what seemed to be fishing. Our lips were parched, and they immediately brought water for us; the sudden burn on our lips were stinging but satisfying at the same time. They took us to their village and housed us, clothed us under a thatched-roof, lepe-floor house that gave a smooth final finish that kept essentials off the dirt ground. They spoke in a native Pacific islander language that I had no hope of understanding, but perhaps Kaiko may have a chance when he comes to.

They gave us some hot tea, warming our insides as it went down our throats. The natives offered us some fresh breadfruit and plantains for lunch as we all started waking up from our stupor. Their clothes were simple, but the people were cheerful and happy. We mainly saw elderly persons sitting at a table, drinking something out of a gourd and giggling uncontrollably. I looked outside and still saw it was windy, with icy pangs sweeping through where I would think would have hot tropical climates at this time of the year. However, I had to admit I wasn't too sure what time of the year it was anymore.

After our meal, the older women guided us down to a river to take a bath before returning. They threw away our clothes before giving us a new set. We hobbled our way back up the slope into the hut where the men were heartily chatting about something and got silent once we returned. As expected, Kaiko could speak their language and carried on a conversation with the men, explaining to them our predicament and that we wanted to get to Point Vauvillier as soon as possible.

They nodded and pointed out that we had landed on the Island of Tofol, the bay we crashed on was called Infal Malem, and this village was called YascrYascr. We thanked the village chief for his kindness and asked what was the best way to move around. He didn't understand the question as almost everything they did was on foot.

Around dinnertime, the ladies went to the river to wash clothes, while the men ate their helping of buttered cassava and taro root and washed it down with *sakao*, a local drink made from the sakao tree that gave a natural high. They passed it around in a gourd, the village chief indicating the next person to drink, and I assumed it would be rude not to partake.

I proceeded to chug down the drink, not realizing everyone else sipped it. Sakao definitely was an acquired taste, as the slime-like texture slithered down my throat with a strong aftertaste of tree bark and sap and a strong burn at the back of my throat that probably won't go away for the next few years. The drink immediately went to my head, and the room started spinning. I needed to take a seat, so I started feeling around, panicking to find a seat, much to the amusement of the other men, the problem being that I was already sitting.

* * * * *

I made my way to the floor and lay on it while the effects of the drink wore off, waking right at the same place the next morning and hearing some voices down by the riverside.

I stumbled down to the river and spied a few of the ladies taking a bath, so I stopped in my tracks and waited for them, even though a part of me deeply wanted to join them. After an hour of waiting, they emerged, and I tried to converse with them but to no avail. I had to wait for Kaiko to arrive before engaging them in conversation.

Eventually, Kaiko arrived, and I was able to ask the questions I needed while they continued washing their clothes. I inquired mainly about the point that I needed to be at and also asked about the weather. They explained that the weather was in fact strange and that for all their lives, they had never encountered this level of coldness. I had to conclude that the Fimbulwinter was in fact at hand, the sign that Lance forewarned.

*I have to act faster now*, I thought.

They pointed in the general direction of the Point Vauvillier, but that direction came with a warning.

"The north of the island is a place of great darkness," they said in their tongue, as translated by Kaiko. "A shadow had been cast over that area from since the coming of the missionaries in the earlier part of our history. The missionaries formed a church and positioned it on the cliff of the north, overlooking the village below. That village soon became witness to several strange happenings on the island. The church acted both as a place of service and as a boarding school; the headmaster, Father Faraday, was their founding father.

"In the late 1990s, the boarding school fell apart, with the disappearance of the children of that school and their main guardian, Sister Mary. After their disappearance, water became very difficult to get in the village, most of the springs and wells dried up, leaving only a wet, foul sludge in the springs. The church is still there but in a dilapidated state, and the village below is now abandoned."

"So how do I get to this village?" I asked eagerly, Kaiko again translating for me.

The ladies hesitated before pointing out the path we would have to take, but they warned me again of the perils to get there as we would have to pass through the Forest of Ka, a wretched piece of greenery that became cursed from the disappearance of the children. They told me no one has ever entered the forest and left thereafter, so passing through it is at our own risk.

I didn't see any choice, and time was running out as the winter storms grew stronger with every passing day. That evening, we packed our things and said our goodbyes, thanking the village chief and his people for their hospitality, noticing upon leaving that no children existed in the entire tribe.

# 19

## HAUNTED FOREST

We packed some provisions for the trip, and I headed out with my trusted cage and Jimmy on my shoulders. Unbelievably, the tote bag and cage survived the onslaught of the storm and the boat crashing. We also had a couple rice bags that held the provisions, and Cliff graciously agreed to carry it on his head as we walked along the dirt track moving north from Infal Malem. We walked for hours, cutting through thick bushes with spiny thorns to make our way north, following the coastal track as our guide, sometimes changing direction eastward but generally heading north.

The ground consisted mainly of something called coral gravel, a form of compacted coral pieces that was very porous but acted as a great substrate for pathways and roads, standing up to the high amounts of rainfall in the region. The winter-like winds didn't let up, a haze still clearly present and sweeping through the land, making it as inhospitable as humanly possible, ushering us at every turn. We had to make a single climb that took us up a steep slope, and my calves burned on the ascent. Eventually, we made it to the summit and climbed over the peak. There it was—a thirty-odd-acre monster forest of dense, strange-looking tall trees sporting a deep green color and overarching canopy that made it all look like a single tree from our vantage point.

"The Ka Forest," started Kaiko, the first time he spoke since we started. "The last of its kind on the planet, the ka trees being present only here on earth and with it, many superstitions and mythologies about its power and resilience. There have been recent attempts to construct roads, houses, community centers, everything possible through it, and for one reason or another, these efforts just kept falling apart.

"This forest is oftentimes referred to as the 'Forest of Mirrors' as during the day, it looks like the greatest life-giving spectacle on the island that should be guarded and worshipped by all. As night descends, however, its face starts to change. The trees take on a form of their own, building with it an anger and fury that claims the lives of all that cross their path."

We all watched each other gingerly, then sped up our trek. It would be close, but if we made good time, we may have a chance of being able to beat the forest before dark.

The dirt road gradually disappeared until we came upon the base of Ka Forest. Each tree was at least forty feet tall, hovering over us like giants from the earth and looking down on us with raised aerial roots and gnarled barks covered in moss and fungi at its base. A light coat of snow started to cover the canopies, which made the scenario seem even more urgent—we had to power through.

We all took a deep breath before entering the forest, slashing the underbrush as we walked through. The forest from within was a totally different beast altogether. The floors were carpeted with leaves, the vines grew from the canopies to the floor acting like walls, and the floor bases were covered in large mushroom pads poking out where they can. The forest was so connected, I felt as if it breathed and moved together like a single living organism.

Upon passing the first ka tree, Kaiko took out his machete and marked an *X* on it for safety as we continued battling the torrid underbrush in our way. Eventually, we passed by many exotic banana trees, ferns, and spiny palms that released their spines at maturity, covering the floor with the six-inch needles scattered among the leaves. An hour later, we kept listening for the water, trying our best to keep it on the right so we could continuously move north. But the light started to die while Kaiko kept marking trees. We picked up the pace and tried drinking less water, but it felt like we were no closer to any end of the forest, not even to break out into a field or meadow or clearing.

"We have to track back," Kaiko said dejectedly. "We have to restart from our last marked tree."

We all agreed, as the dying embers of light started to fade. I lit a torch, and we saw a ka tree in the distance and bolted toward it.

Kaiko looked upon it and said, "Wait, something's wrong, this can't be."

He retraced his steps again on the single path we moved back and forward on. He came right back to my position, but there was no *X* sign on the tree.

I sat next to the tree, and several trees in the vicinity stared down on us as if in amusement. Kaiko checked them all, but none bore his mark of conquest. It was too late to press on. We had to pitch tent and hunker down for the night.

The crickets were deafening, and upon carrying the torch near the ka tree, I noticed the fungi had started to bloom, A dull red flower and several other parasitic plants throughout bloomed in their usual dull fashion. Loranthaceae, Viscaceae, and Orobanchaceae littered the forest with their vampiric stalks and ferns, digging into the intersections between branches and trunks where the moisture and life-giving forces were juiciest. A haunting chill fell on the forest floor with every tiny grasshopper and spider making noise as the crew huddled together to try and stay warm under the cold conditions that still seemed to penetrate the tough exterior of the forest.

I was the first to nod off, drifting into different spaces in my subconscious as the dark, gloomy forest loomed over us all. I could then here distant laughter coming from someone, a young child; and while all I saw was a blank slate, the voices were unmistakable. I took off in the direction of the voices, calling to the young girl, asking if anyone was there. I found myself running so fast, I couldn't control the momentum, moving at full tilt toward the sound.

In the distance, I could see a child, a young Caucasian child, playing in a pile of leaves while a swing blew in the breeze behind her.

"What is your name?" I shouted above my footsteps.

"Jennie" was the response as she retreated slightly to the swing.

I continued running to reach out to the girl, but just before I reached her, I could feel myself stumble and fall headlong into a ditch. I was falling for nearly ten seconds, which felt like an eternity at that time. The experience of vertigo caught up with me, straining my bladder and stretching my faculties to stay alert and focused on the voice of the girl.

I hit the ground with a tremendous thud and blacked out, woken only by the stinging sensation of something biting me and biting hard. The sandflies were back, and they were back to haunt me. I awoke alone on the forest floor with a groggy feeling and strong headache. As I felt my temple, I could sense a sizable bump that formed right where I fell in the dream. It was all very puzzling until I could hear the voice of the girl again, coming from a distance off from the northeast. I had to follow so I hobbled my way over to the voice and was careful to look out for ditches, fighting off the swarms of sandflies that descended on me, attacking my skin as if it was their God-given dinner for the night.

I could see a small but definitive speck of light coming from behind a few forest vines, and it got larger as I approached. There she was, Jennie, sitting in the swing and singing a lullaby with the sweetest tone as her matted blonde hair fell over her face, disguising most of her facial features. She couldn't have been more than seven years old. The swing, however, was covered in moss; and her knees, elbows, and knuckles were bruised and covered in dried blood as if she fell and her body couldn't heal itself.

I reached out my hand, asking her to come with me; and with a single motion, her head rotated but the rest of her body stayed in one place, locking her gaze once she caught sight of me. I too could see the other side of her face—it was another daemon the size of a small person. Half of the face was that of a little girl; but the other side was worn and old, charred and bony, and with hanging dead flesh, its daggerlike long tongue flicking out, ready for its next prey.

A slow mist seeped out from under her feet, and as her jaw opened, a nest of sandflies took flight once they could. She started walking to me, which was my sign to run. I took off to wherever I believed camp was, stopping for nothing, trying my best to outrun the flies and the child ghoul. Razor grass tried to slow me down, but

I took on the scrapes and cuts along the forearm like it was nothing, considering what was waiting for me behind there.

In midflight, I had to use the small knife and cut a stick off some of the small trees and sharpen it while I ran, knowing full well I may only have a single opportunity. As I ran, I could hear the tiny footsteps of the miniature ghoul creep closer with a remarkable speed and precision, closing in on my location. The flies were, however, too fast; and within a minute or so, they were at my back and eventually overtook me, attaching themselves to my face and all biting in at once. The pain was unimaginable, digging into my flesh, some tapping my blood vessels and starting to sap me of my life, bringing me to the forest floor.

I hit the ground hard and turned on my back quickly only to hear the footsteps of the creature slow down until it was right above me. Jennie walked over me, and the flies immediately withdrew. I stared down the horrid creature, looking like a doll in some places and a gremlin in others. And then its tongue came out. With its daggerlike tip flailing about, its drool fell on my stomach like a wet dog. The tongue was covered in strange small spikes like stiff white hairs that stood on end when it sensed prey was near.

It drew itself closer to within a few inches of my nose. I breathed hard and stayed focused on the creature, as the tongue stood erect as a cobra and got ready to strike with lightning speed. It was now or never. I grabbed the stick next to me and swung it wildly, connecting with the tongue. The monster screamed in pain from the blow, jumping backward. Its movements were awkward, so as it retreated slightly, it was exposed. I got ready to move in, and just as I was about to make the final lunge, I felt my hands go numb—I couldn't move them.

*It has to be the flies*, I thought. *Some sort of neurotoxic venom that causes temporary paralysis.*

The vines of the trees then started to ensnare my body, and before I knew it, only my head was exposed, left that way for the beast to feed. I looked up at it and spat with disgust at the creature, the mist now everywhere on the forest floor. I could now hear not only distant laughs but now multiple distant cackling, similar to a witch's cackle from fairytales with cauldrons and broomsticks.

I panicked among the vines and tried to fight it, but it adjusted like a boa constrictor and just squeezed tighter. I could feel the oxygen draining as the creature's tongue once again emerged, ready to claim its victim. I then heard an unnatural rustle to the right, then left, and then in an instant, before the beast could react, a wooden stick went straight through its skull. It was Kaiko!

The creature screamed in pain, and I could hear the entire forest reel in unison with the creature as the vines started to loosen their grip. The impaled beast stood motionless on the floor with the pole through its head and melted away until only bones and dead flesh on its ligaments were left.

Kaiko used his blade to clear off the vines from around me before grabbing my arm from the tree's embrace, holding me up on his shoulder, insisting we stay on the move even though it was night. The cackles continued but only for a short time as we limped around the underbrush, cutting anything in our path looking suspicious. Kaiko didn't mark any more trees as he was convinced the forest was indeed alive and haunted so it would keep playing tricks with us until we died.

Within a few hours of hard pressing, we finally came upon a wall of vines, which we tore down until it revealed another clearing, just like the one we saw upon entering. I looked at Kaiko fearfully.

"Worry not my friend," he triumphantly mentioned, out of breath. "Our entry hill is no longer present at the other side. We have finally made it through the cursed wood. Come, let's get you cleaned up before going any farther."

We made camp a few hundred meters north of the forest and could still hear the distant howls and whistles emanating from within. I couldn't sleep another wink and neither could Jimmy, constantly on edge being so close to dreaded creatures. We came into a clearing and a coastal village with dilapidated huts and palm trees. Finally, we had made it to the Ghost Village.

# 20

# THE CHURCH OF MALEM

The scene spread out before us was like an abandoned warzone, devoid of any life or hope. Single-story, thatched-roof structures littered the coastal community, bordered solely by the dirt road next to the mangrove trees and tide. The lap of the waves on the dirt path was louder than usual, owing to the storm conditions, which kept beating on us like a drum as we continued our trek forward.

I squinted under the weight of the water drops—"white rain," we would call it in New York—allowing visibility only for a few meters ahead, forcing us eventually to take shelter periodically in the abandoned houses just to get some reprieve from the elements. It was cold, very cold, and now wet. But I felt as though my body had become impervious to the common cold after what I've been through, and still my immune system remains resilient. We had to keep pushing forward, and so we did.

We walked along the coast, jumping a little as the slightly warmer seawater bathed our feet when the tide pushed further inland under the storm surge effects. My jeans, shirt, and hair were now completely soaked; but we had to keep moving forward. We could see a large rock now blocking our path—at least ten feet high and thirty feet wide. The shale rock looked to be carved by giants, so we had to climb to make it to the other side. As we reached the top, we could scarcely believe what we saw. There were people, hundreds of people, gathering on the shore ahead of us.

An old tugboat was offloading passengers on to the beach and a series of tall men, seemingly shepherding them farther north toward something else. Part of me was happy to see the scene, so we quickly scuttled down the other side of the rock and ambled to the crowds, anticipating some sort of support.

I spoke firstly in English for Point Vauvillier, then French, Spanish, German, and, finally Dutch. No one responded. I could hear the tall guards then announce something in a foreign language I had never heard before, a native tongue apparently that most people understood. After glancing over to one of the men, I noticed he carried a machete, covered in thick blood, along with his left hand. He was by far the most animated of the lot.

The waves crashed on the pier and tossed the boat around before it turned back and headed into the open ocean, hurrying to leave these shores. I had to ask these men. But I got very little cooperation from them beyond a quick shove into my back, ushering me into a factory-style line that continued up into the mountains that now became visible as the rain subsided slightly with the winds as strong as ever. I squinted up to the top of the cliff and something was there. It was a church, a large church, precariously positioned on a rocky cliff that overlooked the bay below it. That cliff jutted out and over the ocean, but erosion ate away at the cliff's base, making one wonder when the entire church would come crashing down with the mountain face. Beneath it was a series of sharp rocks protruding from the ocean in the nearshore, looking similar to what we encountered when our boat was torn apart.

Suddenly, I got a strong push from my back ushering me on. We had to join the assembly of persons heading up the hill to the church, no one being able to tell me where we were going or what those herdsmen were going to do with us. I looked over to my left and noticed a series of palm trees struggling in the wind to stay stable, and on it, the tree was covered in bats—horseshoe bats! The bats covered the top of the tree trunk looking like a bunch of coconuts and several others on the branches gripping firmly on to tree and looking on the scene, ready to pounce and claim us for their prey. Jimmy was on edge, screaming at them from the cage. But with the strong winds, nothing could hear us—we were simply more bodies.

We passed a tall guard on our left. His lanky stature, hooked nose, and long beard gave him a holy look that condescendingly looked down on us all, holding a torch to let us know the way we are to head. I stepped in mud, trudging my way along the bay before heading up the hill to the first turn en route to the top of the cliff. There were hooded guards everywhere, their torches held unnaturally far from their bodies, remote enough to let us know that they were not interested in conversation as if we were being sent to the slaughterhouse.

The water draining along the center path forced us to fight its currents along with gravity, slipping from time to time on the rounded coral gravel surface of the pathway to the top. It took about an hour at this pace to reach the final slope to the peak, which overlooked most of the island. I could see the Ka Forest, where the tribe was, and possibly where we entered at the mangrove forest. My legs burned as we approached the final steps, and Jimmy was forever on edge, his senses feeling the paranormal everywhere we turned.

The dense foliage helped in giving some shelter to the icy winds, but that all changed once we hit the summit. There it stood, the famed Church of Malem—a European Gothic medieval church, centuries old and now repurposed for an unholy use by the church faithful and island governance. We were being ushered into the main gates as I watched the dilapidated dark structure that towered over all else.

The ragstone finish to the church was all black and grey, littered with old iron doors and stone inset windows with iron bars to keep the unwanted out of the fortress. Gargoyles sat motionless on each of the steeples that went up at least ten feet before terminating at a point, except for the one closest the ocean that had caved in completely. The stained-glass windows were the newest of the features, stretching over fifteen feet tall in traditional rainbow colors and etchings of priests and saints for the followers to praise. A drawbridge welcomed our entry over a moat and into the massive structure that I supposed would be our chambers for some time to come.

I finally entered the main hallway of the church, with forty-foot ceilings throughout and grand arches to welcome our arrival with open-flame torches to give light to all newcomers. We bled out into a courtyard that had several piles of rope on the floor for reasons I didn't want to contemplate fully at that time. The strange design of the church now saw a second floor, which made our courtyard seem as sort of a pit, cordoning us in like livestock and for someone to come in and hopefully shed some light on our situation.

After a little over half an hour of restlessness, a priest in his upper seventies arrived with his pale skin, pointed nose, and ear hairs to match, fully adorned in white and red robes of what I could only make out as Coptic wear. He wore a pontiff's hat and stood on a podium, looking down from on high to address us, everyone now getting silent to hear his speech, which was primarily in Latin. Thankfully, I knew that language too, so I could translate while a short local next to him spoke in the local tongue.

"*Reciperint Hominum moerum*, my brothers and sisters," the priest began. "I have gathered you here today to speak of God and his purpose for you in his grand plan. The day that we have been speaking of for centuries at the pulpits around the world is finally here, the Great Tribulation. In Matthew 24:6–8, it speaks of the great tragedy to befall this earth, which reads, 'Our Lord hath said: And you shall hear of wars and rumors of wars: see that you be not troubled: for all these things must come to pass, but the end is not yet. For nation shall rise against nation, and kingdom against kingdom: and there shall be famines, and pestilences, and earthquakes, in diverse places. All these are the beginning of sorrows."

His voice then grew louder.

"But worry not, this pestilence that is raging across the globe is all part of God's plan, and we must trust in it. It is divine, it is ordained, it is the truth! The coronavirus has now claimed the lives of 163,000 of our fellow brethren and infected upward of 4.1 million people. This, my dear friends, is an unprecedented situation that has never been faced in the history of humanity, so great is our Lord! But there is more to come. The planet will survive this scourge of pestilence as it wipes out the sinners of the world and leave the rest for us, as the rightful descendants of the divine to inhabit this space as our own, to rule as kings, to live as we ought to have lived before the vile plague of nonconformity and liberality spread through our treasured race like wildfire. We shall endure, we shall survive, and that is why we have you here, as you must prove yourself to be children of the one true God.

"You will be in quarantine in this holy facility for fourteen days, and as the moon turns new, you will be assessed for your purity. Those alone who are pure will be taken to the kingdom of deliverance. All else, well, they must perish with the other sinners. I speak these words of benevolence to you on this day, my children of the one God. Seek ye forgiveness of thine ways and offer yourself unto him, and only then can you possibly leave this place a new man, born again in the blood of righteousness and piety."

A smirk dawned upon the father's face as he lifted his hands in the air and pointed to us as if showering us with a grace of which only he knew the benefits. The torches gleamed on his form as I noticed the purple, swollen fingers of hypoxia on his outstretched hands.

*He's infected*, I thought quietly.

"I speak to you as your humble servant, Father Fulton, just as those before me spoke, just as Father Faraday once spoke, Ite per voluntatem Dei et gratia tua ad guide."

With that, he closed a massive hardcover book on his podium, his piercing eyes looking down upon us with pity but no remorse.

We were let out on a balcony that was depressed into the rock, making it impossible to escape. A windswept plain into which the unlucky overflowed from the courtyard faced the icy tundra winds tossed in from the sea. I looked around to find Kaiko and Cliff. Eventually, I was able to locate them as all the guards simply stood on the first floor looking down on us like animals, but they would generously give us our last freedoms as an act of mercy. It was all a very surreal and dark experience, the looming guidance from an overarching power to guide us into our next step in life. I chuckled at the arrogance but was also mindful of the reality of the situation.

"So does anyone even know that this church at some point in time was a boarding school for little children and they all went missing?" I bellowed to the mass.

A hush descended upon the group before someone came up to Kaiko and whispered something in his ear after which he bowed to the gentleman in thanks prior to giving me an update.

"Umm, so they don't want to you reference that story anymore," Kaiko said. "They consider it blasphemous and that it will bring bad luck to their already troubled existence. They are very finnicky here about the dead, which is why you will not find any morgues on the island. They prefer to simply read very specific and traditional rites to the bodies, and the extended families tend to get quite involved. Talking about the dead after they are buried is seen as invoking their spirits from the land beyond and drumming up more trouble than they might be willing to take on."

I watched Kaiko with a suspicious frown on my face as I did see some semblance of contradiction of this to the ease with which they accepted the deliverance from the priest. But I knew that the less waves I could make, the better.

"So what now?" I asked impatiently. "Do we simply wait for these men on high to foretell our future or do we take action?"

The guards started murmuring among themselves before out of the corner of my eye I saw an opening in the wall to the back of the open courtyard. After going up to it, I noticed it was a window overlooking the bottom of the cliff, and something unusual was hidden among the beach swash.

# 21

# MALEM SEA CEMETERY

The window was a dirty, moss-filled abomination with rusted bars to prevent anyone from jumping off the two-hundred-foot-high cliff through its five-foot opening. It had a wide inset into the cliff rock and overlooked the shoreline very clearly, which shone under the bright moonlight. I peered at the beach hard, and there were some oddly shaped rocks in the surf causing an unnatural backsplash on the coast. Myself, Kaiko, Cliff, and Jimmy all peered through the window at the same time, entranced by the scene.

"Look!" said Kaiko under his breath so as not to attract too much attention.

The backwash was exposing more of the shore, but the tide was still far too high to see much. It looked like a fairly regular shaped rock from where we were but still too difficult to discern the particulars of the object. The stormy ocean beat relentlessly on the shore as if punishing it for something it had done in the past, and then I could see something floating—a wooden plank with an engraved cross.

"The top of a coffin!" I gasped, my eyes bulging.

I looked over at Kaiko as he seemed undisturbed, eyes still glued at the floating piece of evidence. He took out a toothpick and started fiddling with it nervously.

"So it is real," he said grimly.

"What? What do you mean? What is real?"

"The Malem Sea Cemetery, an old wives' tale from the villagers that spoke of, well, misgivings of the operations of the church in its days as a boarding school."

"Kaiko, I sense your hesitation but I fear we have little time left before our incarceration by these creatures. Whatever you may know, let it out now, we must trust each other if we are to get through this together," I implored Kaiko for his good sense to prevail.

"The sea cemetery, a place that was once behind the church that was used to bury its hidden secrets," he began his story. "The cliff was once much farther out than what it is now, a place for learning and joy that uplifted the island, it was a source of hope for the village. Until, well, until the twelve girls came to Malem, and with them, a strange feeling of dread descended upon the school.

"The operations changed completely—services changed from four times a week to one, the curriculum became more regimented and militant. This was also the time of World War II. Some suspected it was the gestapo trying to influence the education in the Pacific by getting a foothold in the church. No one knows for sure. At that time, Father Fulton was a young monk, eager to advance the cause of the church as he served under Father Faraday, the principal pontiff of the church in the region. Many cast very dark aspersions about Father Faraday, none of course substantiated, but Fulton never believed any of them. He simply continued his service. Then there came the fateful sermon of Father Faraday that marked the beginning of his end."

Everyone was glued to Kaiko's story as the winds picked up in speed and my nose could feel the ice starting to form, sandflies starting to bite.

"The 'Tribulation of God,' he named the sermon, foretelling this very same prophecy of the coming of the end of the world. He spoke of it with gaudy brilliance as a point of deliverance for the faithful, as a time where God's children will be lifted up from these wars and rumors of wars and that he would be the shepherd to lead the way. The congregation, too, supported Father Faraday—they loved him, a love that was blind. But not to the twelve new girls.

"They continuously heckled the father, disrespected him in the worst ways, and accused him of being with the younger boys of the village, pointing out the chores he would always have them do outside the deacon's chambers. There was one boy in particular—his name was Yho, a young local boy barely of seven years old. Father Faraday always had him rake the leaves at his backyard, even when there was little or no grass to rake. One Christmas day, Father Faraday was accused by the head of the girls' troupe, Jennie, that the father was using church funds to buy gifts for his boys, one of which was the swing set on the back of the yard. It was located right behind the deacon's chambers.

"Wait, what was that name?" I interrupted. "Jennie you say? Hmm, curious indeed, go on."

"One Sunday, in the middle of Sunday mass, Jennie accused the father of sexual misconduct with Yho in front of the entire congregation. The father was furious and ordered the clergy to take her away and punish her for her wrong deeds while reminding her of his role as the pastor of the church. The scene never truly went away. No one saw Jennie for a few days, and when she emerged, she had several bruises around her body, including her face. One evening, she waited on the cliff behind the church for Yho. He sat on the swing and swung gently as it was his favorite toy. Jennie then came up behind him and pushed him. He was frightened, but Jennie was also very convincing, egging him on. She kept pushing, and pushing, and pushing until finally he went too high and flew right off the swing and off the cliff, into the bed of nails—all the jagged rock emerging from the surf, as you can see is still there. Since then, nothing was ever the same again at Malem.

"Father Faraday lost all his energy, and the sermons dropped to a bare minimum until he finally died in the 1970s. This marked the rise to power of Father Fulton, who left the swing out of respect for his predecessor, but then used the cliff as a church burial site for important church members. At least five people were buried there in the 1980s until the incident with the twelve girls happened in the early 1990s. From there, the twelve girls were buried near to the father, and a year later, the entire cliffside came down, tearing right off the edge of the mountain. This was seen as a haunting omen in the village, and all stayed away from the church since then. The waves still relentlessly pounded the cliff below, taking the graves into the ocean.

"Since then, the space below was called the Sea Cemetery of Malem, and yet if you notice"—Kaiko pointed above the courtyard—"the swing still stands. A lot of people believe it was Father Faraday's revenge against the girls for killing his love, leaving the villagers to come up with a saying anytime the concept of death arose, 'The dead march out to sea.' That is all, the dead march out to sea."

I rubbed my eyes with the harrowing weight of Kaiko's tale—a sea cemetery and spirits that kept haunting the stables of this church, an institution that I now had to spend fourteen days in while constantly hearing the hammering of the sea on those poor people's graves. I pondered this reality with a heavy burden descending on my heart. I leaned on the wall for support on the already leaning floor that naturally prompts gravity to push you to the sea, calling you to join the marching dead.

# 22

## THE MISSING KIDS

Kaiko went on to continue his story about the history of the twelve girls, now ignoring the murmurs from the group to not talk about them. Their spirits clearly still haunted him for whatever reason.

"Jennie," he began, "was clearly the ringleader of the troupe, a troublemaker but a focused leader as well. She and her group of miscreants came here on the order of the pontiff from the main Coptic Church in Kiev. Father Faraday had no choice in the matter, simply to put things in place to accept them and be gracious hosts while maintaining the guiding principles of the church.

"They made a name for themselves everywhere they went and were also a charismatic group. Their energy levels were always off the charts and raising the vibration in any room of the church they saw it fit to visit. But Jennie—Jennie was a little different. She had an air of chaos about her. Coming from a damaged household of abuse and adultery in Latvia, she had little to lose and much to gain, using her feminine wiles even as young as she was, barely turning nine. Still, she flaunted her sexuality where she could in order to get her way. This pushed her over the edge beyond the capabilities of the other girls. Put here as their alpha, and what a dangerous alpha she became.

"Upon arrival, her mission wasn't just to become the alpha of her little girl group but also of the church. Within the first month, everyone noticed the lengthy times she spent pursuing Father Faraday, and gradually she became less and less obedient to the church staff orderlies and Sister Mary, the headmaster of the church school and main disciplinarian on the grounds. A few more months passed, and she gradually became problematic, until she was an outright blasphemer, as accused by Sister Mary in school one day. This forced Jennie to focus her guns on the sister, naming her the beast and spreading rumors about her and Father Faraday behind closed doors and how she would often inflict her beastly abuse on her at detention, which happened more often than anyone would expect.

"After those rumors got little traction, Jennie spent more time with the gardeners and started using them to get her and some friends off the church grounds and into the village below. They were a hit among the locals. The blue-eyed blonde troublemakers sent the boys wild, and they took full advantage. Jennie, however. was a smart one, waiting for the right opportunity—in this case, Easter season—to then spread a damaging rumor about the father, which is Sister Mary only abused her because she was jealous, jealous of the father's secret love for her. The rumor quickly spread like wildfire and, with their connections in the village, took hold over the entire island.

"The father tried in sermons to manage it, but it was too late, the congregation already buckled under the pressure of the gossip, and it was now the church staff to turn. Jennie had the control she needed, and she had the Father where she always wanted him—at her feet. She waited until Holy Thursday to enter the Father's chambers while he was deep in contemplation to confront him.

"'Father, I wish you to know that I am deeply troubled about the rumors circulating about us, I don't know what to do or how to deal with it. I was hoping, maybe you can help me understand better?' She batted her eyelashes like a common whore to the father before he became enraged with anger and disgust, berating her for her behavior and promising that that would not be the last she saw of him. Jennie stormed out of the chambers weeping, no doubt to try and make as big a scene as possible.

"After all her twisted efforts, the father still wanted nothing to do with her—the attention she craved was still being denied. In her mind, that was a minor setback, and she kept visiting the father at odd hours, trying to get him to cave. But he refused, his derision toward her simply growing, fueling his hate and anguish. The father also kept Sister Mary in the loop, and she too grew in anger at the audacity and temper of the little monster. And since the sister was a creature of habit, she had noticed strange happenings started to rear their ugly heads at the church. Of course, some believe the sister's behest.

"Like clockwork, she would settle in the living room after eating a bland dinner in her nunnery frock, cross her legs while watching the news, nod asleep in front the TV, and switch it off before heading to her quarters. Sometimes she would retire later than usual, but in the morning when the helpers come, the TV would always be on, even though the sister would swear by Almighty God that she turned it off. But for some reason, it always came back on. Naturally, everyone suspected Jennie, but everyone also knew she was on a strict night curfew, much more so than the others. Because by 9:00 p.m., she would be banished to her room, and the orderlies would pass a few moments later, locking her within. It was a puzzle that troubled the on-call night staff and the help that came in the morning, forcing the father to spend time every sermon explaining the powers of the church to exorcise demons and bless the ground on which we walked to protect the space from darkness. This, however, did little to appeal to the staff or remaining congregation.

"They were quickly taken up into the hype of a paranormal presence in the church and that it was the ill deeds of the father that brought this fate upon them. Jennie thought that was the opportune time to return to the father's space and further plead her case for love. But something was now different, Father wasn't just resisting anymore—he was cold. This happened around the same time of a new addition to the garden staff, a young refugee boy from the Philippines called Yho, barely ten years old but very proficient with a rake. The father's attention was now for something or someone else.

"Jennie quickly realized what had happened and left the father's chambers in a blaze of fury, throwing all the things that could break on the stone wall of her bedroom, cutting herself several times against the broken glass. She, too, then changed, turning her attention now on the village. The fishermen, basket weavers, potters, and market vendors—she spent all her time with them, encouraging her friends to join her on days of wine and dance with the villagers, the gardener continuing to help her on her near daily escapes from the church citadel confines. Her rumors and gossip now started to claim the lives of the fishermen at the wharf, and they didn't know any better. Every time a big catch was made, she saw herself as the prize and would ensure their families would get to find out about the bragging of the fishermen as they tried to claim her as their own. Slowly, Jennie started to groom her accomplice, an equally vile human being in Debbie. But the difference was that she pleasured herself with the pain of others.

"On occasion she would take the girls to the edge of the mangrove forest on the shoreline and lay siege to the pig pens near the ocean that the villagers had been rearing for years and saving for a big feast on a special holiday. Debbie would take the pigs and assemble them with the girls, carrying them far inland before tossing them all into a hole she dug before, burning them all alive, reveling in their acidic screams for help and scrambling to climb the sides of the hole, which was always proved too steep. Neither Jennie nor Debbie could be controlled. They were both sirens of mythical lore, loose temptresses that caused havoc in men's lives who were too weak to stand up to their ways, and there were very few who could.

"A problem then began when the effects of Jennie's gossips started to overlap between the tight-knit families of separate tribes. The women of those tribes were very close and eventually banded together to find out exactly what was happening. The church bell once rang one afternoon to commence afternoon chores on the grounds, and the girls were forced to mop and remove the cobwebs in the courtyard, an apt punishment for the errant children in her class, thought Sister Mary. This was greeted with scowls and jeers from the twelve girls, but they still did it as the sister kept her hickory twigs close to her chest, looking out for any form of uprising or mutiny.

"Jennie was the first to claim she was done, so the sister inspected the work and failed it, tossing the bucket Jennie's way and instructing her to do it again. Jennie was full of rage but didn't feel like receiving any more burning lashes that day, so she hunkered down and tried to redo the task as, one by one, each of the other girls finished and were allowed to leave. She spent two hours extra before she was given permission to leave, a smirk on the sister's face anchoring her satisfaction within Jennie's psyche. But there was not much light left in the day. It was a big haul day, and she wanted to be on the wharf to receive the fishermen, dragging all the girls with her that time. All twelve of them paraded themselves on the shores for the fishermen, each one with their tongues hanging, lost in contemplation of what could be. But as the alpha, Jennie had her pick of the lot—except for one whose name was Albino.

"Ironically, he was the most handsome of the lot—chiseled physique and warm smile, with buttery-soft skin. He did his work diligently without partaking in the games on the wharf, as he was loyal to his wife and family. However, that day, something different happened. He approached Jennie, pushing for her to take him. She was smitten by the proposal and lunged at the opportunity to feed on that forbidden fruit.

"As she advanced on him, he hesitated, asking her to bear with him and to go a place more private. Jennie agreed, but only on the condition that her followers could accompany her. 'You will see this time, girls, how your queen treats a man, so you may learn and aspire towards this someday,' she told them. Her haughty words entrapped the bunch of girls as they all ran off from the coast further inland to an estuary that naturally formed within the bay a little over thirty thousand gallons.

"A storm then descended upon the land as the girls ripped off their clothes and dove into the water, Albino still being the most hesitant of the lot, not even able to make eye contact with the girls, treading carefully on the water's edge. As the storm landed white rain battered the shores and waters, causing a rough surface, making it impossible to see anything below the surface. And in an instant, Albino was gone, disappeared. Jennie glanced around, and after not seeing him, she called his name. The other girls then got suspicious, and as they looked around, they only saw seven of them. 'Where are the others?' screamed Jennie, but it was too late for them all.

"The estuary water turned blood red. Though rare, someone had released a bask of saltwater crocodiles in the pond, and within a few minutes, everyone was gone. Under the storm conditions, little was left of the girls, not even a change in water as the tides were high and washed the bloodbath in the estuary clean. As the news spread of the girls, it quickly took hold of the island and morphed into a paranormal tale of spite and revenge. The father, while mournful of the loss, was slightly relieved. He gave the girls burials in twelve caskets filled with material items of the girls' rooms, except for Jennie. Someone found her hand. Her wrist was chewed off but was still added to her casket—the casket branded with a golden cross."

As Kaiko finished his tale, he watched me, my eyes bulging based on what I just saw.

"The church then descended on the scene," continued Kaiko. "Eager to find answers, they launched a full inquiry into the deaths, sending their best cardinals and one in particular, Cardinal Devereaux, wanted blood for the demise of the girls. He poked and prodded at everyone, interrogated staff like a general at war, but to no avail—nothing serious came of the investigation beyond temporary sanctions against the church. Even Father Faraday didn't seem to care anymore. After Yho was lost—and now the twelve girls who were the bane of his existence—he couldn't take much more pressure, and within a few years of the start of the inquiry, he died leaving, Father Fulton to take over in his stead."

The story was a gripping one, and it left my jaw unlocked at the depth of despair.

I looked at Kaiko and asked, "So how do you know so much about this? How do you know all this about the church?"

Kaiko shamefully looked down on the floor before looking at me in tears.

"I was the gardener who let out those girls, and Albino—he was my father."

# 23

# VOICES FROM THE OCEAN

The icy winds bit through the tension of the conversion like a sharp chef's knife through fresh lettuce, everyone's face starting to turn blue. A bitter cold rose from the depths of the open ocean and flooded the courtyard, bringing everyone to their knees.

The guards watched us still, several of the captives started pleading for mercy, pleading for the humanity of the guards to bring us in from the cold. But I knew better. I knew that their humanity died a long time ago. This was just the surface of the tale; I knew I was getting closer to the foul nest from which those daemons were born. I would find Liz, get the protein that she needed, and bring an end to this nightmare plague before it goes beyond the far extents it has already reached.

My resolve alone kept my mind sharp amid the cutting winds, and then I could hear a low groan emanate from the ocean that silenced everyone. I rushed to the window and looked through, and there they were—an entire pod of corpse brides, bellowing at the beck and call of their master. And as they breached the surface and released their cry, mist clouds floated above the rough waters and rose until it settled into our courtyard. Within seconds, the courtyard was covered in the mist, the guards seemed to have grown stronger upon its arrival, breathing it in like fresh air and nourishment.

The loud ring of the church bell resonated throughout the cathedral, its steeples vibrating as a high pitch spread its message of doom throughout the land. I looked behind me and saw an elderly gentleman collapse on the ground. We all ran toward him without anyone else batting an eye. I tried to keep him awake, sharing my jacket with him, Jimmy fighting to lick his cheeks and keep him warm. But it was too late—he died of hypothermia and froze stiff.

The guards then instantly jumped off their high balcony atop the courtyard and into the mist-covered floor, hoisting the man over their shoulder and bringing him with them on the top floor. A great ruckus ensued, as if they were fighting over the body. I knew the look, sound, and smell of that frenzy; it was just like the one of the mermaids—they were eating his corpse.

I shouted at the top of my lungs to stop it. I screamed as if I too were being eaten. Kaiko had to hold me back as the guards didn't even budge. Within a few minutes, it was all over. They replaced their hoods and continued watching over us as if nothing had changed. No one knew what they were or what they could do, but I did.

Suddenly, we could hear a creak coming from outside—it was Faraday's swing. The haunting screech of rusted metal-on-metal rubbing pierced the atmosphere and dug into everyone's hearts, the associated stories and weight of the plight of the little boy bearing on the entire courtyard as we all tried to catch a glimpse on the back of the church. Within a couple minutes of silence, you could see people's spirits starting to break under the pressure, murmurs turning into whistles, whistles into shouts, and shouts into maniacal laughs.

Out came Father Fulton; at high moon, he rose to the pulpit, unhurried and unbothered about our gathering, a blaze of greed dug deep into his eyes. He looked unto us all with a smile of satisfaction and lust.

"Hear me now, my children," he started as everyone was glued to his words, still out in the winter tundra. "I bring to you tidings from the lord, tidings to bring you to redemption, to make you holy again, for as I have said, you are mired in sin. But not for much longer. You will enter our conversion program and be purged of this sin. You will be stronger, you will be holier, you will be more."

His lips pursed and arched to the dome-shaped ceiling as he spoke his words with conviction.

"I remind you of the tale of Nicodemus from John 3, when he spoke of the sinners and the need to have them purged through the fire of water and spirit to be born again, 'Truly, truly, I say to you, unless one is born of water and the Spirit, he cannot enter the kingdom of God. That which is born of the flesh is flesh, and that which is born of the Spirit is spirit. Do not marvel that I said to you, 'You must be born again.' The wind blows where it wishes, and you hear its sound, but you do not know where it comes from or where it goes. So it is with everyone who is born of the Spirit.'

"Now go forth, my children, be washed in the spirit—be born again!"

His eyes burned a red blaze in the iris as he rose his hands to the heavens, the hordes of daemon guards descending on the crowd, tearing off the clothes of men and women alike. They were too strong to fight off.

I released Jimmy with my tote bag and told him to find me once the hellfire was over. He flew to a safe spot of a steeple near the black gargoyle and watched over the vile scene not meant for mortal eyes. All the people's clothes were torn off and gathered in a large pile to the back of the courtyard, closest to the ocean. And with the pull of a lever, the clothes fell into a vat of acidic chemical that frothed and fizzed violently under the artic winds, overflowing into the raging sea, until nothing was left but the original liquid. The vat was closed, and I could feel my extremities now starting to turn numb.

I gazed up at the guards now drawing some hose and, with the pull of another lever, let loose a gush of what seemed to be water on the crowds like a police cannon in a Hong Kong riot. Shrieks of pain could be heard across the island, but it all fell on deaf ears. I bent my head to try and withstand the pain, but it was excruciating. Like a hammer coming down on your skull, it was not for the faint of heart. This went on for at least ten minutes before everyone found themselves fully doused in a liquid that had a strange smell to it, some sort of treated acetate, but I could not place the chemical off the top of my head, so I had to bear out the pain as the residue burned on your skin like hydrochloric acid.

The screams now turned to pleading wails, many falling to their knees—at least twenty not able to remain conscious. They were thrown in a pile to the rear where the clothes were, like ragdolls. The father had left, and the guards now stole the show as the primitive beasts they were, placing us in single file and having us enter the castle one at a time in shame and disgust. I could hear the ravenous growls of the monsters as they tore into the pile of carcasses behind us. I could not turn back, throwing up slightly into my hands and keep moving forward. My bare feet trembled on the cold stone floor, blue from the cold and trembling with fear I didn't know I even possessed. I was so close to breaking down, but for Liz's sake, I could not.

We were led along the corridors of the church, naked and forsaken, like sheep; my face was now in a state of a permanent scowl from what I witnessed, but not for a moment was I surprised. The guard now walked us down long, winding corridors that had multiple levels like a prison—at least four levels, to be exact—all barred up with the same rusted iron bars that could give you tetanus just by looking at it. I looked up, and there he was, good ol' Jimmy, crawling on the ceiling, waiting for his opportunity to swoop down and rejoin me.

One by one, people were shoved into their cells; and a hundred cells later, I was still outside, no cell identified for me. I then passed a tall stained-glass mirror, at least twenty feet tall and wide, clearly blocking something. I searched for a clear spot and peeped through it; it was a wall, a wall that shot all the way down to the surf. It was a strange feature, a single ragstone wall proceeding along the cliffside no more than a few meters wide like a vertical walkway, covered in moss but very deliberate, disappearing into the ocean. I couldn't imagine what use anyone could have for such a structure, until it was almost outside my sight. And then I could see it wasn't for anything to go down it—some creatures from the deep were climbing up.

They came in droves, scampering up the wall like crabs, but they looked awkward when they moved. And then I realized those creatures were the ghoul mermaids, the creatures from the depths. They came to have their fill from the corpse pile on the back of the courtyard. My hands started trembling again at the thought of them scuttling up the sides.

And then the guard's outstretched hands halted me in my tracks, directing me to the room on the right. "Room 108," it read. He opened the door and looked behind me, and I too did the same. I was the last one, so I gingerly crossed over the threshold and into my cell, Jimmy ushering me in as well, climbing to the top of the ceiling to hide then.

With a tremendous clang behind me, the door was slammed shut, I was now a prisoner of the Malem Church.

# 24

# IMPRISONMENT

A loud crash came from behind me as the iron bars were slammed shut, and a cold wind blew over my naked buttocks and nape, sending a chill across my extremities. The room was barely six hundred square feet and had a gentle natural slant that angled toward the wall closest to the sea. I saw a wrinkled thin, cream-hooded robe lay folded on the thin lumber board bed that looked harder than the floor itself.

My legs trembled under the condensed cold that entered the room, a full-blown winter wind blew incessantly outside as the low growl of the sirens savoring their meal in the courtyard echoed in the church walls, vibrating to the very marrow of my bones, forcing me to curl up in bed as I slipped on the robes, several splints from the lumber sticking me in my sides while I tried to internalize the sheer scale of the position I now found myself in—quarantined for two weeks in what felt to be a prison cell on an remote uncharted island in the Pacific at the dead of a winter that came in April.

Jimmy scuttled down to hide under my robe as well for both warmth and comfort, bringing the tote bag with him. I had a towel in there that was wet from the ice outside, so I spread it on the floor to dry while I took out an old pocket watch I received as a gift from my grandfather years ago. The faded old, gold Longines Equestrian still seemed to work, still ticking loudly. He got it in the early 1920s after the time of the Great War, and it had a compass on it that now pointed north northwest. The ticks were sounding louder than ever now, showing up as a little after 2:00 a.m. when I clicked the latch release on the crown to see the time.

My breath still released mouth vapors, the mist showing up only as a thick cloud of ice reminding me of the dreaded mist of the ghouls that guarded outside. They and their swollen feet passed from time to time so their prisoners stayed in check. I could feel my eyes starting to bulge under my glasses, my hands trembling as I took it off to place it on the floor, rubbing the dark seats that formed under my eyes, my breathing getting more labored and shakier as ever before. Jimmy squeaked in fear as well, huddling close to me, as his nerves were on edge the entire time, feeling the daemons' presence all over the church grounds.

Eventually, by force, we nodded off to sleep, the cold and dampness in the air refusing to go away.

* * * * *

A loud clang at the bottom of the door jolted me awake. I turned around only to see an iron bowl pushed through a little slot at the bottom of the door, a bowl of hot porridge. My senses allowed me no time to inspect the dish as I quickly brought it to the makeshift bed and fed off the heat in my hands, a minor reprieve to the conditions we were forced to occupy. Jimmy too was being grateful for the warmth of the tasteless porridge sliding down his esophagus, warming his stomach, if only for a short time.

We devoured the meal within a few minutes, and I crawled to the hole at the bottom, placing the bowl there but keeping the opening ajar, waiting for them to retrieve the container. I stayed and waited a couple hours, my legs starting to chafe on the raw ground covered in moss and soot from the years of inactivity. I could hear footsteps in the distance, marching their way over; and when it reached near me, I could see their grotesque hands reach out and grab the bowls, their swollen fingers and purple edges characteristic of their disease, barely sparing a moment's pause at each door beyond the collection.

It was satisfying to witness some activity, even just after a few hours. I felt myself feeling restricted, suffocated, and bored under the quarantine conditions. I returned to the bed and huddled up, blowing gently into my right fist to get some warmth, the porridge now spoiling my body into desiring heat in the current circumstances. I glanced around the room, for the first time noticing its morose features creeping up on me as some light entered the room.

The walls were painted at least a decade ago; a rushed job of a thin layer of pale yellow paint attempted to cover the past cream job that was covered in mildew and dirt, the rough newer sheet of paint barely covering the raw ragstone construction, giving a very rejected feel to the room. Its corners were covered with cobwebs. The toilet was nonexistent, only a bucket with a cover lay next to the bed, and the only way to get rid of it was the stone sink or the window, if you valued sanitation. A damp, old, withered rag hung over the tap which had no flowing water through it at the time, a foul scent of old trapped water emerging from the bowels of the sink as I stood over it. The window was at least three feet deep, perhaps spanning the entire width of the church, barricaded with iron bars each square at two-inch-wide openings.

*Big enough for Jimmy to escape and feed*, I thought, *but too small for anyone else.*

I paced along the wall to give my legs a short workout to try and ease my restless leg syndrome symptoms and hopefully generate some heat that would help my mind settle. I eventually lay on the bed, staring up at the ceiling, the concrete box just looming over me, with nothing to do, nothing to try.

*But what of Liz?* I wondered. *How close am I to Point Vauvillier? Have I failed in my mission? The father promised a fourteen-day quarantine, and I must hold him to that. Whether he could be trusted or not, it was his word, and that, well—that is unfortunately all I have.*

The first two hours awake was a drag; I couldn't return to sleep as it was too cold. I had to rely on my sense of hearing. The sound of the surf, the sound of raw sewage splatting against the window, of pacing—they were all I could do to stay entertained. Listening to the sounds was all I could do to give purpose to my waking state.

I rubbed my eyes and pressed hard, trying my utmost to stay sane, looking around for a short moment. All noises went silent—there was nothing, even the sound of the wind died down. A few seconds, minutes, and then at least an hour had passed in absolute silence. I broke down in tears, sobbing uncontrollably; the silence was too much to take. It was deafening, and the pressure was crushing my spirit; it was too much to bear. Suddenly, a hiss came from the pipes.

My eyes immediately went to the tap. I cracked the lever and let out the air pocket that was trapped therein, and with a great rush, water gushed forth, disrupting the quiet. I cheered to myself in glee, dancing around the room, clapping and praising as the water fell to the bottom of the sink bowl. It started off like sludge, but I didn't care until it eventually rolled into a brown but laminar flow, cold but potable.

I drank several gulps as Jimmy clambered up into the sink, having his fill as well. I didn't realize how sweet fresh water could taste. My taste buds stood alive at the touch of the water; and something fired off in my brain, setting it at ease, and now I could use the bucket. I had to squat—something I was never accustomed to—and felt my bowels breathe a sigh of relief as I released myself into the bucket; surely the largest turd I've ever done in my life. It was something that usually would gross me out to the point of puking, but under the circumstances, all I felt was the release.

I placed the cover on the bucket and filled the sink bowl with water and rubbed the bar of soap in it to extract some disinfecting suds. I could now toss the raw sewage at the window as it had a natural downward slant to the ocean and hurriedly went to scoop the suds water from the sink to further wash it down, ensuring the wind didn't have a chance to regurgitate it back into the confines of that small chamber. I rinsed out the bucket and replaced it in the corner, satisfied that at least I could find a way to maintain some semblance of human hygiene while I was there.

My face beamed with pride, and as I sat on the bed, I looked over to the window and noticed that some fecal matter still lay in suspension, the rotten smell returning to haunt me in the room. I had to rush to make another disinfectant bath in the sink before washing down the window more thoroughly, hoping this time to be enough, cutting myself on the rusted iron flakes of the prison bars in the process. By my pocket watch, it was midday, so I sat on the bed, expecting lunch to arrive. Alas, nothing of the sort was forthcoming. The expectancy truly was an ingredient in the mad pot that added a spiciness that was difficult to control.

I could hear the clicking of the second hand on the watch, bringing my mind back to the present as it drifted away on thoughts of Petra and my lost life of New York, fresh scones and bagels, and French toast with wine and cheeses—oh how I missed them. My lips grew parched at the thought; I had to awaken from my daydream as it did more harm than good to my psyche.

I couldn't see the sunset from the window, but I could spot the light as it died over the Ka Forest, which lay spread in the distant western edge of the island. I took notes to relate the position of the sunset and how much the forest it covered, relating it to the actual time, in case the pocket watch would not survive my time in the prison there. By a little after 3:00 p.m., I found myself staring out at the greenery, wishfully gazing out onto the island, watching birds, insects, gnats, and spiders enjoy the luxury of freedom as I wallowed in my extreme circumstance.

I started replaying my journey on the island by that point, wondering if there was something different I could have done to escape this hell. Alas, I thought of nothing. Even though I was there, I also was still alive, and in that lay hope. Hours continued on. I started scratching the wall, letting dirt gather under my nails, as my blood crawled, forcing me to wince uncomfortably at the sound and feel. The scratching kept my mind alive and awake to the pain of touch; there was no other way.

And then like an angel's horn, I heard footsteps approaching the same as before, eventually releasing a bowl of porridge through the slot. Myself and Jimmy devoured this odorless, tasteless bowl of mush as the first almost purely for the temperature with our bare hands, licking the bowl clean like animals. I set the bowl back in the hole and waited for the guards to collect it, and as they did, I stared through the hole and noticed the guards had no shadow. I stopped and thought for a minute about that and what it meant. Aside from the fact that my life had now become an endless cycle of admiration and tail wagging when food came to greet me, it was fascinating that the guards had no shadows.

I went back into the bed and leaned on the cold wall, taking the now dry but cold towel from the ground and covering my toes with it. Jimmy opted to head outside to find some fruits, ascending through the window and darting out. I was happy for him, but after a few minutes, I realized that one truly was the loneliest number.

# 25

## LOSING MY MIND

I just stared out at the window for what felt like hours, checking the watch every ten minutes to see how much time passed. I shook my legs from time to time just to keep them awake. I felt like an angry spouse waiting for their significant other to come home from a late-night party—it was torture.

A little after ten at night, Jimmy returned with a piece of a banana. He dropped it on the bed, and I hugged him with gratitude, gobbling up the banana. Though it was a little green, my body craved the starch; so as it went past the jaw, my body was none the wiser.

"So how was it, bud, where did you go? I bet you went down to the bay, right at the rise after the forest, there had some nice banana groves, did you go there?"

Jimmy looked up at me, puzzled and disinterested, rummaging through the sheets before settling under the towel for warmth and then nodding off.

"Hey, hey! I'm talking to you, don't you dare go to sleep on me!" I shouted at him, my mind at the brink.

I laughed, and I returned my gaze to the window, feeling the bulge in my eyes getting larger, the depths in my stomach getting deeper, my beard growing thicker and longer. I went back to clawing the walls, grating off the dirt as I pulled down the masonry grout, the whole scenario just so wrong.

*What have I done to deserve this?* I talked to myself. *Officially they are saying it's the virus, we shouldn't be a threat to regular citizens, so we must quarantine. Okay, but what of our rights?*

I nodded off to bed to those thoughts as they started picking up steam.

* * * * *

I awoke the next day to another bowl of porridge. As usual, we ate and returned the bowl, and I kept thinking from where I left off.

"One nation under God, that's what we were taught, one nation under God—hey!" I shouted out toward the guards. "One nation under God, indivisible with liberty and justice for all! You hear me? *Liberty for all*! I demand my liberty, I am an American citizen, you cannot do this to me, *liberty and justice for all—all, I tell you*!"

I screamed as loud and as long as my strength allowed, my voice soon starting to crackle under the strain, and my head felt winded until I wobbled and hit the deck, murmuring, "Liberty . . . all indivisible."

I had to crawl back on the bed, the hiss of water from the pipes returning so I knew what that meant. My excrement became much more fluid than usual with a diet of porridge and bananas, so it was easier to wash down. I sat on the bed after doing my chores, looking out at the scratches where I dug my nails into the wall. My beard itched, so I scratched it; unable to touch skin, I lay back on to the cold stone floor, staring up at the ceiling, letting my mind do its worst.

There I was, barely past thirty years old and lying with my last threads of psychic stability before another sinking feeling started to creep in—hopelessness.

*This is only day two*, I pondered on my predicament. *How could I possibly manage another twelve days in this hellhole after growing up on a diet of justice, liberty, and freedom for all? Is it so easy for all of that to go away? In times of extremes, is it so easy for the power class of* Homo sapiens *to so quickly turn on those with congregations and mass followers in positions of power, just by virtue of the number of bodies they have behind them? How did I reach here? How is it so easy for them to usurp my rights? How could my individual rights mean so little that I could lose my freedom so easily? I know I showed no viral symptoms, yet I am being punished as if I had a full-blown episode.*

The pit of my stomach sank. I stared at the edge of the bed because there was nothing else to stare at—no internet, no Wi-Fi, no TV, no card games, no human interaction, little pet interaction.

*Why? Just because people are afraid and ignorant to what to do with this virus so they take it out on us? Us, the plebs—democracy was based on a principle of "of the people, by the people, and for the people." Good ol' Abe Lincoln had an idea of what us plebs went and are going through, now it has turned full circle,* I reasoned with myself. *Here we are again, needing an Abraham Lincoln. But who will stand up to fight for our rights when every leader around the world is just as afraid as we are and want to protect themselves and their family first before seeking praise for being the selfless nature-building personality they were elected to be?*

My head felt heavy, weighing on my neck. I pulled it toward the floor, and my breathing went on effortlessly but subtly that barely ensured life. The life I once had was gone. This was my new norm—a state of existence that you read about in concentration camps and distant lands of constant civil war, a new reality that barely fueled my urge to live.

Another bang came on the door, surprising me.

*More porridge*, I thought, looking up and around, wild-eyed. *What time is it?*

Time, I realized, was not as relative as we thought it to be. It was also a measure of life itself, a quantifiable property of reality that gave purpose to our existence.

The guards walked past to retrieve the bowls, and I sat at the slot, looking at their boots to witness their lack of a shadow like a good boy. I couldn't help myself; the impulse was too great. Time felt like it was slipping away; the fourteen-day marker was all I had to keep everything I did within context as without that, I would be floating in endless space with no point of reference, no finite goal—I could only just be.

I stared at a point on the wall as Jimmy was soon off again for the night. It was a crevice that formed under the paint, forming a miniature crater. I walked up to it and stared at it, trying to burn a hole through it. I then thought up a story to go with it. I thought of the microbes and dust particles that lived in it, how their day must go, rolling in and out of the space, at the total mercy of the wind currents that swoop in and out—in many ways resembling my own existence.

I used my nails to dig at the crevice to make it larger. I spent hours behind it, eventually making it as large as a few millimeters. I was elated—now the dust particles have so much more space to play. I made their day so much better, so I lay on the bed and rest comfortably. My work, though just beginning, had begun with a bang.

* * * * *

By the next day, I was waiting at the door to receive the bowl, determined to get the first bite before Jimmy. I started to see him as competition for the food. But he didn't even show for the food that morning. He must've had his fill from heading out last night.

I waited on the ground there, eating until I was full and looked around the room in suspicion, staring at the dents in the wall for more cultures to grow by making larger holes. I stared at the cracks for hours and noticed they started to form little shapes—oxen, trees, butterfly, a dog—and I smiled when I saw these shapes.

*This is art,* I thought to myself, *pure and simple art.*

I took out the pocket watch to look at the time; the compass was now saying southeast, and the time showed 3:00 a.m. I went to the window that still wreaked of sewage, and I could not recognize any discernable line of light. I let some time pass and looked at the clock again. It now read 1:00 a.m., so I closed the cover on the watch, placing it back in the tote bag, trying to avoid the confused time that was bubbling up from the bowels of the watch.

I sat back down on the floor, looking around at the same dull room, breathing heavily before my breath started to speed up. My heart rate rose to an astronomical level before I felt the room spin uncontrollably and I blacked out.

* * * * *

Upon waking, I stumbled over to the bed and lifted up the blanket, noticing Jimmy lying there, and he brought back three bananas with him. He was starting to look weak. I immediately awoke from my stupor and ran to the sink bowl to put some water on the towel and bathe him with it.

"Hey, man, c'mon . . . you have to stay with me," I whispered to him. "You're all I have, man, c'mon don't do this."

I scraped together of what's left of the porridge and placed it to his mouth to feed him, and he turned his face, refusing to eat any of my food.

"No, no, I ate already, you have to eat to keep whatever is left of your strength."

I paced around the room, pulling at my hair, and tears started streaming from my eyes. The room started to spin again. I turned to the window and grabbed on to the bars, its rust digging into my palms, drawing blood. I let out a loud scream into the wilderness before falling to my knees.

*No, it can't end like this,* I sobbed inside, running back to the bed, peeling the bananas, and holding it out to him, nudging his nose.

My tears fell on his face, and then, suddenly, his nose started twitching, gravitating to the banana, before getting a whiff of its rich, creamy center and eating it whole. I thrust my hands to the ceiling and pulled my hair, falling to my knees and rolling on the ground, laughing uncontrollably. His spirits too rose in light of my chirpiness, though it was bordering on the edge of insanity. I laughed so hard I was out of breath, and my skin turned red at the oxygen coursing through my veins.

I went over to window, Jimmy squeaking again with his beady eyes. I looked over to the Ka Forest in the distance. It was dark, and as I looked at the canopy, I could see it form an expression, a face that resembled Jennie.

*Yes, my work here is far from done, it has only just begun,* I thought. *I'm coming for you, Liz. No daemon is going to stand in my way.*

# 26

## SURVIVAL

I felt suffocated in the room as my mind started to grow in sharpness, my body now able to live off the porridge during the day and the bananas Jimmy brought during the night. I used the edge of the bucket cover to scrape more and more mortar chips from the wall so I could draw my plan once I emerged from that hellhole. There was no more time to lose.

*I know as much as we were far north, but perhaps not far enough to reach Point Vauvillier,* I deduced. *This would involve trekking back down the hill and walking along the mouth of the sea cemetery, heading farther north, crossing whatever other treacheries lay ahead.*

I drew out the plan of the courtyard and church as best I could and how I could make my way out on the side and under without arousing too much suspicion. There was a blinding level of clarity that descended on my psyche, and I intended to make use of it. The rope in the corner of the room would have obviously been placed to show mercy to any occupant who wished to take his life by hanging. I too often contemplated the mechanics of the set up and how to make it as painless as possible. But this time around, I only saw opportunity.

I reached into the tote bag and found the bamboo vial of holy water intact. I needed some way to put it to use. The only sport I was any good at when I was younger was archery, but I wouldn't possibly know where to get a bow. I looked around the room and tilted my head when I noticed the lumber. It was not made of pitch pine or mahogany, as usual beds are—this was made of a local wood, pliable and very flexible, making it the perfect material for a bow.

I quickly took off a plank and used my nails to try to split it, but the wood was far too dense. Several splints went under my nails, drawing blood from me in the process, but I felt nothing. I then turned my attention to the rope. It was a fairly long piece of good sailor's rope that they used to tie down the heavy masts under storm conditions.

*This should work fine*, I thought.

I split the rope and unraveled it into its threads before using its tensile strength to split the grains of the board before knocking it on the floor, holding both sides of the rope to cut through the grain. It worked marvelously, and before I knew it, I had several pieces of lumber, each a little larger than an inch and about two meters long. Taking a few threads of the rope, I wove them together and formed the perfect bowstring, tying it on each end before carrying it to the rusted iron bars to sever the string. I took out another plank and worked it to the point where I could split that as well, but in quarter-inch pieces a little over a meter long for the arrows.

The rest of my time I took was whittling away at the edges to make it nice and sharp before tying pieces of string to its end to act as the arrow's fletching to keep it steady in flight. It was finally ready to test it, and I went on a marksman's spree, testing the equipment. Some bows broke as they were too rigid; some were too supple so I had to break them to get it at the right length to create the propulsion I needed. As soon as I got that, I kept the prototype close, breaking only for food and sleep, starting to feel as if there weren't enough hours in the day.

I could hear the screams of the sirens from time to time scaling the wall and heading to the courtyard. This only fired me up more—I couldn't wait to take on the beasts with Kaiko and Cliff, ready to be free again. I kept track of the days like a prisoner marks the days on the walls, and by my estimate, the next night would be the fourteenth day. By late evening, I could feel anticipation grow in my stomach, the excitement giving me butterflies. I looked out the window and tied off the bow and arrows by connecting one thread after another until it hung on the beach below, waiting for me to eventually come collect it. I was focused and ready to embark on the next part of the journey, and then, the time came.

A strong banging on the door signaled for me to step back. Jimmy took the tote bag and crept to the top of the ceiling and await his chance to leap out. The guards ordered me out, and as I stepped out the room, I could feel my heart skip a beat. The floor felt cold and fresh, the air felt free and lucid, it was colder in the hallway, but I kept myself straight and my head held high as we were all ushered into the courtyard once again.

The group was now considerably smaller, no more than eighty as I scanned the top of everyone's heads. We were instructed again to strip down nude before being hosed down under the icy windswept cliff breeze, the wind giving us as much a bath as the water. Father Fulton then emerged, his eyes red with demonic hunger and rage. I could hear the swing starting to call, blowing in the wind, creaking above the rustling group trying to stay warm.

He pressed his thumb and index finger against his pointed long nose and pulled in before opening his good book.

"Welcome, welcome again, my children, you have proven yourself worthy, you have proven yourself defiant. Now, as I give to you my blessing, my God-given right to bestow upon thee"—I scoffed in derision—"I bring you to remember that you are God's children and that the Lord and no one else is your shepherd. I am simply, the Lord's humble servant on earth, a mere child of Gaia."

My eyes opened wide as I heard his open profession of his allegiance to the viral cause, but I couldn't lose my cool now; his time will soon come.

"As you leave this place, be cleansed of your earthly sins, go forth to meet the Father," he continued. "After leaving behind all wealth you would have accumulated along the way, be reborn as the new children of Gaia!"

His thunderous voice echoed through the cathedral as the riot hoses opened onto us, burying our bodies under the pressurized water, tossing us about like ragdolls, like animals being sent to slaughter.

"Repent, my children, repent from your wicked ways and be reborn!"

His eyes now were fully ablaze as he pointed to the rear of the courtyard—the acid pit! The door lifted, and the guards poked and prodded the group toward the acid pit, ushering us toward the sea. They never planned to release us; the plan was always to throw us into the sea, to see who could survive. I was determined to find a way to survive. The pile of clothes we had was tossed into the acid, and our time was now. We had to cross.

In our numbers, we scampered across the ten-meter-wide acid lake. We had to try and tread lightly, practically walking on water, using our momentum to try and keep us afloat. The acid felt like liquid fire, eating away at our skin against the laughter of the guards like it was a simple game to them. I had to stay focused, I had to stay on my path, and as I waded through the final meters of the pool, I emerged from the pit, diving off the edge into the ocean—my skin begging, pleading with me for some cool reprieve.

I hit the water below with a tremendous splash, several others following thereafter. I scuttled underwater quickly, knowing what lived there, heading for the shore. I ran hard and fast, looking for my window and for the gift I hung from it. There it was—the rope extended from my window tied to the bars on one side and the tote bag on the other floating in the surf at the bottom with the bows and arrows intact. Jimmy's head poked out the tote bag, still trying to garner some warmth from it. I took what I needed and headed back toward the shore, moving north.

As I reached the western point of the cliff, adjacent to the sea cemetery, I could hear more marching. At least fifty persons were now on the shore, completely naked and shaking in the cold as the daemon army descended on us. The father looked down from on high. I couldn't believe it—they were going to slaughter us as we stand. The nightmare has no end.

The mist then came, and with it, I knew the sirens would be with us soon as well. I could then see an old tugboat reverse onto the shore, the guards blocking our northern retreat. People murmured and complained, but there was no escape—they were ushering us onto the boat. God alone knows to where, but we had no choice. We rushed onto the deck where the same cream robes were waiting for us. We slipped it on quickly as the mist brought visibility almost to zero, a small platoon of soldiers ambling on to the deck with us. We were about to head back out to sea.

*But what is their plan?* I thought. *Why are they doing this to us?*

I held my hand in my head until I bumped into one of the passengers. It was Cliff! I was ecstatic to see Cliff, and he managed a smile but quickly returned to a despondent, glum expression.

"Hey, hey, don't worry about it, let's find Kaiko, and we'll figure something out, don't worry," I said as he shook his head in despair while pointing out at Needle Cove.

I looked out to shore, and there he lay—Kaiko impaled on one of the rocks, his head and legs being devoured by the sirens. I fell to my knees in pain as tears rolled down my eyes under the icy winter tundra.

"Kaiko." I glanced over to the corpse again, seeing his life disappearing before my eyes. "Kaiko, no . . ."

I stood up and ran to the edge of the deck, shouting at the cursed beach, "*Kaiko*!"

My voice and its echo died as the boat continued heading out to the open ocean, the dead walking out to sea.

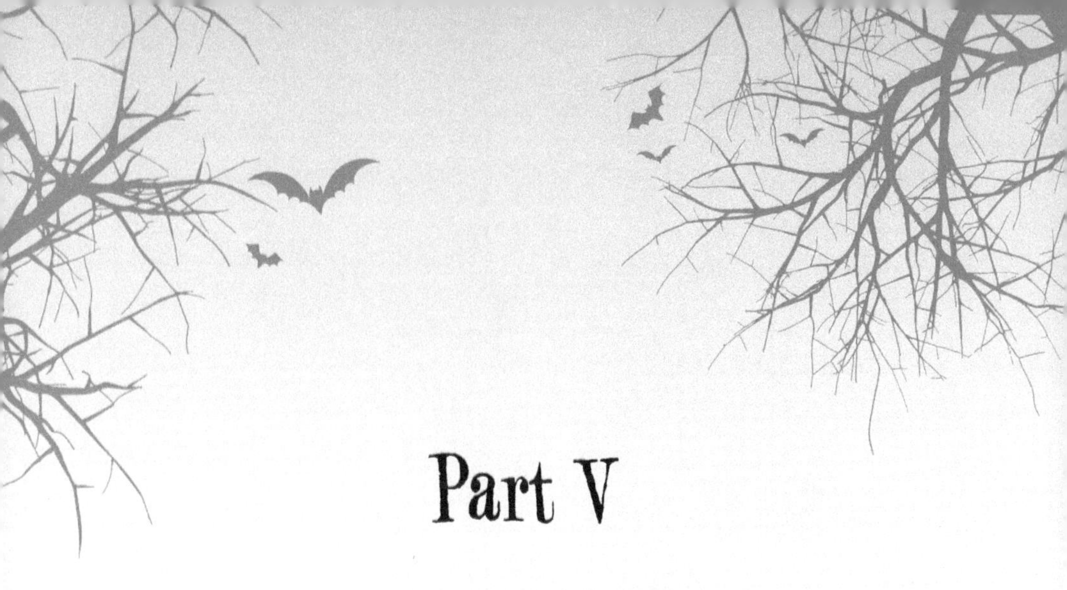

# Part V

# ASYLUM

*October 30, 2020*
*18,554,345 Deaths*
*654,776,980 Cases*

# 27

## TO ROMANUM ISLAND

The seas churn grew stronger with every passing minute as the boat got deeper into the open ocean. I could hear bloodcurdling cries of the sirens in the shallows, clamoring for more life to devour, more to claim as their own. The ship quickly took a sharp turn to move along the reef before heading on to the final straightaway to exit the lagoon.

I could see the shores of the island, some lights on but not much. We were close enough to the shore to recognize a few lone people drifting around the shoreline, God alone knows what for. I could then hear the loud screeches of bats emerging from their caves and descending from the haunted forests, ready to lay claim to the lame and feeble livestock that were left. The squealing of pigs and dogs shot through the atmosphere, ringing above the turbulence of the shoreline reef waters, the last embers of life on the island being completely snuffed out, a lasting testament to the future the father saw for humanity. I sat on the floor, troubled, hanging on to the railing as we rolled out to the open ocean. And then I could feel a rip current yank us forward, dragging the boat and its passengers into the mouth of incoming surf.

The waves were massive—at least seven feet high—raising the ship well above sea level and dropping us back on the surface hard and fast.

*Oh, what new hell is this we have been condemned to?* I thought. *Man and woman alike wearing nothing but a wet thin, cream robe that gave none an inkling of protection from the harsh elements of open sea travel.*

My resolve was strong, but freedom kept eluding my grasp. The enemy was always one step ahead of me, dangling freedom like a carrot on a stick in front my face, part of me now wishing only to stare at it, unfazed by the sweet taste of its fruits. As we left the rough surf of the inner ring of the lagoon, I could feel the deepwater waves lop against the sides of boat as a deafening silence returned to our trip, the mist completely subsiding from the sea at our sides. The winter winds held true, though, cutting through the deck like an arctic gale. A cold and wet journey awaited us—if only we knew how far or where we were heading to.

I went over to talk to Cliff, but he was of little use as he was still distraught over his recent loss. I couldn't give up, but no one else on the boat spoke English—or human, for that matter. I wasn't sure what my next move would be, and then I remembered I still had the pocket watch.

I headed to the poop deck at the back of the ship and took out the watch, and I did get a heading, one I could only hope was right, given the last time it conked out on me in the room.

*North northwest—that's crazy,* I wondered. *Why would we be heading back toward, well, I can't even say Hawaii. It seems to be more to the Mariana Islands or to the Philippines. Why head in that direction? And if we are going that far, we have at least a couple weeks on our hands again to head back through that route.*

I sat on the deck disparagingly, frustrated with what felt like a missed opportunity from the church to head north and leave this nightmare behind. I just couldn't shake it. It was early morning, and I huddled on the deck, trying to get behind a few barrels to protect me from the wet sea spray and icy winds. I looked out at the horizon; dawn was still a few hours away. I was tired, but I couldn't fall asleep. I couldn't miss a chance to spot some piece of land and possibly triangulate our location, give the journey a greater sense of purpose.

I looked around the boat, and everyone who survived looked like livestock—no real purpose or drive but a willingness simply to keep the days turning over and their existence continue as long as possible—a herd mindset. There was little I could do with a herd mindset of people who didn't speak a language I knew, but there still was a way; there had to be another way to find Liz.

Then amid the silence, I could hear the now-familiar roar of the corpse bride pods. They were far off, but I'd recognize that low-toned drone of death anywhere. They were off the starboard, and as sure as I knew night followed day, the mist crept back on the sea surface, which meant land wasn't far off. The ship moved quickly, and the currents and winds were at our backs. We had reached another lagoon with a reef border surrounding a smaller set of islands. I could feel the surf starting to pick up again. It was time to break entry once more.

# 28

## SICILIAN PASS

As the surf rose, Cliff sprung to life as he rushed me to take out some pieces of paper where he wrote down "Sicilian Pass—dangerous" on it. He had been here before. From a distance, I could recognize the barrier reef that blocked our way, except for a narrow passageway that drew us in with a tremendous force.

This lagoon was closer to the open Pacific, and as such, much intense wave activity was everywhere. We braced for impact as our speed shot up exponentially, dragging us by the barrier reef as the monster waves crashed over the reef with loud furor, the white water tossing us around under a strong central current. It felt as if we had little or no control over our trajectory, but the boat driver had a good idea on how to navigate the pass, maneuvering the edges of the reef gingerly as he shepherded the cargo across into the northern edge of the lagoon.

The mist was everywhere, thick and putrid, but we still moved forward at a remarkable pace. However, something felt different—the viscosity of the water felt as if it had changed. Cliff tugged at my robe again, scribbling on my pad, "The ghost fleet of Truk," as he looked nervously around.

It didn't take much time to notice that he was right—the mist was thick at the surface, but there was a lot of structures jutting out of the water. It was a graveyard, a ship graveyard. I remember reading about this once on one of my dive trips, the infamous "Pearl

Harbor" for the Japanese, the result of Operation Hailstone. There were 250 airships, 16 warships, and 32 merchant ships that was sunk in the Truk Lagoon in 1944 and is one of the largest wreck sites in the world. Some say the deaths that came from that operation was catastrophic, to the point where the souls of the fallen soldiers still weep to return to their loved ones.

I could hear the screech and creaking of the rusted old iron as we entered the graveyard, the boat now slowing to a crawl. Everything in the lagoon looked rusted over and covered in moss as the water barely trickled past it, as if the water itself was afraid to flow through. I stayed alert even though my eyes burned like hell, trying to stay awake and to see fifteen feet ahead.

After passing through the eerie fleet of the dead, we finally emerged into a short shoreline adjacent to a pack of arches and stacks.

"The Den of Fools," Cliff pointed out—he knew the space.

As we turned the corner to come around, I noticed a rusted long, old schooner beached onshore. It had a name on it—*Leonora*. My eyes opened wide. Liz's letter mentioned a boat called *Leonora*. She used it as a marker to get to Point Vauvillier.

*I must be close*, I thought.

The surf oozed its way onto the black-sand beaches of volcanic rock, the captain bringing us as close to the shore as possible before the guards instructed us to disembark. Everyone came off the boat, looking around in the dark, trying to gather as much information as possible about the space. The light cracked on the horizon, so I got a short time to glance around, the topography of the land definitely more rolling than in Tofol, still filled with rocky cliffs and tropical foliage but definitely more gentle slopes. I could also make out a lighthouse on the cliff and something else far behind it, something not connected to the island, like a little islet almost completely covered in mist. I tried to peer further but was ushered away by the guards as a shower came down on us, giving another soaking, which felt more common than staying dry at this time.

There was a single road climbing the gentle hill on the left as we came up the beach, a dirt road covered in coral gravel, just as in Tofol but much wider, big enough to take a car. Our group was much smaller this time around, barely making thirty persons, guided by torches under the strong winds up to a house on the hill. As we came closer, the details of the house became more apparent. It was larger, much larger than the church. It was a well-manicured manor perched atop the gentle hill overlooking the bay where the *Leonora* lay at rest. We all made the final few steps up the hill and came to an outstretch of manicured lawn to greet us and a large stonework sign to the front that said "Chateau du Vauvillier."

*I . . . I think I'm here*, I thought, and my jaw dropped without fighting it.

# 29

# CHATEAU DU VAUVILLIER

The manor was huge, and as dawn broke on the horizon, I could now fully appreciate the extent of the sprawl of the campus. Upon looking around, I noticed the island was smaller than Tofol. From the top of the manor greens, you could see all around the island, which was mainly rolling hills of a red volcanic rock peaking at an extinct volcano on the southern edge of the island covered in tropical greenery. Flowers and palm trees adorned the entryway and well-trimmed lawn covered the rest, all the way to the edge of the cliff. I felt almost confused.

I touched the grass and felt the wet morning dew dampen my palms to prove it was in fact real, a fact that left me even more perplexed than before. I looked back and noticed none of the guards that escorted us off the boat were there anymore. My first instinct was to get ready to run, but then another part of me saw the sign of the manor so there perhaps was no reason to run and that this was in fact my destination.

We all arrived at the entrance and a grand double wrought iron gate belched open to reveal a tall, slender gentleman, very refined in his posture with two other helpers next to him welcoming us in. They ushered us to the back nearer to the cliff edge, which immediately made me nervous, and I immediately looked over the cliff past the schooner to see if the islet was still there. Under the sun, nothing odd could have been seen. I rubbed my head strongly, wondering what the hell I have gotten myself into this time, and then the tall man spoke.

He was a little over six feet, had a pointed nose, and wore a pair of horn-rimmed glasses that sat on his nose bridge, forming a reddish indentation on it. I immediately looked at their hands, and the tips definitely were swollen and redder than usual, but not as extreme as the cases of hypoxia noticed in the daemons. He raised his hands to quiet everyone, as the lady next to him translated to the majority of the crowd.

"Greetings all, my name is Dr. Edgar Frey, I am the supervising patron of this manor, the Chateau du Vauvillier," the tall man began. "I know you have been through a trying journey to get here, but I guarantee you that there is no need for further worry. You are now here at your destination and need to look no further. This will now be your home, and we will give you the best possible medical support that money can buy on this planet.

"I am a medical psychiatrist originating from Frankfurt. My family and the Vauvilliers have been close friends for centuries, and with their passing in the early twentieth century, I have taken over their estate to see their vision carried out to its entirety. I assure you that now that you are here, you are safe from the pandemic now ravaging through the planet. Our extensive testing regime would have gone through to ensure you all who are left are the ones who have survived the pathogen in all its mutated forms and functions. In other words, you, my dear friends, are the current batch of evolved humanity."

A smile came upon his face, a haunting and eerie smile that showed no sign of remorse or joy, but the satisfaction of a madman's ploy coming to fruition.

"As mentioned before, most parts of the manor grounds are free for you to roam, and as your cognitive behavioral therapy sessions with me continue and you demonstrate a return to psychiatric normalcy, this grace will be extended accordingly. This is called the Romanum Island located in the Truk Lagoon in the middle of the Pacific, far from the reach of the virus and its contagious victims so you may live here in peace. You are free to create, enjoy, and participate in the group activities that will make our community stronger with every passing day. But I know you must be tired as well. Hal our groundskeeper and Connie our cook will take you to your room schedule where you may get freshened up, take your medications, and rest before our first therapy sessions this afternoon. If you are not up, someone will be sent to fetch you and ensure your medications have been taken. Thank you and have a good day."

I started twitching with anger, and confusion.

*Am I hearing right? Is this guy nuts? Does he know what we've gone through coming here? Does he even care? What is this place, some sort of twisted fantasy island for the rich and famous?* I asked myself.

I looked at my clothes to see I still had on the war-torn thin robes to remember what I had gone through. I saw a birdbath behind me, and I doused my hands into the water and splashed it onto my face to make sure I was alive. And for sure, I was indeed alive. I looked over at Jimmy perched on the nearby tree, and he looked just as perplexed. Cliff seemed taken up by the doctor's offer, much like most of the other people.

*How could they, how could they just move on?* I asked myself further, confused.

Even the staff seemed like professional hoteliers acting like we were here on a honeymoon vacation; it was so extreme for the past few weeks. I felt that much closer to the edge of insanity, but I too had to play the game. After coming up to Connie and asking for my room, she pointed me to the schedule, and I calmly asked her the date and time. She told me, and I immediately felt my knees go weak.

"Are you okay, sir?" she asked me.

I nodded and assured her not to worry. I took the key and went upstairs to my room, which again was at the end of the massive hallway. The interior was the epitome of a French chateau and grandeur with carpets, paintings, and statues at every turn. My room was number 108. I stood outside the door and stared at the key. This was no idle coincidence; something was going on, and I was determined to get to the bottom of it.

The end of the hallway continued out into the second floor balcony, which opened out over the manor's baroque garden, a sign of power and prestige in the Renaissance started by Andre Le Notre and based off mathematical principles from the philosopher Rene

Descartes. I entered the room and placed the tote bag on the coffee table, and Jimmy crawled out the bag as I closed the door. The room was the picture of luxury, although the same size as the room in the church. It was a peculiar design that didn't feel like it fit but carried with it a hidden evil behind the curtain. Fruits were laid out on the table, and we immediately devoured it, continuing out to an adjacent room that opened into a modern toilet and bathroom that nearly brought a tear to my eye.

I wrote down the date and time, October 12, 2020, 7:14 a.m., staring at it for some time, snapping out of the hypnotic reality that something went awry over the past few months to warrant such a sharp alteration in my world. I also took out the bows and arrows, looking at it, feeling its form, passing my fingers over it, and rolling over the grains of sea salt from the long trip to make sure I hadn't been going crazy. I looked over at Jimmy as he was munching down some grapes.

"Something really weird is going on here, boy, but we're closer than ever to finding Liz," I said. "I could feel it, something is still very wrong, and that doctor is the center of this horrific mystery."

Jimmy squeaked in agreement before I lay down on the bed, a soft queen-size Posturepedic bed that sank under my weight when I lay in it. I could feel every joint in my body crackle from the relief when I sank in it, groaning as if under the touch of a maiden's hand. I rested for a few hours well, and as my mind drifted off to dreamland, I could feel the pull of several emotions—Jennie, Liz, Kaiko, and the father, all wrapped into a confusing dream of voices. Pleads and advices streamed forth from the characters, none of which I specifically remembered when I arose, except for the swing. The swing was in every part of the dream.

I ran outside and looked over the balcony, but no swing was there. I rubbed my eyes, cleaned my glasses, and looked again. But nothing was there—just the golf-retreat-quality lawn and broderie hedged with several forms of shrubs and trees to form the baroque setting for the garden. I got my bearings using the compass again and hurried downstairs after putting on some clothes that made me feel like a French aristocrat. I arrived downstairs well in advance of my appointment with the doctor and noticed some oak doors leading to what seemed to be the library.

I opened it and peered in. I was the only one there but continued further into the shelves, looking for anything of interest. At the rear of the library, there was a painting of the Duke and Duchess of Aquitaine, Reginald III and Anne Vauvillier, friends of the French crown and lords of that region which formed part of the larger area of Bordeaux. I found the biography of the two royalties nearby, which I opened to learn more of our deceased hosts.

They were a distant Celtic people that identified more with Iberians. Slender and upright, they were groomed for their royal inheritance from an early age. Being friends with the crown perpetuated the doctrine of the church throughout their land, outlawing paganism and strongly attached the rules of the church to those at the state level. The people loved them and they the people as they lived most of their lives in their vineyards in Bordeaux on a twenty-six-acre pasture that was owned by their great-great-grandfather, a gentleman by the name of Reginald Vauvillier, a name the then-current duke decided to adopt.

Their family estate consisted of the pasture and an old castle that was said to be haunted by the locals at one time but dismissed as foolishness by the coming of Reginald II. The duke's father was a medical doctor by training and brought in an era of science to the otherwise dark ages in rural France. They were both touted as fairly eccentric aristocrats, constantly splurging on their material lives of luxury and being obsessed with living life well beyond their human bodies allowed.

They turned to all forms of science and sometimes occult sorcery to support their efforts, engaging in several ceremonies of human sacrifices and orgies in order to gain favor against the rising tide of their age. Their king tolerated this as they were one of the wealthiest contributors to the crown and were very loyal to his will. But all in all, there was nothing of unique interest to me as my time came to an end.

Connie came calling my name as I headed out, replacing the book and emerging into the courtyard, joining the doctor on the terrace while he offered me a cup of tea. I politely declined and requested water instead to which he gladly provided before starting the session in earnest. His skills at psychiatry were very sharp, and I noticed he bore several signs of the hypoxia as he sat speaking. But I could see he was trying to use medical means to manage the sickness, to mask the symptoms.

"So I have heard, Mr. Huxley, from many others of the very colorful experiences in our quarantine center in Tofol," he started. "But tell me, I understand you are a man of science. I would hope that your experience was more—how do I put it—rational."

He looked at me out of the corner of his eyes like a master playing a game of chess as he moved to my king. I knew I had to stay calm, focusing myself only on the end goal, which was to find Liz, and I could only do that by suppressing any suspicion toward my behavior.

"Oh, of course, Doctor, I too had a pretty torrid time of the quarantine, but I displayed no unusual experiences that would not normally plague any other human subject to the stresses of his sudden loss of freedom. It was, however, manageable, and with your medication, here I am confident I could rebound to full health very soon."

He watched me and smirked.

"So this torrid time you speak of, what was some of the worst, um, times, you would say you experienced?"

He was baiting me—I could see Kaiko's corpse, Jennie, and the father's raging mouth blinding my mind's eye. But I had to remain steady.

"Oh, some of the worst was simply the howling of the wind in the night," I recounted. "It made such terrible noises you couldn't imagine, the crazy dreams I would have, struggling to keep my psyche in check."

"Try me," he replied calmly.

I adjusted myself uncomfortably in my chair.

"Well, it was mainly those associated with claustrophobia," I lied. "The room was in fact very small, so it was difficult to breathe sometimes, particularly coming to the end of the fourteen-day period, but I hung in there, and it was all well and good at the end."

He nodded conspicuously, saying, "But the rooms here are exactly the same size as those in the quarantine centers. They are done that way intentionally, for patients to see how powerful the mind can be in controlling your emotional state and sometimes even the perception of your reality."

He went too far, but it was my time to pounce.

"What do you mean by 'perception of reality,' Doctor? Can you expound on that?"

"Well, of course, this term has to be taken into context," he countered defensively. "And it will mean different things for different people, but mainly I need you in this first session to appreciate the similarities and differences between your quarantine experience and your sanctuary experience."

*Nice save*, I thought of his response.

"I totally understand, Doctor, and I couldn't agree with you more," I said out loud. "I also appreciate your fantastic level of hospitality here on the island and the quality of patient care. After such long travels for us, it is a welcomed relief to the journey."

We both presented fake smiles and agreed to meet again the next day to discuss any progress. As I was walking away, I couldn't help but notice the gradual drop-off on the southern side of the cliff. It was filled with bungalows stepped on the hillside and a large communal space overlooking the ocean a little below.

The doctor noticed my interest and walked over sullenly, sensing my curiosity.

"It is usually used for our special guests," he said. "We also have worship in the central cathedral, as you see down there."

"The communal space?" I replied.

He nodded, and I thanked the weirdo for his kindness and promised to return to him in a couple days so we may chat more.

We both knew I planned to do a lot more than just walk around with my free time until then.

# 30

# ROMANUM SANCTUARY

Night descended quickly on the inactive volcano island, revealing a sleek spread under the gaze of a gibbous moon on a clear night still dominated by winter winds. After the last person had finished his session on the large terrace, I noticed everyone more or less retired to their rooms for the night, leaving an open yet silent space for me to pursue in search of truth about the area.

I started once more in the grand hallway that led to the library, a family crest that stood on a large canvas terminating the end of the hall. It stood proudly with two merfolk holding up a shield with a trident, sporting the local colors of red representing the blood of the people and blue, its connection with water as the main hub in France, where most of the aqueducts and groundwater wells passed to feed the countryside full of water for their farming and livelihoods. I went on reading the biography of the duke and duchess, finding their focus on music and art as admirable, at one time working closely with Pierre-Auguste Renoir, the famous French painter of Limoges to paint some of their family portraits that they mention still remain hung in the Bastille du Vauvillier, the original castle in Bordeaux.

By 8:00 p.m., I could feel my eyes starting to droop. I had to persevere and spend some time outside to survey the surroundings before going to bed. The terrace itself spanned the entire garden, which was a little over five acres by my estimation, its charm really floating to the surface under the pale moonlight. I looked around and saw no one before hearing a searching tune drifting up from the southern hillside. It was a piano playing in the background, the notes seemingly dancing on the icy winds of the ocean, perfectly complementing the tune of the waves. A warm, rich and singing tone that played a familiar melody—I had to find it.

As I ran out to the sound, I found myself standing squarely in front of the garden's broderie, each hedge at least six feet high and characterized by a series of logarithmic spirals that melted into each other, making it feel like a looming maze. I tried running off in straight lines, with Jimmy following close behind, darting along the gentle and sharp curves but only finding dead ends of shrubbery. I tried bursting through a few of them, but the hedge was well matted together and grew on a fine wire that made it difficult to break through. I tried retracing some of my steps, the tune growing louder and farther away as I headed closer to the surf.

I closed my eyes and tried to listen harder, the song carefully drifting away. It was without a doubt Minuet in G Minor, BWV, the Christian Petzold classic that Liz loved so much and played for me when she saw I was down—it had to be her.

The curves were very unconventional of the baroque gardens I knew of, but I suppose the duke and duchess were considered very unconventional people. The sounds restarted and grew louder on my left, so just hugging the walls wasn't a good idea—I needed to follow the sound. It wasn't for a few seconds that I saw an opening on the left and took it with haste. I ran in and came upon a Y intersection, the music lulling me to a false sense of security, but I could also hear a water fountain. I took off to the left and ambled down a set of short steps before crossing a small bridge. I had to be on the right path.

The scene opened up into a classic baroque arch that perhaps would have looked quite stunning in the day but was clearly guiding me to my goal for now. I took off through the space and saw something that shook me—mist. I moved slower, and the music died again. But after a couple sharp turns to the left, the corridor entered into an open terrace to the ocean, the floor completely covered in mist and a water fountain at the center. I looked around for a piano, a person—something—but found nothing, just the open ocean. I had no time for this.

Then out of the corner of my eyes, I spotted it—the swing. I gasped when I saw it; going up to it and feeling its legs and seats, it was identical to the one in the church. My attention left the cursed structure and headed out to the ocean, contemplating the underlying but deliberate pernicious connection between this sanctuary and the church. I had to keep moving, retracing my steps to the intersection, but alas, I could not find it.

I punched the ground in frustration, wondering where next I could go. The song was faint now, but I know I still heard it. I kept pressing toward it, eventually coming upon a gloriette, with mermaids adorning the top stone edifice and a trident at its center. It pulled me in that direction, my trek now moving downhill at some speed. I could hear water taking over the music, so I hoped that I wasn't returning to the old water fountain that I now departed. It wasn't, but there lay a *jeux d'eau*, a network of intricate small waterfalls that cascaded into a gentle pool at the base and with a man-made canal at the bottom.

Jimmy took flight and found the entrance to a small cave a little farther downhill, and as I approached the entrance, I noticed that it was adorned with a mermaid with a perky bosom that greeted you as you came upon it.

Heading into the water, space forced you into a limestone cave that gleamed even in low levels of moonlight and trickled over several sensual statues precariously placed across the flow of the stream. Even the walls had a long carving of the original painting from Titian, the Italian Renaissance painter, and one of his most famous pieces is the *Diana and Callisto* (1556–1559). The scene depicted Callisto being seduced by Jupiter as he took the form of Diana and the moment of judgement when Callisto's pregnancy is revealed as she is forced to bathe with the nymphs. Titian set the drama under an evocative sky and shows an array of naked female figures, the soft flesh beguiling the eye of the beholder—in this case, Phillip II.

I had to grope the several bodies in the picture in order to walk past the deeper parts of the grotto, trying my best not to become aroused from the duke and duchess's ostentatious garden tricks while I had a mission on my mind. Eventually, I came out of the cave on the side of the mountain surrounded by a green mound of thick turf grass. It honestly looked like a spring cascading down the mountain or maybe like a hobbit house on the shire. After looking around a bit, I found what I was looking for—one of the bungalows precariously perched on the edge of the hillside and propped by wooden columns. The faint remains of a classical piece still drifted in the air like a ghost haunting the house.

I sprinted to the house and peered over the veranda, finding nothing there. The mist was still everywhere, but I had to find the sound. It had all but stopped now of course, but this the closest thing to where the sound was coming from. I climbed up the sides and peered into the living room; and on the carpet of the wooden floor, there stood a Bösendorfer, the only piano on which Liz would play classical music. I smiled when I saw it.

I looked ferociously around the house to find her, but I found nothing until I could hear an unnatural rustle in the bedroom. I stood up and stood on the edge of the foundation to get a better look—someone was in the bed. I tried looking around the curtain to see who it was, but I could only see a man's figure. I waited for the person to roll, and with that roll, I could see it was Father Fulton. My face went numb as my thoughts raced uncontrollably through my mind.

*This is insane*, I wondered, nearly exceeding my sanity. *How could he have gotten here so fast and what is he doing here?*

I could see he motioned to head outside, so I had to be on my way, darting back into the cave and fighting for half an hour before coming out onto the terrace with no one in sight.

I quietly returned to my chambers and dropped into the bed with far more questions than answers—the hard, merciless face of the father imprinted on my psyche from seeing him that up close, too close for comfort. As I took a shower and finally settled down in my bed, I thought it best to take time and return to whittling, making sure my arrows and bow were ready for a quick attack. Even though more comfortable than Malem, Chateau du Vauvillier was far more dangerous as it naturally lulled you into a false sense of security, a feeling of normalcy that wasn't real. But the question is, how could I prove it, firstly to myself then to others, breaking apart the charade the doctor had carefully crafted for his own twisted game?

* * * * *

I fell asleep on the couch and found myself being awakened by a loud church bell that rocked the silence on the island.

Everyone found themselves downstairs in a hurry in time for morning communion to occur at the community center. We followed the winding path along the hillside led by Hal, and Jimmy followed closely behind, hopping from tree to tree but staying hidden. It was a little after 6:30 a.m., and the sun was already up. We were all covered in thick clothes from head to toe and sat cross-legged on the floor of the large open space, around the size of a school auditorium situated under a giant peak thatched roof that reflected traditional architecture to the Pacific region. There was a podium and regal chair to the front, so it didn't seem like something the doctor would want as he always preferred to operate from the shadows.

A few moments later, he emerged, the famed Father Fulton, reaching the podium with a sly smile and received gasps from the crowd before applause prompted by Hal at the front of the stage. The father gave a simple sermon addressing standard church matters of loyalty and being your neighbor's keeper, but all I heard when he spoke was his condescending tone. He didn't even feel the need to address us on what happened in the church; it was almost as if he considered here a sort of promised land that only a chosen few would be able to reach.

I found my anger starting to reach a boil as he kept speaking, his red eyes were barely visible in this daylight, but he still tried to stay in the shadows rather than the direct sunlight. My legs started shaking from restlessness before finally I could hear him thank us for our patience and that he would like us to come forward as the first sermon to take his blessing. This confused me, and some were reluctant to oblige. But Hal was a convincing gentleman, giving each person little choice in the matter.

They all came up to the Father, and he muttered a prayer in Latin before placing his palm on their head and asking them to kiss his ring. I was one the last to go up. I was so enraged by the time I had reached him that Hal had to force me to my knees as I bowed and the father reached out his hand for me to kiss it. I looked at his gnarled old hand, the stink of the daemons still strong on his knuckles, the blood of innocents covering his garb.

Hal stepped over me to encourage my next steps, and so I did kiss his ring. I looked up at the father to think about confronting him about Liz, but his eyes weren't even open; he wasn't even watching—we were just a group of plebs to him, to amuse him and to add to his forced following.

I breathed in deeply, walking off and back up the hill. Jimmy fell back onto my shoulder, looking back at the creature, hissing under his breath.

"Don't worry, boy, we will not be fooled," I told Jimmy. "His time will soon come."

# 31

## THE ILLUSION OF FREEDOM

I immediately returned to my room to vent and expend the pent-up energy I had built from being in the same place with that filth. I broke a few more branches of a stiffer wood I found in the garden and continued my work whittling arrows and adding to my stash before dipping them in the holy water and placing them in the tote bag. I had to take a long bath to get my mind screwed on right; I couldn't foresee how long I could keep my lid on, but I did notice my patience steadily dropping as time wore on and basic questions started to pop into my head that didn't have answers such as how bad it really was in the world.

*Do we have any reputable newspapers from the outside world to confirm where the virus spread has reached?* I asked the empty room. *Are we really safe here? Where is the islet I saw on the first day? Where did it go?*

I buried my head into my palms while Jimmy curled up on the chandelier to get his day's worth of rest. I couldn't stay and wallow in self-pity, so I headed downstairs to the library. I knew time for my second session was close, but they possibly may have some sort of external access to information.

Connie found me again while I was looking around, and she asked politely if she could help. When I told her what I was looking for, she pointed out that the island doesn't get any internet or cellular service and that newspapers were never delivered to the island.

I nodded in acceptance, anticipating that kind of answer, before finding a book on psychiatry at the back of the library.

"*In Liberty We Trust* by Dr. Frey," I read the title. "Hmm, this should be interesting."

It took time to get through the lengthy preface and dedication, but then eventually, I found the overall premise of the book quite intriguing. It essentially followed his own personal research into the psychology of the human mind and the specific areas that relate to the perception of the reality around us. Sense perception, limbic system, data storage, reasoning, subconscious, and the human DNA's role in it all—I sat and absorbed the arguments in silence, marveling at the doctor's ability to connect very abstract concept of perception in such a way that builds a platform through which humans can contextualize their experience of what they consider reality.

A few hours passed by, and his ending thoughts expressed the need for humans to pursue the fabled gene X—what he considered a rare genetic DNA sequence that few humans possess that makes them resilient to most states of evolution of the earth and gives those people the ability to see a different reality, a future reality where the present is already the past. He went further to claim that he already possessed this gene and that he would dedicate his life to finding others with a similar disposition, growing the movement to a global phenomenon, creating a better and more resilient world than the one we currently live. I shut the book, and my thoughts drifted off to the doctor's proposition.

* * * * *

Connie then woke me from my daydream as she mentioned that the doctor was now ready for me, and so I headed out to the terrace.

He smiled and shook my hand before pleasantly offering me tea or coffee. I once again declined before accepting water from Connie when she brought it.

"So how goes it today, Mr. Huxley?" the doctor asked. "You would have gotten time with your thoughts and questions. After our first session and a couple sets of medication, your mind may be a little clearer, but I expect a surge of questions for an inquisitive mind such as yours. After all, you have been spending a lot of time in the library. Tell me, what is driving your research? What is it you seek?"

"Freedom," my single answer shot back at him like a rifle.

He was taken aback as I was chuckling at my response. He then adjusted his glasses before he too started laughing.

"Of course, Mr. Huxley, a natural human concept that I assure you will weigh on your mind for some time—at least, your current perception of it," he concurred. "And I am nothing if not flexible, so let us delve deeper into your desire. Tell me about this freedom you seek."

I stopped and thought a little further before answering, "Well, freedom, as I understand it, is a human right. Whether a person has it or not doesn't matter—it is something that humanity should all strive toward and also be wary of those preaching something else, especially if they are the ones holding the key to your own freedom."

"I think I understand a bit of your perception, kind sir, allow me to expound a little. You foresee your experience over the past several months as an imposition on the way you normally would function. Travel-wise, house-wise, interaction with peers—this disruption, you have classed it into a series of entities, organizations that perhaps may have managed the situation better that prompted you in particular to lose what you would consider freedoms, is it not so?"

"Why, yes, I think you are correct, Doctor, but even simple freedoms such as knowledge—should knowledge not be free to all? I think everyone could agree that it is a universal good. So if more people have access to it, is this not a freedom that people should enjoy?"

"Yes, but in rationalizing the concept of freedom, I need us to also stay objective as the discussion progresses," Frey was quick to respond. "Compare apples with apples so we may remain in the realm of science. By doing this, I can offer the entire modern education system, filled with public and private schools, Ivy League universities, and local colleges, even the universities that you attend, Mr. Huxley. Do you not have tuition to pay for those forms of knowledge? And if you do not pay, would you not be suspended? But I'm sure you can agree that if you were to gain the knowledge of that university, then you would in fact be a better human. If knowledge were free, we all would have been better prepared for the situation we found ourselves in."

"And what situation is that, Doctor? The pandemic? The situation of a rampant plague that shows no sign of stopping? A scourge on humankind that man is yet to find an answer to?"

"Actually, I do not agree that that is factual or scientific, Mr. Huxley," he responded calmly. "The coronavirus pandemic is simply a response to something anthropogenic—the problem is actually overpopulation. Our population on the earth, as you know, has grown eight times over two centuries alone, and a lot of scientific arguments point to the increasing connectivity of societies to blame for this. At one point in time, China saw this problem coming and instituted the one-child policy, which was met with wide criticism of the humanity of such policy when in fact it was a reasoned response to what the leaders saw as a growing plague. A necessary evil, if you will."

I started losing my cool, but I had to restrain myself and bring my thoughts back to the facts.

"And what of the pandemic, how are we to track its progress on this remote island?" I said, incredulous. "We don't get newspapers or internet?"

I thought I had the doctor stumped, but he had a calm response to that as well.

"In the context of the past, Mr. Huxley, you are in fact correct, but not in the context of reality," he replied. "Unfortunately, the situation in the world has greatly changed over the past several months, and it was due largely to competing economic powers for the right to claim the title of most dominant. As one would expect, the virus would have brought several countries to their knees, and they lost significant economic strength as a result. In so doing, it created a strange void in the trade world that prompted a mad rush toward reopening the world for business in an attempt to secure fiscal dominance. This short sightedness caused a second and third wave of the pandemic that decimated the built world, leaving us today at a little over 18.554 million deaths worldwide and 654 million confirmed cases."

My throat went dry when the doctor uttered his numbers; he too noticed my shock.

"You see, your perception is based on a past reality, but it is not the truth," he said again. "The truth is in fact only a future reality based on a group of individuals in possession of gene X, which I am told you are familiar with after reading my book. So you see, Mr. Huxley, we are not stopping you from going anywhere—as a matter of fact, it is our remoteness and self-sufficiency that is protecting us on this island from the scourge that has taken over the planet. That is our current reality, and within that reality, your perception of freedom is simply an illusion."

I hurried to drink some water and reflect silently on that reality. I also did not bother challenging his data as it is in line with what I projected in my model months ago. An instant headache dawned on my skull.

"Are you sure you don't want some tea, Mr. Huxley?"

I nodded finally in acceptance, and as I drank it, I felt a calm fall over my body.

"A mixture of Ayurvedic herbs designed to return your energy centers into balance," Dr. Frey said. "It works wonders, and I wouldn't recommend a day without it, Mr. Huxley. Now, I also wish you not to worry about the outside world—that is simply nature running its course. We are free out here and can proceed to live as we have known humans were originally designed to live, in civility."

A strange gleam returned to his eyes, and his smirk grew as my vision got slightly blurred. I rubbed my eyes in an attempt to clear my vision, trying to show as little emotion as possible.

"So what now? What are our next steps? Is this simply the final stage of inpatient flow before being able to be released?"

He smirked again, saying, "You are persistent, Mr. Huxley, but yes, from a technical standpoint, you are all still within the context of a medical care system designed to return you to a natural state of health, and so in our sessions, I monitor your progress, and we take steps to improve your momentum toward that state of health."

I took a deep breath in and said, "I understand better now, Doctor. I appreciate your time and attention, but tell me, when will the father's next sermon be? I am interested in doing more for his community so I may be of greater service."

The doctor's expression changed before directing his gaze to Connie.

"Connie, won't you be a dear and confirm when the next session of the father will be? I'm sure once Mr. Huxley attends, he can pursue his dream to support the father in a new reality then. Do not worry, sir, all will fall into place shortly. We will heal together, and together we will form a strong new reality for the world to emulate, even in this state of turmoil and chaos."

I thanked the doctor before ending the session, feeling like I lost most of my chess pieces but still holding the right ones close to my king. I had to make my move. I had to go on the offense, and it had to be tonight.

# 32

# THE SINS OF THE FATHER

I returned to the room feeling ill, but I had to sleep it off in anticipation for a big night. I couldn't help but notice that the father kept a journal on his nightstand adjacent to a candle in a silver antique holder that I assumed he used for light for his late night writing. I needed to read that journal; it was my only chance of finding something resembling the truth. The doctor was crazy, and listening to him nearly had me fooled until I remembered that he barred us from leaving the manor grounds. In his twisted world of freedom, he was the architect, judge, and jury—just like a corrupt government and dictator, not the same but not that different either.

I sat at the window overlooking the southern end of the island, a quiet serenity descending upon the land with mist plumes starting to rise from near the shore and soon covering the entire beach with its wicked fog. It was maddening to hear the serenity and frustrating to witness the everyone else's level of compliance. My sanity gradually slipped away from me. I had to keep it together, wondering soon what Cliff was up to. I sneaked out the room and headed up the hall to find Cliff in room 75, which was on the western wing along the regal carpeted hallway.

I knocked gently and waited outside, staring at another painting of the royal couple. While waiting, I studied the painting—its edging, framing, tone, and brushstrokes to get a feel of the quality of the work done—before something caught my eye. Their fingers, even back then, were slightly swollen! I looked harder and pressed up to the image to be sure and shone a light on it before I was certain. Yes, the fingertips were swollen with a slight discoloration under the nails. The artist was true to his art, and I thanked him for it.

Cliff then called under a groan for me to enter, and so I turned the door lever, barging in with Jimmy.

"Cliff, you wouldn't believe what I just found, it's the duke and duchess"—I looked at Cliff lying on the bed and realized something—"no, Cliff, no, not you too!"

I rushed to his bedside and noticed he had wasted away, showing advanced signs of hypoxia. He was sweating profusely and groaning in his bed as if on his last breath. His bedsheets were soaked from the sweat, so I turned him over and placed him on another end of the bed, his eyes partially closed and his mind seemed to be in a daze. I saw some of the doctor's meds still on the coffee table, and he reached out to them, as if he wanted me to bring them to him to take. I did not question him, but he was almost just skin and bones now.

"Cliff, what has happened to you, what can I do to help?"

Cliff smiled a half-hearted smile, glancing up at the ceiling but only for a short moment, as he swallowed the pills with some water left out in a glass.

I sat by his side, holding his hand, wiping off the sweat from his face. But he only got worse, until finally, his hand went limp. Jimmy squeaked when we both saw Cliff's body go cold. I couldn't be found in the room—I had to stay under the radar.

"Gosh, Cliff," I breathed heavily, dropping his hand on the side of the bed and clambering out of the room, trying to return to mine as quick as possible.

My nerves were on end as I paced around my room, and then I could hear a thunderous crash off the coast. I ran out to the balcony and saw a strange sight—the ghost fleet, coming closer to shore and erupting over the surface, causing the rough seas to look even more dangerous, forcing waves to break further offshore, with rusted large pieces of metal jutting out from the ocean. I could hear the creaking of the ghost fleet all across the bay, totally out of sync with the winds and forcing us to pay attention to it.

Looking across the bay, it was a sight to behold; and when my gaze drifted north, I saw what I was looking for—the islet. It was small and dark but definitely present a couple miles north of where we landed. Something sinister was going on there, and I needed to find out what it was.

*I need to be smart about my approach*, I planned.

Connie and Hal were now loose on the grounds with the crash on the shore, so I had to be very careful of how I moved around. The night was completely dark, but I had an advantage—I had Jimmy.

I took threads from the bedsheets and unraveled them out until it was long enough to form a leash, which I tied it on to Jimmy, telling him it was time to go. I took out a piece of the lumber from the father's bungalow and had Jimmy smell it. He was hot on the trail.

I peeped out into the hallway and noticed a lot of traffic on the ground floor, so I slipped out the balcony and climbed down of a nearby mango tree, staying out of sight. Jimmy was ready to move, so I waited to see Hal and Connie head along our morning trail toward the community center to meet someone, some of the occupants following after them. I took my route through the maze, and even though it was dark, Jimmy remembered the way using echolocation. It was like having a bloodhound on a leash. We didn't take a single wrong turn en route to the father's bungalow, and as soon as we broke out of the water cavern, it was within my sights.

I crawled up the side and looked in the bedroom, but no one was there. I looked in all the other places, and no one was home—that was my chance.

I snuck into the living room and saw the father's coat was off the hook. He must have headed out to meet with Connie and Hal at the community center to tell him about Cliff, so I had to move fast. With every step, I felt as if I was being watched, so I kept my guard up looking through his most personal things until I found it hidden in the cupboard—*Quarens Veritatem*, the father's memoirs.

I headed out quickly out of the bungalow, heading into the cave while, taking one of his candles to light hid memoirs so I could read the innermost thoughts of this man of the church. The entire journal was a letter-size book of over seven hundred pages. It was old and bore the stains of having travelled with the father in his early life.

The entire book was written in Latin, so I was thankful for being fluent in the dead language. I started his preface on his earlier years as a child in a Protestant home in Ukraine, just a little after the First World War. That meant, of course, that the father was in his nineties and was ending the era of his natural life. I went on in the story and noticed some places were smudged more than others. A feather-tip ink pen seemed to have been used, but the ink bore a strange consistency.

I bent over to smell it, and the smell also was very strange so I plucked some of the thick parts of the writing and brought it to my nose. It smelled fresh, so I passed water on it, and it immediately dissolved. I know I did not have to, but a part of me wanted to, and I tasted the ink, immediately spitting it back out and washing out my tongue. There was no doubt in my mind that the ink was human blood. A headache instantly crashed on my skull, but I had to be strong as I read the plight of the poor soul who has brought so much misery to mankind.

His early life was indeed a godforsaken one, spending most of his time like a nomad, moving from house to house. He and his mother tried to escape the violent abuse of his father who was a veteran from the many civil wars with the Soviet Union. They were persecuted as Christians in those times and often ran out of town, out of fear from the consequences of the much larger Marxist government and their following. These policies were written into their laws, to the point where Red Army soldiers acted like crusaders, converting mass regions through violence and plunder.

In his early teens, he eventually escaped the reach of the Kremlin by fleeing to the countryside of France, living and working in Bordeaux on a potato farmer's land for free but with meals and lodgings. Eventually, he felt obliged to further the cause of his following and joined the regional church there, the one also attended by the Duke and Duchess of Aquitaine. Even though their titles were ceremonious, Fulton respected it to its fullest. His twenties were the only period of stability in his life, and from his writings, he felt heavily indebted to the Vauvilliers for that.

He wrote at length of the musings of the duke and duchess and their elaborate life and how it caused tensions across the land as the faithful saw their lives as sacrilege whereas the church itself tolerated it. Soon he joined the church as a clergyman and started actively participating in the church's efforts to spread their message to a wider audience, but he also got closer to Anne, the wife of the duke. Eventually, this acquaintance grew into a forbidden love that morphed into an affair that would eventually destroy both their reputations, should anyone discover it. He spoke so fondly of her that he would do anything to protect her and her lifestyle.

Many times the father too would dabble in the occult with the Vauvilliers' special priests, and he wrote at length about his first animal sacrifice and the thrill he got from it which was nothing compared to his first human sacrifice. The writings grew progressively darker until it all fell apart when the duke learned of their affair and had Father Fulton banished from France to Tofol, where he served under Father Faraday for the rest of his life. He wrote of Faraday's misgivings and his attractions to young boys and how he despised him for allowing himself to revel in the sins of the flesh. He also took pity on Faraday's plight later on, writing that he now understood the reality of loneliness and what he would do to see his Anne once more.

In the 1970s, apparently the French government could not protect the Vauvilliers from the wrath of the Vatican anymore, and they too were banished from France. In the duke's race, he allowed the government their wealth and servants, one of whom was Dr. Frey, whose family served theirs for centuries. The Vauvilliers eventually arrived at an uncharted island in the Pacific and claimed it in the name of Rome. Thus Romanum Island was born. The journal went on to describe how Father Fulton fully prepared for the coming of the duke and how he wrote to him expressing his apologies and how he is devoted to his title and wished only to serve the House of Vauvillier.

Eventually, the duke forgave the father but under the condition that he supported their lifestyle and set up churches in Tofol and Romanum to always be of service to his crown as the Lord and Lady of Romanum. The father so did. The local church still served their mainland counterparts, but upon taking over Father Faraday's role, Fulton came into his own, supporting a cult called the Reign of Gaia, the same secret society Kaiko spoke to us of on Maui that had existed for centuries in little pockets around the world.

Within a few years, Duke Reginald III died and Anne a few years later. The news devastated Father Fulton, leading him to question his existence and forcing several suicide attempts in the 1990s, until he partnered with a more mature and learned Dr. Frey. The doctor had just returned to the Vauvilliers from his long study break in Germany, and upon realizing they didn't live in France anymore, he immediately charted a boat to take him to their whereabouts. Since then, he had been on Romanum Island, guiding and acting as an advisor to the father, shepherding him through the vagaries of the cult, its ways, traditions, and prophecies.

The father's journal writings then became more academic, analyzing and taking cues from the doctor after, for logic and internalization, before regurgitating it to the congregation. It seemed that his story of Gaia, the fallen earth titan aligned similarly to Kaiko's, except there were more theories of her return in the father's memoirs—the Fimbulwinter, the blotting of the night sky and the rise from the flames of the *Grumarim*, the champion of Gaia, on earth. He also wrote briefly of Alderbron Maeghus and the first sorcerers, their ability to perform transmutations and levitate, things you would normally hear of in a magic show. But I suppose nothing was beyond my comprehension anymore. The clan and their operations were traced to a French colony in upper Algiers, north of Tamanrassct in Northern Africa. This is where they secretly practiced their religion, and until they married into the money of Reginald III, they then became more brazen and open.

I stopped reading for an instant and looked up at the cave for a moment.

*That means that the Vauvilliers are descendants of the Maeghus Clan*, I concluded.

I continued reading to be sure, and as expected, Anne Vauvillier's real name was Annelise Maeghus, born to one Grumarim Maeghus from that French colony in Algiers. I had to stop and take in the wild ride of this journal for a few moments before continuing. It was a truly tumultuous history that seemed to be playing out before my eyes.

Father Fulton spent the rest of the journal simply aligning existing practices of the church to the cult to make it less conspicuous; and after a hundred pages, he fully explained all the operational tenets of the religion, its restrictions and its hopes—centered, of course, on Dr. Frey's concept of the illusion of freedom and the coming of Gaia. The symbol of the movement was an enneagram, a nine-pointed star that represented Jotunheim (the home of Gaia) and a crescent moon at its center, representing one of Jotunheim's moons. He still continued to speak of Anne, as if she were still alive. It was sad, really.

The journal started to overwhelm me slightly until I reached near the end where words about the new recruits—us—started to take shape in the final set of pages. The ink was much lighter on those pages, and as I turned past the page, I noticed he spoke of his sermon to the faithful on the night of Gaia's moon, a night he described as the one after our new moon. That means it was tonight.

I flipped forward and noticed there were no more writings, but as I flipped back, more writing appeared. I dropped the book, and it was writing even as I was there reading it. That sermon was happening now! The new lines that came across the page speak of Father Fulton's anticipation toward the sacrifice for Gaia and the turning of a new page for the clan—a page of prosperity and greatness. That, of course, meant that something was going to happen tonight, and that sacrifice might be one of us.

# 33

## THE INNER SANCTUM

I had to act fast. Retrieving the book, I flew out the cave and onto the porch of the father's bungalow, replacing the journal within his closet. I made sure Jimmy smelled it and some of the father's clothes before heading out to look for them.

We went back through the maze and overlooked the island from the terrace, but nothing looked beyond the ordinary. I quickly went to Cliff's room to see if they had found him, but there was a strong stench starting to come from his bed as he started to decompose. I covered my nose and exited onto the balcony, and then remembered I saw Connie and Hal heading toward the community center.

*Fulton must be there*, I thought.

I packed the tote bag with the arrows and headed along the trail to find the father and confront him about his ways, as what he had set in motion had taken things too far. We eventually reached the center, but no one was in sights. My spirits dropped a little until I noticed Jimmy's disappearance.

"Hey, Jimmy, Jimmy, where are you?!" I started calling before going into a panic.

I heard some squeaks, and upon looking at the pulpit, I could see Jimmy's head poking out from under the boards of the stage—it could move!

I pushed until I was nearly blue in the face, until the stage gave way a little—enough for me to slide in and join Jimmy below, heading into what I would assume to be the father's real gathering. I walked carefully along a three-foot-wide rock hallway with torches lighting the way. I could hear the low drones of a congregation chanting and an organ to the background to add to my uneasiness of the situation. The rock was the same reddish rock from the island, so the passageway was almost certainly dug by hand. The hallway went on for a little over a hundred meters before spilling over into the upper circle of a theatre-style cave.

It was a lot to take in, seeing Dr. Frey and Father Fulton at the top of the ceremony in their regal thrones while the rest of the congregation was standing in lines. I looked for pews but saw none, all I saw was the red glow in each of their eyes, unhindered and hungry for their next victim. I tried to stay hidden, wondering if I could make a shot from up there, and even so, if I take out the father, what good would that be to my search for Liz, which had now started to yield some fruit?

The cave itself was at least sixty feet high and sported a huge horos and templon, with a large banner to the back in black and gold with the nine-pointed star and crescent moon. At the end of the organ song, which sounded more like a funeral hymn, Father Fulton asked for silence as he addressed the congregation, his eyes fully ablaze in its red glory as I watched from behind one of the chairs on the upper tiers. There were candles and torches everywhere, but what was also strange was that water came and went from the right side of the cave. It was the ocean—they were right next to the ocean, and the tide was just about receding into the waters.

The father was fully decked out in all his regalia—a golden staff with a crescent moon at its horn, his gold-and-black Saturno and robes, all against the backdrop of the doctor and his wry smiles.

"My children," the Father began, "I come to you, as I always have, your humble servant once again to celebrate our near coming of the one titan Gaia."

Cheers and grunts erupted from the crowd.

"'Woe to the earth and to the sea,' says Apocalypse 12, 'because the devil has come down to you, having great wrath but knowing that you have only a short time,'" the father quoted, leading to a crescendo to capture the attention of the crowd. "This devil is here, and he is the plague that we call mankind."

Another set of cheers and grunts went up.

"I want you to understand that man has spread about this earth like a plague, claiming it for his own to do as he wishes. Men on this planet have been enjoying the spoils of their ill deeds for centuries at the expense of the men of lesser means. They start wars, they start monopolies, they destroy our beloved Gaia for the sake of growth of their own wealth even for their short life spans."

The father's eyes now blazed even stronger.

"The real question is, can Gaia tolerate it any longer? And the answer is no—she has watched on as her followers were cast aside into the shadows, forced to feed off scraps while the men of the world plundered and raped her assets, becoming richer than entire nations. To what end, I ask thee? Their time is so short, so to what end? Gaia hath come to us in our time of need when the populace of mankind has grown almost eightfold over two centuries, wiping out her richness and natural beauty for their own gain, and so she has said enough. She has drawn the line, and we—her ardent followers, her steadfast hopefuls—stay with her, protected, safe from her wrath in the form of her own plague, just as the humans have done to her.

"This is nothing new," the father continued. "This coming hath been foretold since the early 1900s when the innocent trio of Portuguese children saw the three secrets of Fatima as an apparition, but instead of reveling in their discovery, they were silenced. We live in silence no more. Now, just as the plague spreads across the world and men and all their science fail to thwart its spread while their economic desires fuel their ignorance and wanton greed, forcing them to return to their wicked ways, Gaia's victory is certain. It is in that certainty, just as was done to Polyxena—the youngest daughter of royalty in Troy as she, just as mankind, betrayed the home that gave her life—so too shall we offer a sacrifice to Gaia. Under the full moon of Jotunheim and the setting tides of the ocean, we give our offering."

It was hard to watch—it was Connie. For whatever reason they targeted her, I knew not. But no matter what she had done, it was wrong to set the father and doctor as the judge and jury of an innocent woman, a woman barely in her midthirties, as she was tied to a granite slab, clothes ripped off, exposing her human flesh.

The beasts in the crowd grew thirsty with the premise. Drums started rolling as the father returned to his throne, and the entire crowd got behind Connie as she screamed and cried under the ignorance and mad rule of an angry mob. The march out into the ocean floated on the churn of the organ and the rise of the mist, as one of the executioners drew for his machete and, in several mad attacks at her neck, eventually hacked off her spine, bringing the night wailing and a vicious feast I could not bear to watch, turning the ocean blood red, to a haunting end.

*How could the father have done this?* I asked myself in pain. *Is he so far gone that he couldn't see that what he was doing was wrong? Can he not see that a basic moral compass, a facet common to all mankind, is lost?*

He sat unnerved on his throne, and then I understood—it was not the absence of a moral compass that drove him, as I saw in his journal he still experiences very honest and human emotions; the issue is power and its promise of dominion. There are few things on this earth that gives a man the nectar as sweet as power; it is what all men crave; it is what they work for their entire lives; and, in his case, he was perfectly positioned to grab it. This Gaia movement was simply a means to an end; the truth is, he is living a life of regret, one that never allowed him to be with his dear Anne. And now, poor Connie must atone for his sins.

*I cannot put a stop to it this night, but trust me when I say, Father, your time is slowly coming to an end*, I said to the heavens.

# 34

# THE THREE SECRETS OF FATIMA

Jimmy and I rose to press on, my paces became a run. I could no longer feel my feet and body; only my mind was alive. I sprinted back up the chambers through the caverns in an attempt to return to the father's bungalow. I had to read what his dark journal had to say about the sacrifice.

Within a few minutes, I was able to return, prying open the stage boards and emerging into the community center under the cover of the winter winds. The winds were the perfect cover for my reconnaissance, trying to follow whatever trail I can to locate where Liz could have gone. I could hear a low rumble emanating from within the father's bedroom—it had to be the journal pages writing.

I entered and opened the closet, the book bursting out the space with a cloud of black smoke and the smell of burnt cinder in its trail. I covered my mouth as I tried to handle the charm, using one of the arrow to slide open the book to the most recent pages. As expected, many new pages were written, the book's magic being appeased by the blood of the sacrifice. I could see the ink was rich and smooth, as if a new ink bottle was bought at the store. But I knew better; I knew it was Connie's blood, the smell as fresh as the deed was done.

I took a vantage point on the roof so I could see when people came out from under the center, giving me time to peruse the pages and their contents, as the father continued his story. He spoke at length of the greatness of Gaia and how well his speech served to vilify the existence of humankind and perpetuate the movement of the great titan. He also wasted no time disparaging Connie for her disrespect to his crown, sometimes meeting him eye to eye and refusing to bow. Her fate, he wrote, was a direct result of her insolence toward the order; and if nothing else, it demonstrates the strength and swift dispensation of justice within the community, a strength best suited for the coming of the new earth.

My eyes started to hurt just watching the words as they formed beneath my eyes, a draining feeling coming over me as if I was donating blood myself in a hospital bed. The intriguing next few pages shifted the focus off his mind a little, returning to Annelise and her relation to the Fatima children. Lounging in his mind, he circled the personalities of the three young Portuguese children, a girl named Lucia Santos and her two cousins, Jacinta and Francisco Marto.

The girls started their schooling at the Sisters of Saint Dorothy in Vilar, Porto, where their supernatural powers started to manifest. Later on in life, Lucia Santos was encouraged by the then bishop of Leiria to write her memoirs; perhaps the bishop at that time understood the importance of their prophecies and the impact it would have on the world. The girls claimed to have been visited by the Virgin Mary six times as apparitions between November and May 1917, only allowing their first two apparitions to be made public.

Their first vision was that of hell, a land of demons and fire related to the Nordic *Muspelheim* and spoke in fear of the vision as if the end-times were near. She mentioned that the Lady of Fatima showed them a great sea of fire, which seemed to be underneath the earth, a principle that aligned with Galilean astronomical theories. But more so, it was believed to be residing on Epsilon Indi, a planet south of earth but considered part of the solar system—all within the confines of the Maeghus Order. Both daemons and men were plunged into the sea, writhing in pain and agony as flesh melted under the extreme conditions and raised into the air by the pervasive flames throughout this planet, together with great clouds of smoke.

Fear descended upon the girls as they witnessed the horrid scene, as the subjects fell back on every side like sparks in a huge fire. All the daemons bore remarkable likenesses to repulsive animals never before seen, all blue and some transparent like ghosts or ghouls. The first apparition ended with the Good Lady promising the sisters to be delivered to heaven, a future they had, and all felt relieved to know this fact after being petrified at the sight of what awaited them within the confines of hell, praying they never be subjected to such misery and suffering in any lifetime.

The second apparition spoke of a war, a war unlike any other born out of the thirst for greed and power in men. This was seen as the prophetic vision of World War II, a state of horrific proportions plummeting several nations into depressive economic states that would bring widespread suffering and plagues across the planet. This came in the 1940s, right after the great influenza killed over fifty million people around the world. This truly was a set of events that so far acted as a form of confirmation for the Gaia following to add to their case for another apparition that would fuel their current state of being.

What couldn't escape me, however, was the depth to which the father intimately understood the knowledge and innermost feelings of these three girls and how their perceptions aligned perfectly to the fear-based rule that he himself perpetuated in his following. I still reserved judgment, as the children's concept of hell is one that aligns closely to what I read in Chinese myths from the 1200s that seemed to fit a similar persona.

Annelise, in her time in Algiers, became very bold and opposed to the rule of the Vatican, sniffing out any contention she could find. And for some reason, this topic was of great interest to her. After marrying the Duke Vauvillier, she maintained a close relationship with Portugal and the Diocese of Leiria to learn the final secret apparition against the version that was released by the Vatican. Although nearly passing in the 1940s due to influenza and pleurisy, Lucia Santos went on to live to 2006. She was instructed by the bishop in 1944 to release the third apparition for the sake of the faithful at the time. Though hesitant, Lucia released it on the condition that it only be revealed to the public in 1957, a time when she believed the Holy Mother will allow her to share the news with the world.

This dedication deepened Anne's faith, and she took time to try and acquire the actual letter from some friends of the French government in Rome. She believed with all her heart that she has found the original letter, and it is this apparition that formed the basis for the current struggle of the Gaia faith. The third apparition was revealed at the Cova da Iria, Fátima, on July 13, 1917.

"We saw an angel with a flaming sword," I read her recollection. "In his left hand flashing, it gave out flames that looked as though they would set the world on fire, pointing to the earth with his right hand. He cried out in a loud voice, 'Penance, penance, penance!' This angel will be the final saving grace of the earth, the champion of Gaia."

I could read the words now slowly imprinting on the book as it came to the father's mind, "I shall be this champion, I shall bear the sword of which my sweet Anne spoke, and I shall be the man she always wanted me to be—deifying the grace of Gaia and her coming. Our time is near, and I will not stop until Gaia can reclaim her Earth from the heathens who have now occupied her glorious planet."

I was shocked to read these words but not surprised; he was completely in love with Anne and had turned into a fanatic in the process. Yet there was more.

"After receipt of the letter and pronouncement of its contents, Anne knew of her importance to the progression of the cause," I read further. "It was then decided that she changed her name to Faucet Vauvillier, the Lady of Romanum and saving grace of the people of Gaia, renouncing her ceremonial title as duchess and returning to where she belonged—born again and ever with me even after death."

I was confused with the father's words but also not surprised. The part that confused me most is that he wrote of Anne as if she were still alive.

*The grave, I have to find the grave of the duke and now Lady of Romanum, Faucet Vauvillier*, I decided. *The answer I'm looking for must be there.*

I closed the book and shimmied off the roof as I could hear voices approaching, scuttling off to the cave in order to return to my room. The Father was returning to his retreat, the hunger of his red eyes appeased by Connie's sacrifice, the beast in him devouring his soul completely. As I headed up the water cavern, I could hear the tune of Minuet G start to play, and I froze in place. I had to bow my head and fight the urge to return.

*I must leave and head to my room, lest I be caught and tried for my crime of breaking curfew,* I thought.

I still returned to the edge of the cave and peeped over the edge to get a glimpse of the piano. I saw it, and someone was playing it beautifully, just as Liz used to.

*But who could it be?* I wondered. *Who is that soul who has the softness to reproduce a tune with such simplicity and sweetness?*

I watched in horror, noticing it was Father Fulton—he was the one playing the tune.

# 35

## AN END TO THE ORDER

Seeing him playing the tune just enraged me more. I quickly escaped through the maze to try and avoid any further confrontation, but this time, as I reached to my door, I crossed the last step to the upper rooms when I remembered that with Connie gone, Cliff would most likely still be in his room. This irked me even more. I went around the side to check, and indeed he was still undiscovered.

I looked at Jimmy and said, "No more, Jimmy, tonight is the last night the father will draw breath. Tonight we make a stand. For freedom, we make a stand."

I went into my room and grabbed my tote bag and rope, clambering up the vines by the balcony as I headed on up to the roof. It was a far stretch, but I could see the father's bungalow from the top of the roof. I tried looking harder so I could spot his moving frame. The mist was still thick, and I looked out at the bay with little light to aid my sight, but it had to be now.

"C'mon, Jimmy, let's go," I said to my friend, and we darted down the side of the building and through the maze, moving like panthers among the grove, swift and quiet.

We barely made a splash while wading through the water until finally coming upon the mound surrounding the cliff on the gentle turf. I could hear the melodic tune coming from the piano, hypnotic and alluring. I shed a tear watching the beast play the song—play our song.

*Liz, I can't let him play that,* I said in my head. *How did he know to play it, Liz? I would rather not let my mind wander its shadows as there are plenty there to take carry it to places where there is no returning. But that tune—he plays it. But not like a master, not like you. I will not let him defile it any further. Today, his reign as the daemon of Malem will come to an end, and as his time as father comes to an end here, it will mark the beginning of something new, something born not of fear but something greater.*

I drew my bow, pulled the string taut, and bent the bow. It was now up to my mind.

"This something will be a spark emanating from the humanity of people, not the daemons," I whispered in prayer. "They will keep their hellish reality to themselves. If I have to draw my last breath to do that, then so be it. I am coming to find you, Liz. I know you are near. Let this mark the start of the final phase of my search. Let this be the end to his evil reign."

With those words, I let fly the arrow. It tore through the wind, moving against the humidity and currents coming from the ocean, forcing the tip of the arrow to bend to the left as it started to rotate, its point still holding true. The holy water oozed down the stem of the arrow as it moved into the straightaway. The song reached its crescendo as the father heard the arrow burst through the mesh window, tearing it out like a bear after a pot of honey, moving straight for his forehead.

His red eyes gleamed with fire as his jaws hyperextended in his true form, releasing a roar beyond any I have ever heard. He moved his arms to try and block the projectile, but it was too late. The arrow had too much intent and certainty behind it, pushing through his evil ways. And within its final approach, brushing past the dust settled on his partial unibrow, the arrow tore into his fake flesh and finally burying itself in his skull. Something different happened this time.

His head convulsed as the arrow sank in, and then a spark started reacting with the arrow tip until a full blaze ignited on his forehead. A blue flame burst forth from within him, grabbing hold of his head before engulfing his entire body, forcing him to flee his house rolling on the ground in agony. I looked at him with the same condescension and indifference he showed us in Malem, the flames crackling with an otherworldly ferocity. His true tongue escaped his mouth, dragging on the ground searching for someone to pity him. But none stepped forth.

"This time, beast, you die alone," I said.

And as if hit by gas, as an upsurge in cold winds came up to the house, the flames exploded on him, consuming what was left of his flesh and no doubt the eaten flesh and blood of many others. The luminous zone of the flame leaped up to at least five feet above his head, and he finally stopped moving after about twenty seconds of fighting it. Eventually, he fell to his knees and slumped on the spot, the flame will do the rest of the work.

Jimmy squeaked in delight as we put away our stuff and made our way back to the house. I crept into Cliff's room and looked at him. His drawn face was so young, yet he met such a tragic end, brought on by the unscrupulous treatment by other men calling us their superiors. I left a bow and arrow in his room, placing it in his hand and using a knife to bury it in his heart.

"My friend, even in death, you serve our cause," I told Cliff as if he were still there. "I cannot thank you enough. Just know that my thoughts are always with you and that I will do everything in my power to fulfill our mission. Rest in peace, brother."

I kissed him on the head before leaving the room, heading back to my room for a shower and to give Jimmy the bag to hide it on the roof for the time being until the upsurge in interest dies down. I got down on my knees upon coming out of the shower to thank Liz, Cliff, and Kaiko for their help. The water on the arrows and Kaiko's whittling skills proved to be a surefire method to combat these daemons, to give me a fighting chance. I lay on the bed that night exhausted as cries of hysteria and general panic started to set about the manor. I headed outside simply to show my face but was quickly ushered back in by Hal and a few other burly-looking Eastern European gentlemen, instructed only to leave the room when they allowed it and deemed it safe to do so.

* * * * *

The next morning, Hal came to fetch us from our rooms for breakfast, allowing us only to eat and return to the rooms. Apparently, the doctor had begun an inquisition into the father's death and had suspected one of the new recruits to be the guilty party. Each of us, one by one, went down to see the doctor as he asked us a series of taxing questions to determine our exact whereabouts and corroborate that with his people's understanding of the events of that night, which I know would have been difficult for them as they were busy sacrificing Connie at the same time.

More places around the manor was set as off limits in light of this event, and the doctor called a meeting of the new arrivals on the terrace later that afternoon.

"By now, you all may be aware of the tragic events that befell the manor last night," he began. "That brings great sadness and loss to our cause. Our Emeritus Father Fulton was murdered last night."

Hearing the news from him still caused murmurs among the crowds, but he knew as well as I did that all evidence pointed to Cliff.

"We currently have a suspect in mind, but two were found dead last night," the doctor continued. "It was our colleague Cliff, and honestly, I find it hard to believe Cliff to be capable of such a heinous crime against humanity."

I snickered when I heard this, the audacity of the doctor to speak of crimes against humanity.

"Rest assured, we are doing everything we can to confirm the murder suspect, and justice will be served once convicted by the council of Gaia. But until then, you will be under stricter restrictions, and I ask that you bear with us as we work together to make the space safe again. The funeral arrangements for the father are currently being made, and members of the continental church are expected to come to read him his final rites within a few days. Until then, the charred remains of his body will be stored in a safe place and our sessions will be temporarily placed on hold. I thank you for your understanding and maturity in this trying time."

This move definitely shook the congregation, so while my next aim was to find the grave of Faucet Vauvillier, I also had set my sights on the doctor. No doubt, he would have his guard up now because of what has happened to the father, and naturally he is a more careful man, making him a much more difficult target to overcome.

I returned to my room that night and endured the struggles of staying there, my body no doubt getting accustomed to moving about again. The grounds were far too active tonight to head out, so I had to stay put and wait them out, thinking mainly where the doctor's quarters could possibly be located on the compound and how I could access it.

* * * * *

The next few days passed fairly quickly as arrangements for the father's funeral were in full swing, both for his ritual ceremony and for the receiving of the cardinals from the head churches in Ukraine and Moscow. They arrived from a boat and, with much pomp and ceremony, carried off to several bungalows where their contingent were staying under heavy security and much attention.

I noticed the next few nights brought with it little or no mist, but the winds were still cold to the point where I swore I saw hints of snow and some hail coming down on the terrace in the late evening. I also took the opportunity to retrieve more books from the library and study the works of a peculiar painting at the end of the corridor near Cliff's room, which was now taped off and we were ordered not to go there. It was a painting by Goya of St. Francis Borgias helping a dying impenitent. Goya captured the popular exorcist of time in his work freeing a victim of his demon possessors using something called the *Rituale Romanum*, the rite of exorcism.

I headed to the library to find some writings on it and was fortunate enough to find quite a bit, clearly someone on the compound with influence had some interest in the art of exorcism. In 1999, the Vatican, after several revisions, promulgated the final version of the *De Exorcismis et Supplicationibus Quibusdam*, an eighty-four-page document that encompassed the entire procedure and ritual prayers for expulsion of demons and devils alike. I thought it useful to add to my arsenal, if possible, rather than just arrows and holy water.

It took me several hours and a couple nights studying the literature before I got familiar with some of the arts and tools used to cast out the demons, which meant little room for trial and error but more for practical application. I couldn't shy away from my duty now, but I assumed very little will be easy moving forward from here on out.

* * * * *

I slept off the text as a loud horn woke me when the father's funeral procession commenced in the early morning. I got up and started dressing in an attempt at least to hear the lies these men would try to spew about the father so I could better understand my enemies.

Much of the proceedings were filled with food and familial obligations, supplanted with flowers and poetry, with greetings from the church headquarters. And then came the doctor's speech. He showed no sign of breaking down emotionally, but I knew he had something planned.

"It is with a heavy heart and on the cusp of such a great victory that we lay the great Father Fulton to rest," Dr. Frey began. "He was like a real father to us all, providing comfort and support when we needed it most, in his ripe old age of ninety-six."

I tried my best to stop myself from scoffing so as to avoid the attention, but Jimmy was very much enjoying the proceedings from the tree canopies nearby and stopping in for a bit of the treats from time to time.

"This time is the time of the father, and I will not sully his name with any ill words. But I will say this—we have a good idea of who did this to the father, and trust me when I say that your church will protect you, the true congregation. Those who spit on our gratitude, there will be dire consequences to their actions. But I will let this continue to be a celebration of the father's life as we work toward restoring normalcy to the manor. I promise that I will work tirelessly in the pursuit of maintaining the order set out by the father and to continue in his work."

Until he said that, I didn't realize then that the doctor actually was an active part of the church and played a strong role in its executive branch.

A few moments later, the church announced the doctor as the stand-in father until a confirmed replacement could be found. He, of course, expressed his gratitude and pointed out that his therapy sessions will be restarting in the next few days and will increase in frequency to every day.

I felt the grip of the order squeeze tighter as the colony rejoiced at the graft-skinned father as he lay in the coffin, no doubt wanting to be buried next to his beloved Faucet Vauvillier. But security was far too tight for me to breach it to find the grave; all I saw was the procession disappearing toward their bungalows while leaving everyone else at the reception on the terrace to eat, drink, and be merry.

Being merry wasn't something I had felt in a long time, so I gave Jimmy the smell of a piece of the father's journal again, as they did mention that they will be burying it with him, if not now, in a few days when things die down. I will find that girl's grave and get to the bottom of what he hid in there. This battle was far from over.

# 36

# FREY MANOR

The doctor was the next pillar of support of this corrupt system, and I had to find a way to bring down his empire, much like I did with the father. I waited for nightfall for some more cover before heading out in search for the doctor's quarters, looking out for the daemons that roamed the grounds by night. I could see the doctor still wining and dining his guests from the church on the terrace, so it was time to make my move.

Jimmy led the way as we headed down to the community center, scorch marks still apparent on the father's bungalow as a mark of my past victory. To my surprise, Jimmy continued ambling past the center and walked along a pathway after it, just a couple feet wide, earthen and rocky, forcing you to descend slowly.

I held on to the cliff as I made my way down its side, the salty air penetrating my nostrils and clearing my sinuses. The path continued around the cliff, straddling just a few meters above the high tide before breaking off into a forked path—one heading down to the beach, the other heading back up the hill but, this time, on the other side of the cliff. I hadn't noticed that before, but that side of the cliff was usually concealed by the maze or the direction of the main manor, along with a small thicket that grew along the cliff face, making it impossible to recognize that there was a built structure behind it. The doctor must have direct access to it through the maze, but finding that access would be near impossible if one hadn't played a part in designing the original maze, a role I'm sure the doctor found all too satisfying.

We braced ourselves against the cold winds, which were now beating on our backs, ascending the wet clay slope for a little over half an hour before arriving at the back plateau that connected to a small house on the edge. The two-story building was small in footprint but still bore the design of medieval luxury, with a soft gray-and-peach color that made me want to barf a little. I could notice the iron-hinged wooden back door stood there, waiting for me to break in and unearth its secrets.

A little sign stood on a half-rotted pole outside, partially covered in moss with the writing "Frey Manor" barely visible. This corner of the world was claimed as the dear doctor's little space, notwithstanding the fact that it was out of sight and out of mind—a fact that tempted my curiosity even more to figure out what he had to hide.

I used Kaiko's old knife and a flattened book staple to jiggle the lock free, just taking a few minutes until I heard the satisfying click that let me know I got in, a gentle hiss emerging from the inside of the house as I cracked open the door.

The house smelled musty and was filled with cobwebs as if no one had been living in it for years, but there was definite use. I could see footprints throughout the house as I too sneaked about on the wooden floors, the creaking noises shattering the windy silence from the ocean upwelling. A nearby vulture flapped its wings violently and gave off a strange whooping sound that let me know I was not welcome in the space, almost as if they saw the house as their own like a weird set of interconnected undead. But I prodded on.

I looked up at a painting that stood over an extinct furnace, by the Spanish master Francisco Goya. I looked carefully, and it was his 1788 piece on St. Francis Borgias helping a dying impenitent, the same one I saw in the book from the library earlier. The saint was seen as a hero in that time, and I remember from my early history courses of Europe, he was considered by some as the chief exorcist and a master of the art.

I walked on and noticed the wind started picking up speed, violently shaking the windows, causing a tremendous banging sound that made it hard to concentrate. I made it to an empty bedroom to the back. This bedroom also had a painting on it, one titled "The Torture of the Maccabean Brothers." This sixteenth century German piece was painted in Cologne and showed a public village torture scene of the brothers using various popular torture machines—a head crusher, rack and furnace, for example—as the men and child were publicly killed for a crime about which I knew little. It was a haunting scene to witness in the house, looking almost as if the doctor enjoyed the concept, reveling in it.

I walked closer to it, my breath starting to fog the painting's seal as the sound of my footsteps hollowed. I looked down, confused, as I used my knuckles to tap the floor and listened intently—it was a false door. I felt around for an edge and finally caught it. Using my strength, I lifted it up and revealed below was another room, a basement. But this was no ordinary room.

I walked down the narrow steps and saw a low-ceiling dungeon. I had to find a light source as it was too dark to see anything. I took out a lighter that Connie gave me I thought would come in handy and lit one of the torches in the room. It revealed a part of the doctor's mind that even I wasn't ready for.

The smell was overpowering, similar to the basement in David's house in Maui. It was very possible that human parts existed down here in some form of preservative liqueur. I took up the torch and started to venture into the room, and at the back and staring at me with its gaudy eyes was a massacred daemon, half its face squashed in and its tongue on the floor, with the head crusher machine still mounted up right in front of another of Goya's pieces, *Saturn Devouring His Son.* A story of the mad titan Cronus and how he ate each of his sons to prevent a prophecy of one of them returning to kill him. In the end, Jupiter escaped his grasp and did live up to the prophecy but not before Saturn was able to devour his wife, the scene which was graphically displayed over the chair of work with the titan's rabid eyes and wild hair gleaming with the rage of cannibalism pulsing through his animalistic veins. His hands were covered in the blood of his victim, his knuckles white with rage, along with an erect phallus, speaking to the excitement and thrill the demonic act brought him.

The wind now started to die, and there was also a strange allure of the painting, so much so that I was tempted to drift closer to it. I stumbled over a few medieval torture tools on my way but eventually was right under it, my breathing growing heavy and the creature's eyes now following me to where I now stood. The painting replica was almost the size of a man, sending a chill of desperation and repulsion throughout my body. And then, the wind simply fell, and the torch started to flicker.

I placed my hand over it to keep the flame alive, but to no avail, it went out. I closed my eyes to adjust to the darkness and looked up at the painting. I could still feel the mad titan watching me with its mouth ajar, the blood on the canvas stained with a shade of red I could still see in the dark. A strange smell then started to emerge, a fresh smell, and then the paint started to tremble as if starting to take on a life on its own.

I stumbled backward onto the lifeless daemon, tripping over it and making a ruckus. I was out of breath watching around the room, crazed, drawing a small stick I carved with the tip ready to take another life if it had to. The red on the canvas now started to spread, the fibers on the canvas started to get moist, and the red started to bleed onto the image, the eyes of the Titan glued on my fear. I thought to run, but it was too late.

My pants leg was already caught in a device called the ripper, so I began fighting to break free. But as I sat on the ground, I could feel see the painting start to not only redden but bleed profusely, bleeding until the floor, my hands, my pants—everything—were completely covered in fresh blood. The pungent smell of death filled the room, and something was moving in the painting, something heinous. I could see something trying to escape from behind the painting, and eventually, it broke the fiber.

I could see antennae, its head, and then its jaws. It was a cockroach—no, several cockroaches! They started streaming out from this hole in the canvas, right where the Titan's tongue would have been.

As thousands of the roaches crawled out from their den of darkness, a lone tongue came out and plugged the space. The tongue was at least a foot long, with the same dagger-tipped edge and fine white bristles covering it as it waved around like a snake. Eventually came its hands, then its naked body, like a muscle-bound seven-foot-tall human with the lean body of a ninety-year-old bodybuilder with scoliosis. The daemon's red eyes burned bright in the darkness as its mouth opened, its lips completely torn off, warts growing on its gums and fang-like teeth. The creature watched me with one thing on its mind—dinner.

I drew Kaiko's knife as I cut free my pants, darting up the steps to block the creature, slamming the door on it, which barely bought me a few seconds. Vultures with flaming red eyes also entered the house by smashing the windows, coming after me. I had to run for my life. I darted out the back and closed the door, but the creatures smashed into the wall and door as if they weren't there, so I continued sprinting out to signpost to the back to get some sort of height on the creatures. I lit the torch one more time and finally got it to catch fire, waiting for the right time.

As soon as they were within range, I launched a lit bottle filled with fuel at them, the kerosene bursting out its glass prison, engulfing the birds and the creature in flames. It slowed them down as they burned, and Jimmy needed no further invitation to act. He immediately darted after them and sank his fangs into the heart of the first bird, causing it to scream in pain as the flames gradually changed to a blue color. Jimmy then turned his attention on the other before biting the third vulture's head clean off.

I ran forward with a piece I recognized in the living room. It was the Saint Benedict Medal! And with one of the prayers I found under the exorcism books, I jumped into the flames with the beast and held the medal over his head, reciting, "Vade retro Satana, vade retro Satana! Numquam suade mihi vana! Sunt mala quae libas. Ipse venena bibas! Begone, Satan! Never tempt me with your vanities! What you offer me is evil! Drink the poison yourself!"

With the final few verses, I pressed the medal on the daemon's forehead, being burned myself. The flames turned blue before my eyes, and they harmed me no more while the daemon writhed in pain and agony on the ground. I got off it as it ran for the ocean, diving off the cliff in a blue ball of fire as it fell to its death in a mighty thud on the rocks below.

I fell to my knees, panting and out of breath, only scorched earth left behind while Jimmy stood in victory against the buzzards. He spread his mighty wings in victory as I gave off a wry smile as the burns on my body still hurt. But there was no time for thar—we had to get out of there immediately.

# 37

# TWIN NIGHT TERRORS

We ran at full speed along the cliff in an attempt to return to the room without being detected. The news of the disturbance would definitely be heard of by now, but due to the doctor's guests, he would try to keep it under wraps. I returned to the room out of breath and closed it behind me, pondering the might and gruesome nature of the daemon.

*Is the doctor breeding those daemons in that cell? What sort of place was that?* All these and more filled my mind as I took a long shower and got in bed in an attempt to try and sleep off the eventful night. Within a few seconds, I fell asleep; but this time, I felt as if I was fully awake. The sights and smells all felt very real as my room stayed alive well after I felt I had nodded off. My hands started to feel clammy until I broke out into full night sweats, soaking the bed beneath me.

I woke up and was totally naked, opening the door to the terrace as I stared out over it. No one was there, and only one thing was on my mind—Frey. I dove off the balcony and ran to the father's cottage as Minuet G continued to dance with the ocean winds that nipped past my skin with surprising sharpness and guile. The ghost fleet also croaked continuously, forcing a large storm surge up the hillside, consuming the houses along the southern edge and barely reaching the community center. I couldn't believe how far it came, and I stood as the wave edge washed up. The moment it touched my toe, I could feel a gigantic unseen force pulling my body toward the sea.

In the blink of an eye, I found myself in waist-deep water. I knew immediately that something was wrong. For almost ten minutes, I tried as best as I could to run back up the hill to get to the center, but the swash stayed a few feet ahead of me. Gravity was against me, and after trying the third and fourth time, when I was inches away from escaping the ocean, the sand sunk beneath my feet, the ocean taking me again.

Mentally I started losing energy, so I decided to let the ocean take me. The surge came from the depths and pushed me onto the shore in an instant while forcing me to float, dragging me underwater, forcing me to fight for my last breaths. I was just as violent as the ocean, fighting underwater to get a chance to feel the surface wind again. My air started to run out, and now I felt a shackle on my right leg. It pulled me down, dragging me to the depths. I stared up at the glistening surface waves shining some light that kept me focused on some prize, a prize beyond the depths to which I was being dragged and the reality that now faced my being. My lungs screamed out in pain, begging to die, but the ocean didn't let me. I settled on the floor, tied to a chair, my body hanging over on its right side, leaving me completely flailed across the sandy floor.

Suddenly, I felt the water gravity pull start to change; the surface started to come closer and closer until it began rushing toward my face. I covered my face in defense and found myself on the floor of the doctor's basement, still naked and under the light of a surgeon, out of breath, soaking wet, and cold, shivering under the winter winds. I looked over to the other side of the dark room, and there sat the doctor and two other men from the church, muttering gibberish among themselves, contemplating my fate.

I gradually sat up before I started pulling and tugging violently at the chains until the doctor held the palm of his hand upright, instructing me to stop. I breathed out shivering, and a gunk of phlegm flew onto the ground, splattering among the blood that was let out before, slightly hardened on the ground like spilled oils. The doctor gave his evil smile as he looked at me. I saw only a reflection in his horn-rimmed glasses as he stared in my direction.

"Close your eyes," he instructed. "What do you see?"

I closed them, but I saw nothing.

"Look deeper, what do you see?"

I closed my eyes again and saw nothing, but this time, the darkness started to shimmy, starting to take form. It was a bat—was it Jimmy? No, it was me; I could fly. I immediately took to the skies and sped off in another direction to escape, my wings still heavy form the night sweats.

"And what else?" the doctor continued. "What is behind you?"

I turned around and looked behind me. It was a panther—a black panther with red eyes and the tongue of a daemon staring at me, stalking me, hissing like a snake, before picking up speed running in my direction. I flew as hard as I could, as fast as I could; the chase lasted for hours.

I flew all over the island, finding every nook and sinew in which I could hide, until I reached past the schooner. I could see it now, the islet—it was in plain view, but there was a swamp before it. As I flew over it, I flew too low, and something grabbed me. I flapped viciously in vain. I looked back, and the panther was in midleap with sharklike fangs in its hyperextended jaws. It reached out for me, devouring me whole as I watched my body disappear piece by piece.

As I started to feel my body move into shock, I awoke, staring at the doctor and his group. Their mocking laughs were no comfort as I could feel my hands and legs tied to a wooden plank-and-pulley system—it was a rack. The doctor then came upon me and started turning the rack, my legs and arms completely tired from the chase but still elongated as the pulleys stretched them well beyond limit. I could hear my bones start to crack, until my right knee popped completely, only tendons now holding it in place but blood red from the internal bleeding.

I screamed in pain as he started the saw and furnace beneath my back. He then set up two knee splitters, each with four half-inch stakes on them and placed them under my knees before giving each of them a series of turns to crush the knee joints completely. I wanted to pass out from the pain, but I couldn't. I kept moaning and screaming as the group looked on.

"And let this be a warning to all those who oppose the Order of Gaia," the doctor warned. "Let your death not be in vain."

He took me off the rack half conscious and placed me on a wooden wagon wheel a little over five feet in diameter. Each of my limbs were nailed to the wheel, and a hammer was used to crush whatever joint in my body was left intact, leaving my spirit broken and body mangled.

A few daemons were summoned, and they carried me to the terrace, placing me on an axle and a stand so the wheel stayed horizontal and I lay flat on it, my limbs dangling over the edge of the wheel as I lay suspended for all to see. My extremities started turning blue, and the lack of blood pulled me in and out of consciousness. The church bell rang louder than it usually did as the sun came up on the eastern end.

The entire manor populace was summoned to the balcony and terrace to witness the humiliation of my naked body, in plain view and for all to see, torn and beaten by the order. They left nothing behind, not even my spirit to fight on any further.

# 38

## AZRAEL

I fell silent as gasps of horror and fear gripped the masses. Emerging from the maze, the doctor proclaimed himself as their savior, giving them assurances that he kept his promise to find the murderer of the father and to keep his legacy well after the doctor entered the grave. I lay there, looking at the crowd, my vision blurred and my speech slurred. But even though my body wanted to rest, a part of me, my spirit, could not allow things to end like this.

I reached to the floor and got Kaiko's knife. I used it to pry free my left hand from the nail, forcing it to burst through my flesh and carving in the left forearm "Draco ad Mortem." As the blood seeped from my forearm, another gasp silenced the crowd, which turned into more fear as my body now burst into blue flames. I rose on the wheel, standing shakily as these flames then engulfed the wheel, forming a mass of fire that didn't hurt even the slightest.

The crowd was petrified as the flames spread, engulfing the entire terrace, taking one daemon after another under its wing, burning them into a crisp. A massive explosion erupted, blinding everyone and everything, forcing me to hit my head on the floor. I could smell burnt flesh and wood as I groggily stood up and looked around. The islet was within my sights; and as I headed there, far in the distance, a grand gothic basilica stood tall. I could now see the top tower overflowing with flowers. And after squinting, I gathered a freshly dug grave where the Father lay, right next to his eternal love, Faucet Vauvillier.

A shrill female scream then forced me to jump as I approached the tower, and there, on the uppermost steeple, a man from the shadows fighting a woman. My eyes could scarcely believe it—it was Elizabeth! I shouted her name loudly as I ran to help her, the other being slinking away into the shadows as he heard my voice.

The tower was a single silo so I tore up the stairs, my arm still burning and bleeding profusely from my carvings. As I reached the top, I noticed this tower had a balcony of its own, and upon walking into it, something was buried there. The balcony was made of soil—at least, its surface was—and there were two graves, one freshly dug and the other a tombstone was there. But try as I might, I could not read it.

A daemon stood over the grave on the right, exhuming the body and gnawing away at the feet of a woman. As soon as it caught my eye, its red eyes changed its focus to me and immediately dove my way like a rabid dog, catching me on my shoulder, sinking in its teeth. A woman in a flowing white nightgown then fell upon the creature's back and started biting at its face until it too burst into flames. The flames were blue and cool, just like mine. My breathing was shaky as my consciousness gradually restored; the walls of the room 108—they returned to life, the dull decor and luxury carpet still there as I rolled around on the floor. I couldn't believe that it was all a lucid dream . . . or was it?

My mind started adjusting to this reality—the dark and dingy wall corners and my soaked bedsheet. Jimmy stepped up and started licking the sweat off my face as I could see some of the bite marks left on my left forearm when I turned on my back, staring up at the ceiling.

"We're far from finished, buddy, but trust me when I say we're getting closer," I told my winged friend.

My breathing remained heavy for some time, and eventually, I took out the pocket watch to notice the compass going berserk again, as the time said it was around lunchtime. I then went and took a bath, taking off the sheets and heading downstairs to try and get something to eat. Everyone was on edge when I arrived in the eating hall. Connie, of course, was no longer there, and Hal was looking particularly stressed, having to take up her duties, in addition to keeping his groundskeeper portfolio. I went up to get some food, and I gave him a smile, as if to assure him it will soon be okay.

He seemed to have understood, bending over to give me mashed potatoes from his six-foot-five Icelandic frame, his bald head sweating beads of perspiration in ironically what could only be described as a global winter like no other, even degrees above the equator. His beard was a massive work of art, tapering off from his ear with a slightly red hue, reaching as far as a foot long at its longest point. He was a solid persona and no doubt would have been shaken by Connie's departure, but I suppose he probably thought of his concerns of little importance here, trying to color within the lines of compliance set out by the order.

I ate in my own silence but could hear the murmurings of the crowd, word of a disturbance at the doctor's dwelling slowly creeping through the commune, suspicions being raised about the father's killer still being on the loose and several different theories about who it could be. The arguments just turned a corner to involve the paranormal, some saying it was Kaiko's ghost, some saying it was the ghost fleet, and others saying it was Connie, which was why she was no longer around. Speculations stayed high as the doctor and his visiting group stayed alert to the prospect of the killer being one of us.

The doctor then passed through the area a few minutes later, keeping his gaze mostly to the floor, his mind clearly on something else as he was asking Hal a few questions before leaving the area and returning into the maze, disappearing into the greenery. The doctor's personality started to play on my mind, how he would be different to what I faced so far, why he would be different. I supposed, like the father, he would have some minor supernatural abilities. But the difference is that I sensed a lot of mystery with the doctor, a lot of depth to his character, also a lot of pain.

I quickly returned to my room after eating, hoping to finish my notes on the exorcism books so I may be fully prepared for the night, should my dreams be any indication. The key to the fight tonight will lie within those prayers. I wanted to rest for the sake of my body, but my mind didn't allow it, racing nonstop. All I could do was stare at the ceiling for a couple hours while the sun gradually set and the cover of night gave me the opportunity I needed to begin the hunt.

I took out a staff I cut earlier and started shaving it down to an Olympic javelin but just a little easier to manage. I made the point as sharp as humanly possible, almost seeing my own reflection in the sheen of the wooden edge, now ready for combat. I tied a string to it and slung it over my shoulder, with the bow and arrows in the tote bag. There was no coming back after tonight—this was the final push, and I had to make it count.

I walked out onto the terrace, the winds particularly inhospitable tonight, blowing so hard; cold visibility was cut to just over twenty feet ahead of my strides.

*Twenty feet is all I need*, I told myself as I strode through the maze, trying to find a way out to the other side of the house, knowing it was on the other side of the cliff face.

It took me some time as I heard footsteps approaching, coming from the doctor's lodging. There was no place to hide, so I crouched on the side of the hedge, trying to blend into its shadow. I had to be ready to pounce. Two daemons then emerged, walking side by side. They were busy on their own mission until they walked past me and I thought I had escaped, but then one stopped and smelled the air like a dog. I knew I had to act.

I drew an arrow and ran up behind him, stabbing one of them furiously at the nape of the neck as he blazed into flames, and after dodging the wild swing of the other, I buried the arrow in the other's forehead, setting him alight. I watched as the gruesome creature burned under the blue light—no mercy for the humans they betrayed. I closed my own heart to their pain, opening it instead to their suffering even more.

I left the arrow in his head as they burned before heading down to the lower levels of the maze in an attempt to escape it. Jimmy helped here; being able to fly above the maze, he was able to guide me through the incredibly complex set of curves and sharp turns that took me a little over twenty minutes to navigate before emerging on the other side, facing the front of the house. From there, the house looked abandoned, the wind picking up a set of leaves from a nearby willow tree and tossing it my way as if to tell me "Begone." The ground was damp, and my footprints sank into the ground, the trees on the upper part of the hill either dying or already dead, scattering its twigs and branches everywhere, making it even more difficult to move about silently. I walked up to the porch and cracked the door, still seeing footprints and tracks heading out to the back from my struggle with the beast from the painting last night.

I pushed the door open, and the hinges creaked slightly, the wooden floor also whistling as I entered. I could hear some movement at the back room, so I drew my spear expecting a confrontation with the doctor. I carefully moved to the back and noticed that no one was there; the empty fireplace still empty, but the painting was a different one. I could still hear movement as Jimmy started to bare his teeth on my shoulder, sensing something sinister nearby. The movement then turned into scuttling, the scuttling then into dead silence.

I walked closer to the painting to observe it, it was *The Angel of Death*, an 1888 painting by Evelyn de Morgan of her vision of the divine being. The doctor must have switched them. Right at that time, I could hear footsteps approaching—it had to be him. I readied my spear and faced the door, about to spring into action, and the doctor emerged, calm and well put together. He smiled at my presence. I didn't know what to think. I gazed at his form and wasn't sure how to deal with the situation.

*Should I lunge for his throat or should I wait?* I asked myself.

At least ten seconds of waiting passed while we stood there motionless in the silence until he snapped his fingers. A blood-red flame spurted forth from the fireplace, startling me to the point where I dropped the spear on the ground. The light in the room showed hundreds—no, thousands—of rose-haired tarantulas on the ceiling, crawling everywhere, some dropping to the floor and scurrying along under the heat of the fire.

The doctor motioned me to sit on the floor as he took to it, sitting cross-legged before he went into discussion.

"Tell me, Mr. Huxley, do you despise me? Do I revolt you in some way?" He exhaled heavily, pausing and reaching for a tarantula on the ground, bringing it to his face, biting off its head and chewing it until he swallowed. His large Adam's apple moved under the strain of the mass of food heading to his stomach before smirking and gazing my way.

I too breathed in deeply before exhaling loudly.

"No, I feel no hate for you, only pity, as you have chosen a twisted path to what you consider enlightenment," I said. "But I respect that you live by a code, and in that space, there is no wrong or right, only existence and the resolve of each of the parties to bring their dream to a reality. Dare I say, Doctor, your resolve is strong, but so too is mine, and I will not rest until the state of humanity is restored to what it once was."

The doctor stopped and thought for a bit before chuckling slightly.

"So what you are saying is that your goal is to be humanity's savior? Is that not so?"

I tried to disagree with him a little as he seemed to have taken my words and made it into an ego thing before he chimed in again.

"But is it not you, William Huxley, who have been travelling the world, pursuing a cure for the virus only on the premise of finding your older sister. In other words, you really couldn't care less what happens to humanity—you only want to find your sister, and the truth is that if she hadn't devoted herself to save humanity, you wouldn't be any closer yourself, is that not so?"

It was a painful demon of mine to face, but I had to admit he was right. My heart—even though Liz believed in me to be that person—was never really there. All I truly believed in was being able to save her so our lives could return to what it was before.

"So in essence, Mr. Huxley, you are living a lie because your desire to return things to how they were is a selfish desire because the truth is that things could never return to how it was. The virus has already wiped out over twenty million people and infected close to a billion, all scientific means of culture modification is simply to allow humans to exist in a modified state of being where the planet can handle an eight-billion population. But you must also ask yourself, what is the truth of this scenario?

"We have faced the truth centuries ago, which is that the world is far too overpopulated and that Gaia has to now lay a hand to return the earth to its natural potential, to allow for its continued survival for all its species—and that, that is the truth. There is nothing more, nothing less. We are living up to the execution of that truth. What are you doing for your selfish conviction, Mr. Huxley? Where does your resolve lie?"

He turned now to face his painting as if I barely existed.

"Do you like it?"

I looked at him now with contempt. He was toying with me, like a lion playing with its food.

"Oh, come now, we are scientists, you shouldn't get offended when the truth is spoken. It may hurt, but it is truth—it its pure, holy, simple natural state. It is perfection. So tell me, what do you think of this painting, *The Angel of Death*? It has been around since the 1800s, and its beauty has yet to be surpassed. It's true, it is no Goya, but if you think of the perspective and beauty that emerged since the Renaissance, it really was a shining light in the history of humanity. They accepted both life and death as integral parts of their existence, take my torture chamber below."

He reached for the trapdoor and opened it, walking down below, beckoning me to join him.

"This chamber is a work of art in itself. It gives praise where human ingenuity shined. Whether life or death, it is still celebrated."

I carefully followed him to the basement, noticing the half-torn painting of Goya still standing to the back, blood still everywhere on the floor, and flies in every corner of the room. I nearly convulsed upon entering the room. But there was a play here, a play that he was sure he would win so I tagged along.

"Look at it, William, it is all true beauty, is it not? And though I was not able to find one to share my vision for this type of appreciation, I know one who will."

I was perplexed by his statement.

"Oh, it's Gaia, of course."

"Gaia, *the* titan Gaia?" I asked, confused.

"Oh yes, her time is near, and I must commence preparations for her arrival within the next few months, and oh what a celebration it will be. Unfortunately, though"—his eyes now changed as the red veins in his iris started to pop, the hue starting to evolve until it burned the color of red-hot blood—"you cannot be around to receive her. The father was weak, corrupted by what he thought love could be. He never took the time to understand true love, what it means to be equally yoked, and if I am not normal, William, how could I expect to find love in something that is normal? That is just not scientific."

I immediately felt a series of straps grabbing my arms and binding my legs, pinning me to the ground, as my face fell flat on to the floor where the half-dried blood stood still.

The doctor rolled me over and placed me under one of his contraptions, as his face started to change: his flesh started to tear away from his face, melting off, peeling away little by little. I struggled on the ground as the belts squeezed tighter. I looked down, but all I saw were shadows holding me. They weren't actual ropes. It was suffocating as he continued to speak. His voice started to change a little, getting a little higher pitched and having a slight tremble to it. His teeth started to sharpen as his body continued to grow into something beyond what I could have previously conceived, into some sort of daemon lord. He broke out of the basement and tore off the roof so the basement was open to the sky, laughing maniacally as if feeding off my fear in light of his transformation.

His skin turned to a pale green that extended only as far as his jaw. The rest of his body transformed into a mutated mess of muscle, and he grew hooves for feet. Several hundred wings burst out of his back, each positioned in clockwise, so all formed a complete circle when finished. His one face broke into four half faces, each showing a different emotion—despair, rage, excitement, and hunger. He had four hands, two behind his back that held a book with pages that seemed to be made of flesh, and his hands constantly writing something down on one or the other. His body was fit to the point where I could say he showed no signs of body fat or skin, just the underlying look of red meat. His front hands grew claws the size of talons, and scattered all over his body were hundreds of eyes and daemon tongues, flicking in and out as if to say he would always be watching.

"Look at me William Huxley," he bellowed in a haunting, hissing tone of whispers. "Look at the angel of death in all its glory. I stand before you as Azrael, the grim reaper, and just as the millions who feed me know, you and your fate will be no different. But I shall enjoy your feast that much more. You have caused me so much grief, William, so much grief. Here now I stand, your reckoning that you cannot escape, but rise to accept it graciously so I may make this comforting to you."

I looked at him as he gathered a fistful of shadows in his right front hand, letting them spill over as if he clenched water.

"I am sorry in advance, your highness, but I choose not to be your subject," I hissed back. "Your theories and concepts, while convincing, is not the absolute truth. You ignore one fact, the same fact that sparked the human creativity that painted the grotesque paintings you like so, the same human creativity that gave you this island space, and the same creativity that even bowed to you to give you their service. What do you offer them, Azrael? Sacrifice? Hmm? Is that their truth or yours?"

"Deliverance!" the disfigured doctor screamed. "I give them deliverance, child, just as I give you!"

# 39

## DELIVERANCE

He swung his hands downward to slash my abdomen. I turned in time, but he caught my back, leaving me with foot-long. quarter-inch cuts and a burning sensation that did not go away.

"Do you feel that, son of man? That is the power of the shadows," he boasted, his tongue waving in front of his chin like the lowly daemons. "It allows emotions such as pain and despair to linger, allows you and I to savor the experience."

I looked at the room and noticed there was enough fat and human oils around to make the space flammable. There was no time to waste, so I reached in my pocket and flicked the lighter; the flame slowly caught on the floor and eventually exploded across the room, setting everything to flames. The shadows around me were gone, as Azrael wailed in agony.

"My room, my perfection, my vision—you disrespect me so, boy, you despise the one science!" he growled. "By Gaia, I will make you grovel!"

"Grovel? That is still your idea of freedom?" I said as I watched the creature through the flames. "It sounds to me like we're on a pretty slippery slope of principles. I think it best to bring this charade to an end, for all our sakes."

I laughed, but it was the first time I could see the creature stand straight. The once doctor was at least eight feet tall, and its wings extended another three feet beyond that, as it bore its fangs. I, however, did not feel any fear. I knew that.

"I was here because someone believed in me, this battle is one of belief and resolve," I told the daemon lord. "I will not let them down—they are counting on me, I cannot fail them!"

I ran toward the beast through the flames, and it went in shock as I tackled it; no one was ever so brave enough to attack it. I drew out an arrow and sunk it into the creature's chest. It let out a loud howl like a wolf. I got up to my feet after the blow and turned for a second attack, but the shadows caught me as I turned, wrapping around my face and head. They turned me to kneel and face it while the beast pulled out the arrow. As soon as he pulled it out, the wound healed instantly, the blue flame extinguishing itself on the ground.

*This thing could regenerate, that's different*, I observed.

It flew forward with a massive right hand punch that felt like it broke a few of my right ribs. I coughed blood on to the creature as I flew backward with the tremendous force of the punch. It wasn't done there. We were all now rolling in the flames as I tried to get the creature off me, but its hunger was too great. Its jaw hyperextended as one of its faces rotated on its neck to show the face of hunger, leaping forth and biting down on my shoulder, starting to suck the life from me. I was brought to my knees.

Every time I wanted to stand, the pain sank deeper; and as I settled into the pain, a sleepiness started to grip me until I felt my consciousness starting to fade. The arrows fell from my hand, and I started to lean off to the side as only the creature's jaw kept me upright, but there was hope yet.

With a loud shriek and a high-pitched screech, Jimmy tore into the scene! He used his talons to grip on to the creature's face, and with his massive two-meter wingspan, he used his spurs and dug it into the daemon's skull and bit down ferociously. He tore and tore at the creature's flesh until it howled in pain, and its flesh went alight with the blue flame. Jimmy kept fighting it until he tore one of its faces right off, spitting it out on the ground.

I woke up, grabbing the spear; but I barely had balance, blood spurting out my wound. The creature was now infuriated. It got down on all fours and ran full gallop toward me, aiming for a killing blow. Both Jimmy and I knew we couldn't withstand another attack now, but we still believed, digging in our heels.

We were ready to thrust in, and then I saw a blur come in front of us with a spiked mace delivering a glorious blow. It was Hal, the 450-pound Icelandic force! He turned, and although he was a man of few words, he understood what I was trying to do.

I looked at him as we crawled out the burning basement to the backyard. Still in shock from Hal's surprise attack and with only half a face left, the creature stumbled out eventually, some of its wings still on fire as it continued ambling forward to prove its point. It picked up speed again, bolting toward us, but Hal raised his mace, ready for another blow. With all his might, he swung, but the beast was too agile. It turned in the air like a corkscrew, its wings giving it an advantage when airborne, and it stabbed Hal in the stomach, lifting him off the ground.

"This would be your last day, groundskeeper, you are now fired, and your fate will be worse than that of the cook."

The beast shoved his hand further into the innards of the large Halvak, now forcing him to spurt blood out on the floor which seemed to feed the strength of the beast.

*No, it can't continue like this,* I thought, running toward the creature and was about to deliver a blow.

Hal heard my footsteps, and he thrust down with his elbow, right on the beast's humeral capitulum, and it worked. The creature lost balance, and Hal could now turn the tide, wrestling it to the ground. They were both rolling their way near the edge, and as they reached a few feet away from the two-hundred-foot drop, they put the brakes.

I wasted no time. I got the momentum I needed and ran headlong into the beast while shouting at Hal to get out of the way. As he tried to get up, we both went over the edge. I held on to the creature as Jimmy flew in after me, biting as much as he could to set parts of the creature on fire. We fell with tremendous speed. The tide was high, but not high enough to cover the rocks; my timing had to be just right.

I guided us toward one of the sharp outcrops, and as I passed terminal velocity, I kept the creature on its back so the wings will be virtually useless. About ten meters from the target, I kicked off the creature with all my might, changing both our trajectories and giving me just enough time to draw my bow and arrow for one last shot. Seconds before landing on the rocks, I released the arrow. I had to hit and right at the center of its forehead, and I let the arrow fly. It made contact almost simultaneously with the spike of rock jutting out from the ocean. I too hit the ocean hard, getting knocked out on impact.

* * * * *

I felt someone tapping my cheek and calling my name, and I eventually awoke, still groggy from the encounter. I could see it was Hal, I smiled to see his face but quickly looked around for Jimmy. He was right next to me eating a banana, and there in the surf, the beast of Azrael, impaled on the shoreline and ablaze under a blue flame, only some bones left before disintegrating to pure ash.

The surf was loud and the winter cold, and I could barely breathe as Hal picked me up in his gigantic arms. He carried me for almost a mile downcoast until we came upon a massive cave. It was the inner sanctum of the church!

I looked around, and it looked just as I saw it before. I could see Hal leave me on the floor and went to get something. Upon his return, he had a set of dandelions in his hand. I fought all my pain to follow him to see where he was going. He led me behind the church, and there was a freshly dug grave there with a tombstone marked "My Love" on it.

"I only got some of her bones left," Hal said. "She was my wife you know, Connie, secretly. But she was my only true love. Connie was my reason to wake up in the morning, why I shaved my head, and why I brushed my beard. She loved my beard, she loved so hard, but I couldn't protect her."

He sank into a great despair as tears flowed down his cheek. I hobbled up to him and placed my hand on his shoulder. He gave off a stern grunt that made me withdraw my hand and stick to words of comfort.

"There's nothing we could have done then, Hal, but now, we're fighting for a dream, fighting for the final hope of humanity, a sunrise beyond the endless Fimbulwinter."

He looked at me, surprised I knew about the phenomenon.

"There is still much work to be done, Hal, but I think together, we could find a way," I told him. "We have to persevere, but we could find a way."

"But what else is there?" Hal asked. "Both the doctor and father are now dead."

"No, they were just the effects. The cause is something greater, and it resides on that cursed islet somewhere north of here that disappears under the sea. In that place, we will find what we're look for. We need to be ready."

# Part VI

# DEATH

*March 30, 2021*
*93,566,234 Deaths*
*5,425,359,120 Cases*

# 40

## DESCENT OF THE MAD TITAN

We rested in the corner of the inner sanctum for the rest of the night, trying to get some shelter from the bitter cold winds. My wounds burned strong, and I was sure that some of my bones were cracked or broken, but there was no point in bemoaning the fact. I just had to suck it up and power through the pain.

The blood on my shoulder had also dried, but it started to ooze pus, the creature's fangs leaving an infectious wound that sought to bring me down even after its death. Jimmy too wasn't in the best shape, but we both knew we couldn't come this far without finishing what we started.

As some semblance of minor warmth crept in with the rising sun, we ambled out on the dirt path back to the manor, hobbling and dripping blood from our wounds. Within the hour, we eventually made it up the hill, and Hal immediately brought me to his shop where he had a first aid kit with which he tried to start patching us up. We stumbled and hit the walls in our frustrated state, making a lot of noise until a middle-aged Chinese woman came down from her room to see what the fuss was about.

She spoke little English and was shocked to see our condition. I felt Hal knew her as he immediately relaxed and fell to the floor once he saw her. She immediately went into action, taking charge of us all, bandaging and treating our wounds like a professional medical care specialist. Later, Hal did mention that she was a retired nurse, working with the outlying arms of the church, supporting them in training their staff in first aid and medical capabilities, and a good friend of his. I smiled at our luck as the medications started to take effect, my body starting to feel sleepy again.

* * * * *

Within a few hours, I awoke to loud commotion happening outside. I got up gingerly and proceeded to the terrace to see what the matter was. One of the members of the church was speaking to everyone off the podium in a tone to force us to comply with curfew restrictions until his superiors in the central church could be contacted to determine what our next step could be.

"It's amazing how quickly people gravitate to a void of power and try to fill it, even if they know they aren't right for the role," I said, as myself and Hal shook our heads and walked up to the balcony where he was speaking from.

His voice got progressively more hysterical as we approached.

"Get back in line, get back, I tell you! If you take one more step this way . . ."

We both ignored the self-appointed acting father, after what we saw and went through. We knew the space of wickedness and control he was coming from, and Hal wasn't having any of it.

Hal walked up to the man, and he towered over him both in height and size, before grabbing him in a bear hug, breaking most of his bones. Under the usurper's screams, Hal then turned him to the crowd, snapped his neck, and threw him over the balcony to the cheers of the crowd below.

There were a little over forty persons left as I went ahead and explained the progression of proceedings so far, making it clear that my intent was for everyone to return home, to break out of this twisted concept of freedom practiced here on that remote island, and continue supporting our respective countries in their attempts to fight the virus and restore some semblance of normalcy to the planet. The entire crowd cheered me on, and I took the opportunity to raise the fact that the battle was far from over and that now the order would move into the final gear.

"The night of the dark moon," I called it—a waning gibbous moon was scheduled for that night. All my efforts would be to find the man of shadows and take him head on tonight, bringing an end to this mad cult and their repugnant daemon tribe of beasts. I went on further to go into details of the mad titan Azrael and how he masqueraded as the doctor, where his house and corpse still lay, and where his concept of freedom lay, in plans to enslave us for eternity. This brought a hush and some murmurings in the crowd.

"And this is not the worst of them," I continued. "As I said before, this man of shadows seems to be the architect of the entire show. The islet that only seems to arise on certain nights is its home, and it has something to do with functioning as the source of this cult and its intent to inflict mass control measures across the globe. They try to usher in a new world order, much like those of the economic superpowers that exist now, dictating our norms and trends for us subconsciously as we do their bidding, and sacrifice our God-given right for freedom as humans in the process.

"If there is anything this pandemic has taught us, it's the value of personal and collective freedom and how closely it is linked with our core nature as human beings. Our right to choose our own future—whether good or bad—is our choice, so I tell you now, as the sun sets on the horizon this fated night, I will be making one last march on the shadows to bring an end to this plague. When the coast is clear, I will fire a flare into the sky. Those who wish to fight alongside me are welcome. If you prefer not to, that is understood as well. But one way or another, this hell will end tonight on these winter Romanum seas. For that much, I give my word."

Cheers from the crowd went up as I left the balcony. A feeling of satisfaction and warmth descended upon the crowd as I went back to my room to pull my final set of supplies together. I emptied my pockets; seeing that I still had Kaiko's knife brought a smile to my face as I went outside to cut more arrows and a new spear. The vial of holy water from Bali was still intact, so I coated the tips of all the weapons in it before heading up to Hal's quarters and brushed the same liquid on his mace. I thanked him for all his help as he gathered pitchforks, pickaxes, shovels, and machetes in long leather duffel bags, along with some provisions and water to last us out for the night.

Hal went ahead to cook supper for everyone. A fish broth made up our last meal before heading out for the evening. I could see the warm setting orange sun now start to signal the dawn of our plan as my anxiety started to build on the coming of the long winter night. We sat out on the balcony as we overlooked the bay, and the sun gradually set in the west as we both reminisced on stories from our childhood and individual countries, a few others of the manor choosing to join in and share as well. It was enjoyable, and it took my mind off the reality, if even for a few moments at a time.

"But what of the cannibals, sire?" one older gentleman to the back asked with a grave tone. "How will you challenge their might? They are animals, and they are settled right where you are considering to go."

Myself and Hal watched each other curiously, thinking over the strategy carefully as we pondered the old man's question.

"Cannibals, you say?"

"Yes, cannibals," he responded. "They guard the only landmass on that side of the island that they worship as their god, the thorn mire. Their entire tribe is positioned right in front of it, and they promise to kill and eat anything that comes too close to them. That is when they don't choose to come out and hunt us on the rest of the island at night anyway."

A shudder embraced the recently cheerful group, as I scratched my head in thought.

"And these are humans, correct? Not daemons?" I asked.

The old man nodded in confirmation.

"Well, I guess we would have to fight our way through them as well," I said. "Anyone willing to come along to help would be welcome, but I'm not gonna force any of you. But if we have to carve a path to make our way, then so be it."

The crowd quickly dispersed as morale drained from the group. The sun almost completely set as the loud creaking of the ghost fleet of Truk signaled the dawn of the winter night. Its creaks sounded particularly loud this time around, shattering the silence from the retreating crowd on the manor.

We went to the balcony overlooking the manor lands that looked like a ghost town, and just like clockwork, I could now see the islet to the north rise up.

"C'mon, Hal, time to get moving," I said as I could still see from the balcony the remnants of the scorched bungalow from the father's quarters, smoke still emanating from the burnt basement of the Frey Manor.

I took in a deep breath, knowing that little odds were in my favor to reach this far and that now wasn't the time to stop pushing forward.

"Fight on," I whispered to Jimmy, as he squeaked in agreement.

I went down to the terrace to check our supplies before heading out, wondering how we were going to carry it that far north. Hal came up and asked about the cannibals again. I could see some fear in his eyes, so I had to take the time to think through the process on a way forward.

"I think we have to be careful with how we proceed, but we must proceed," I said. "We have defeated some great daemons so far, and these cannibals are just aggressive humans. Their main tool is fear. Not their weapons, not their strategy, but the fear of what they will do to us if they kill us. By that time in my mind, it won't really matter, making them no different from pirates or robbers.

"This power that fear has on humans—I'm sick of it, Hal, first starting as a seed, germinating into anxiety, building up as lactic acid in the body, and dropping the brain's serotonin levels from stress leaving us with a cloudy mind. By then, the battle is already lost. I'm tired living in fear, aren't these people too? Through the coronavirus, they set up fear in the virus. Everything they want us to do is based on fear of this happening or fear of that happening because they see a fear-based population easier to control."

Hal nodded in agreement.

"Well, we can't continue like that," I said more forcefully now. "We aren't worth pressing forward with that mindset—we would be sure to lose! Instead, we have to power through that fear, push through in a space of courage and determination to build a different future, a stronger future, a fairer future. Only then can we truly claim our birthright as humans. If we throw away the cloak of fear and stake our claim to the throne of our destiny, only then we can move forward."

As soon as I mentioned that, I heard a low drone come from the ocean, and the mist returned, an eerie, villainous fog clouding our visibility.

"This will work for us this night, Hal, stealth will be our friend against the cannibals," I told my friend. "Come, let us get moving. Tonight, that Gaia Order will fall!"

Hal then placed his hands on mine when he saw I was ready to take up the bags and walk with them. He shook his head to show there was a better way. I followed him as he carried me to the back of the manor where there seemed to be a small barn, but something was moving in it.

As he opened it, there stood a large Victorian carriage, fit out with magnificent black horses and reins, each horse trusting Hal with its life, and so they were very happy to see him. I smiled watching the carriage as it barely looked used.

"It's a Clarence, brought here by the duke and duchess for their evening strolls, more than able to carry our supplies with my black Friesians, Mark and Dave, here ready to take us to the ends of the earth," Hal said.

They whinnied in agreement, flashing their magnificent manes and tails as they stomped, getting my adrenaline running again, ready for the attack on the islet.

Hal was just about to guide me into the carriage when I could hear a few people asking me to wait. It was the nurse and a few others, imploring us to take them along.

"We aren't much of a bag of soldiers, but we're some extra bodies that are willing to help you out if you'd have us."

I smiled and looked at Hal as we nodded in agreement, suiting them up and placing them all around the carriage with the supplies. As I stuck my head into the carriage, I could see a piece of paper stuck to the underside of the seat. I motioned for everyone to load in while myself and Hal sat on the driver's seat on the front. I opened the piece of paper and noticed it was a newspaper, *The London Herald*. I looked over at Hal, as it was no more than a week old.

"I didn't know we got newspapers, Hal?"

He shrugged his shoulders, pointing out that maybe some of the recent visitors form the main church probably brought it with them and forgot it there, not knowing the doctor's strict rules regarding it.

On the front page, we read where the pandemic numbers were at March 30, 2021, clear as day. I was perplexed as I thought it had just been October.

*How could five months have passed by so quickly?* I asked myself.

The headline with the World Health Organization numbers published as bold as possible read:

HEADING TO EXTINCTION
93,566,234 DEATHS, 5,425,359,120 CONFIRMED CASES

My knees went weak when I read the article about the global spread of the virus that had now reached every corner of the earth, infecting over 70 percent of the global population count and with a total body count second only to the Black Death. My hands started to tremble, but I couldn't show fear in front of everyone when they needed a leader in this time.

I motioned for Hal to get the carriage moving, and as it started, the jolt forced me to throw up on the side as the numbers truly hit home.

# 41

## THE THORN MIRE

Hal watched my eyes closely as my expression slowly changed from shock, to fear, and then anger. The horses picked up speed as the carriage tore through the dirt roads and rummaging over the stones, making a low growling noise while kicking up a cloud of dust in its wake. The road remained mainly on the coast, and I could feel the sea spray on my jaw and salt in my hair and beard, which had now been fully grown, making myself and Hal look like a team of hobos heading to war.

The mist still followed, and I did feel as if eyes were watching us carefully. But I didn't care—the adrenaline kept me moving forward as we approached our campsite. The growl of the carriage and the gallop of the horses just drowned out the rusty creaks of the ghost fleet and the drones of the surrounding corpse brides.

As I glanced over the rough surf, I could see the winter swells coming in and the water breaching the high-water mark further inland and making our path more treacherous than usual. From time to time, I also noticed a few corpse brides breach the water surface, their ghoulish red eyes hovering over the choppy waves to keep an eye on our every move. I smiled as clearly we were making someone nervous. We made a sharp left turn that nearly threw me over the very ominous–looking cliff edge, as I got a peek of the waves crashing below. We entered a thicker part of the forest, so slowing down was imperative. I noticed the foliage start to evolve.

We moved through the forest to an area where more sinister gray forms of moss grew on dead branches, with vampiric, thorny vines that wrapped around each of the plants, projecting their spiny quills and thorn hooks to pierce and poison anyone who dared passing through. The cut from the vines burned ferociously, forcing rashes to break out on my skin. We eventually came into a semiswampy clearing that wasn't too far from the cannibals' camp. I could hear some of their voices and saw the tent city and torched lights through the thick network of trees.

We came out the carriage there, and I thanked the horses for their strength and support to get us to this point before Hal went ahead and tied them to a tree stump within the vicinity. We reached in for our weapons; there were nine of us in total, and Jimmy made us ten. Each one of us had axes, spears, pitchforks, or, in Hal's case, a spiked mace all dipped into the holy water, in case we encountered any daemons. That would not help us in any way here, so we had to be smart.

I asked them to wait by the camp while I marched on to the edge of the jungle and climbed one of the trees to get a better vantage point. The first acre of the area was littered with tents for the cannibals and before the mire started. Our target was hidden after the five-acre mire, which is where I noticed a ten-acre spread with a silo at the water's edge but couldn't make out any more details than that. The cannibals were up and active, so we would need to wait out their high energy levels before heading in. The mire seemed to be a beast all its own.

I went back to them to explain what I had seen, focusing on the mire and the science behind how it worked.

"The mire has several parts to it, but essentially, think of it as a floating football field that could swallow you whole, depending on where you step," I warned. "It looks like a regular swamp, but it's rich in methane in a space called the Smoking Catotelm that decays the main meat of the mire, be it peat litter, or trees, or animals, and releases the noxious gas to the air, which is highly flammable and toxic to breathe in.

"The turf in some areas would actually roll and form depressions in other areas, which would be underwater. The water would not be potable as it's probably pulling from the saltwater right next to it and would have several pockets along the way that would act like quicksand. Once it swallows you, that's it—you're gone for life. If the cannibals are there, then I'm betting they would have staked out some safe pathway across the mire that we could follow to the back to the castle where I couldn't really see much. But be on guard in the mire as it seems to be at least ten meters deep, and there's no sign of anything living on its surface, which means that it ate everything it came into contact with.

"The moon isn't gonna be much help to us, but it would help a little with the cannibals for us to head through the camp and try and find the path they might have had set up to walk through. So for now that's the aim, we wait for them to fall asleep, sneak behind their tent city, and try to find their marked path past the bog into the back of the castle. Does that make sense?"

Everyone nodded, but one guy put up his hand to ask a question.

"So what if any of us get caught?"

I sighed when I heard the question.

"Don't get caught, but if you do, that's what these weapons are for. Know that being caught may mean certain death so make sure you are aware of risks before heading out there tonight."

Another loud groan erupted from the direction of the mire, almost like a belching sound, before we felt the ground tremble a little as if in fear. We sat around in the wet, swampy dampness next to one of the mangrove trees, waiting for our opportunity to strike. After a couple hours of facing winter chills piercing through the forest foliage, I could finally see the torches start to go out one by one.

Within half an hour, all the lamps were out as I assumed the time approached midnight—it was time to act.

We came out to the edge of the forest, and I peeked out the vines under perfect silence. Everyone seemed to have retired to their tents. Suddenly, I felt something swish in my boot and clamped onto my toe. I had to bite my tongue and stomp on the creature when I watched it was a yellow-headed hairy crab, probably brought out by the light moon and tides trying to reclaim his hole. I held on to my little toe in pain, but for now, I just had to suck it up.

Hal took lead as we headed out into the open, walking around the fringes and trying to make little noise. We were able to stay in the shadows for the most part, and as we reached about halfway into the camp, we all noticed their campsite. There was a recent butchering and kill. We looked at the corpse and could see the mangled body, mutilated under the venom of a dull blade, only its skull and legs left and everything else carved off the bone. The fire in the center was still smoking from the night's dinner special.

The stench was fresh and horrendous; the smell of burnt flesh and blood was everywhere and wafted straight into our brain centers. I looked around and saw a pile of reject parts accumulating on the edge of the village filled with fingers, toes, noses, and hair; just rotted on a pile of a couple meters high. I covered my nose as the flies were everywhere, motioning for the group to keep moving on.

We were in the final third, and we noticed there were some people at the back nodding off. It was a coop of tribespeople—women guarding what I would consider the entrance to the mire. There were several instances where I saw the same nine-pointed star either carved on trees or etched in the sand, so they too must believe in the whole Gaia cult as well.

The women guards were formidable, bare breasted, and moved with a sense of certainty about them. Long, flowing, straight hair and tattoos adorned their arms as they held a machete in one arm and a spear in the other. Oddly enough, though, they were always facing the castle area, as if guarding from creatures that might emerge from the bog. They also sported a knee-length loincloth made of sheep's leather and stood straight at their post. They were our target.

Hal and I went quietly behind them, barely making a sound, and grabbed them from behind, drawing our weapons to their face, ordering them to quietly surrender while forcing them to their knees into submission. They dropped their weapons after we forced them to turn around. We pointed our weapons at them as they looked at us in disgust, probably unable to speak English. We motioned for them to guide us through the mire when they turned their backs to lead the way through. I called for the others to follow as we headed through the village without a problem and walked into the mire, its repulsive smell hitting you the moment you enter. We all had to be very reserved as we breathed.

Hal kept a close eye on the captives as I could see they thought of taking us on a couple times, only to think better of it after examining Hal's gigantic stature. We continued marching into the mire as I dropped markers along the way, pounding in stakes I cut before. Each stake slid in to the mire with no resistance; in some cases, the mire swallowed the stick whole and spitting it back up a few seconds later. I felt the ground rumble, and then another belch from the mire roared into the ocean, drowning out the sound of the waves; and with that, a roll into the soil came across the mire like a wave, the surface turf rolling like a chocolate layer of icing on fresh cake batter with no stability or solidity beyond the crust but purely fluid beneath.

The women of the tribe rode the waves beautifully, so we had to stay on our feet. We did so and was able to barely recapture them a few paces in, not before they released a series of clicking noises that no one knew what it was for. We continued to snake through a series of fairly complex pathways that would have been impossible to reach, had it not been for the guidance of the women. The grass on the mire became filled with thorns and interspersed brambles, with stinging nettles along the way. Eventually, we came upon a point in the mire that worked its way into a sort of small hill a little over ten feet high, and at its summit stood a willow tree, a lackluster weeping willow that blew in the strong winter winds. Then things took a turn for the worse.

We could hear the winds start to whistle, and the women with us started to panic. They tried to run back to their camp, and I and Hal had to wrestle them to the ground, bringing them to stand again. But they stayed in that state. We looked up, and the tree was adorned with corpses, hanging from the tree with nooses, and a strange whistling noise could be heard coming from the distance behind it.

"Ghouls—it's the ghouls of the Thorn Mire, they're here!" shouted one of the older men at the back of the pack.

I turned around and couldn't help him, and he shot off toward the village as the corpses on the noose started to become animated.

Their eyes turned red so I drew for my spear, knowing that daemons were near. I instructed the others to do the same and stay calm, but it was too much for the women. They broke free from Hal's grip and in a panicked craze ran into the mire. They barely got twenty feet in before they started tripping on to the mire's soppy ground, and we saw the beast at work. Mud was everywhere; and the more the women fought it, the more the mud reared its ugly head to cover them in the smear of muck, dragging them down farther and farther in the ground.

They screamed and yelled, but none of us dared move a step further; and as their bodies descended into the mire, we could see a paranormal poltergeist with a scythe of some sort emerge from behind the corpse tree, severing their scalps from their body, taking two fresh scalps, and nailing it to the trunk of the tree before returning to its hiding place. The whispers and whistling was deafening at this time, to the point where I felt as if I should kneel to ease the pain to my ears, but we had to press on. "The corpse tree," as I called it, spoke to another of our team from the back as we watched the tree devour the long lush hair of the women, piece by piece, like flesh-eating worms, savoring each mouthful as it disappeared and metabolized into the weeping willow's structure. Everyone shook with trepidation, but I had to be careful and steady of mind.

After staking out the path for so long, I noticed that the path generally followed a form of clumpy nut grass that grew on the Manor Hill as well. I assumed it to be a variety of tough Savannah grass that needed hard land to grow. I think that is how the women knew where to step, but there was only one way to know.

I trod very carefully, moving forward as gingerly as possible, using the spear to test the stability of the ground before inching forward. As I did, I could feel myself being immersed in the environment of the mire more and more—the brambles getting thicker, the smell of methane becoming more enveloping—until I could start to feel become nauseous as I stumbled through the field. It was like a minefield from World War I. The team followed me carefully but winced as we passed the area where the two women were eaten by the mire, their hands still exposed to the air.

Eventually, we reached the latter half of the mire; but with still some way to go, I could see the obelisk that was the castle at the back much clearer. Although it was a single silo, it was a truly imposing structure that we had to power through to reach. Coming to the last few steps of the mire, the dirt path came to an end. I wasn't sure how to proceed, as we were standing purely on a collection of muck.

*But what is it really?* I thought, using my spear to move some of the collected muck.

I soon realized it wasn't just muck—it was a graveyard of bones, animal and human bones alike. Judging from the curvature of the wave of the collection point that spanned the entire mire, it was likely the result of subduction of the various layers of the bog; and when we heard the belching of the mire, this was where all its indigestible refuse piled up due to its internal currents, a sedimentary boneyard of sorts, really.

We had to keep climbing to push through, and so we did. Stumbling over the mound of bones, we all fumbled our way to the next side, exhaling heavily to prevent much inhaling so as not to inhale more toxic fumes than we had to. I noticed a horror came upon us—one of our team members who ran back awoke the entire village. They were now running our way to claim our lives.

"They're coming, we have to run!" shouted another from the rear of the line as at least a hundred warriors stormed the path from the cannibal village, bearing down on us in the boneyard.

In the process, I could see some stumble off the path, providing more food to the mire. The mire was claiming its share of death that night, and as we crossed the boneyard, I could see a discernable finish line where a beach spit accreted significantly to the rear of the mire on which the castle stood firmly. I ran to it, only to be greeted on the path with another horror. Just as the mire claimed death from the cannibals before, here, it was giving life.

Hands started emerging from the muck of the soggy parts of the bog; and daemons emerged in the hundreds, roaring as they broke free from their swampy prison, waving their tongues like dogs that had just been let loose to hunt, thirsty for flesh and blood. We were nearly there, but it felt like we wouldn't make it through in time. The hordes were upon us from both sides, and I had to think fast.

As we ran, our feet got caught in the mire in some places, and one of our team members was caught by a diving daemon, dragging her to the depths of the mire like the others.

"Hal!" I shouted. "I need you to trust me, we must stop here. Wave your mace ferociously enough around you to clear the air, I need only one shot."

Hal did as I said, and in so doing, the immediate surroundings above Hal's head was clear of the thick methane, allowing me to use the machete to decapitate one of the creeping daemons, skewering his skull with an arrow and on one knee.

I pointed my bow to the heavens and shouted to everyone, "Run straight through now!"

They didn't have to be told a second time, as they darted past me in the final haul for the back of the castle. I released the arrow to the sky with hordes of daemons and cannibals on our tails. The final few seconds before I thought I was going to be caught, I ran like my life depended on it, darting out and diving to the spit on the back of the castle, just evading the grasp of my hunters as they too clashed in the mire, turning the scene into a vicious battle ground.

"Duck!" I shouted as the skull reached its apex with the arrow and started descending.

The moment it reached around ten feet in the air, the blue flame ignited the skull; and once the thick layers of methane caught on to it lower than that, a tremendous explosion caught the latter third of the mire, wiping out all the hordes, setting them all on fire, some imploding with the force, others being thrown backward and set alight. But all fell victim to the appetite of the Thorn Mire in the end.

# 42

## GRUMARIM CASTELLUM

I groaned in pain as my bones crackled in the naked sand on the other side of the mire. Plumes of smoke leaped up into the sky as the Thorn Mire claimed its next victims. Its belches came as satisfying reverberations along the floor as it begun its consumption process, digesting its spicy meal from death and life.

I called for everyone to make sure they were alive as we gathered whatever was left of our weapons before staggering over a decorative ragstone bridge to the eerie castle at the peak of the islet. I hobbled over in pain while Hal continued on, expressionless, like a man on a mission he is yet to complete. I tried to breathe in, but I felt my ribs were really broken from before, making breathing very difficult to accomplish.

My left foot dragged behind as we walked through some thickets before reaching the actual castle grounds. Hammerhead bats were perched everywhere in the trees, their beady, globe eyes staring out with vacant expressions at every turn we make as if we never got permission to make them and would have to pay dearly for that soon. The layout of the castle was like a keyhole, the base being the main cuboid silo tower with each side being forty feet long and two hundred feet tall. A circular terrace to the east was connected to it, housing something in its tallest tower that I couldn't decipher from this far below.

The silence was broken again by the ear-shattering creaking of the ghost fleet; more than anything else, it felt like the sunken ships and planes were directly beneath me. All these were superfluous details to the real mission at hand.

*But what is the main mission?* I asked myself, quietly looking back at the tortured corpses in the mire, their flesh burning to a crisp in the ravenous mud that awaited them to cool. *Am I here to find Liz? Am I here to free the people on this island? Am I here to save the world from extinction? Why couldn't it be all three?*

I felt confused, not knowing which was my priority, but I made a promise to see this through. I'd have to start at least by heading into the castle and confront what lies there.

It was a strange design for a castle, a single tower protruding all the way up to two hundred feet, no windows, a single door, single moat—nothing remarkable. It also felt abandoned; the weeds surrounding it and the creepers that started to scale the castle walls were already halfway up the building. The sides were covered in moss, and there were no signs of life, as if no one wished to be found and simply wanted to be alone with the ocean here. What was strange, though, was that the moss on the walls weren't alone. Along with the algae, there were several species of barnacles, acorns, goosenecks, *Balanus trigonus*, and *Balanus crenatus*; and they were all attached to the sides of the walls of the castle, at least for the first five to eight meters. This was strange; even though most of the vegetation was dead or near dying on the island, some vegetation was still thick, particularly on the north, near the small river at the base, and the creepers also survived. I left it alone and gathered everyone before we headed into the castle.

"Okay, guys, this is it," I said. "Our mission is to confront anything that looks like a daemon inside there and kill it, anything we find is likely to be a daemon, and we have the tools to take them down. We need to stick together as a group and move in ordered steps, just as we did crossing the mire. We're almost on the home stretch, guys, let's go take the rest of our freedom."

Everyone smiled in response as they gripped their weapons tighter, moving to a standing position before heading over to the main door.

As we approached, we noticed the main castle door attached to a moat that was over something. We looked over the edge and realized it was a snake pit, a pit that awoke once they sensed something alive. The hisses were loud, and the pit sported every snake known to man in this deep moat. We basically had little or no chance of coming back once either one of us ends up down there. Corals, vipers, cobras, constrictors, and rattlesnakes all comingled in that pit—not necessarily harmoniously as I spotted a king cobra devouring one of the pit vipers for dinner. It was an edgy welcome, but we expected more of that.

Out of the corner of my eyes, I noticed a pod of agitated corpse brides offshore, breaching the surf and circling the area. Their red eyes focused on our next step in our mission, spewing mist indiscriminately into the atmosphere as if out of rage. We got our weapons ready, and under the noise of incessant hissing and snake fighting below, we walked up to the door and kicked it, trying to pry it open. But the door didn't move.

I went up to it and tried pushing the center gently, pulling first, and the hinge gave way, allowing the door to open fluidly. We expected a horde of daemons or something similar waiting for us inside, but we were half disappointed to find nothing, no one—anywhere.

The stench of marine decay hit strongly as the door opened, and I slipped and fell as soon as I entered. Getting up as quickly as I could, covered in soft sea moss, I looked around, expecting some sort of attack; but nothing came. The door stayed open, creaking on its hinge, as the cold breeze drifted into the castle in a mystical tone, allowing us to look around. But nothing of interest beyond the same barnacles were here, albeit a lot less than those outside.

I did find a small glass window to the north of the castle eventually, but it was totally covered in moss, so I had to clean it. I felt something drop on my face like a little bead and realized it was some sort of feces. I wiped it off my face, and upon looking at it, I turned to Hal.

"It's poop—bat poop," Hal mentioned.

We all looked up and realized that the first ceiling was very high, a little above sixty feet, and clinging to it were hundreds of bats shimmying around for a good sleeping position. They were the same hammerhead bats that were seen outside, with their globe, red eyes and three-meter wingspans. But they didn't seem to be aware we were there. Nothing else special existed on this floor, other than a helical staircase with no railings, wrapping around a central column and seeming to head all the way to the roof.

I went back to the window to try to clean it off so I could at least get my bearings. Only one side got clean, so I could only make out the outline of something outside.

"Hey, hey!" I started shouting.

Hal came over and took a look, agreeing that someone was turning something outside. Suddenly, we all felt the ground shake, and the thunderous cry of the ghost fleet broke the air again; this time, it sounded like a splash, like something dove under.

"What was that?" I asked, panicked.

I ran to the outside of the castle, and as soon as I reached the moat, I could see it—torrential fifteen- to twenty-foot giant waves barreling down on the castle, and mist was everywhere.

"C'mon, guys, we have to get to higher ground!" I said.

We started running up the stairs, but it was blocked at the higher level. I told Hal to try slugging away at the door—we had to break it down now. Then two massive doors on the north of the silo opened, and with it, a rush of water crashed into the first level of the castle, barreling into the walls, filling it as fast as my breathing had become. First, two inches, then four, eight, sixteen inches, all within the first minute.

We all took to the stairs, and I realized the vegetation I saw outside was there because they were floodgates. I looked out to the entrance door, and before the pressure from the inside could close the door, hundreds of snakes found their way in the castle from the moat, hunting everything that could move within the water, the falling bats being their main victims. There was nothing for us to fight, nothing for us to do but to depend on Hal and his strength.

He kept banging on the trapdoor above, and we kept sitting on the steps, watching the water rise. The scariest thing happened when I looked around the walls for a water mark and I realized there weren't any, which means the entire chamber would soon become totally submerged.

The waiting was killing me, just watching the snakes get closer and closer, until the first couple snakes realized that there was food at the top of those steps. I felt my vertigo start to set in as the staircase started vibrating subtly from the pressure of the water from the outside. Before long, the water rose to the twenty-foot mark and kept rising, and a couple vipers made their way on the stairs and started sliding toward us. I glanced at it and thought to act. But Gretchen, one of the women in our group, beat me to it, diving in with the shovel and giving it a mighty swing, connecting head-on with the first snake before turning it to expose the sharp edge and decapitating the second one, each of them bursting into blue flames when struck.

*They were daemons!* I thought.

A sinking feeling filled my stomach.

*Wait, if this silo is filling, does that mean that things could enter from the ocean?* I concluded.

No sooner than I thought that, I could see the red-eyed beast enter the castle—a full-size patriarch spanning at least twenty meters long. Its movements, while still whalelike, also had an extra agility of a reef shark, smelling the fallen chum in the water and circling its prey. Its large frame came out in the form of a dark outline viewing from the top, circling us like a band of hyenas, waiting for us to make a mistake and join it in the water.

Time was not with us as the water continued to gush into the castle and rise with every passing second. Hal incessantly thumped at the trapdoor above us, starting to slow as he got tired. I turned my attention there and noticed he was burned out. His fatigue was a combination of the repeated banging and the struggle just to get this far, and his body was not accustomed to these stresses. I couldn't ask any more of him.

I climbed the steps behind him and laid a calming palm on his shoulder with a smile, telling him not to worry. I devised another option, but it would be dangerous.

Right then, the elder in the group came up the stairs to try and meet us; his enthusiasm to help the situation got the better of him. As Hal and I continued discussions over the options, the elder continually moved closer until he felt he was within earshot, and then I heard the fated crack.

"No," I whispered.

I immediately looked to his feet to see his left ankle buckle and twist, falling back and over the edge in the absence of any sort of railing. Hal and I lunged in but only barely caught his sandals, which quickly slipped off as he flew headfirst into the water pit—it was gruesome. We all watched in terror as the corpse whale swiftly positioned itself and leaped into the air, its fangs, young and strong, skewering the abdomen of the old man as it threw him in the air before chomping down the elder with its jaws, making a tremendous splash. It left the lower half of the body on the surface twitching uncontrollably as the snakes and bull sharks had their way with the remains while the bats took to the sky in a frenzy, picking off whatever they could get their hands on.

Both Hal and I remained in shock, visibly shaken from the incident and witnessing the reality of what was now directly below us. We had to act fast.

He nodded at me as this was the distraction we needed to execute our crazy plan to escape this vice grip.

I ran around to the northern side of the helical stairs, and as expected nothing was there as all the creatures were occupied with the commotion on the southern end. I took off my shoes and dove off the edge, leaping into the water, trying to minimize my splash, heading straight for the tunnel to the ocean. I held my breath and knew that that was a long stretch, but that was our only chance. I kicked hard and ended up in the tunnel, a shot ragstone Crete tunnel mossed over with age standing a little over twenty feet tall before ending up on what was the shoreline. The problem was, the water was still pushing its way into the castle, creating a massive current to swim against.

I put my head down and used my arms to swim as hard as I could, swimming as if I was on the surface, using every last bit of strength I had in my body. As the currents started to ease on the backwash, I could look back into the castle. There were the red eyes again, and I think they saw me—I had to move fast.

Eventually, I barely reached the end of the tunnel, with the whale a couple feet behind me, biting away at my feet. I could feel the warm dead recirculated water regurgitated on my heels as its jaw reopened. I was finally able to swim above the main current and clamber atop the past shoreline and all the way to the surface outside. It was a tormenting sight to behold—not a single ghost ship in sight, just rough, stormy seas and several large creatures thrashing in line with the tunnel, fighting to get in as they too must have gotten the smell of food.

I grabbed on to the creepers on the wall, holding on for dear life. I had to retrace my steps to where the window was and where I believe someone was turning a mechanism of some sort. I saw it just by estimating the distance along the wall from the edge. I needed to move a few more meters west, but I had to have my strength as the current will not be with me. Thankfully, the draught was shallow enough to prevent a whale from following me here—but not for long I supposed, as I could see them waiting and watching on the effluent spout a few hundred feet offshore.

I saw my opportunity, and I pushed off the wall and dove down, looking around quickly to locate a mechanical apparatus that might be controlling the flood gates. After a minute, I found nothing and had to resurface. The whales and now bull sharks were closer, the bull sharks careful not to take first lunge as the whales were the recognized alphas in line and jumping that line meant certain death for them. On the second dive, I refined my search a little, using the creepers and vines as a guide as I expected they would have tangled themselves around any mechanism that was located on the beach for a while. I was right, and I could see it: a black wellhead stopcock valve at least six inches in diameter lying at the bottom. I didn't have time to resurface—I needed to do what had to be done.

With all the strength I had left, I tried to turn it, but nothing gave. I realized then how much easier that would have been to do when on land. But underwater, the competing hydrostatic pressures would make that turn very difficult to achieve. Still, I kept turning but to no avail.

Out of the corner of my left eye, I then saw a flash of gray; it was one of the bull sharks, ready to make a swipe at me, his eyes blood red. He grazed my shoulder and was about to make another turn. I looked over to the whales and realized there was a scuffle taking place—although more like a massacre as the four whales continued mauling the sharks that were there, bursting them into several little pieces for not being able to hold their position. But one got away, and that one was at least an eight-meter specimen, more than enough to take me out of the equation.

I was running out of air and had hunters bearing down on me from all sides—I had to try again. But the valve would not give. And within the last ten seconds of holding on, I was never so happy to see a burly Icelandic knave come to my aid!

Hal brought his mace and smashed it in the face of the oncoming shark, drawing blood and forcing it to scurry away. He quickly turned his focus to the valve and slipped the handle of his mace through. We both pushed hard on the longer lever, and at long last, we could hear the sound of the crying ghost fleet.

*It was steam!* I thought. *This valve released steam into a set of pipes that controlled gears that tightened a series of structural cables similar to what holds up suspension bridges.*

And just like that, the ghost fleet started to rise, and with it, the displaced water started to fall rapidly. I rushed to the surface, gasping for air; and within a couple minutes, the ghost fleet was visible again, and so was the shore as the floodgates dropped behind it once all the water had evacuated.

# 43

## JUDGMENT

I gasped amid the wet sand, coughing out water, as the final inches of water drifted back into the ocean. There was a bloodbath among the daemons still in high rage near the shore. We both rolled on our backs, looking up at the dismal, clouded sky, barely opening our eyes as the winds felt even colder than before.

"Thanks, Hal, I needed that," I said.

He nodded gently and gave me a fist bump, which prompted a chuckle from me.

"Since when do *Íslendingars* fist bump?"

He shrugged his shoulders, slightly recognizing the humor in it all. I took a deep breath in before forcing to my feet, knees still wobbling under the close call.

"C'mon, Hal, lets head in and get to the others," I said to my Nordic friend. "Talk to them for a bit before moving on."

Hal too struggled to come to his feet, so I had to help him up before I held him under my shoulders, both of us hobbling back to the entrance of the castle. The structural cables were still creaking violently under the weight of the ghost fleet in the ocean. I could spot a shimmy on the roof in my peripheral vision, and I glanced up but saw nothing. Yet I was certain we were being watched.

On the moat, everything was soggy and covered with moss, but I had to open the door. In doing so, the final few feet of water from the ground floor escaped, along with the few snakes that survived the flood, ushering the reptiles to their original space under the moat where they clearly felt safest. I had to jump back from this scene.

The doors let out a fresh stench of death that would make even the most avid fish market patron convulse. I could still see the old man's sandals on the floor, blood discoloring in the surrounding water. The remaining six in our team were shaken but were happy to see we had survived, and after a brief exchange of hugs and kisses, we were ready to head beyond this dungeon.

"We have done a great deal to come this far, but it would mean for naught if we do not press on," I said. "We are far from the top of the castle, but we are slowly getting there and we need to persevere. I, however, do appreciate the value of human life and know good well that what we saw here was not easy to witness. I will not, as I always do, force any of you to continue with me. The danger will only get worse from here on out, so you must be ready for this."

Everyone nodded but was confused about how I planned to get to the next level; but as I expected, it was all a test, a game to the man of the shadows.

As I walked up to the trapdoor—this time around—it creaked open, half its outer shell battered from Hal's efforts but far from breaking. As we all clambered into the new chamber, each of us appeared even more haggard and drained than before. This chamber, however, was a single corridor lined with rooms on either side and torches along the way to keep the place in light. I appreciated this and heard the trapdoor and latch shut behind us as soon as we were far enough forward, prompting a couple muffled yelps from our group. We kept walking and eventually came to a circular lounge that split two ways.

I asked everyone to stay together as we went down the left corridor. I looked down and noticed my vision getting slightly blurred. I shook my head and looked at the others. They also were having problems with their vision.

*Is it the floor we're walking on?* I deduced. *What is causing this reaction?*

Then as my sight extended, I tilted my head and could see it in the distance—the mist. It was being channeled within this confined space, so that was all we have been breathing for the past few minutes.

"C'mon, we need to speed up," I shouted impatiently.

And as we sped up our walk, I noticed we eventually ended up in another circular lounge; fifteen minutes later, another; and another and another. By the next time we reached the same thing, Hal reached out his hand on my shoulder, pointing out that the building was not that long and that we have been moving in circles, that someone was toying with us, and that we should try the doors. We all agreed to head down the right corridor, and each person tried a different door.

As I entered the room I picked, I could see the lights suddenly go out, and the door close and latch hung with a sentencing cling before being thrown onto the bed and clamped by it, forcing me to stay stagnant.

* * * * *

Four candles were lit on the four corners of the bedposts as I lay motionless on the bed. It was extremely comfortable, but the comfort was too much for me, like I had to fight to stay awake in a circumstance that demanded more than 100 percent of my attention. I looked above my head and saw a message carved into the ceiling by a crude instrument. It read, "Senentia."

*Judgment*, I thought. *What on earth could that mean? Is this the man's way of dispensing a self-proclaimed right to be judge and jury?*

I exhaled deeply, tired of the crazy individuals and their twisted concepts of existence that I had to keep fighting against as I clearly entered another dream state prompted by the toxins of the mist.

The mist now gathered to the height of the bed, as if someone opened the window to let clouds enter, and the strange smell of charred flesh accompanied it. Suddenly, a shrill cry for help shattered the silence in the room, blowing out all the candles, returning the room to darkness. I then started to feel something prick my right shoulder—first, a little and then a lot—forcing me to grunt in pain. The candles came back on, but this time, the scene was different. I immediately lay back on the bed, but a spider's web of a very intricate network of bridge and anchor threads were now connected to the bedposts, a series of spiral and auxiliary threads crisscrossing with radial threads, all hovering millimeters over my body, suspending thousands of needles of differing thicknesses and eye types.

I immediately turned my head to give it a little more breathing room as the web started to creep closer and closer to me.

"Is this another dream?" I shouted impatiently, to which I had no response.

I could then hear a whisper come from the shadows.

"What do you fear most in your blind spot?"

It was confusing at first until I started to turn my head to consider the ludicrous request until the web started to press down on my chest, drawing blood across it, forcing me to wince in pain. I had to return to my original position, breathing short, shallow breaths. I looked off into the darkness as I started to pass memories throughout my mind. The fear of blind spot had to do with psychological work done in the 1950s from Joseph Luften and Harry Ingham who believed that acknowledging your shadow self was one of the greatest ways for the mind to progress past deep trauma by facing your fears. "Blind spot fears" were ones that everyone else sees you have that you have not been able to see.

I started to scan recent times—the daemons, David, Azrael, losing Kaiko—but as I proceeded in that direction, the needles kept piercing deeper and deeper until I started joining the others, screaming in pain. My mind then started scanning deeper until I came upon Elizabeth. As it settled there, I could feel the pinch of the needles ease.

I focused on it, internalizing the emotions I felt when my father came home drunk one night and started beating me. Liz intervened and took me to a motel, promising she would never let me near that man again because he didn't know how to be a man. I hugged her; I was barely twelve years old when it happened. Soon after, we left Florida for New York, and I never looked back. I could feel tears starting to well up in my eyes, as things started to approach current times in New York where she paid for my undergraduate study, encouraging me to believe in myself at every turn. I looked up at her. I started breaking down and I told the air how much I missed her. And then I could feel the needles start to return.

Liz's face started to turn harder.

"Tell me, what do you fear, child?" a voice that resembled Liz's said.

"I don't know, I'm afraid that I was just a weight on you," I replied. "I'm afraid that I haven't helped you the way you helped me."

"Tell me, why you are afraid, boy?" it said again, as a haunting tone started to emerge from her throat as I felt the needles draw blood again.

"I'm afraid I am too late to save you, to keep my promise to save you," it said, Liz's face now softened and returned to her smiling state.

The scene returned to darkness as the needles started relaxing even more, pulling themselves out of my now-open wounds. I coughed blood and sputum as they drew out of my skin, pulling the final layer a few millimeters upward, and the skin on my arm looked like it was covered in tiny volcanoes, leaving me with a sickening feeling when they finally left my body.

"Tell me boy, what are your arena fears?"

I started thinking again, as these would be fears what I see and everyone else is also aware of. I felt like I was drawing a blank; but as the needles starting pressing again, I could feel my jaw, neck, upper chest, and thighs pierced. The muscles started to tremble, but the piercing at the ankle and hip touched the bone, which brought me into convulsions. I had to stay focused.

"Uhh, it was my father," I shouted, and the needles eased.

I had to think fast again.

"He was never there for us," I continued. "He was a deadbeat"—the needles tightened—"umm, he . . . well, he is my father. That lack of care toward kin is in my DNA. I have his genes, and I could very well end up like him, not caring for anyone or anything other than myself, a truly selfish person. I fear just becoming a reflection of him, that I am no different to him."

The needles eased before heading to what I perceived to be the final two windows. The pain was too great, so before the practice went on any more, I turned over; but the shadows kept pinning me down again. This time, I lay on my stomach, exposing my back, buttocks, and the back of legs to the needles.

"Tell me, boy, what are your facade fears?"

I thought in silence, thinking of the gravity of the situation I was in, before wondering about what I feared that no one else knew about me.

"I-I-I . . . want to love, but I fear that I would be just a burden to someone."

The needles tightened sharply, forcing me to wince as it quickly pierced the top layer of my skin.

"My fear is that I may not meet Liz again."

The needles tightened further. A needle on my hip jabbed the bone furiously, forcing my back to arch and my body to stick into other needles, drawing my first scream.

I fell back down on the bed, its surface now drenched in my sweat and blood as they both oozed out of my pores and wounds while I tried my best to separate the apparent physical reality from my mind. I once again brought up a vision of Liz and wondered what I feared.

*It couldn't be losing her*, I debated myself. *She herself never feared death, doing all her work in biohazard level 3 or 4 labs. She always went to work thinking it may have been her last, but is it that I felt that I needed to offer some form of reciprocity to the care she showed me?*

The needles dug in further, and my wails now stifled to a mere cough.

"I'm not enough . . ."

"I can't hear you, boy," the voice that sounded like Liz said.

"I'm not enough, I'm not Liz's love, her support, her belief—I am just not worth it."

The needles stayed at that level in my skin, as the piercings stayed at different levels throughout my body, not digging further but also not releasing.

"I am just another boy who out of circumstance was lucky enough to be there to receive Liz's love, to be there to witness what a great human being she truly is. But I don't deserve the faith she places in me."

"And what about Lance, Jimmy, Petra? Is their faith misplaced as well?"

"I think so."

The needles started to advance again as I looked out into the darkness, pondering my uselessness.

"Hal, Gretchen, Kaiko? Cliff? Their faith too?"

I fell silent.

*They could easily find another champion, someone else to carry them over the finish line—anyone but me. I'm just another worthless competitor, barely deserving of their care.*

"Unless you actually do?" Liz's voice rang out in her usual cold, firm tone. "It's easy to be a pessimist, to approach the world with a mindset of cognitive bias that fits well with your existing beliefs, but that was never you. This battle you fight here, this battle that you fight for humanity—it is a battle that has been going on inside of you. The fact that you have reached this far merely cements my assumptions about your talent and skill, but you also have to understand that fear is also a function of your mental toughness and resolve, so I ask again, what is your facade fear, boy?"

I looked up at Liz, surprised at the change of tone of voice, as blood now covered my face. My body was now completely inundated with the needles, and I struggled to stay alive.

"I fear . . . I fear that I am not good enough," I admitted.

The needles immediately halted their progression as I could see Liz's face let out a smirk.

"Fight on, boy."

My vision got blurred, and I glanced over the edge of the web of needles before I recognized the spider spinning the web. It had red eyes—it too was a daemon. My arms were nearing immobility, but I struggled to move my left hand. With all my energy, I snapped it forward, grabbing the spider and crushing it between my thumb and middle finger, releasing me from the cursed web.

I let out a strong exhale, coughing on to the floor. The web folded with all the needles, losing the strength of the taut line, falling to the ground, and breaking upon impact. And just like that, I could see my vision in the dark room returning as if awakening from a bad nightmare. I had been struggling for hours to awaken from that dream. I woke up, drained, with needle holes surprisingly all over my body, leaving me in excruciating pain. I had to stay on my side, so as not to lie on much puncture wounds. But I also had to keep moving as I could hear the screams from the other rooms and also an infernal scratching at my door.

As I popped open the door, Jimmy flew in, enraged for a battle.

"Hey, man, don't worry, I'm fine. C'mon, let's go finish what we started!" I gave him a pat on the head before we hobbled out to look for the others.

Each door I opened, I could see the team completely mesmerized by the spider's web and struggling under the pressures of their own fears. Jimmy just flew in onto each one and ate the spiders, crunching them into little pieces, setting them on fire as he did, allowing Hal, Gretchen, and the others to wake up from the nightmare and start regaining consciousness—all except two.

We came to the end of the hallway and found their torture was too advanced, their jaw slacked and they were drooling all over the floor. Their vacant expression told us we had come too late. I closed their eyelids before anyone else could enter the room, covering their heads with sheets.

"Come, we're finished here, we must keep moving," I said.

I could sense the morale of the group low, but what's important is that we survived. At all times, we had to survive.

# 44

# THE GRAVE OF FAUCET VAUVILLIER

As we all walked down the hallway, our limbs trembled from the needle torture until we came once again into the lounge circle. This time, there was a window and a wooden ladder, one that surely went to the roof.

I looked out onto the roof terrace, and I could see a short tower on the top of the terrace poised under a dilapidated gothic steeple with a gargoyle sitting on its perch watching over the terrace. A short movement caught my eye that prompted me to speed up and burst open the trapdoor to the roof, letting in a gust of cold air that nearly forced everyone back down into the castle. I forced myself up on the deck, which was a stone-finish rooftop that extended far and wide, the end of which stood that steeple.

One by one, our team of seven emerged and had to use our hands to slightly block the incoming wind to make it toward the steeple. Under the steeple gave some protection. But the eerie eyes of the gargoyle—a two-meter-long statue of a wailing hunchback priest, with a daggerlike tongue, staring over us with beady eyes—was not a very comforting feel. We had to step into what seemed like a small chapel that had its own gothic stonework and ceiling fresco the portrayed the battle between angels and demons and the rising of the serpents in the context of the plague.

I remembered seeing the piece by Tintoretto first at Scuolo Grande di San Rocco in Venice, Italy, where the depiction showed the scene of the coming of a plague, characterized by the serpents biting people on their thighs, the first place that showed signs of the bubonic plague that killed over two hundred million people. I stopped at the time to wonder how far the pandemic had now come and if they found some reprieve to the spread or it was still ravaging the earth at its current pace.

Two grand Roman pillars greeted me to a golden templon in a design all its own, fit for royalty. It set up a crypt made of solid stone within a cradle that was fit for royalty. Large tombstones showed the Lord and Lady of Romanum, formerly the Duke and Duchess of Aquitaine, preserving their ceremonial titles from before.

On one side of them lay a freshly dug grave and a smaller yet still prominent tombstone for Father Fulton, right next to his precious Annelise, the one who eventually drove him crazy but still retained her title next to the duke, forcing him to retain his place in the social strata as the father.

*Both endearing and sad*, I thought as I perused the tombstones before eventually coming upon a large epitaph at the back of the duchess's tombstone.

It read her final set of thoughts on the progression of humanity:

> I see a world free from persecution, free from separation and the anxiety of judgment. Within the world of men, there is no place for this, as its very nature is one that epitomizes the pursuit of wealth and power and with that comes a natural separation of powers that resembles a Darwinian theory of natural selection.
>
> To see beyond the horizon, you must possess a vision beyond this world, a solar vision, and that is what we profess in the Gaia faith—one where the one true titan rules over all, preserving the sacred and holy name of our Mother Earth, raising it above all else as the ultimate goal and living in accordance with this foundation principle. Many have gotten lost along the way, but it was the founding fathers of the Maeghus Clan that returned us to our moorings, asking us, pleading with us to keep the faith. And so we have.

> I will not be here with you for much longer, but my love for you as the children of Gaia will never wane. All I ask is that we continue to live for the earth, to keep her health as our ultimate goal. Wars indeed are no longer the business of men alone—now we all have a part to play in the coming of Gaia. We must be ready when she calls upon us. We must be ready to serve.
>
> *Omnes quoquq si ambulaveris coram omnibus serve meus*—"all must serve, all will serve." Fear has no place in our movement. Greed and power have no place in our movement. We are only here for the earth, she for us, and together, we will fight to the bitter end.
>
> —Faucet Vauvillier, Lady of Romanum

I passed my hands over the stone when I read the profound words.

*How could something so dark emerge from something this pure, this well intentioned?* I asked myself.

But I already knew the answer, but in this case, as it was trying to defend humanity, its imperfection felt like a cop-out, trying to explain the theory and reality of the Gaia movement. I was finally here, the object of my travels—the grave of Faucet Vauvillier.

*But what now?* I thought. *The only fresh grave I could see is the father's. Is there some other trick I'm missing?*

The mist started to creep into the crypt, covering a little over a few inches over my ankles as I knelt down over the grave looking for an answer to my question. The graves were open top, with the grass growing over the bodies. On my hands and knees I could feel the cold soil below as I placed my palms on the top of the grave, staring down on the grave. The needle wounds all over my body burned as the mist started to encapsulate my entire body. And then I felt something suddenly move under my palms, causing me to jump.

I looked again, feeling the top of the dirt, but there was nothing—just grass. I started to apply more pressure as the mist buried me, to the point where visibility was almost nonexistent and I could hear Hal start to call my name. And then I could feel something reach out to me; coldblooded human hands touched and met my own, our fingers interlocking. I could feel the smooth touch; it was feminine.

*It has to be Liz!* I wondered.

I buried my face into the mist and inhaled deeply before I could feel something place its arms over my back and start to pull me under. Usually, I would panic, but this was the closest to Liz I had felt in months. I had to see it through. The soil around me started to give way as I started to disappear under like a crab trying to escape the attack of a seagull, slipping under the first, second, and then third layer of soil until eventually I felt as if the earth gave birth to me into its birthing chamber.

I landed on a layer of soft soil, moist and rich, with a few inches of water in it. The air was still suffused with the mist and had an expected earthy smell to it as I was totally covered in wet soil. I took out my lighter and broke off a piece of root I was holding on to, setting it alight so I can see around. And there, in the corner of the room, a small room barely nine feet high and thirty square feet, was Elizabeth. Tears ran down my eyes when I saw her.

"Liz, oh, how I longed to find you!" I said. "I can't believe it is indeed you, even as I look at you here, I feel at ease. Despite the suffering to get to this point, it was all worth it. Now come, we must move with haste. I have found some friends of mine, and they will help us escape this cursed place. At least now we have each other."

I walked up to her slowly and embraced her, her long brunette hair and pointed nose and soft skin flowed effortlessly on her body. She was dressed in a cream nightgown, which now was well soiled under what seemed to be her current living conditions, and though I had my share of questions, there was plenty of time for that once we left this place. I held her head in my palms, looking her straight in the eye, her smile radiating the familiarity and nostalgia of the good times we once knew. But I quickly realized that something was wrong. Even she couldn't hold on to the warm, radiant disposition for too long before I started to see tens then hundreds of cockroaches start to burrow their way into the chamber, crawling around her as if she was their queen.

"L-Liz, what's going on? Liz, what's happening? Why are you down here, Liz? C'mon, it's time to go home," I pleaded with her.

My words triggered something in her.

"What do you mean by *home*?" she said, still in a childish tone of voice.

"I mean home, as in New York, Hawaii, Cyprus—anywhere you want it to be, anywhere far from this hellhole."

"Home, William, is a matter of perception," Liz responded, her tone started to deepen. "Humans spend their entire life seeking out their own reflection in partners, in their home, and in their work, until they find a suitable enough combination that reflects what they feel deep inside. I never felt that where we lived, and truth be told, neither did you. It was why you were so hurry to go on that trip to Shanghai and why you felt no real attachment to the apartment in New York or our previous home in Florida because none of those things were our true reflection. Up until recently, I didn't know what that reflection was."

My expression dropped as she started to spew the Gaia gospel.

"But I found what I was looking for here, two of us and the master—we are a unique breed of human, we are part of a super race that is immune to all current and future forms of epidemics to hit the planet. That is why we are still here," she said. "Did you ever wonder why you never got sick from the COVID-19 virus? It is in your genes, William, and we must preserve those genes."

I started pacing around the room nervously, twiddling with the arrows in my tote bag.

"So how do you and your master plan to do that, Liz?"

"With the earth, Gaia," she quickly responded. "Gaia healed me, and she could do the same for you."

"Elizabeth, what were you doing in Faucet Vauvillier's grave? Why are you almost stationed under it?"

"No, you have it wrong," she said. "For us, there are no such thing as graves—only earth. I can move seamlessly through the earth and mist like a teleportation machine so I don't have to travel above ground like regular humans. Sometimes I sleep within Faucet's grave. I consider it a great honor, actually, to gain some of her regenerative powers as she was so close to the Gaia consciousness."

I scratched my head as I started to hear those words coming out of her mouth.

"But what of humanity, Liz, do you remember them? The people you spent your entire life with, working toward developing a cure for the coronavirus? Don't they get a say?"

She paused and unnaturally cricked her neck to the side while staring at me before suddenly responding, "No, they have been the most cruel to Gaia, and they must be punished. But don't worry, their punishment is soon at hand, and with you here, we could complete the process and fully realize our destiny."

I didn't even bother to finish that thought process as I realized I was no longer dealing with someone rational anymore.

"I don't know what your master has done to you, but I am here to keep a promise," I told her. "I am leaving this place with or without that guy's blessing, and you are coming with."

She stopped showing the cheerful facade she was trying to put up, and with her back now the entire time to me, I could slowly see her neck rotate until it faced me head-on, her skin tone now changing to a pale blue as it started to harden on her face.

"I don't think that would be happening, William. I am now reborn, you too are almost reborn, I could see you have conquered your fears, the last weight of the old world that bound you to it. Now you are strong, let Gaia revive you, and together we will help shape a brighter future for humanity in the vision of our lady of Romanum!"

She started giggling then laughing maniacally, the cockroaches responding to her haphazard thoughts.

I started to walk forward to embrace her, to reach out, to talk to her—something, anything—just to bring an end to this nightmare. I didn't realize that my feet were rooted to the ground; several roots had already grown over my ankles and now held me in place. I still reached forward far enough to grab on to her shoulders.

"Liz, listen to me, this talk—it's not you, you are a scientist, you are rational, you are filled with hope for a better future for humanity. You are more than this, come on, Liz, snap out of it."

I shook her continuously, pleading with her to awaken from her stupor, until she faced me directly, releasing a wide smile that reached well beyond the reaches of normal humans, baring all her teeth that were filled with countless patches of dead flesh, gum sores, and the ill-fated daggerlike tongue. As I stared, I could see her tongue emerge from her lower mouth and rest on her lips, dancing about with the white bristles on the edge, getting ready to attack. Her body then crawled up the side of the wall, her back legs looking more like spider legs and two arms looking like two front legs. An emaciated structure and balding skull revealed an animal I could barely claim as being familiar.

"Liz, wake up from this nightmare," I pleaded with the creature who was once my sister. "Liz, I need you, Liz!"

She exhaled, and the breath of rotting corpses rushed forth, putting out the torch I had in my hands, blinding me. I took out Kaiko's knife and severed the roots from my boots, but as I moved around, all I could do was keep talking to her.

"Liz, c'mon, you are better than this, Liz."

I yearned for her response but heard no footsteps in the shallow water.

*Where could she be?* I wondered, lighting my lighter momentarily.

She was on all fours on the ceiling, recoiling with her roach friends before leaping forward with a deadly lunge, but I jumped out of the way quickly.

"You are either for us or against us, William," she hissed. "And so far, I am disappointed in your maturity."

I clenched my fists when I heard her words, trying to stay as mobile as possible, wiping my eyes when I could, feeling more and more hopeless in the circumstances.

"The master," she went on, "is an amazing man, William, you will like him. But if you will persevere on your current path, I will be your reckoning."

I could hear her second lunge as she pushed me to the floor.

"Liz, I am not going to fight you, goddammit, you are more than my sister, stop this!"

"Prove it then, join me!" she retorted as her fingers quickly slid on to my shoulders, pinning me to the ground.

I could smell the corpses once her mouth was open.

"No, Liz, don't!" I shouted.

A hiss then roared through the chamber as she clamped down on my left shoulder, biting into it and ripping at the muscles. I howled in pain as I tried to wrestle her off. I could hear the commotion outside as the others was trying to get in to save me.

"You had so much potential, now you wish to simply throw it away?" she insulted. "Why, for humans? They hunted us like dogs!"

*Did the humans hunt us?* I asked myself, confused.

"I could sense your confusion," she said. "Do you think the daemons that came after you were the same ones that had me on the run? No, child, it was the humans who hunted me down like a common rat, to every end of the earth, to try and exterminate any chance of a vaccine. It was only when I got here in Romanum that my brilliance was truly appreciated. Those daemons were simply sent to get you so you may join me here."

She lunged at me again, slamming me against the wall, forcing my shoulder to bleed profusely on to the floor. I pushed her off but felt my body started to feel the drain of the last few battles.

The ground continued shaking above until finally it gave away, Hal and Jimmy and the others breaking into the chamber with streams of light, shouting for me. Liz screamed like a mole whose sight couldn't stand the bright lumens as the light started to enter the chamber. Hal immediately drew his mace as he was ready to attack until I held them back.

"Guys, I have to deal with this alone," I told them. "This is Elizabeth."

Hal watched me, surprised, asking, "Your Elizabeth?"

I nodded, responding by shouting for everyone to stand down. He knew this was deeply personal.

"Our DNA is unique," Liz said.

I looked over at my shoulder wound, and it wasn't even septic. I wondered now a little deeper why the daemons couldn't harm me and why I never contracted the COVID-19 virus. I knew what I had to do. I could barely watch her as we fought, trading blow after blow, flooring each other to the ground, wrestling, stabbing, biting until eventually I could see her strength too start to wane.

"I'm sorry, Liz, it's time for this madness to stop."

I took out Kaiko's knife and carved the message I saw in my dream and ran toward her.

She screamed in agony, lashing out at me. Hal had to hold Jimmy back as he too went into a mad frenzy, ready to chomp someone's head off. And in the heat of the moment, I felt oddly at peace.

Using my hands and feet, I held her in a hold she couldn't escape from; and as we rolled around on the floor, she continued roaring with anger.

"Draco ad Mortem," I uttered the chant. "Draco ad Mortem, Draco ad Mortem!"

The blue flame leaped out from my forearm and consumed us both, the power of her screams doubling in intensity as she bit and tore as hard as she could, but I would not let go. I just held on to her, crying incessantly. The tears scorched any part of her as they came into contact. Eventually, she started to lose motor functions, then her voice, and, finally, her muscles started wasting away, leaving only her bones left in my lap as I hugged them dearly.

"My dear Elizabeth, what have I done?" I cried. "Why, Liz, why did it have to reach all the way to this hell? Please forgive me."

I could hear her voice trailing off, and then, from the depths of the silence she returned.

"I forgive you, Bill, you are the cure."

# 45

# THE MAN OF SHADOWS

I felt every muscle in my body drained of energy as I left the underground crypt, leaving Liz's remains below, emerging onto the floor, gravity doing a cruel number on my joints and legs. One by one we spewed over onto the floor, taking stock of the mist that was still present everywhere. I could hear the creaking strain of structural cables as the wrecks of the ghost fleet begged to submerge again.

All through my search, my journey, along the length and breadth of the earth—all brought me to my goal, only to have it ripped from my heart again. Oh what a cruel lady fate can be, leaving my body and mind in shambles with business still unfinished. And then I noticed the mist start to grow again.

Hal came up to me, offering a hand to bring me to my feet, reminding me that one daemon still breathed. And in that, we must find our purpose.

"Dig deep, my friend," Hal beseeched. "Dig deep for rage, dig deep for disgust. It will bring us to the end in the salvation we craved for so long."

I nodded as my knees trembled, stumbling on to my feet, Jimmy now perched on my shoulder as if built for the battle yet to come. I looked at him, remembering the effect of the holy water. I reached into the tote bag to retrieve the bamboo vial.

“Do not use it all, but you know what we must do, from the mire to the crypt,” I said, tossing the vial to my friend.

Jimmy caught the vial in his mouth and took to the sky to spread the good word. The last of us six who were left came out the crypt, but I noticed a current to the mist. It was being drawn to the rear of the crypt on the terrace roof. I walked around it, and behind there stood another weeping willow with hung corpses, just as in the mire. Reeds covered the top of the terrace, and the mist moved in and out of the roots of the tree as if it breathed from it.

Just beyond the tree, I could see stormy waters, rough and antagonistic, several corpse brides lashing out in the water and undead sirens circling the tower as we looked down two hundred feet below. The bats also hung from the tree where they could, almost shuddering from the blistering cold winter winds and torrential storm clouds that were coming our way. A sharp drizzle started, forcing some of the mist to disperse as the ice-cold droplets from Helheim fell onto our faces with no mercy or remorse for what I had just gone through.

From the shadows of the tree, a man stepped out, slowly but with certainty. It was definitely him. He brought out his cane with him, an odd-shaped, cream-colored support stick that looked a bit like bone. He faced to turn me, and for the first time ever, I got a chance to confront the lord of the daemons.

My breathing shook with rage as I stared upon his piercing red iris; sharp, pointed nose; and aged skin that would bring him to his late seventies, I would estimate. His posture was proper as he was dressed in a black Slavic cloak that extended to well beyond his shoes, whipping in the violent winds behind him. His chin was strong and shoulders broad, with a slightly overweight shape. A golden ring adorned his right hand.

I started to walk forward in the reeds, and he put up his hand as if asking me to stop. We all stopped advancing but wasn’t sure why. He then spoke with the voice of an Athenian general—clear, loud, and it felt as if it were coming from the mist surrounding us, confusing us from where the sound originated.

“It has been a long journey, Huxley, a long journey indeed,” the lord began. “But you have come far, as I had expected.”

This was not the time for clever comebacks—this was kill or be killed. And to do that, I had to understand more about my opponent. The corpses swung in jerks under the winds and the gentles movements of the willow tree, creaking at the knots, pleading to be let go so as to join their brothers in the earth.

"As you would have probably already realized, my plague has now lain siege to most of the earth, leaving only a few months left before the human race's complete extinction. With that, my destiny as the champion of Gaia will be fulfilled, and the prophecy of Sister Lucia would have come to past. But even before this, you probably wonder who this old man in front of you could be—the man of shadows, you call me. Your sister knows me only as master, as many others also do. To put the story in perspective, you will know me as Grumarim Maeghus, the direct descendant and third generation of Alderbron Maeghus, the first sorcerer of our clan, and this is my castle.

"This world, William, is filled with mystery and uncertainty, but it is also filled with destiny and purpose. Riddled within that mystery are the stories of the wars between men and gods and how we, as men, seek the title of gods in our pursuit of wealth and power through greed and desire." He chuckled at the concept. "Machiavelli once told us that all armed prophets have been victorious and unarmed prophets have been destroyed. It follows then that the key to world domination lies within the strength of a nation's army and the leader of that army. But I challenge this concept, William. I brought to the world an enemy that no army could fight, no warhead could challenge, and no mercenary could kill. I brought a plague unlike anything the world has ever seen—a virus that will keep mutating until the job is done."

"And what job is that?" I asked.

He turned at my question, raising his brow condescendingly.

"Extinction—the goal has always been that," he thundered. "Now, the conversation among world powers is to get their hands on the core nature of the disease so it may be engineered, as no known weaponry has ever been as effective as this virus. All the economic powers—they come to me, begging for me to support their order, an order of man.

"This will mark my third century on this earth, child. I have seen the full depths of the human spirit, and I want you to understand that their impermanence makes them weak, and in that weakness is born a selfishness that you will only see when they are cornered and when the hungry wolf approaches you for dinner. But our business is greater than this—our business is that of men and gods. Our business is how we came to being from the merging of the energies of the daemons, daeorums, and titans, which brought about the near extinction of the titans on Jotunheim, their last savior being their champion Ouroboros and the new grace offered by our guardian titan Gaia that will bring our earth into deliverance."

"I knew you would be deranged, I didn't think you to be quite this mad," I responded, seething with anger. "Everywhere you go, chaos follows you. These titans are no different from the so-called leaders of earth who seek economic dominance in our time of greatest suffering. Are they not mired by the same thorns of greed and power as we are? Are they not subject to the same emotions as we are? The only difference is that their battle falls with a different class of beings."

Grumarim looked at me with a quiet poise before responding with a long exhale.

"I have started this holy discourse, boy, with predefined reality that this about titans and gods. I am the chosen champion of Gaia, and she is almost strong enough to rise and take her rightful place on the throne of this earth. Who are you to deny her that right? Look around you." His tone now became deeper, his hand gestures more animated, as veins started to pulse along his forehead.

"Is the earth not healing for the first pause in anthropogenic activity from mankind since the Great Depression? Are highways now not starting to repopulate with wildlife? Is the smog in city centers not dissipating? And with that, you must also ask yourself, is Gaia not healing herself? If your answer to any of those are yes, then it is time for me to welcome you too to the Gaia order, and we must discuss posthaste how we may finalize the coming of our god."

I was still far from convinced and continued to plea the case of humanity, citing the needless deaths of Connie, Cliff, Kaiko, and Liz, just to name a few.

"You know, there was a final part of your fear training you are yet to complete—the shadow window, the fears that you do not see and no one else sees," the man of shadows continued. "This window is usually saved for death. But in your case, like Liz, you do not fear death, no. The antithesis of life for you all is hopelessness, unworthiness, uselessness. I could act as your guide.

"You could join me, and within that space, you could assist in ushering in a golden age for the earth, free of the real plagues of capitalism and daily strife, free of the contaminants that undermine the health of our god. This era is one only for the strong and the clear of mind, and you—you can play a key role in this resurgence."

I took a deep breath in as the mist once again encircled us as the rain started to subside slightly. Jimmy had returned with a quarter of the vial still left. I placed it on my waist and looked up at the crazed old man.

"Sorry, your offer is crazy, you are crazy," I denied his offer. "This entire setup is a fantasy world because even within the context of all that you spoke, you have not been able to effectively tell me why you, who were once human, are supporting the extinction of that very same race and why you believe rule under a titan would be any better than our governments now.

"What we have now isn't perfect, but that isn't bad either, and in humanity there is hope. That hope is what drives us as a species, it is what makes us feel belongingness as a community. What you offer is a constant state of war and vigilance that mankind has always rejected, as history dictates."

He looked at me, shaking his head.

"Well, I tried, and Elizabeth—she was a bright star, your sister. But she always held back, never fully gave herself to Gaia. And when you proceed in the order as deep as she had, that has its own, sometimes fatal, consequences."

"You do not get to speak of her choices," I shouted. "You lost that right when you turned her into your puppet, when you chose her from so many others and plunged her life into your misery, just because she was good at what she did."

He started laughing uncontrollably for few seconds, well before addressing us as we were stunned at his response.

"Good at what she did?" he mocked. "The Elizabeth Huxley you know, boy, was Annelise Maeghus. She was my great-granddaughter and the Duchess of Aquitaine. And you are the next generation of the Maeghus Clan. All descendants of our clan are blessed with the extremely rare KAT6A gene that she was able to splice through a drink to give us immunity to the coronavirus."

I was in shock, and I fell to my knees as my nosebleeds returned.

*No, I shouldn't let him get to me,* I tried convincing myself. *He's lying!*

"Oh you think I lie, boy? Why do you think you are here, hmm? It is because you are the final piece of the puzzle," he said. "None of the daemons could survive for any extended period, which means the mutated version of the virus has a limit. Your version of the spliced gene, however, has a wonderful protein hidden within it that, when combined with my proteins, can bless daemons with immortality. But as Liz is now gone, you will help me finish my mission. Even if you won't, all I need are your snRNPs. This I could extract from you dead or alive. Welcome home, child. Welcome home, Lazarus Maeghus!"

He began laughing maniacally again as I started throwing up. Hal and the others urged me to gather myself, but I was rattled and I wasn't sure what my next move could possibly be.

# 46

## REAPER

He continued laughing hysterically at me, reveling in my pain, to be so close to him, to be so much like him.

Out of rage, I kept shouting that I was nothing like him and that it ends here, that I had come to take his life. He immediately went silent.

"You have come to end my life? me?" he chuckled, not letting us wait any longer. "Have at it, I'm right here!"

A strange glow started to pulse on the ground around him in the shape of the nine-pointed star as he broke out into a series of Latin chants that were moving too fast for me to pick up. The wind speed whipped up even further as he started sucking in the mist, almost absorbing it. He was morphing into something greater, something more sinister.

"I shall remind you, I am no ordinary man," he said. "I am the champion of Gaia, and as the reaper, I will be your reckoning."

He glanced at the ocean, the storms raising to almost hurricane-level winds.

"Look at how beautiful Gaia responds to me, my flesh. She tears it off, a burden she knows it to be, bringing the gift of the Fimbulwinter to the last cannibal. I would relish the last morsels of dinner. Now who wants to go first?"

His words came with a snarl as his skin was raw and the roots of the willow tree almost completely entangled him into a ball.

He absorbed a series of oozing fluids, eventually giving birth to something totally different—a monster, at least ten feet tall, fangs the size of knives, no gums or lips. I couldn't even see its eyes; it was just an exoskeleton anchored to the ground by several tentacles waving in the air, ready for an attack.

He drooled incessantly as the famous daggerlike tongue protruded from his mouth, his reptilian poise still remarkably flexible, given his rigid and robust exoskeleton.

I had to pull everyone together quickly, letting them know that it would be feeding on their fears so there was no time to show them.

"The beast is big and scary," I began. "We could see and accept that, but we have to move on. It's still an animal. We all need to attack it from different angles, do you have your weapons ready?"

Everyone nodded in agreement and turned around to charge in, just after I whispered to Jimmy to stay back and observe before diving in. I drew my spear, and the others ran in from all sides. The creature's attacks were difficult to track but not impossible; its tentacles had a long reach, and it was in its home environment—mud and slush—which made movement challenging.

Hal connected with a mighty blow, knocking the beast to the ground. But this only made the reaper mad, returning with its own attacks. Hal had to be agile enough to dodge them. I released an arrow while running in and caught in on the upper chest. It howled in pain as that area caught on fire. The tentacles were somehow impervious to wood—only metal made any real damage to it. Gretchen's shovel was able to bludgeon one of the tentacles until it turned limp.

As one of the tentacles fell off, the creatures tried to retreat behind the tree. This was our time to pounce. I noticed the skeleton covered everything but its neck.

"Aim for the neck!" I shouted, and everyone followed suit and bore down its neck, attacking it relentlessly.

The beast was able to shield the first few blows, but the third and fourth broke through, connecting with what I would call its windpipe, sending it reeling backward bleeding all over the ground.

I didn't expect to see blood. As Gretchen saw blood, she lost her head, running in screaming for a killing blow. By this time, the beast was on to her strategy, shifting around to avoid her, until it countered and descended on her.

"One more martyr!" the beast shrieked as he caught her with his tentacles, his mouth wide open as his tongue waved like a snake, thrusting forward like a scorpion's sting, connecting two, three blows on Gretchen.

The kill was instant, but he didn't stop there. He wanted to make an example of her, devouring her corpse in front of us, ripping it apart, limb from limb, as we watched enraged. He tossed her legs over the castle and into the ocean, leaving the rest on the ground around him like his trophies, blood dripping out of his mouth onto his grotesque frame.

We had to make out next move, and I told them before we headed in to listen for my signals to focus and charge in. We all circled the creature as it reveled in its kill, falling into the trap of complacency, allowing us all to come at him from different directions. Hal landed the strongest blow with his mace, tearing off part of its flesh and setting it alight, sending Grumarim into temporary shock.

I was right where I needed to be—high ground on the willow tree, using one of the corpses' skulls as a prop for my forearm. The mist was too thick for him to find me, but his height was his greatest weakness. I could see his wide-open skull level with my chest, and with a single release, I let fly the arrow, embedding itself into the brain of the beast, flooring it, causing it to scream in pain.

I jumped down quickly onto the terrace, running over to check the others. They were fine, and the beast was very hot, to the point of boiling over, as putrid steam evaporated into the air. We all watched in horror as all its muscle matter just slunk away into the soil, finally allowing us to breathe a sigh of relief.

"So is that it? Is it finally over?" one of us asked.

I was fearful to answer, keeping my eyes glued to the area near the willow tree, as the tree itself started trembling until the corpses fell off its branches like ripened fruit in a storm, devoured by the ground once it landed. Several daemons unearthed onto the terrace, only to be swallowed up by the earth again. I could feel the soil get wetter with every passing moment. Something was happening, until eventually I lost my footing and fell onto the turf.

Jimmy was about to shoot out after me, but I told him to stay. The other tried to grab me, but it was too late. I could feel some force pulling me in, dragging me under. It felt like my perennial nightmare of the oceans, just being dragged to its depths, and it was just that—getting dragged past the soil and into a bog of water, with minor cracks of light getting through the layer of soil between the bog and the surface.

I looked at the creature and realized it had morphed again. It was now an amalgam of the skeletons of all its prey, a large blob of interconnected ghouls, still with the infamous blood-red eyes and full set of fangs arching on either side of its jaws like an abyssal fish. Its jaws hyperextended and its skull split into four, breathing through that hole. A wretch of a monster if there ever was one. It still had a large exoskeleton but much less muscle mass and appeared far more ravenous than before. It walked on its massive front arms as it didn't have any legs, swiping when it could and biting when within reach.

Another two of our guys broke through the surface and reached beneath with me. I could feel my air starting to wane. But the key was to move between the light cracks and the bog, so the beast could be seen coming. I pointed that out to them, and they went after the creature.

The reaper tried to duck and shimmy, but the blows were too accurate. The guys used their spears like harpoons, connecting on its shoulder and back, piercing whatever muscle was left and pulling out the spears to spew out whatever blood was left into the water. However, they got complacent.

No sooner had they withdrawn their spears, they turned around to swim back for air, turning their back on the creature; and its massive arms stretched out from the darkness like a monster from the depths of hell, grabbing hold their legs, stopping them from getting any farther. The beast opened its jaws wide, anticipating the meal to come, before skewering both of them in multiple bites, swallowing them down by opening its head and pulling in their body parts, relishing the strength that came with the victory. It still continued to bleed out into the water, so I had to swim out before I ran out of air and couldn't see anything.

I thankfully saw the hole through which the guys came so I was able to pop through it, gasping for air as I did. Hal yanked me up as we ran off the muddied part of the turf as it kept rumbling like a volcano that was about to blow. We ran to the edge and gathered ourselves. It was just down to the final three of us, and we held our weapons tightly as the bog threatened to form into something yet again. And then we all heard was a flushing noise.

Just like that, all the water from the bog was gone, some mechanism was apparently lost.

"No, this can't be it," I said.

Hal then called to me, watching over the castle edge, as the wind still tried to push us around on the roof. He pointed to the mire, which started to bubble ferociously, and mist started streaming from it as if something big was about to emerge.

"He's coming up through the mire," I warned. "C'mon, we have him on the run!"

We all darted down the ladder into the corridor and down the trapdoor, racing down the helical stairs, fighting to keep our footing along the way, until we ran over the moat. There we were once again, at the stone bridge, facing the gruesome Thorn Mire. I remembered the bushes to use to walk carefully into the mire, but the problem was that it was all singed to a crisp, leaving us no trace or guide through that valley of death.

Hal then walked over; using his mace, he kept testing the mire and walking and testing and found the ground to be solid.

"Think of it like a burnt pie crust," he said. "Until it gets weathered again, it would be pretty firm, so come on."

I was excited when I heard this, running over the mire's burnt area, until we arrived next to the willow tree. This one was much larger than the one on the terrace, and the ghost with scythe still sat patiently behind the tree, mumbling some incantation to itself. I could see some movement under the tree, and as it bubbled and morphed and wove its way forward, the mire let out a tremendous belch of toxic gases that shot right through the ghost.

It filled itself as its own cloud of shadows, forming into the "ghost of Thorn Mire," as Hal called it. Its fangs were just as sharp and long as those before; except now, the beast was twenty times larger. I looked like a man facing a god. Its face was still that of Grumarim, but he was ready now to end the battle.

The last guy with us grabbed his shovel and got ready to run in until I stopped him, pointing to the softer side of the mire. We had to go around and face it on the ocean edge along the sharp rocks of the coast. That coast was lined with sirens and daemons for miles releasing their own mist, feeding the cloud, as their red eyes glowed with terror under the dark skies.

At first look, I felt beaten, until Hal reminded me, "Look, it's the mire, that's what is feeding these ghouls!"

"Hal, you're a genius!" I said.

I whispered something in Hal's ear before I took off on the beast's left flank. It swooped down to devour us, but we dove down to the coast, deep enough to escape its fangs. As we stayed down, I could hear the plan in action until a massive explosion erupted. Only then we surfaced and returned to shore. It was the holy water Jimmy had spread.

Hal went on and set one edge on fire, and it spread all over the castle, now setting it ablaze. I watched as the blue flame engulfed the entire structure, and the steeple above the crypt of Faucet—of Elizabeth—continued disintegrating. I was silent for a while. Then I heard a strange wailing start a chorus on the mire and the ocean. The daemons were reeling from the blow; they were feeling the end was near.

We looked back and saw Hal coming to join us on the shore, as Jimmy perched himself on a tree to make his final lunge in. And as I looked up, I realized I had been careless. Two sirens leaped out of the ocean and pinned me to the rocks. The same thing happened to Jimmy before they started devouring his body; he screamed in pain, until he could scream no more. The ghost of Thorn Mire now descended upon his body to strip it of all life, only for Hal to dive in with his mace. But I knew that was too rash.

The beast left its mouth ajar and swallowed Hal whole as the sirens continued biting down on me, but nothing happened to me. And then it clicked.

*It was the cereal,* I deduced. *The first cereal in New York—the one that made me sick and vomit for days, that was the trial serum.*

*Liz pumped me full of it. That is why she said I'm the cure! I have the proteins for the cure in me, that's why Jimmy draws blue flames when he bites because he bit me around the same time, getting the same antidote!*

With both sirens pinning me down and with whatever strength was left in me, I flew into a mad rage. I bit into each of them, chewing off their faces, sending them into instant flames. I ran over to the ghost to try and save Hal, but this only got me devoured—the creature was just too large.

As I was falling into the stomach of the beast, I thought how I got there, how I could have done things differently.

*No, I can't give up like this, I'm too close. No!*

I could feel the internal muscles and teeth start to try and gnaw away at me, and just like so many time before, I could hear a strong, high-pitched screech—it was Jimmy.

"Jimmy!" I called for him and heard no more, starting to panic. "Jimmy, no, Jimmy!"

And then I could hear something fall—it was the vial! Jimmy brought the vial, and with the vial, a potent dose of the holy water from the Heaven's Gate Temple.

My hands were trembling as I grabbed the vial as the creature's muscles started crushing my body. I broke open the vial and poured it, out chanting the words of the most powerful exorcist prayer in the *Rituale Romanum*:

> *Adiuro vos magnus serpens antiquus qui in judex vivorum et mortuorum, per te Creator, est Creator universi, per eum, qui habet potestátem mitténdi te in gehénnam, ut ab protinus timorem, una cum vestris sinum recúrrit, ex hoc servus Dei. Exi ergo, operatur superbiam. Exi, sedúctor, plene omni dolo et fallácia, virtútis inimici, innocéntium persecútor. Cedant diríssime, cedere monstrum, da locum Christo, in quo nihil invenísti de opéribus tuis.* (I adjure you, ancient serpent, by the judge of the living and the dead, by your Creator, by the Creator of the whole universe, by Him who has the power to consign you to hell, to depart forthwith in fear, along with your savage minions, from this servant of God. Depart, then, transgressor. Depart,

> seducer, full of lies and cunning, foe of virtue, persecutor of the innocent. Give place, abominable creature, give way, you monster, return to the depths of Hell from whence you came and never return.)

The fire was everywhere, until eventually the creature started turning solid, like a translucent jellyfish with bones for teeth.

I broke out of its stomach first, and then Hal. I barely hit the ground when I went up to the creature's mouth, prying it open and reaching out for Jimmy, wailing, with tears in my eyes. I saw Jimmy impaled on one of the creature's teeth.

"Hey, buddy, c'mon, don't give up on me, buddy," I told my winged friend. "I can't go on without you, man, not you too, c'mon."

I was so overcome with grief, I didn't realize the creature's eyes still moving; and in a single motion, its jaws clamped shut, coming down on me, severing my body in half.

"No, no, it can't end like this, Grumarim, Grumarim! You hear me? It can't end like this!" I shouted.

Grumarim's body was rejected onto the shore, spewing out the original human form that I saw originally in Maui. I went up to it, crawling there. I could see his eyes barely opened as he was now feeling the burden of being three hundred years old.

"You piece of garbage, what did you do?" I cursed him. "What is wrong with you, what is . . ."

I could feel my body going into shock, and he sensed that and pounced, biting down on my shoulder again, chuckling, as blood streamed out from my body. I then dropped Jimmy and grabbed on to him, biting down into his throat, tearing it right out, before rolling over with him and Jimmy over what was left of the Thorn Mire.

Soon, the rest of the body also floated onto the mire, causing a huge explosion, completely destroying the bog and everything in it. All I could see were the blue flames everywhere and an exploding force in front of me, throwing me backward, leaving my vision completely blank.

*And so, I guess this is the end of it all.*

# 47

# UNFINISHED BUSINESS

My consciousness drifted aimlessly for a few moments before being grounded. I didn't see anything around me—just darkness.

*Where was I then, did I lose? Is this what the end of humanity looks like? Is life no more?* I started to panic just thinking about it. *What would befall me if life were no more? How would I feel? No more waking up, no more eating, no more baths—this is a trip. How long will I be in this state? And what state is this?*

I tried looking around, I felt the sensation of looking around, but I saw nothing—just blank, nothingness. But the weight and burden of sharing the cure with the world was still on my shoulders. I could feel that obligation, that dragging weight just ringing as thoughts over and over again in my head.

*But what could I do? There's only darkness everywhere, I could move around, which feels as if I'm sort of underwater, except I could breathe fine, or at least I think I'm breathing.*

I stopped to try and feel my breath, but nothing—it was all pure emptiness.

The sheer gravity of the circumstance threatened to overwhelm me, but where would I go? I looked around, and again—nothing. The fire, the rage was still in me; the drive to help the world was still there. I looked again, but now, I could see a small speck of light over on the horizon.

I tried moving or swimming toward it; I felt my body drift toward it like I was an amoeba or something, and within a few seconds it was upon me—the light. I didn't know what kind of light it was; all I knew was, it was light.

*What could this be?*

I tried staring into the light, which blinded me for a few moments. I felt a slight, subtle feeling wind coming from the other side. The opening started to get smaller and smaller, until I could make out a little shape. I looked again, and it was a gate, a gate of some sort—those red Japanese gates.

*No, wait, I think they called them Shinto gates or something, and they're connected with the afterlife, I believe.*

But I wasn't ready for the afterlife yet; I still had unfinished business.

I swam to the gate in my amoebic state until I reached the gate. I felt a little resistance coming upon the gate, but I had to push through, and that I did.

Upon pushing through, I could see something on the other side—it was a cave. I looked hard, and I made out a set of Chinese symbols. They were the ones I saw in the Mountain of Illusions that now felt so long ago:

盖亚将生活

But now, I think I could read the sign—"Gaia will live." This was a little disconcerting to see, but I could read it.

*I have to be looking at the Mountain of Illusions, but why is that space so important? All can't be lost, I have to keep pressing on.*

The visions I had underwater felt nothing more than a really bad trip from some heavy mushrooms, so I had to push through.

I started pounding the rock and pounding and pounding, until it gave way. I noticed I had fists; my knuckles were bloodied, but I had fists. I needed it, and it took form. I crawled up into another chamber that was hidden somewhat behind a mountain chasm. I held on to the side of the mountain as I walked forward, realizing that all my body parts were in fact intact. My legs were a little wobbly, but I managed. I still bore all my scars, but I was still in one piece.

My breathing was now labored and challenging, but eventually, I turned the corner and noticed I walked out under a full night sky, with bright stars and two moons lighting my way. I looked down and saw I was completely naked, and there lay an open desert ahead. It seemed I was alone.

It was in the night, the sand felt soft to the touch, and the grains gathered at my toes; and I rolled over the sand while I dug it into runnels. It was a satisfying feeling of reality starting to dawn on my existence. Noticing rocky stacks ahead, I felt the need to walk to them. It still seemed like I was alone, but the gentle dunes along the sands looked real enough, enticing me to keep moving forward.

It took me what I would consider a couple hours to reach to the strata. Huge goliaths of schists projecting from the sandy desert floor covered a lake of some sort with a gentle tide. Suddenly, I heard voices in the distance—more like screams, which made me uneasy. I found a piece of driftwood and immediately plunged into the water to see what lay around the corner by drifting downstream.

A few minutes later, I could feel the water starting to feel a little cold so I got off and started to walk again, which apparently just made me colder. The stacks then opened into a desert village at the bottom, a village from where the wails and screams came.

At the mouth of the rock openings, I saw something on the ground. I stooped down to retrieve it and saw it was a vermillion feather. It was large, at least two feet long. I looked up to see what bird could have possibly left such a feather, but nothing was there.

# Part VII

# EXTINCTION

*March 30, 2021*
*93,566,234 Deaths*
*5,425,359,120 Cases*

# 48

## LOST

The desolate desert landscape stretched on for miles, ending in shadows and thunderstorms on the far end of the horizon. I had to gingerly make my way down the steep incline of the rock before coming into view of this town. It was a haunting scene, covered much like the mist I have come to be so familiar with. But this mist was thicker, cloudlike, with a heaving presence that grabbed on to the people below like prey.

The people there were thousands, drifting aimlessly on the desert floor, wandering its ends. I came through a winding path upwind where I could fully form a vision of what exactly lay there, but there were more and more humans emerging. Everyone had no clothes on, being ushered into the space like a horde of animals, bringing to mind my time in the Church of Malem.

An instant headache dawned on my head, except I wasn't sure that I could fathom the pain in that state. It felt real, though. The memories were filled with pain, and the weight was crippling. I kept looking at the space, the central desert, looking as if people were losing their minds—or as if they were already lost to begin with. Who were these people? I looked closer and saw they were not alone.

The closest thing I could describe them to are the Chinese demons guards, the *yaoguai*—muscular large, lanky, twelve-foot-tall demons with horns like goats and fiery red eyes, with long, silver hair and large cleaves that kept everyone in order. They each had their own rock to stand on, their ankles chained to the rocks, cleaves in one hand, and a pipe in the other. As they exhaled, the smoke added to the mist below. They had dark blue skin, as if they were in their eighties, but appeared very trim, and they wore golden bracelets and large circular earrings. They also wore a skull necklace connected with chains and a long red loincloth that would blow around in the wind. Occasionally they would usher the wanderers back into a general space of the desert when they wandered too far off track, a truly fearsome sight indeed.

There were at least ten of them I counted in this region, and I thought about how I may be able to avoid them. I started to walk around the village when I was confronted by three beings, each with empty smiles on their faces. They introduced themselves as the three judges of the Jade Court: a bull with a scroll in its mouth mounted on a single human leg, a beast that had a panther's face and torso but the lower body of a water monitor, and an old man in regal Chinese wear.

I tried talking to them but quickly noticed no words came out my mouth.

"Greetings, we are the three judges of the Jade Court," the man spoke. "I am San, this is Ti, and that is Shi. Every being passing on from the realm of earth must be judged to determine their worthiness before moving on to the next world, starting with this place, the Town of Suicide, a place for those who gave up the gift of life so easily now must live with their decision, as life returns to them in a barren plane with their problems still hanging over their souls. Your deductions about the yaoguai were correct—they are there to keep order and to carry out executions as necessary. But there is no way around your deeds. You must see the results of your actions, and as such you must pass through the village."

Each of them had a scroll on their person, but I couldn't ask anything or try anything clever, as nothing seemed to present itself at this time. I was forced to play along—at least, for now.

I walked down to join the influx of humans jostling for the center stream, and in so doing, I was on the outskirts. It felt like a naked version of a day on Wall Street, everyone hustling toward something that we're not all sure about. But the difference was those guards. Upon passing, there was a sense of compliance that dawned upon the crowd that forced an order until everyone was allowed to bleed out into the main desert, wandering where they pleased. For some, I could see impatience; others anger, malice, or discontent; but, generally, most people were fairly frustrated.

As the lines progressed through, only a few had the mind to continue on. Most actually stayed behind, wandering around. I know I needed to get to the thundershowers area, but many just stood watching the desert in awe or wandering around aimlessly, unable to escape the pressure of their deeds. After pressing on for a couple hours, I noticed a single man on a rock, sitting on the edge in deep contemplation. I looked closer, and it was Kaiko! I rushed up to him.

"Kaiko, Kaiko, it's me!" I told him, "You're gonna be okay, Kaiko, I'm so happy to see you. I wonder if the others are here too."

I looked at him, but something was strange. He didn't even hear me; I wasn't even sure if he knew I was there. I was in shock but also a little hurt.

"No, Kaiko," I whispered. "His jump…"

He knew where the rocks were, and he jumped to meet the rocks—he jumped to kill himself. He couldn't take the oppression anymore. But this certainly couldn't be considered fair; he had to get a second chance. The spirits appeared behind Kaiko.

"Every man would be judged on his own merit, but taking your own life is a serious karmic burden to bear," San said. "His heart is now very heavy as a result. He doesn't see or hear you as you all exist in different dimensions to the same universe—that is, same space but different times, therefore different realities. You must continue on."

I felt a deep sense of sadness looming over me upon seeing Kaiko, even more so that I couldn't do anything to help him with his current fate that in my mind was cruel and unfair. But I stayed obedient—I kept moving forward.

After clearing the next dune, I noticed the crowd got significantly thinner, but I could hear the beating of drums—large drums—in the distance. A strong light was coming from over the next hill, which made me start to run toward the scene, where I could notice another line of humans, each walking up a hill then disappearing down the other side. I walked cautiously as I could see two yaoguai very involved in tossing people over the hill.

As I approached the peak, I lost my footing on the dune, and I noticed a figure at the apex. It was Grumarim! My heart suddenly filled with rage. I looked down and could see my arms started to turn red and blood started to drip off me onto the sand, steam started escaping off my skin. I was ready to lunge at him again before he made another step; and then one of the demons leaned over, grabbed him with both hands on either end of his body, and pulled like an angry gorilla. The screams were deafening, shattering the desert sounds and drums, and seemed to pleasure the demons; their smiles grew wider with every extra inch he stretched.

My emotions became so mixed, I wasn't sure what to think. In a few minutes of torture, his body broke, and the blood seeped onto the floor before he was tossed over the edge. When it was my turn to reach the top, I was shaking with fear, understanding now that there was a reality to the concept, that it was a natural reaction to pending pain and misery that every human must feel—it was inescapable.

When I reached the apex, I was simply ushered on. I looked below and saw a gargantuan pool of blood, looking as large as a football field. As I started walking along it, I could smell the stench of human blood, boiling in the pool, bubbling with thousand others, and human parts everywhere. My blood curdled at the very sight. I then could see the reflection of the judges.

"This is the Pool of Blood," San told me. "These are filled with those who have no respect for the sanctity of human life. For those who have lost that quality, they will spend a long time here until the lesson is learnt."

Their image faded as I picked up speed, walking faster in case they made any mistake with me. As I walked past the horror of the Pool of Blood, I realized that the sound of the deep drums did not yet leave me—it did not originate from there. Through an hour or so of aimless walking, I noticed a group of people gathered at another dune and more yaoguai on at least three massive *tanggu* drums, beating it incessantly as if their lives depended on it. Here the demons sported pitchforks and spears, ushering the humans into a large cauldron filled with boiling oil.

I ran to the center of the crowds as one by one people were tossed in to the pot. A singing sound kicked off as soon as they entered. I again avoided the pain of being dunked into the calamitous bowl that gave off a foul smell of death that saw the demons lining up after to eat by scooping out pieces of the floating hides at the bottom of the pot. I turned and could see flesh burning raw on the surface of the cauldron and a face—a familiar face. I peered closer, and I couldn't place where I saw the face before.

I ran, ran hard and fast, until I outran everyone else; my heart and mind felt as if they couldn't take anymore. As I reached open desert again, I threw up on the sands, a vicious tension gripping my body and chill coming over me. I stared up at the starless sky, and I didn't know what my reference could possibly be, where I would go or what new hell would await my arrival.

# 49

## DESPAIR

I crawled for a while, keeping my skin on the soles of my feet close to the sand as that feeling was the only thing anchoring my sanity at this point, and then I fell on the ground. The loose sand now felt like a solid slab of rock.

Turning over on my back, I looked up at what seemed to now change into a night sky. I couldn't distinguish what was real and what was a dream at this point, the relativity of it all. I picked out Orion's constellation and a few others, so I guess maybe the earth did survive her second coming after all.

I stopped and looked back at the Cauldron of Boiling Oil, still able to hear the beat of the drums in the distance. I looked up at the sky again, only to see the faces of the three judges peering over me creepily. I jumped up from the ground, panting hard before San spoke.

"Why have you stopped?" he asked me. "There is much still to go. Guilt is not your burden to bear. Many of those humans—they have earned their fate, the Cauldron of Boiling Oil is for rapists, thieves, and abusers. Their fate is nothing more than the simple reciprocity of energy. All actions have a price of weight on a human's spirit. Even if denied, every human could feel it and either accept it and change their ways or deny it and proceed in spite of such feelings."

As he said those words, all of a sudden, my time in the church came flooding back to be. The face—it was Father Faraday's. I remember seeing a painting of him in the inner sanctum, so it was him boiling in the cauldron. I buried my head in my hands, sobbing at the intensity of it all.

"These lands—are they real? Where exactly am I?" I asked aloud, but they just disappeared as if I said nothing.

*I have to try and keep it together*, I guessed, my scalp pulsating with tension through all its veins.

I ran my hands through it to try and ease it, but I wondered, *If all of isn't real, why am I giving this place the satisfaction of torturing my soul?*

"Because that is precisely what it was created to do," a voice emerged from the emptiness.

I spun around but found no one to pin the voice to. I had to keep pushing, keep walking, and so I did that. With no footsteps ahead of me to guide me, no one behind me to talk to—it was just me, no one else.

I started snickering, mumbling gibberish to myself, telling myself jokes that for some reason sounded hilarious. I kept walking forward, tried walking in a straight line, placing one heel ahead of my big toe, and then repeating the process—one heel ahead, then repeat. I kept going like that until I lost count. Before long, I noticed the consistency of the soil started to change, silt and clay started to arise, so I looked up. And as I did, I felt lightheaded, toppling back and falling on my ass in the process.

I got up again, looking forward, and didn't realize I came upon a forest. It looked like a pine forest, with thick spruce trees going up at least forty feet. It looked like the smell would be something to relish, and my mind and body kept expecting it. But I smelled almost nothing. I got lured into the apparent calm of the forest, its branches blowing in what would be a cool evening breeze. As I walked down the hills, I could hear a distant rustle in the bushes.

Upon following it, I could see something dart off into the distance, passing through some sparse meadows and running into a denser part of the thicket. The trees were just like before, but now, they were all towering directly over me. The light was completely blotted out, and I found myself grasping for direction, still trying to follow the rustling I saw rather than heard. Then the creature slowed down until it settled under a fruit tree.

It overlooked another space that reminded me of where I was, where more screams and the cracking of whips cut across the atmosphere with dread and horror. I leaned on the tree, only to see its fruits were stitched human faces in bunches of three.

"I am the Ninmenjou, welcome to the Forest of Chaos," the tree said. "I see you meet the Douen Fu Shi."

I looked over at the deer and realized it was something far more grotesque; it looked more like a horse with a cyclops's eye on its nose bridge, with a foxlike jaw and a human forehead with tiny horns where the hairline usually recedes. I looked at it, and it glared right back at me. I could feel my stomach turn again, but the tree kept talking.

"This area is the Forest of Copper Columns. This is where arsonists are punished for their wicked ways by being tied to red-hot copper columns and forced to keep shedding their skin by tearing themselves off it and back on over and over again. Our yaoguai particularly enjoy overseeing this job, so they bring along their whips for those who haven't stayed on the column long enough."

Some fruits smiled, and then another set of fruit heads turned and smiled, then another, and another—until all the tree fruits turned and were smiling and giggling at me. All parts of my body were jumping around, going totally insane at the revelation.

"Go now," the Ninmenjou ordered, and so I walked down the hillside and saw a small cloud come down, low enough to the ground to almost touch. It had a strange black cat on it that looked like a shadow.

I started walking quickly by it, then jogging before running at full speed.

"Hey, hey, where are you going? What are you?"

It too acted as if it couldn't hear me, and eventually, I found myself in the middle of a muddied clearing. I could see a small pool ahead, and as I walked to it, the fog cleared to reveal hundreds of other people there waiting. The fog was cold, and I shivered when the winter winds came down from the mountains, which surprisingly felt pretty close to me now. I bent over to take a drink of water from all that running, and the three stooges again appeared in the reflection.

"Here is the Chamber of Oxen," San began. "All men who have tortured or mistreated animals in their lifetime will now face reckoning."

Their image disappeared as the surface of the water started to tremble. I got up off my knee and stood, and the surface then started to shake. I looked behind and saw only a cloud of dust racing toward us. Everyone else was still unaware of what was happening, and I started walk quickly, jostling my way to the back of the line before breaking into a full-blown sprint.

I was gasping for breath, and as I turned, there they were—sure enough, thousands of oxen bearing down on the open meadow like the bulls of Pamplona. With their sharpened horns, they ripped through the crowds. The group of oxen roared in terrible groups like lions, a noise I didn't even know an ox could make. They stomped and bulldozed their way through the crowds while I spotted a few of the yaoguai up in the trees overlooking the massacre. A snake-tailed ox with a single eye led them, and it didn't not stop until the group charged through the entire forest. The last few hundred meters of running were up a hill and under heavy thunderstorms. I imagined I was pretty much climbing the dark area I spotted from the desert earlier.

Out of breath and alone, I could feel the wet, soggy turf turn into hard, steep rock. I was tired, frustrated, and listless from the scene. I had to stop and look back at where it all came from. I could see from the wastelands and the canopies of the forests a distant mountaintop awaiting me above. I let the thunderstorms lash down from above, pummeling my face and spirit, wishing I had a cigarette to smoke or some ale to bury my troubles in at that instant, even though I usually wasn't one to use under pressure.

"My threshold was usually pretty good, wasn't it, Liz?" I whispered, and my nose couldn't help but crinkle up.

Bawling my eyes out and in tears, I shouted at the forest and deserts—at anyone who at least could hear me. Of course, no one responded. I was the proverbial tree in the forest that fell and no one heard it fall, so it didn't really fall, did it? My shoulders hung, I stared at my hand, and I forgot even having a rock in it. The sharp edges now were dug so deeply into my palm, it bled out while I stared at it. The rain, of course, didn't want to ease up, but why would it? What's in it for the rain to something so kind to me?

*Humanity, did we get what we deserved though?* I mused. *Are we all blameless in all this struggle? Or do those Gaia clowns have a point to their fight? Hmm, maybe I just messed it up for everybody, as I usually do—reach 90 percent of the way to restore hope, then miss the mark, just giving everyone the hardest drop back to the ground they could possibly get. Taking a nice great swell and reaching the apex of that fifteen-footer then wait to reach the top to realize I can't swim. They should've gotten someone else. Too late now. It'll just drop me like a ton of bricks, smashing my board on the reef. I guess that's what I deserve, though, what else is there for someone like me? I can't run from the truth. This is the reality of it all—I just am not good enough, I never was.*

The rain started to pour even harder, wind battering my body with shards of water that hit like punches in the face. But I just sat and took those punches. I think a part of me figured I deserved it. Pieces of rock then started to come down the hill, so I had to move from my spot. I could feel my vision starting to go, and the vision before me started to slip away.

Struggling to keep it together, I reached the cusp of the hill and noticed a little over fifty men and women strewn about the ice. The judges returned to tell me I had reached the Hills of Ice, a place where schemers and deceivers of elders were left out in the cold and naked to die.

"Just for scheming?" I asked, surprised at the harshness of the penalty.

As I walked onto the frozen lake, I could see everyone just shivering and shaking, most of them emaciated but struggling to try and stay awake while some of their skin stuck to the ice slates. At the end, a tiger sat on the rock, overlooking the scene. Coming to the end, an elderly man saw me, and I could see kindness in his eyes; so I helped him to his feet. As we sought to walk past this place, the tiger leaped down and blocked our path.

It was gargantuan, with a larger-than-normal mane. It looked well over two thousand pounds; on all fours, it was taller than I was standing up, but I felt like I had nothing left to lose. But I felt something for the old guy.

"He earned his pass, you have to let him through, he doesn't deserve to suffer anymore," I said.

The tiger roared and suddenly started approaching. After going as low as I could, a sense of purpose once again started to refill my spirit.

"I said, he earned his pass, his days of suffering are done," I said as I put the old man down and ran forward to the tiger.

It came at me full tilt, looking to charge me to the ground. I would have none of it, and even though the odds were stacked against me, I tried to pivot and got the sole of my feet on a piece of dry ice. I could feel the soles of my right foot tear off the bones, leaving the sole still on the ice below, but I just kept fighting.

I shifted enough to get behind it, and as I was about to mount it from behind, a gleam picked up my eye—it was a blue scale with razor-sharp edge. I grabbed on to it, lifted it high, and plunged it down the spine of the creature. It bled profusely and threw me off, trying to pry the scale out.

It was in a state of confusion, so I took the opportunity to run back at it, and its massive arms connected with my ribs, breaking something, while I grabbed on to its lower fang and bit down onto its neck. Just like the daemon I knew it was, it went alight with a blue flame.

The tiger ran off as a ball of fire while I hit the deck with a few broken ribs and a badly damaged right foot.

"I could feel the pain," I thought aloud. "This place—it can't be an exercise in futility because I could feel the pain, the guilt, the hunger. I could feel pieces of my humanity."

# 50

## RIGOR

The old man smiled at my victory, and even though we were weak, we both appreciated the fighting spirit that could still exist in a godforsaken place such as this. We both gave each other a hand, leaning on our own body weight to try and amble forward into a tunnel that lay ahead. He found a tree and tried picking some of the leaves and used whatever teeth he had left to strip the bark, wrapping it over my foot, and it immediately felt better. We couldn't communicate with words, but we didn't need it; we both had the same goal and route to take. We had to stay focused to the end. I could hear the voices return again.

"Thieves, robbers, and the corrupt will perish in the flame of hell's volcano," San said.

And sure enough, there was a mighty volcano on our left, moving us from frigid ice to boiling heat. Hail came from the sky as fire rocks as you walked out into the open, and the only way around the massive crater was hugging the mountain edge along the single-foot pathway and doing your best not to fall into the mouth of the volcano's lava. The edge itself wasn't the sturdiest, but we came this far.

I reached out my hand to the old guy, he held on, and I nodded as we started with our backs to the volcano inching forward along the path. Very soon, this seemed to be a stupid idea as a couple stones nearly pushed me off balance, and I could not pull myself to the mountain face or pivot my toes. I took another deep breath in as the crowd behind me started to pile up and get antsy. This time, my back was on the mountain face so I could see when and where the rocks were coming from and lean toward the safe side.

We were halfway there until I could see the rock falls starting to get larger, taking out at least ten people ahead of me, leaving loud screams and massive splashes to fall on my skin and remind me what pain felt like, in case I had forgotten. We continued inching forward, and I could see the old guy sweating and starting to lose his composure. We had less than fifty meters to the other side, but he wouldn't make it. I had to think fast.

I kneeled down, motioning for him to get on my back. I honestly hadn't given a piggyback ride since early days of childhood with Liz, but I knew the key was balance and speed. As soon as he jumped on, I shot off to the finish line.

Rock after rock came my way, hitting, pulverizing, and spraying hot lava all over me; but I would stop at nothing. I leaped over the edge to head over to the next chamber, just happy to have made it over. I was sweating nonstop, but we had to keep the momentum.

I darted off, bringing the old man with me as we stood motionless in front of a putrid lake. It smelled like pure sulphur, the scent nearly knocking me out, and then I realized I could smell again. The old man realized it too and we embraced each other at the victory. As we looked at the limestone cave, we noticed the only way out was to jump on to the pillars that were scattered around the pool. Hundreds of stalagmites with rounded edges stood at varying distances from each other, some people holding rocks over their heads and standing on the stalagmite.

We took the path of least resistance, careful not to drop into the pool, which seemed like it would have us for dinner. As I said that, I could see several water eels swimming in the pool, looking very hungry. Eventually, we made it across, and the judges appeared before us, letting us know that we are halfway up the mountain.

"That was the Chamber of Rock," San said. "For those who abandon or kill babies, they will be forced to hold a rock over their head, surrounded by a putrid lake, until they have learned the wickedness of their ways."

The old man started coughing, so I took a little time before heading further in. I could hear drums restarting in the distance, which is never really a good sign. The yaoguai were in their numbers for this one, and there was barely any walking room as a snake with nine human heads calling herself Xiang Yu spoke from atop the hill.

"This is the Chamber of Saw," Xiang Yu began. "This is for those who exploit the law for their own gain. They escaped the laws of man but not nature."

The drums rang out, and as we passed through the center, random men were yanked up from the crowd by the yaoguai and mounted on flat tables and inverted vertical tables using two-man crosscut and single-man crosscut saws, sawing the men in half down the centerline.

I was nearly completely bathed in blood after passing through the scene, and upon looking up, I could see Cardinal Devereaux. I recognized him from paintings in the manor—he was being sawn in half, screaming for his life, as the saw penetrated first skin and then bone. I winced under the sight, fighting to get out of the space as fast as I could. We both threw up upon exiting the space, only to hear the drumming continue and witness another chamber right behind it looking very similar, except this one had a different demon presiding. It called itself Mogwai, an old-looking demon with horns emerging from under its jaws like tusks, a hunchback, and disproportionately thin hands, with a creepy smile so he looked like what you would think an old pedophile would.

"This is the Chamber of Mortar and Pestle, the land where those who waste food will be punished for their sins!" Mogwai announced.

I continued with the similar strategy, sticking to the center of the crowd and trying my best to hustle through, and then, I felt the pull of a giant arm lift me from the crowd—it had caught me; I was going be tortured in this chamber!

My heart started racing, and I didn't know what to do. The giant bent me over to one of the giant mortar and pestles to the center of the room as they force-fed food down our throats while whipping us with leather-spiked floggers. I could hear the wind wisp in the air, just before the whip came down with a cracking sound. The only thing to bring relief was to swallow the godawful liquid mixture of purely unidentifiable garbage. My back went from being icy, to hot, and now to raw, taking over thirty lashes within a single hour while being held beneath the foot of this yaoguai.

I looked ahead of me and saw some of the other men or women already keel over in death yet still taking blows as if the demons didn't care.

*I can't give up, I've come this far, I can't stop now*, I told myself.

I was moved to another mortar and pestle while the force-feeding continued, and as the whistle in the air restarted, there was a strange terror that came over me. It was the anticipation of the blow, that anxiety it brought—even that, that was worse than the act itself. Yet there I was, taking these blows, these lashes, with no end in sight. How can I surmount this battle?

By the fourth mortar and pestle, I was practically being dragged there, as my body started to go into shock. I could definitely feel pain, but my back started to go numb. I didn't know how much more of this abuse I could really stand, and by the end of this session, food spattering all over the ground. The yaoguai shut down the punishment for the day. Almost everyone in the chamber was dead. I think they thought I too was dead as they returned to their posts to await a new shipment of fresh meat.

I lay on my stomach, mashed food all over my face and chest, blood all over my back and neck. But the demons were gone, and within the hour, my purpose didn't die. I rose to my feet, hobbled on my ankle, and stumbled my way to the end; I spat out blood and perhaps a tooth or two; but I served my time—now it was time to get on with it.

I tried standing and could feel the skin burn as I straightened my upper back, forcing me to throw up again with disgust, hobbling my way to the end while briefly looking back to see if the old man survived. But it didn't seem like he did. I saw a rope bridge on the edge, connecting the top of one mountain to another. I rested for a while, while my strength gradually started to come back to me. My breathing started to even out as feeling gradually left my skin.

The winds were still strong as I started to cross the rope bridge at least three hundred feet high above the river below. It rocked in the wind violently while I grabbed on to the rope for stability but found that to be as unstable as the wind itself. All I could worry about was keeping one foot in front of the other, pressing forward in small but certain steps, as the ropes groaned under my weight at its anchors on either side of the mountain. I could feel the snow starting to gather on the walkway as my footing got less and less certain, the massive drop below not helping. But still, I persevered. Unrelenting I pressed forward, but the fates were having none of it.

After reaching two-thirds the way across, I could hear the threads in the rope start to give way. The bridge must be unaccustomed to many people crossing it, so the dry rot destroyed most of its materials, especially with the thawing and cold at this extreme height. In one fell swoop, my footing was lost, and I came tumbling to the rope planks. And as I hit them, the ropes gave way, swinging headlong into the mountain face on both sides.

As I was falling, I could see the storm, see the mountains upside down, and now see the river beneath me.

*Oh, how cruel a temptress fate could be—90 percent of the way, you dare give me hope, dare give me belief, and now you wish to take my goal from me,* I wondered as I fell. *I will not let you win this day, daemon! I will not let you leave, I will not roll over, I will not be defeated! This day is the day that the earth will find victory beyond anything else it has witnessed in its history. I will conquer, keep my promise, keep my word.*

With those words of defiance, my left foot got tangled into the rope ladder; and as I hit the mountainside, I could hear something snap. The pain shoot through my entire body, but by now I was numb—my body had fulfilled its function.

I crunched my way to a sitting position, pulling myself up; and with one foot, the other hanging like a dead mass, I started climbing up the other side. One pull at a time the sweat and rain mixed to make a perfect cocktail to drive me harder, to propel me faster, to egg me on.

I felt my hand touch the rock of the mountain plateau, and on that plateau, the grip was a holy one—one that could raise a lion from the dead. And so it did. As I crawled over the edge onto the mountaintop, I noticed a black turtle rush off the edge, diving into the river below. But now, my time to finish what I started was upon us. The end was near, and I could smell the finish line.

# 51

## RAGE

Blood was pumping through my veins at an alarming rate. I pulled myself along until I could find a branch off a tree I could break off to help as a crutch to get around on this final approach to the mountaintop. The winter snows and torrential rains were endless, battering on the summit like a monsoon in the Sri Lankan peninsula. Still I fought on.

Foreign faces and body parts were everywhere, but I still pushed past this. I came upon a wooden driftwood sign that read the "Chamber of Dismemberment—for those who raided tombs and hypocrites, your punishment lies ahead." Its name was self-explanatory, as I entered the chamber to wails and screams of men and women being chopped into several constituent pieces, many being hung up as signs of warning.

I thankfully passed through without being called upon and noticed a man's upper torso nailed to the side of the cliff. He was just blowing in the strong winds.

"Traveler, traveler, I beg thee, show mercy on your fellow man," the man said.

I took pity on him, so I took his bait.

"What do you need, other than the obvious?"

"Water," he replied.

And so I veered off the path to retrieve some for him, which he drank heartily before I took him down from the mountain face. His hands and face were bloodied in his last encounter with the demons.

"You have reached far, young one, I'm afraid I am not long again in this world," he said. "But for you, there is still hope I see."

"Why do you say that?"

"Your eyes—you still have the fire of resolve in your eyes. It is that purpose that keeps you pushing to the end you know. Preserve that at all costs, it is your ticket to reach the end."

His hand started to stiffen before his entire body eventually went limp. I called to him but heard no answer. I thought a bit of what world he must be going to now, but there was no time to lose. I pressed on into the next chamber, tossing him over the edge of the mountain, lest the demons get the rest of him and devour that as well.

"This one is called Iron Cycads for those who caused discord among family members lives," San said as he appeared.

There were trees here, groves of trees scattered around but growing on the edge of the cliff where I could barely see its canopy. Upon coming closer, I could see the tree branches were actually metal or, at the very least, an alloy of some sort, with pointed tip ends for its branches. The stomping feet of the yaoguai covered the area, moving people from the crowd and tossing them onto the trees where they were impaled for most of eternity.

I could see the mangled frame of the bodies in twisted, painful positions, impaled by multiple parts of the branches, some still bleeding out from their wounds. They looked like tree corpses, and after passing a few trees, I noticed one familiar face—Dr. Frey. His eyes followed me as I passed by, showing piercings through his abdomen, leg, and skull and an old scar on his chest.

*He must be in glee,* I thought, *to be able to be so close to pain even in the afterlife after spending a lifetime of perfecting the art.*

The path went on for hours. There were people moaning, some screaming on the trees, twitching and flinching, giving the trees lifelike movement, while their blood painted the cliff edge red. As we moved farther downward, I could see bodies stretched out before us on the ground, crawling forward as if unable to walk and paralyzed on the earth through fear. I looked at their faces: pale white with ghostly expressions, bearing the signs of addiction—sunken eye orbits and hungry faces but not for food. I continued past them, moving back to an incline into a space called the Mountain of Knives. This is the hell for people who knowingly killed or tortured sentient beings; this is their punishment.

I was eventually brought to my knees as well, as several dagger-shaped blades littered our pathway and came up at least two feet from the ground. It covered the ground we walked and was easier to avoid on all fours. All of a sudden, I heard a wretched screech of a mighty eagle.

I looked around and saw it come from the depths of the cliffs, amassing at least ten people it picked up from before. A nine-headed vulture came and flew over, dropping the people on the stakes, their screams and silence equally deafening as they fell to the ground. I remember reading about that demon, the Garuda, a nine-headed vulture the size of an ostrich just blessed with flight and massive talons, nine elongated heads, and a single one chopped off through a fight centuries ago with another yaoguai.

Higher up, I could only hear tortured screams; and as I passed the place where people were being dropped, I now saw a place where they were being pulled off the stakes and thrown into an open hole and set on fire alive. I looked below and recognized one of them to be Debbie, the cruel girl of the twelve who had set the group of pigs on fire. The screams now were just as punishing to hear.

I continued crawling through the road of blades on all fours, careful to avoid any new deliveries that kept dropping from the sky for some miles. At the end of the trail lay a tunnel with steam pouring out and one of the judges at its gate. It was the one-legged ox with a scroll in his mouth.

"Here you have reached the Chamber of Tongue Ripping," San informed me. "This is for those who gossiped their entire lives, bringing grief to others in the process."

It was truly a horrific sight to behold—a massive open space being ploughed by humans and yaoguai masters. Each human was in pairs, chains attached to their tongues, which then was attached to a plough that they pulled through the plain like oxen on a farm. Some stumbled; they were unfortunate to get a whipping with a wrath I had never seen before.

I continued walking by, as my energy started to drain to its minimum. I could see some tongues handle the pressure, being ripped clean off, leaving each human to scream in silence while writhing in pain on the bare ground under the thundershowers. I looked over and saw Jennie as one of them, her decaying frame and harassed spirit still evidently in some sort of limbo. The eternal tongueless punishment crippled her very existence, trapping her within her own impulses.

The sound of wolves beckoned. It was a howl that was relieving to hear, but soon fright then dawned on me with what they would do should they find me, the only cripple out in this wilderness alone. I could hear the endless clanging of weapons like a blacksmith's shop and saw the second judge waiting there with a scroll in its mouth.

"Take witness here to the Yard of Stone Mill," the judge said. "These are for those who performed wanton misuse of power and oppressed the less fortunate beneath them."

I was a little nervous to witness the new horrors that awaited here. In this chamber, I saw mortars large enough to hold several humans at once as the demons pounded their flesh together in a single cauldron. Vultures and wolves were everywhere, devouring the scraps that would squeeze out the pots and onto the floor to devour, as the pets of the daemons that they were. The pounding was done with sledgehammers; and as I walked by, thankfully, no one singled me out from the crowd. I saw a single face which brought out a rage in me that forced me to stop—Father Fulton.

He begged for mercy, tried to talk his way out, but the yaoguai have no soul. Within minutes, they tore him limb from limb and threw his pieces into the mortars before pounding it into a delicate mush that fed their pets, a pounding that resounded deep within my spirit as I continued on.

I eventually arrived at a cave mouth, one that looked familiar. I threw up on the side, trying to gather my breath as my left foot felt as if it was ready to fall off, bringing me to my knees. I could now hear the voice of the final judge chanting an incantation behind me.

But before I could turn around, I was shoved from my back, and I toppled headlong into the cave, falling into hot spring pools.

The pools were boiling hot, and the pain was unimaginable. I searched frantically for some place to emerge from the pool and gasp for air but found none. It must have been a closed underwater channel tunnel. I could feel all my old wounds giving out on me as my skin burnt to a welded crisp. I looked around, reflecting on all that I had seen. And now, I was thrown in here, left to die, just like the others I saw.

Eventually I stopped fighting it, and I just internalized the pain. The rage in me was overflowing—rage for the system that separated strong and weak, rage for the unfairness, rage for the pain and suffering I was being put through when my goal I know was an honest one. I tried to shed tears, but my faculties were worn; it would not be long now.

*It was a good fight, I suppose*, I thought. *It's almost inhumane that I reached this far. My mind is clear. Rage is all this damned place has left with me, so rage is what I will carry into the next world or beyond. I will wear it with pride, like a badge of honor, born out of the treatment of one to his fellow man.*

Then I heard a whisper come to me, "Fight on."

I turned in the scalding waters, pain in my every limb, and whispered back, "Liz, Liz, is that you?"

My heart was bursting with so much rage that I forgot why I was doing what I did. Her voice was so soft, so calming, so reassuring. It opened a floodgate from my heart where tears, wails, screams all came streaming out—they all just came out.

I could see my vision start to go dark, and this time, I felt I had reached the end of my rope. This was perhaps all she wrote.

# 52

## FREEDOM

With a mighty heave, I felt myself dive from the depths of the hot water and emerge from an icy surface, gasping for air and drinking it in like a madman lost in the desert for years and finally able to taste water. My skin burned incessantly, and the pain and damage was unimaginable. And yet there I now sat, on the edge of a pool—a placid pool that was oddly calming as it whispered a relaxing tune to my soul. It also looked familiar, and even though I saw only out my right eye, I was still able to make out the surroundings. It was the Lake of Illusions. I had made it back.

I started sobbing uncontrollably, looking at the entrance to the cave behind me. The lake flowed effortlessly as I fell to the floor, the pain now feeling irrelevant. The sobs turned to maniacal laughs, still in disbelief I had made it back. And with the fire of purpose returning to my stomach, I started crawling, one arm after another, until I reached the walking path that I knew so well. I slid down most of it and rolled down the other, unconcerned about the razor grass and stinging nettle bushes that lay scattered around the path.

As I reached to the bottom, right at the house where Lance had parked his van, I kept calling until a middle-aged woman emerged; and as she saw me, she gasped in horror. The old lady returned a few seconds later with a couple younger gentlemen. When I asked for Fu, they repeated his name several times before lifting me on their shoulders to take me to him. It was the last time I had to try and stay awake. I could feel my consciousness drifting away, and as we left the forest, I could see something rustle on the top of the hill near the lake. The shadow turned, and all I saw was the tail—the tail of a white tiger. I smiled as I fell away, drifting into a deep psychic sleep.

* * * * *

I awoke a few days later in the compound of the Ancestral Buddhist Temple to the voices of cheer and playful children on the temple grounds. I could see the abbott sitting on his rocking chair, smiling in peaceful contemplation, and another young monk, not too far away, smiled happily when he saw my eyes open.

"Ah, I see you have awakened, Mr. Huxley, it is good to see you return to us."

"Thank you, Abbott," I spoke with a low, hoarse voice as it escaped from my parched throat.

The next few hours, I spent explaining my story to the abbot, one that he keenly listened to and nodded as the tale unfolded.

"So you see, Abbott, I need to get a sample of my blood to Dr. Fujiakawa," I said. "He will know how to extract the proteins and synthesize a vaccine—it is our last chance to save the world."

The abbot summoned one of his younger monks and had them bring a vial into which I bled a little and wrote a note to the doctor, imploring him to use his genetic splicing techniques once more—this time, using my blood that Liz has suffused with the protein he was searching to create a vaccine that would wipe out the virus from of humanity.

The young monk took the package and escorted it to the post office, mailing it over to the Uppanna University Medical Department, constantly seeking confirmation from the office of the doctor's receipt. We were overjoyed once he had confirmed in the affirmative and was just as excited as I was to conclude his work on a vaccine for the mutated virus.

* * * * *

A month later, word had spread that the doctor had found the cure and mass production had begun, ceasing the spread of the virus and allowing human populations to stabilize before beginning the long road to recovery.

The abbot and I looked at each other as we read the article, knowing how far we had come to get here, shedding tears for the enormity of the process and the challenges we had to surmount.

"No matter how much wars the world may face, anger and hate are never sustainable—only love. Because love is our true nature, Mr. Huxley, it is our only reality," the abbot said wisely.

I smiled as the wind caressed my skin, as I was now recovering from 80 percent burn coverage, amputated left leg, and needle wounds all over my body. Even though I only saw out of one eye and heard from one ear, there was a sweetness to the day that I savored, a sweetness in knowing that I and many other humans alive shared. At least, for now, we were granted the gift of experiencing the every day, and that is enough.

# EPILOGUE

I have now completed my first draft of the book today, Sunday May 17, 2020, in Micronesia in the Pacific. To date, the coronavirus has sadly claimed the lives of 313,212 and confirmed cases stand at 4,719,631. Though the numbers come at a time where nations are discussing the details of exit strategies and second waves of infections, a great deal of uncertainty still circles the pandemic, the timing of a potential vaccine, and life returning to normal. As was truthfully reported in this fictional novel, the earth's population has in fact risen to 7.74 billion people from 1.2 billion in the 1800s and is projected to reach upward of 8 billion by 2030. Life is not expected ever to return to normal and as a resilient species, collectively, I believe humanity has accepted that.

Notwithstanding this, one common facet of the fight against the pandemic was a unilateral push from the world on a whole to do all in its power to fight for the life we have, and after going through quarantine measures, we experienced a loss of freedom that makes you appreciate the beauty and sweetness of life that makes it so valuable and worthwhile to preserve life on earth. And even though a challenging road lies ahead, as humans, we will continue to fight on.

William Huxley the Exorcist is the first of seven immortals to emerge from their individual trials. But this is a tale for another time.

# ABOUT THE AUTHOR

Shankarah Lessey is a writer, born and raised in the Caribbean island of Trinidad and Tobago, with a unique perspective on the world and its peculiar nexus with island culture and history.

www.ingramcontent.com/pod-product-compliance
Lightning Source LLC
Chambersburg PA
CBHW030625310726
48979CB00003B/892